I0633766

BLOOD MAGIC

BLOOD MAGIC

STRANGER MAGICS, BOOK FOUR

ASH FITZSIMMONS

BLOOD MAGIC. Copyright © 2019 by Ash Fitzsimmons.

Print Edition ISBN: 978-1-949861-06-8

Cover design by BespokeBookCovers.com

www.ashfitzsimmons.com

CHAPTER 1

From out of the blackness, as omnipresent and powerful as if it were speaking form to the void, came a voice that whispered and shouted and would not be denied, a directive that sprung sourceless from the depths and echoed in the silent chambers of my mind: *Open your eyes.*

I obeyed.

An instant later, I wished I hadn't. The sun wasn't strong through the curtains, but after the darkness, it hurt. I coaxed my limp arm into motion, flopped my hand over my face, and tried to take stock of my surroundings.

Aside from the light, I wasn't in pain, which was an auspicious start to the day. I couldn't pinpoint an hour, but if I were in my room, and I supposed I was, then the bright light would suggest morning. My other hand patted the surface beneath me, and my fingertips recognized a sheeted mattress. Yes, my room was looking like a solid possibility. Going off of that assumption, it was morning, and I was waking in my own bed. Not a terrible discovery.

But I was parched and starving, and my mouth tasted like something had crawled inside and died, and been left there to decay. I didn't have a headache, but otherwise, I felt like I'd been on one hell of a bender the night before.

What did one use to treat a hangover? I couldn't remember the proper cure, but I recognized a sudden craving for orange juice and thought that seemed safe. Lifting my hand enough to let a sliver of daylight hit my sensitive eyes, I glanced around the bed to see if I'd perhaps left a pitcher of juice nearby the night before, but

I was out of luck. Before I could grow too frustrated, a full glass popped into existence on the nightstand, and I froze for a moment, wondering how this had come to pass, before I remembered.

Magic. Of course.

I struggled to sit up, grabbed the juice, and enchanted a bendy straw into being. The juice was heaven, sweet and tart and chilled nearly to freezing, and I refilled my glass five times before I was satiated. With that task accomplished, I lay back and tried to piece together the previous night. What had I *done*?

And for that matter, who and where was I?

Before I could puzzle through the blackout, someone rapped at the door. I hesitated, then hoped for the best and croaked, "Come in?"

When the door opened, a man with a familiar face let himself into the room. I tried to place him, but instead of a coherent picture, all I could see were features: a gray tunic belted over brown leggings, olive skin, an aquiline nose, scuffed leather boots, close-cropped brown hair, muscular forearms, a crooked eye tooth. His eyes, though, caught and held my attention—dark brown, widened in concern, and...odd...

"Coileán," he said, grinning as he quickly crossed to the side of my bed, "welcome back."

"Back?" I parroted.

He squeezed my shoulder and nodded. "It's been a time, my lord. What do you remember?"

My lord.

That was me, wasn't it? Colin—no, *Coileán*, I was Coileán again, and Coileán was...

...king.

I gasped as the pieces of my memory snapped into place. "Val?"

"Easy," he soothed, pressing me back into the pillows as I labored to rise. "Take your time."

I struggled against his hands as the last moments

before the darkness came rushing back. The bind I'd fought for a seeming eternity, I'd broken through it…and I'd dragged myself upstairs, I knew *he'd* be there…the smells of smoke and blood and the citronella tang of magic…the war cries and the screams of the wounded…Oberon's dead green eyes staring at me as I lay beside him on the floor, watching his pooling blood seep toward my face…and Aiden.

Moon and stars, *Aiden*.

"He's fine," Valerius insisted as I shouted my brother's name. "He told me you'd woken, and he'll be here momentarily. Everything is fine."

But I panted as my heart raced with the memory and the surge of terror. Oberon had been standing a few feet away, snarling and twisted with rage, and the air between us had been filled with the shimmering haze of the shields we were struggling to hold intact. He'd looked worn and gaunt, but his aim had been as true as ever. We'd been chasing each other seconds before, throwing ourselves around the room as we vied for the best shots, and then, in an instant, he'd had me cornered with my back to the wall. But even as I'd tried to calculate an escape, I'd seen a figure swinging something through the fog of shields, something long that caught the candlelight…

Oberon never had time to register his own death before he fell. In the split-second before his body collapsed, I'd seen the swinging shape for what it was: a sword, heavy and sharp, a shining steel blade that bit into his neck and cleaved it. The wound had smoked where the metal had seared his flesh, and then he'd slid off of the sword as he tumbled for the last time.

Stunned and exhausted, I'd dropped my shield, and I'd realized who was wielding the sword as the screen between us disappeared. Aiden, my sixteen-year-old brother, the witch-blood who couldn't have held a glamour together to save his life. He'd faced me over Oberon's corpse, his chest heaving under his blood-spattered shirt, his dark eyes wide and unfocused, his hands wrapped in a death grip around the hilt of the sword. But that sword hadn't been designed for two-handed use—the hilt was too short—and Aiden's left hand had partly covered the pommel.

And it had been smoking. Aiden's hand had burned where it touched the metal, which meant...

No, it couldn't, but...

How?

I'd gaped at him as my strength ebbed. Aiden, Mother's youngest, the dud she had sent off to die, had killed the last of the Three. And if my eyes hadn't deceived me, he'd been exhibiting a new, dramatic contact allergy—the kind that only plagues the fae.

I can't imagine what had to have been going through his mind, how high on adrenaline he had to have been, to go so long without registering the excruciating pain of an iron burn. I remembered saying his name, trying to alert him. When something had finally clicked, he'd tossed the sword aside and swore, and I'd seen the angry, weeping wound on his hand where the burned skin had ripped away.

And then the world had faded as I'd teetered on the edge of a lake in my mind, a pool of unfathomed size whose depths were about to swallow me. I had been falling, helpless against the pull of the darkness, and somewhere in the shadows, Aiden had called, trying to yank me back. But the plunge was inevitable, I was already in motion, and I'd taken his hand...

I'd said...

Awareness dawned then, and I stared up at Val, frozen with the horror of what I had done. "Aiden. I gave him the court."

My captain nodded. "You remember?"

"*Remember?*" I shouted as a wave of guilt crashed over me. "I...God, I did that to him..."

The end of the memory taunted me as it replayed over and over again. *Hold the fort*, I'd told him. I'd named Aiden regent, and I'd asked him to hold Faerie together for me.

Aiden. Who was *sixteen*.

How many days had I left the court on his shoulders?

"How is he—"

"He's *fine*, Coileán," Val repeated. "He'll be here shortly. Please try to relax, you need to rebuild your strength…"

I ignored him, swatted his hands away, and swung my legs over the side of the bed. The room began to spin before I could find the floor, however, and Val caught me as I listed. "What's wrong with me?" I mumbled as he guided me back into the warm hollow I'd left in the mattress.

"You've been healing. Give your body time to readjust."

"Readjust to *what*?"

"To being anything but horizontal." He pulled the blanket over my legs with one hand and kept me pinned to the pillows with the other. "Please don't fight me, I'm trying to help you, and I've been through this process before. Listen to experience, hmm?"

Worn out from that minor exertion, I closed my eyes and felt him draw the blanket to my chest. "I slept," I muttered, finally understanding what had transpired. "The deep sleep."

"Exactly. You pushed yourself to the edge. Possibly a little *over* the edge." The bed shifted as Val sat beside me, and the straw pressed against my lips. "Drink. I know you're thirsty."

He had a point. I sipped and tasted an unexpected sweetness—a white wine with notes of berries and honey. Cracking one eye open, I saw that my juice glass was full to the brim, but Val held it steady and waited for me to down its contents. When my thirst was temporarily slaked, I paused and pushed the straw aside. "If I'm dehydrated, do you really think alcohol is the best option?"

"No," he said, smirking, "which is why I took the

liberty of removing it from your wine."

"Clever." I grunted and emptied the glass. "How long was I out?" When Val didn't respond, I frowned and tried to interpret his silence. "A week?" I guessed. That earned nothing but an uneasy stare, and I tried again. "Two weeks? Less?"

Still, he said nothing.

"More than a fortnight? Surely not a month..."

He cleared his throat, glanced at the stone ceiling, then lowered his eyes to mine. "Coileán...you slept for over a year."

I waited for him to smile, to laugh, to let me in on the joke, but Val's face remained fixed in an expression of cautious concern, and I felt the weight of his words settle in. "A *year*?" I whispered in disbelief.

"Oberon almost killed you. I'm surprised you awakened this soon."

I gazed at the curtained windows beyond the foot of the bed, too dumbfounded to do more than blink. A year. I'd lost a year, and Aiden...I'd left him at the helm for a *year*?

Sensing the direction of my spiraling thoughts, Val offered, "He's performed remarkably well. Better than I could have hoped. The boy takes instruction, he listens, and he...well, he's grown," he continued as I turned back to him, still speechless. "He held this court together in your absence."

After a moment of contemplation, I recovered my voice. "Aiden ruled Faerie for a year?"

He nodded and grinned. "You left it in better hands than you knew. Though I don't suppose he'll weep to surrender the reins..."

Val's thought trailed off as a gate blazed into existence by the door, a bright, jagged streak of white light like a bolt from a summer thunderhead that glowed and ballooned into a hole in the fabric of space. Looking through the gap, I could just see a cluttered workbench, but it took me a few seconds to identify the young man who stepped into my room as my brother.

He *had* grown—possibly an inch or two, I thought, quickly sizing him up as Val stood to greet him. The skinny boy I remembered had bulked, adding a layer of muscle to fill out his chest and limbs. I could see the result in his arms, which were bare under a black shirt with a familiar circular insignia. I knew the logo—Aiden had shown it to me before—but the name danced on the tip of my tongue until I recognized the color palette. Captain America, that was it, one of his comic book heroes.

Yes, the recent king of Faerie was sporting a superhero T-shirt over his well-worn jeans and black tennis shoes, but that wasn't the strangest thing about him. Aiden's blond hair had grown unchecked, and when he turned to Val, I caught a glimpse of his foot-long ponytail. His eyes, dark and round like our mother's, seemed indescribably different, but more pressing to me was the pair of clear plastic lab goggles perched atop his head.

Despite his changes, all of my doubts faded as soon as Aiden flashed a beaming smile, instantly taking five years off his face. "Coileán!" he cried, taking Val's vacated seat on the bed to clasp the hand I extended to him. "About time! Enjoy your little nap?"

I squeezed into his grip. "Not so little, I hear. And you…"

"Kept things tidy and mostly dust-free. It's good to see you, man."

"I am *so* sorry."

Aiden shrugged. "Not your fault. It's not like you forgot to set your alarm—"

"But I…" I looked up at him, shaking my head. "I can't believe I did that to you."

"Hey, someone had to do it while you got your beauty rest. How're you feeling?"

"Weak," I admitted as I released him. "Ravenous. Disoriented…"

My brother held out his palm, and a stoneware pizza plate the size of a tire appeared in his hand. "All the meats and black olives, right?" he asked, plopping it in my lap. "That should get you started."

I looked from him to the pie and back, then tentatively took a test slice and bit into it. The pizza was hot enough to burn my tongue, the cheese melty, the edges of the Canadian bacon crispy and curling.

"Edible?" he asked as I chewed.

I took another bite, then gave up on propriety and shoved half the slice into my mouth. "Fantastic. *Really* fantastic. Where—"

"Astrid gave me a few pointers. And Hel's got a favorite joint in Nashville—she lets me sneak along with Joey sometimes," he said, grinning. "He's on his way back—I called him about ten minutes ago, and he and Georgie were off the coast. They should be here any time now."

I called a stack of napkins into existence and wiped the grease off my fingers, then studied my brother's face. "What happened to you?"

"Well, more or less, the realm knew you needed someone to tag in," he replied, shifting on the bed, "and she suppressed the wizard bits. And then loaned me enough power to take on Oberon."

"Barely," Val muttered.

"With a major assist from Val and Joey," he conceded. "Anyway, she took most of it back when you woke. Glad I can still do pizza, though."

My brow furrowed. "Are you...all right?"

He spread his hands. "Eh, I'm here. Little drained, but I'm sure it'll pass."

"But that much power—"

"Look," Aiden interrupted, "I went from walking to racing a Ferrari, but it was always a loaner Ferrari. There's no room for two kings in one court, right? But Faerie said that since taking all the power back would be unfair, considering my age, she left me with a little boost. It's more like a compact car with a V4, but it's still better than no car at all."

I tried to attach proper values to his analogy, but quickly gave up the exercise as futile. "So…you're half fae now?"

Aiden nodded. "For practical purposes."

"And, uh…Helen?"

He met Val's glance, then looked back at me. "Hel and I are fine. She's on track to become grand magus this spring after she graduates—she's finishing her degree a semester early," he said with a touch of pride. "Dad's still not speaking to me, and Mom's following his lead, but Hel and I are cool. And you should probably know that she and Joey are getting married."

I paused, crust halfway to my mouth. "*Married?*"

"Yeah. You owe me five bucks." I frowned, and Aiden explained, "You bet me that they wouldn't last a month, remember? He put a ring on it. I win."

The news was a shock, but the pizza's siren song was stronger, and I tried to carry on the conversation with my mouth full. "The Arcanum hasn't tried to stop this?"

Val snorted, and Aiden rolled his eyes. "The Council has *tried*, but she's not budging. The Inner Council, I mean. The installation heads would back her if she wanted to go pole dancing on a rocket sled. It's the silo crew that gives her fits, but the succession's in place, and there's not much they can do about it now."

There was an edge in his voice when he spoke of the Arcanum, and I trod with caution. "Have you had dealings with them, or is this all secondhand?"

Aiden's smile was hard and mirthless. "We've had dealings. It took time for a few of them to understand the situation."

"And persuasion, I take it?"

His smile deepened. "I can't help it if certain magi persist in being obtuse."

"Of course. What did Greg have to say about your persuasive tactics?" I asked, folding another slice for efficient delivery.

"He asked me not to kill anyone. I agreed." Aiden helped himself to my pizza and chewed thoughtfully. "Needs more basil. Look, I didn't go in there trying to be a jackass, but..." He gestured to his young face with his empty hand, and I nodded. "They assumed they could walk right over me. I had to nip that in the bud."

Aiden didn't have to explain. Having witnessed the abuse he'd suffered at the hands of magi's sons and grandsons, I could envision the situation he'd faced. Greg Harrison, the outgoing grand magus, had a healthy respect for me, and the few magi I'd met tended to slink around the corners of the room and try to blend into the paint when I was nearby. It had been centuries since a wizard was a match for me in a fair fight, and we all knew it. But Aiden had been the Arcanum's mobile punching bag, and I could only imagine how the Council must have chafed at treating him with the deference and caution due a high lord—especially one whose sister was about to become their boss.

"How many bones did you break?" I asked.

"Only a few. Russell Mulligan does *not* know when to roll over."

"Which one—"

I paused, feeling the pressure of a mind trying to infiltrate my thoughts, and realized that the clumsy prodding was from my brother. Dropping my defenses, I gave him entry, then saw a face appear in my mind's eye: a sullen boy a bit bulkier than Aiden, his brown hair pulled into a short ponytail, his muddy eyes narrow and thickly fringed, scowling at the world.

"Ah," I said as Aiden retreated. "I remember him. And nicely done."

He sighed in frustration and rubbed his temple. "Sloppy. I'm sorry, I'm not usually that heavy-handed..."

"If the realm took your power back," Val murmured, patting Aiden's shoulder, "you'll have to adjust your technique. We can work on this later—don't let it concern you now."

"I guess," he muttered, and finished his pilfered slice. "My gate was sloppy, too."

"You're *seventeen*, boy. No one is demanding perfection."

"By the way, happy belated," I added, putting the remains of the pizza aside as I attempted to ease myself vertical. "I suppose. It's…"

"December tenth," said Aiden, slipping off the bed to give me maneuvering room. "And thanks. I'm expecting one hell of a birthday gift."

I chuckled and closed my eyes, willing the world to stop spinning. "What did you have in mind?"

"It's less of an item and more of a favor. Here," he said, wrapping his arm under mine, "I've got you. Want to stand?"

Though I leaned on him far more than I wished to admit, I managed to push myself upright and stay that way as my heart pounded its complaint. "What sort of a favor?"

Aiden shifted his grip, and I realized with a faint flash of jealousy that he was now taller than me. "I called in that favor you had coming from Grivam," he replied. "Told him that if he helped me find out what had happened to you, the two of you would be square. So if you could back me up on that, I'd *really* appreciate it."

"That's all?" I asked, balancing against him as I took a faltering step across the rug. "If you called in that favor on my behalf, I can't exactly fault you. Don't worry about it."

I felt his shoulders relax and wondered what sort of contingency agreement he had struck with the merrow king. "Thanks, man," he said, and grabbed me as I stumbled over my own feet. "Whoa, there, this isn't a race."

"Easy for you to say," I muttered, but I let him guide me across the room to the sofa pushed against the largest window, and I sank down with relief. Aiden stepped back, giving me space to breathe, and I massaged my knees. "Any trouble from the rest of the family?"

"Nah." He leaned against the bedpost and folded his arms. "Mina made all the introductions—you've met, right?" he asked as my brow furrowed. "She's in the guards…"

"Autel's daughter," Val offered. "Do you remember her?"

"Mina—wow, yeah," I said, connecting a face with the name. "It's been a while. Where's she been hiding?"

"She was out to sea during the transition with some of her cousins. They survived—"

Val's voice cut off too quickly, and I caught the look that passed between him and Aiden. "Survived?" I asked, glancing back and forth for an explanation. "Survived what?"

Val's eyebrow rose as he watched Aiden, and my brother took the hint. "When Oberon came over," he said quietly, "Val got Joey and me out of here before he could find us. Our siblings…weren't so lucky," he finished in a low rush. "Sitting ducks. And then he went after anyone else related to Titania—grandkids, whoever. He didn't get them all, but he got enough."

I felt like someone had kicked me in the stomach. My siblings and I had never been on good terms, but for Oberon to have slaughtered them… "His court," I said as my mind reeled, "what happened to them?"

"Some fled, some died. I imprisoned the rest for a while. I was waiting for you to wake up, but a couple of months passed, and I couldn't hold them any longer."

"You sent them back to the mortal realm?"

"I executed them."

As I stared up at my brother, I realized then what was so different about him. The boy who had come over from the silo had been just that—a boy. But the person who matter-of-factly told me about the punishment he had meted out was a young man, harder and sharper around the edges than the boy had been. He was still recognizably Aiden, but the fire through which he'd passed had burned away so much of the child in him.

Still, he was watching me, waiting for my reaction, and the tightness of his arms betrayed his nervousness. "Good," I told him. "But I'm sorry you had to do that."

"Yeah," he said, rubbing his elbow. "Not something I want to revisit right now, if that's okay."

"We can discuss it later. I'm still waiting for an explanation as to your headgear."

He frowned bemusedly, then reached up, felt the goggles, and groaned. "I *knew* I forgot something," he muttered as he pulled them off.

"What have you been doing, building a bomb?"

"Nothing so exciting." He sat at the foot of my bed and twirled the goggles by their strap. "Vivi said you owed the Fringe a favor, and she asked if I'd help them out instead."

"With *what*?" I asked, momentarily miffed at the slight. The Fringe were mostly witches and lesser-blooded fae— what could Aiden have done for them that I couldn't?

"Building a better laptop."

I beckoned for the pizza, and Aiden obliged. "Seriously? They were due a favor, and they called it in for a damn computer?"

"Not just any computer. They need mobility, and depending on what they're doing, they need heavy tech. You'd be amazed at some of the systems that Fringers have hacked."

I thought I detected a twinge of envy in his voice, but I could only shrug. Computers, to me, were mysterious and highly flammable things, unpredictable and best avoided.

"Anyway," Aiden continued, "their problem is the usual: building something that can handle their computing needs and still be portable. Considering that some of their more ambitious projects need multiple servers, this is tricky…and your eyes are glazing over."

"Sorry."

"Okay, in short, I built the system they needed, then made it fit into a standard field-protected laptop with some heavy enchantment. Of course, if you've got something that big warping space inside the machine, you've got to go back and enchant around the components to protect them from magical interference, and it's a mess." He shook his head and flashed a grimace. "There are, like, two wizards who consider themselves technomages, mostly because it's a headache. Well, that, and the old guard still don't trust anything more advanced than parchment."

"You convinced a wizard to assist you?" I asked incredulously.

But Aiden snorted. "Fat chance. I've been doing this by trial and error—the first one was decent, but I've been tweaking the successive models. Oh, the debt's cleared," he assured me, stopping me before I could speak. "I like playing with my toys."

"And I thought you were going to take precautions," Val interjected. "Proper dress—"

"I did! I left my shirt behind in case of flecks." Seeing my confusion, Aiden showed me his bare forearms, which were pocked with tiny circles and oblongs and lines of scar tissue. "Most of what I've been dealing with is iron-free, but accidents happen. I've got a work shirt and gloves back in the lab. And these," he said, holding up the goggles.

"The lab?"

"Built myself an extra room to keep my gear walled off. I can't imagine why the guards didn't want to be around me when my room was full of shrapnel," he added, cutting his eyes to Val.

The sunlight hit Aiden's left hand, and I saw the puckered patch on his palm where it had scarred over. Before I could press him about the wisdom of pursuing his current hobby, a shadow blotted out the light falling through the window behind me. I turned and pulled back the sheers in time to see Georgie coming in for a landing, beating her wings furiously to slow her descent.

Well, I assumed it was Georgie, as no one else seemed concerned that a black dragon with wings like an overgrown bat was stomping around my roses. As she approached, I watched a figure climb up her neck, then crouch atop her head and hold on to her horns until she reached the palace. The dragon trod cautiously—or as cautiously as a lizard the size of a 747 could tread, that is— and pressed her eye against the windows to my left, then moved down the building until I was face to face with a massive red iris and slitted pupil. The eye retreated as her head turned, and one nostril fogged the entire window as she exhaled. *Hi!* said the familiar voice in my mind. *Going to open that?*

Aiden leaned over the back of the sofa to unlatch the window, and as it swung open, Georgie lowered her head to give her rider a level entry. He stepped onto the sill, pulled off his motorcycle helmet, and beamed as he jumped to the floor. "Boss!" Joey cried, and I found myself caught in a tight, backslapping, thoroughly unexpected hug.

"Hey," I gasped, and tried to thump his back in turn, but my hand hit something hard beneath his black suit.

Joey pulled away and brushed his damp hair from his forehead. "Body armor," he said, seeing my confusion, and rapped his knuckles against his chest. "If I hit the ground, I'll still be dead, but more of me might be intact."

"Hel insists," said Aiden, leaning out the window to rub Georgie's nose. "And if Hel insists…"

It's best to surrender, Georgie finished. *Lunch?*

"More like brunch," said Joey. "Go on, sweetie, knock yourself out."

She lumbered away, stepping carefully over the hedges. As Aiden closed the window behind her, I considered

Joey, whose dress seemed to be a cross between professional biker and SWAT chic. His blond hair was dark with sweat and plastered to his skull, but he'd managed to cultivate a neat mustache and beard, aging his appearance to a respectable thirty. "I understand congratulations are in order," I said.

His brown eyes crinkled. "Thanks! She hasn't kicked me out yet, so it looks like this wedding's still a go. We're on for April—Father Paul's doing the honors. Hey, you'll come, right? It's not going to be anything big—Helen's folks are opposed, and mine don't *exactly* know everything yet, but, uh…you know…love to see you there."

Joey's smile was infectious, and I felt the corners of my mouth twitch. "And what would Helen say to that?"

He glanced around the room, then plucked a cream-colored envelope from my dresser and blew the dust off. "She okayed the guest list," he replied, handing it to me. "And did the calligraphy. I have the penmanship of a kindergartener."

My name was neatly written across the front, and I pulled a letter-pressed card from inside. "You know," I said, scanning the details, "I've never actually been invited to a wedding."

"*Seriously?*"

"Suppose there's a first time for everything." I put the card back into the envelope and resumed my attack on the pizza to disguise the sudden tightness in my throat. "You've registered somewhere, I trust?"

"Oh, sure. Helen *did* pick a silver pattern."

"You're on your own for that one," I said, then reluctantly dropped my pizza again at the sound of a knock and called, "Enter!"

The door opened, and a guard I didn't know slipped inside. "Your pardon, my lord—"

"Yes?" Aiden and I said in unison, and he rubbed his neck and looked away with a mouthed apology when we locked eyes.

The guard glanced back and forth uncertainly. "My lord…my *lords*…she's come early."

Aiden straightened and picked up his goggles. "Already? I thought we weren't planning for her until tomorrow…"

"Yeah," Joey cut in, "but you know how iffy they are on time…"

They stopped and stared at each other, and slowly, each broke into a madman's grin.

"She's here, you said?" Aiden asked the guard. "Now?"

He nodded. "I showed her and her retinue to the throne room, but if this is an inconvenient time—"

"No, no, that's fine. Coileán, uh…think you can make it downstairs?"

"I suppose," I said slowly, trying to decipher the gleam in his eye. "Why? Who were you expecting?"

"Hold that thought," said Joey, already heading for the door with his helmet tucked under his arm. "I'm getting the camera."

CHAPTER 2

I could understand neither their excitement nor why Aiden refused to tell me who was waiting, but I recognized a distraction as he helped me to the throne room.

"I did some work on Joey's helmet," he said, taking my weight as we slowly descended the main staircase. "Built a computer in—the visor's a screen, and there are a couple of cameras around. It syncs up to the mapping he's done thus far, and it can at least give him headings. Not nearly as good as proper GPS would be, but it's a start."

"Aiden—"

"And I built a phone into it, too, so he doesn't have to dig in his bag every time he needs to take a call. Oh, and I put a speaker in the housing. Georgie anticipates instructions pretty well, but it helps if he can actually *tell* her what he needs, you know? I mean, she can read his mind if she's confused, but in a pinch—"

"Wait, Aiden—"

"The hardest part was making him comfortable with the system's commands, but he had the gist of it in a few days. We've been tweaking as problems arise."

"Damn it, stop," I said, tugging on his shoulder before we reached the ground floor. "*What* is going on?"

"There's someone you need to meet," he replied, dropping down a step, "and she's waiting, and if you want me to open a gate—"

"I said no," I grunted, silently cursing my weakened legs, which quivered with the morning's brief exertion. "Now, who's waiting, and why are you and Joey so eager for this to happen?"

"What do you mean?" he asked, all innocence.

I looked over my shoulder at Val, who had long ago mastered the art of the poker face. "Something you'd like to share with me, Captain?"

"Nothing comes to mind."

"Is that so?" I muttered, then sighed as I let Aiden lead me the rest of the way down. I was in no mood for another surprise, but I realized the futility of further interrogation.

A knot of guards awaited us outside the side door to the throne room, standing at attention but hiding their mirth with varying degrees of success. Overwhelmed already, I brushed it off and leaned on Aiden as little as possible while the guards flanked us for entry. When they threw the door open, I mustered up what I hoped passed for a look of regal nonchalance, straightened my shirt, and willed my body to cooperate as I marched inside.

Straight ahead on the stone dais, exactly as I had left it, was my throne, an oversized seat of polished oak carved into leaves and vines. It still bore a blue cushion—I'd learned the hard way that the chair was unforgiving after long hours atop it. A thick-piled azure runner flowed from the dais down the length of the long hall, bisecting the rows of chairs I'd placed around for petitioners. The room was unchanged, as far as I could tell—stone pillars fashioned like gray trees rose to support the vaulted ceiling, while the sun falling through the eastern windows threw jewel-toned pools of light on the flagstones. The place was my architectural pride, sufficiently imposing without stooping to ostentation, even if I had appropriated most of its finer elements from my favorite Gothic cathedrals.

Gritting my teeth against the wobble in my overburdened legs, I let Aiden help me up the steps and tried not to seem too relieved to take a seat. When I was situated, I spotted Joey lurking beside the nearest pillar, holding a phone in front of his face. The newer ones had video cameras in them, I recalled, and wondered again what was going on.

I didn't have to ponder long. Aiden slipped down to the floor, and I finally noticed a little cluster of lights atop a chair midway across the room, a splotch of color I'd mistaken for the glow of one of the stained-glass windows. But these lights were too small to be part of the swirling patterns of the glass, and they were *moving*. As Aiden hurried toward them, a bright purple light rose from the clump and sped toward him, and he stretched out his palm. Squinting, I realized that the light masked something solid at its heart as it landed in Aiden's hand. He spoke to it—I didn't recognize the tongue—then turned and carried the glowing thing back up the aisle toward me.

"My lady," he said as he neared, "this is my brother, Lord Coileán, who has only now rejoined us and so didn't know of your coming. Coileán, allow me to present Lailu, queen of the piq."

"The what—" I began, then faltered and froze.

As Aiden reached the foot of the dais, the fine details of his passenger's form hit me like a bucket of ice water to the face. The glowing thing—Lailu—was a homunculus in a golden sheath of a dress, perfectly proportioned but for her large, dark eyes, which reminded me fleetingly of a loris. Her black hair fell to her waist in a thick braid woven through with tiny flowers…and she sported a pair of wings that wouldn't have been out of place on a swallowtail butterfly.

Stunned into silence, I watched the little thing fan her wings, counterbalancing against the slight movements of Aiden's hand, and I focused on my brother's wide grin to pull me from my shock. "That…what is…"

"The piq," he replied, smiling out of Lailu's view, "live in the woods about forty miles northeast of here."

"Pixies," Joey offered from behind his camera.

I understood then why the moment was being

preserved, but all I could do was shake my head. "Moon and stars," I muttered, "that…that can't…"

Saving me from myself, Lailu took wing and landed on the arm of my throne. "We have had few dealings with your kind in days and days and days," she said, her Fae unremarkable but for its speed and impossibly high pitch. "Not since the daig warred."

"They went into hiding when the Three fought," Val offered, sliding into his usual place at my right hand. "Aiden and Joey stumbled across them last year."

"And we would like to reestablish relations with you," she continued, clasping her dainty hands. "I have come with my brother's son, Kuni"—a little gold light rose from the cluster on the far chair—"who, with your leave, will remain among you and observe your ways. Aiden and I had discussed this…does it displease you?"

"No," I mumbled, conscious that a response was expected of me as I looked down into her oversized eyes. "No, that, uh…that's fine. Sure. As you like." I stared around the room in a daze, then located Aiden as a pressing matter rose to the fore of my thoughts. "Please," I begged him, "please, for the love of all that's holy, tell me Stuart doesn't know of this."

"And *cut*," said Joey, lowering the phone to reveal his smile. "Oh, man, when I'm old and gray and senile, I'm going to watch that over and over again and die happy."

Somehow, I pulled myself together and even produced coherent sentences, despite the fact that I was talking to a creature who was one shower of glitter away from a children's movie. For her part, Lailu was the epitome of grace and tact. She and Aiden conversed quickly in the unfamiliar language, and then the gold light flew over to join us—or, more properly, an almost naked piq landed on my brother's shoulder, and the two of them carried on as if they were old friends. Catching me gawk, Aiden explained,

"They don't go for clothing. It's a ceremonial thing for Lailu," then resumed his rapid conversation with the little winged male I took to be Kuni.

As I continued to stare, I felt something tap my left shoulder, then turned to see Lailu sitting there, smiling at me. "You seem surprised," she said.

"Stunned."

She reached up and patted my cheek. "Poor boy. I suppose my timing could have been better, but no one warned me that you had awakened."

Val leaned over me to join the conversation. "It's only been an hour or so, my lady."

"Ah. In that case, perhaps we could discuss matters at another time. Surely you have more pressing issues to consider than our entertainment." With that, she grabbed my hair as a handhold and pulled herself back to her feet. "Perhaps we could rest? It has been a long journey, and my people are weary," she hinted, gesturing toward the lights down the aisle.

Overhearing her, Aiden jogged up the dais with Kuni still perched on his shoulder, balancing himself by gripping Aiden's ear. "I've prepared a room for you, if you'd like to come with me," he told her. "You'll be comfortable, and once he's got his head on straight," he added, nodding at me, "we can talk. Will that work?"

"Of course."

Aiden held out his arm as if waiting to catch a falcon, and Lailu landed near his wrist. "Back in a minute," he told me, then strode off toward the others. When all the piq had settled aboard his arms like a string of moving Christmas lights, Aiden saw himself out, chatting with his passengers as Joey followed a step behind.

The double doors slammed behind them, and I slowly turned to look at Val as the echo died away. "Pixies."

"I know."

"Those are honest-to-God pixies."

He nodded. "Surprising, but there they are. Lailu

protected Aiden and Joey when they first tried to rescue you. The boys have visited since then, and the queen thought it was time to send an envoy."

"And you didn't think it would be a good idea to warn me about them in advance?"

"I was sworn to silence. And knowing what those two went through, I wasn't going to deny them their little amusement."

He offered me his arm, and I rose from the throne on unsteady legs. "What happened last year? I need you to tell me *everything*, Val, amusements be damned."

His face clouded. "Once you've had a chance to rest—"

"I've been resting for months. This is my court, and…and…"—I gestured at the doors through which the visitors had disappeared, momentarily lost for words—"and a bunch of pixies just wandered over to say hello! *Pixies!*"

"They call themselves 'piq.'"

"Whatever. Where the hell did they come from? How do they *exist?*"

I knew I sounded petulant, but I was too tired and distressed to care. Val, ever patient, ignored my shouting and steered me through a gate that had opened directly ahead of us—a shortcut into my office. "Sit," he said, leading me to the pair of leather couches. Another pizza appeared on the coffee table, along with a gallon-sized bowl of red grapes, a plate of nuts and olives, and a glass jug of something that looked suspiciously like sangria. "Keep eating, keep drinking. You'll be weak for a time yet, but food and drink help," he continued, taking the couch opposite me. "And I'll tell you all."

"Everything," I insisted, reaching for the jug.

"Everything," he agreed with a sigh.

And he did. Calmly, clinically, he recounted every wound, every death, every sacrifice—and then he left me to the silence.

The stars were out when I next heard a knock. I said nothing, but the door creaked open a moment later, revealing Aiden's face in the gap. "Hey," he murmured, then hesitated to gauge my reaction. "Are you feeling any better?"

I beckoned him inside. "Stronger. Sit, if you like," I said, pointing to the empty couch.

Aiden frowned as he looked around the firelit office. "Dark in here, isn't it? You want some candles or something?" I shook my head, and he settled into the seat opposite me. "Look, I'm sorry about the thing with Lailu. It was stupid—"

"I'm not upset about that."

"Oh." He paused as a log cracked and spit embers in the fireplace behind me. "You're not?"

"No."

"Because Val said you wanted to be alone, and I thought maybe you were mad at Joey and me..."

His voice drifted off as he waited for confirmation or denial, and I refilled my glass from the decanter on the table. The sangria was long gone, and I'd moved straight to whisky, sobering myself every few drinks to keep from passing out. "Aiden," I said as the melting ice cubes clinked, "for everything you've done in the last year, you're entitled to a prank. And I still haven't thanked you properly. What you've done on my behalf...I should never have put you in that position, but all reports suggest that you've performed admirably."

"But my timing today could have been better, huh?"

I shrugged and sipped. "I swear, I'm not angry with you."

"Just processing everything, then?"

"Mourning, actually." His brow wrinkled, and I winced as the alcohol hit my throat. "All the deaths last year—I heard about them today. They're fresh." I drained my tumbler, shook the ice cubes, and reached for the decanter again. "Some more than others."

He waited while I poured another couple of fingers. "Siblings?"

"Eunice." Saying her name summoned her face to my mind—the immobile blonde hair, the eyes hiding beneath far too much eye shadow and purple-framed bifocals, the over-rouged lips pulling into a smile that turned every laugh line into a canyon—and I finished my drink in one long gulp. "She was one of the good ones," I said as my eyes watered with the burn.

Aiden nodded slowly. "She tried to save us."

"That's what Val said." I put my glass aside and gripped my knees. "She died for nothing."

"Yeah, she did."

"Damn it," I whispered, then grabbed the glass and threw it at the wall. It exploded in a shower of ice and crystal shards, and I stared at the wet spot on the floor where the debris had fallen.

He considered my outburst, then softly asked, "How many have you smashed today?"

"That makes seven," I said, pulling another from the air. "It's more satisfying than washing them."

"Mm." The evidence vanished with a flick of Aiden's finger, and he helped himself to a grape. "I'm sorry, Coileán."

I said nothing as I thought again of my former neighbor—Eunice Cooper, the little old lady who'd held her own against a bunch of faeries while armed with a teakettle. To learn that she met her end at the wrong end of a wand and died in the road like a rabid dog...

"It never gets any easier," I said, feeling the pressure of Aiden's eyes on me. "Good, bad, or other, they all die eventually. And when it's one of the good ones, the ache doesn't go away." I glanced up from my contemplation of the rug. "That's one of the reasons why I've kept to myself. It hurts every time I lose someone."

He gave an almost imperceptible nod. "You didn't want to bring her here?"

"She wouldn't come. And I don't blame her." I stood, tested my balance to be sure I wasn't about to tumble into the furniture, then shuffled to my desk through the flickering shadows. "That's some of the best advice I can give you, little brother: choose your friends carefully and sparingly. They grow, they age, they die, and you're left to toss flowers onto the casket."

I tried not to think about what might be going through his mind. Aiden was young, and the young think themselves invincible and immortal, evidence to the contrary be damned. But Aiden had seen more than his share of death since we'd been thrust into each other's lives, and surely he understood the future that awaited his sister—and, I reminded myself, Joey. I'd let myself become too fond of the boy, and now that he was tying himself to Helen, his fate was sealed. Faerie could keep him young while he remained within its borders, but every trip back to the mortal realm returned the deferred hours and days to him like grains of sand down a moving hourglass. If he were to marry the grand magus, he wouldn't stay here indefinitely. And someday, not that many years in the future, Joey would leave for the last time. They would die, the both of them, because no self-respecting wizard would ever accept the devil's bargain I could offer: live forever, young and strong, but do so as a de facto prisoner of Faerie.

Surely Aiden knew that. Perhaps he hadn't yet *accepted* it, but he had to know that they would leave him eventually.

But before that happened…well, by the odds, Father Paul would be next to go. My pupil and partner—my *friend*—would face the end, no matter how much I tried to coax him out of it, and go forth in hopes of a short stay in Purgatory. And after him…who? Greg, perhaps—wizards were adept at extending their lives, but not indefinitely. Or Slim, maybe by a heart attack or cirrhosis. Stuart the would-be wizard wouldn't last long if he couldn't accept his mundane nature. Then Vivi Stowe and her hapless beau, Hal—and that one would be all the worse because Vivi should have shared her family's immortality. I couldn't help them, any of them, because the sanctuary I promised was a well-appointed bunker in a radioactive desert, protection from certain death but a prison nonetheless.

And I would be alone again. Oh, I'd have Val and Toula—and by some miracle, I'd have my brother…

Unless I *didn't* have them, my traitorous mind insisted. Unless their lives ended like Meggy's. I could protest all I wanted, but I couldn't guarantee their safety.

I shook my head, trying to dispel the memory of Meggy's eyes, and slid my chair out from my desk. "About Moyna." Aiden cringed, but I held up my hands to calm him. "This isn't a complaint—I want to know where we stand."

His shoulders relaxed. "Nothing confirmed in a year. Rumors and dead ends, but no solid sightings. Toula even got a summoner from the Arcanum's stash, but it couldn't find her. Wherever she's hiding is a good spot."

"Or whoever is hiding her knows a good spot," I said, levitating the whisky across the room with a crooked finger. "And how to cover her tracks. Any idea how many of Mab's people are working with her?"

He shook his head. "Val could pick them out of the dead, but I know we didn't kill all of them in Montana. Probably not even a large fraction of them. As for how many have joined Moyna, your guess is as good as mine."

I produced a new glass and poured my poison. "Val told me you've been having issues about that with the Arcanum."

"I don't exactly run home to catch up with friends," he replied with a smirk, propping his tennis shoes on the table. "Council wants to know where she is. I keep telling them I don't have the resources to devote to that at the moment, and it pisses them off. Your call now, of course, but I'm not going to lie and say I haven't enjoyed being the sand in their shorts."

"Mm. No word from Nath?"

"Not a peep."

That much was reassuring—with everything else I'd dumped on my brother, at least I hadn't left him to negotiate with the new queen of the Gray Lands. I drank and tried to enumerate the places my patricidal daughter could hide, but the hour was late, and my head was fuzzing up again. "What of Oberon's court? No sign of the heir?"

"None," said Aiden, rising from the couch, "but we're getting close. Want to see?"

I spread my hands across the desk in invitation, and with a little grunt, he hoisted a stack of atlases off the floor. "I was wondering about your sudden interest in cartography," I said.

"Not mine. Toula's." Aiden cracked the top book open, a road atlas of Argentina, and flipped through the pages until he found a cluster of white dots of corrective fluid. "That's the raw data. Wait there," he said, walking back toward the bookcase beside my desk, "and let me pull up the spreadsheet."

"What am I looking at?"

"Oberon's kids." He pulled what appeared to be a slim screen from the shelf and plopped it onto the top map, then made a few taps until the screen lit and shifted into columns and rows. "I worked this up a few months ago. There's a neat little piece of enchantment connecting the tablet and the maps—when the targets move, the computer knows it. Makes my life a heck of a lot easier. Fewer paper cuts, at least." He propped the device on a kickstand and tapped the white dots on the page. "Toula's a genius when it comes to theoretical spellcraft."

"So she tells me…"

"She really is *that* good. Gives Hel pointers. Quietly," he added, grinning. "This, now," he said, patting the map, "I don't want to know all the work that went into pulling it together, but the end result is gorgeous."

I looked down at the paper, which smelled strongly of magic but was otherwise unremarkable. Aiden could see the magic around us, but my healing sleep had done nothing to correct my lifelong blindness. "Colorful, is it?"

Aiden's smile widened. "Sufficiently shiny. Anyway, this is running on blood magic. I had a sample from Oberon preserved, and Toula did her thing with it. Each of those dots corresponds to someone in his bloodline," he explained, raising the corners of the atlas's pages to show me the colored circles marking the maps. "Red denotes children, orange is grandchildren, and so on. We're only interested in the red ones, but it's still been a long slog."

He let the pages fall back into place, and I tapped the top one. "And the Wite-Out?"

"The ones we've cleared. Let me show you." He pulled the computer forward—instinctively, I slid back in my chair—and began scrolling through his data. "Identity, approximate age, date confirmed…I've done a lot of work on this," he said, pointing to the columns as proof. "When the maps update, so does my spreadsheet." Seeing my puzzlement, he said, "The spell keeps tabs on them. When they move, their dots move with them. Have I mentioned that Toula's a genius at this?"

"I believe you." The dots on the top page were stationary, but I had no idea of the hour in Brasília. "How many are left to investigate?"

"One hundred ninety-four down, three to go."

"That's *all*?"

"I told you I've been busy." Dropping his computer on the blotter, he began to riffle through the stack until he found a UK road atlas. "I didn't have leads on any of these, so I saved them for last," he said, opening to an overview page of the island. Three red dots popped out of the printed chaos, and he pointed to each in turn. "One in Cardiff, one in Leeds, and one in Durham."

"I think I know Cardiff and Leeds. But check against your records—Mary Newsom and Tobias Black?"

He made a few taps, frowned at the screen, then shook his head. "I don't have either name."

"She's a painter, he's a potter, and they're both recluses. They're also both under two hundred, so I doubt that either is the one we're after."

"Which leaves Durham," he murmured, adding my notes to his spreadsheet. "Hasn't budged all year but for a quick trip to southern Spain."

"You'd run off to the Costa del Sol, too, if you spent the rest of your time in Durham."

"What's wrong with Durham?"

"Nothing," I said, shrugging, "aside from the bit about northern England. The beaches are better on the Med, trust me."

"Well," he replied with a dramatic sniff, "aren't *we* fancy."

I shoved him off my desk and flipped through the atlas until I found a closer view of the city and another red dot. I'd had occasion to visit Durham, and I remembered the place—modest beside London, but impressive for the region. I'd not visited since the 1950s, but the map made plain how far the city's university had spread in the intervening decades. As I peered at the page, trying to orient myself, I watched the red dot slowly move north along one of the streets. "Is there a better map for this area?" I asked Aiden, pointing to him the drifting dot. "Something to give us an idea of where the target might be going?"

"Not in there," he replied, but pulled his computer back into his lap and began working. "I took the liberty of installing Wi-Fi in here." His left hand waved toward the bookshelves, and I spotted a squat black box with a pair of antennae on one of the shelves. "Micro-gate running into Stuart's apartment with the line. I pay for his cable and Internet, and he lets me plug in."

While Aiden worked, I headed to the shelf, then carefully pulled the box out of its hiding place. A gray cord ran from its back through a nearly invisible hole in the fabric of the realm, and it resisted when I gave it an experimental tug.

"There's one in my room, too," he said, "and one in Joey's loft, so I'll take that one out of here if it's bothering you. And it's not going to bite you," he chided as I nudged it back into place with two fingertips. "It's a router, not a land mine."

"You never know."

"Actually, since I bought that one at Best Buy, I'm pretty sure I do. And here's your map." He brought the screen over and showed me an aerial view of Durham. "I put a marker where the dot stopped," he said, then swiped at the glass until the view zoomed in. "It's a university building."

He held the computer out and waited, and I gingerly took it from him for a closer look. There was the main road, a narrow track lined with brick and stone buildings, like so many others in any good British city of relative age. A pair of pedestrians was frozen on the side of the street, a girl and boy in shorts and T-shirts. "This can't be current," I said, touching the glass. "Not in Decem—wait, what did I…"

The picture shifted under my fingers, but Aiden had seen enough. "This is from 2009," he said, restoring the earlier view with a tap, "and you're using a touch screen, so be aware of that before you start poking it. Is that what you wanted to see?"

Wary of the weird computer, I handed it back to its master and nodded. "I know of exactly one of Oberon's children with a reason to be in Durham," I said, heading back to my map-cluttered desk. "She's been there for years in one guise or another. I say 'she,'" I added, piling the books back into a stack, "but it's entirely possible that she's still passing as male. Haven't seen her in sixty years, so it's hard to say."

Aiden turned his computer off and put it back on the shelf. "Who is she?"

"Her true name is Eleanor. When I last saw her, she was known as Richard. Historian," I continued, dropping the maps back onto the rug. "Antiquarian, author, professor. I was in search of a book, and she had a copy in her library."

"Sold it to you?"

"No, but she let me examine it once I swore I wasn't going to attack her. People get so *twitchy*…"

"You do have a reputation."

I brushed it aside. "We never spoke of her age, but Eleanor's no spring chicken. She could be the heir."

Aiden folded his arms and leaned against the stone wall. "So why hasn't she come forward? No one's been hanging around Durham. I've got time-lapse maps if you want to see—"

"I believe you," I said, cutting short the offer before Aiden could bring out his toys again. "Eleanor's half fae, and she keeps to herself. She never even crossed my path until I stumbled into her. If she avoids the rest of her family…" I shrugged. "Up for a field trip?"

He made a face. "Northern England in mid-December? Your timing is *impeccable*."

CHAPTER 3

Though I was eager to be off that night, Val wouldn't hear of it. "You're not going anywhere until you can walk the length of the palace unaided," he decreed as he assisted me back to my room. I led us on the long route, hoping to show him that I was no invalid, but the plan backfired when my knees buckled on the staircase. "She's waited a year," Val told me as I muttered curses at my legs. "She can wait another few days. And if she has a queen's power," he added, hoisting me from the rug, "don't you think you should be in decent form before approaching her?"

Despite my long nap, I tumbled into bed and slept until the sun was high. The rest had done me good, and I made my way to my office with the assistance of a wooden cane. Val walked beside me, ready to catch me if I stumbled, but I clenched my teeth and focused on remaining vertical.

Shortly after breakfast arrived, Aiden let himself in and pulled a chair up to my desk, the better to steal my coffee. "I gave this some thought," he began, helping himself to the carafe, "and I think it would be best to wait until tomorrow to pop over to Durham."

I nudged the sugar bowl his way with a fingertip. "Val got to you, too?"

"Aside from that. Tomorrow's Saturday. I assume the goal's to find Eleanor when she's alone, yeah? Smaller chance of catching her with students if we go on the weekend."

"True," I mused, attacking my omelet. My appetite had

yet to fall from ravenous, and I was prepared to eat the parsley garnish if the eggs and toast didn't do the trick. "Tomorrow, then. What time?"

"After dark. We're not synched with them right now in terms of daylight, so let me study the map today, see if I can't figure out where she goes and when. Her weekend schedule might be different, but at least we'll have a starting point." He sipped his coffee, then added more sugar. "And you've still got a dozen piq downstairs, Coileán."

I lowered my utensils and groaned. "Knew I was forgetting something."

"Which is why you have me. Lailu understands—she had a word with the realm."

"*She* talks to the realm?"

Aiden nodded and drank. "Faerie can be chatty when she wants to be. Or when she thinks I'm about to do something stupid," he added, grinning over his cup.

I hesitated. "Has she spoken to you since…uh…"

"Since you woke? Yeah. The constant voice, now, that's gone—and you can have that with my blessing," he muttered, "but she's keeping me posted while you recover. I think she's trying not to overwhelm you. She said you ignore her when she tells you too much, too quickly."

"Guilty," I mumbled, resuming my breakfast. "So what I am I to do with our guests?"

He leaned back in his chair and propped his feet on the corner of the desk. "Well, Lailu's plan was to leave Kuni here as an ambassador. I went ahead and gave him the language yesterday, seeing as you don't speak any Piq."

"And you do?"

"Picked it up on a visit out there. Joey's intonation is better than mine, but they're nice about it. Now, *Kuni's* speech is going to take a little work, but it's not impossible to understand him. Just tell him to slow down and drop his voice if he gets wound up."

I thought of Lailu's squeak in my ear. "How low *can* he

go?"

"Eh, still sounds like he's sucking helium, but it's intelligible. You get used to him."

The omelet was cooling, so I talked around bites. "Is there any chance of getting trousers on him?"

"Not unless you insist. I mean, yeah, the loincloth is distracting at first, but we got over it."

Nudity was nothing new to me—I'd had enough dealings with the merrow over the centuries to be unfazed by their lack of fashion—but the thought of having a near-nudist around long-term, let alone a six-inch-tall near-nudist with vibrant orange wings, was unsettling. "If you *gently* suggested it, do you think he'd give pants a try?"

"Probably." He shrugged. "If you think it's going to be a problem—"

"I do." I stuffed the last of the egg in my mouth and turned my attention to the basket of toast. "And where did you leave them, anyway?"

"I modified one of the guest suites. They live in a cave and a hollowed-out tree, so I didn't think a four-poster was going to cut it."

I regarded my brother closely over the desk. "How cave-like did we go with these modifications?"

He chuckled. "Not particularly. I put niches in the wall, a pond in the middle of the room, and threw in a few trees. Lailu seems to like it."

"There's a *pond* in my guest suite?" Aiden tensed at my change in tone, but I shook my head. "Faerie left you with more than a little boost, didn't it?"

"Looks like she did. I'll put the room back together," he began, but I waved a piece of toast at him to cut the offer short.

"Aiden, you've managed to reconnect us with a race I didn't even know *existed*. Don't worry about the pond."

He relaxed, but only fractionally. "If I screwed up," he said in a quiet rush, "just tell me, okay? I'll try to fix it. You're not going to hurt my feelings."

I dropped my crust and stared at him. "You haven't screwed up, kid. For that matter, you've done a better job than I would have in your place, all right? I was still pretty useless at seventeen. You kept the court together."

His face reddened. "A lot of that was Val—"

"And you had sense enough to listen to him. Again, *seventeen*." My stomach complained about the delay, and I plucked up another piece of toast. "If something should happen to me, you'd better damn well take the reins again."

"Roger that," he replied, refilling his coffee cup. "Assuming Moyna doesn't come back, right?"

I sighed but kept chewing. "One problem at a time, Aiden. One at a time."

Finding myself with hours on my hands that afternoon while Aiden studied his maps, I asked an aide to invite Lailu to my office to resume our aborted meeting. Ten minutes later, she arrived on his shoulder, then flitted onto the nearer couch and waited while he left and I limped over to join her. She positioned herself on the edge of the cushion and frowned up at me. "You are in pain?"

"Unsteady," I admitted, straining to make out her words across the coffee table. "I'm recovering, but—"

"More slowly than you would like. I know the feeling." Seeing my bemusement, she quickly shook her head. "Not the healing sleep, but a broken leg, a torn wing, these things I know too well. We have no magic to speed the process." She shrugged. "Rest and time. Do not rush yourself."

"Unfortunately, I have matters that can't wait." I paused, remembering that situations like this generally called for refreshments. "May I offer you a drink?"

"Water."

I imagined a piq-proportioned glass into being and carefully passed it across the table. She took it with both hands—I'd overestimated the size and cringed at the gaffe, but Lailu remained gracious as I poured myself a dram. "It has been years since I was among daig," she told me. "One forgets the ease with which these things come to you," she added, hoisting her accidental chalice.

"Daig?"

She tapped her chest, then pointed to me. "Piq, daig."

"Ah. Aiden said you used to—"

"I knew your mother when she was a girl," said Lailu. "And Mab, and Oberon. I watched them grow, and then I watched them go to war. I took my people to safety." She put her glass aside, balancing it on the cushion, and smoothed her dress over her knees. "Some crossed between the realms—my daughters have bands of their own over there—but most of us remained in the forest. I would ask that you respect our right to our land."

I tried not to gape, but it was difficult to hide my shock. If Lailu was older than my mother, then she was positively ancient. "Of course," I managed after a moment. "Show me what lands you claim, and I'll see that your territory is acknowledged. And, uh…my lady, I had no idea you were so…um…*seasoned*."

She smiled impishly. "I do not discuss my age, child. As for our lands, all we claim are our settlement and hunting grounds—perhaps half a day's flight in all directions. Joey says he has been mapping the forest. If he is available, perhaps he could show us his work. To spare you the trip, at least."

"I'll ask him to come in," I said, rising from the couch to collect my phone. Before I could make it to my desk, however, I heard a rattling from the bookshelf, then a familiar, if muffled, voice calling in English, "Hello? Aiden? You in there?"

I froze, cutting my eyes between the router and Lailu, who cocked her head at the disturbance. "Just a moment," I told her, hurrying toward the router and the tiny gate behind it. "Please don't get up."

"Aiden?" the voice asked again—a nasal voice, one that could only belong to Stuart Purcell. "Are you there, kid? Got some mail for you."

I moved the router out of the way and expanded the gate in the back of the bookshelf beyond the quarter-sized hole Aiden had installed. "He's busy," I told Stuart as the brown eye on the other side widened and retreated from the enlarged gate. "Can I help you?"

As I peered through the hole, I could make out Stuart's thin face, chapped nose, and cold-reddened cheeks. A yellow ski cap hid his messy hair, and he held an open envelope with coordinating gloves. In lieu of a coat, however, Stuart wore a fluffy bathrobe. "Colin!" he cried, clutching at his chest. "Goodness, when did you wake up?"

"Yesterday," I replied, willing Lailu to stay out of sight. "What's going on?"

Stuart pulled a folded piece of paper from the envelope in his hand. "New packages from the cable company," he said, holding the paper closer to the gate. "They're offering faster high-speed, and I didn't know if Aiden wanted to upgrade."

I knew that nothing good would come of asking for clarification. "I'll pass it along," I said, sticking my hand through the hole, and Stuart gave me the letter. "What, uh…"—I glanced at my Virginia-synched wall clock—"what time is it over there? Two-thirty a.m. or p.m.?"

"A.m. I couldn't catch anyone last night, and since I was up already, I thought I'd try again. I was doing a little prep work, shoveling snow," he explained. "Hate getting caught in a rush at sunrise, you know?"

The thought of Stuart drawing ineffective circles on the driveway and chanting in the cold was pitiful, but I withheld my opinion. "Good luck. Don't freeze."

He stepped back, and I realized what I was seeing through the gap: the long wall of my old apartment's main room, now painted sandstone and decorated with a replica tapestry. It was Stuart's apartment now—it had been for about two years, I recalled with a pang, seeing in my mind's eye the watercolor seascape Meggy had hung in place of Stuart's tapestry. I'd given the building to Eunice, and she had loaned it to her great-nephew…

"Stuart," I said as I retracted my hand through the gate, "I just heard about Eunice. My condolences, I didn't—"

"Thanks," he said, cutting me short as he bent to pick up the tabby rubbing herself against his robe. "She…" He paused, scratched the cat's head, and sighed. "She tried to do the right thing."

"She did."

We stood in awkward silence for a few seconds, and then I cleared my throat. "So what are you still doing in Rigby?"

He shrugged. "Two buildings bought and paid for, a decent Internet business…I don't have much incentive to move again, to be honest."

"You don't think there are better markets for a wizard?"

The corner of his mouth ticked upward. "Seeing as the Arcanum would probably laugh me out of their silo…"

"True. Any luck with the, uh…wizarding thing?"

"Probably nothing you'd consider proof, but I have several lovely testimonials on my website." My eyebrow quirked, and Stuart sniffed his disdain. "*Skeptic*."

"Not at all. The fact that you're still making a living on that nonsense is magical enough," I replied, conscious that Lailu was watching our conversation in polite silence. "Sorry, Stu, things to do, realm to run, I'll give this to Aiden. Thanks," I said, and shrank the gate back to its original size.

"Just let me know if I need to change the package!" he called through the hole, and then I heard something slide in front of the gate, blocking it from view.

With a sigh, I shuffled back to the couch and dropped Aiden's letter on the table. "My apologies. Something for

Aiden. That was an, uh…acquaintance."

"No trouble," Lailu replied, hoisting her glass for another sip of water. "Daig? Daigul?" I frowned, and she explained, "Daigul—big like daig, but no magic."

"Emphatically daigul. He refuses to accept it, but that's another matter."

"Poor thing. How are you acquainted? A friend of Aiden's?"

I closed my eyes and softly groaned. "Long story short, he moved to my town, and now he's living in my old apartment. When we met, he said he was a wizard, and he was working on a book about fairies—tiny, glowing women with wings and sparkles." I shook my head at the recollection. "He actually told me he'd seen a bunch on the beach. I still don't know what he'd been drinking that night, but—"

"Near you?" Lailu interrupted. "He saw them near you?"

"Yes…"

She smiled. "When Titania died, I asked the Lady about you. She would not tell me much, but she said you spent time in the other realm, and she told me where to find you. I passed that information to one of my daughters, and she and her band followed the coast to you."

"You *stalked* me?"

"Not precisely," she replied, unbothered by my rising voice. "I wanted information. We are adept at going unseen." She ran one hand through the purple haze surrounding her. "One learns to compensate."

"But you were spying on me?"

"Only briefly. There was little to see. But it's possible your acquaintance saw us."

I gawked at her, uncertain whether to be more upset by the piq espionage or by the fact that Wizard Stu might have been *right*. "And leaving your nephew here, is that to be a continuation of your intelligence-gathering activities?"

Lailu's smile faltered as my anger pushed its way to the

fore. "You misunderstand me. I wanted to know what we could expect before I considered bringing my people out of hiding—whether you were reasonable or more akin to your mother. That's all. My daughter gave me a good report." While I considered that, she pressed on. "Consider my position, Coileán. My people have been safe largely through daig ignorance. I suppose I could have made myself known to you sooner, but I could not take that risk." She spread her hands in a gesture of helplessness. "You see my dilemma. There will be no further investigation, but I had to know before I made a move."

Her explanation was sound, even if I didn't like it. "You couldn't have trusted the realm?"

"She is not always as forthcoming as I would like, and she respects your privacy."

"Oh? She told you where to find me, didn't she?"

"In the vaguest of terms. They searched for days and days before they located you. The Lady can be…capricious."

"Fair enough," I muttered, then stood and headed for my desk. "I'll get Joey in here, and you can show me your lands."

As I trudged across the room, Lailu squeaked, "I have offended you. That was not my intent."

I turned to find her standing on the back of my couch, clasping her hands. "Mother used to spy on me," I murmured. "I seldom liked the result. You'll forgive me if it's a sore spot."

"I will. But tell me honestly that you would not have done what I did."

"I can't," I grudgingly admitted.

She waited, letting the silence condemn my indignation, then said, "I assure you, Kuni is no spy. Had I wished to put a spy here, I would have done so without your leave. It would not have been the first time one of my people lived in secret among yours. But I come to you with an offer of friendship. Will you accept it?"

I reached for the phone on my blotter. "If I didn't, I wouldn't be calling Joey in to talk borders."

Lailu smiled and took a seat.

I had told Aiden to pass along to Joey my assurance that I wasn't going to kill him for the stunt with the piq entourage, but he still seemed hesitant on the phone. Nevertheless, he hurried to my office, lugging with him a leather-bound folio half the size of a door. Working quickly, he cleared the coffee table, then dropped the folio on top with a thump and a flurry of dust motes. "I've got to reshoot some of this," he cautioned, "but the aerials should give you a rough approximation."

He opened the folio and started flipping through the tabbed pages. I tried to assemble the glimpses I caught into coherence, but he turned too quickly for the photographs and line drawings to make sense until he stopped on a spread and pointed to the glossy green half on the left, an overhead shot of a tree canopy with a clearing in the middle. "That's the area," he explained, then pointed to the photograph on the right, a false-colored shot revealing the details below the branches. "The resolution isn't great, but that's more or less what we're actually looking at. And here's the final product." He flipped the page to a highly detailed hand-drawn map of the forest floor. "Frances has been doing the cartography as we go."

"Frances?" I asked.

"Your niece. She and Bon are the only two who can draw worth a damn, and he'd rather do plants." I continued to look at him blankly, and Joey straightened up from the map book. "You don't know Frances?"

"Can't say that I do…"

"Oh. Guess she's too young. Well, anyway, you have a niece named Frances, and she's our cartography expert.

Ingulf helps where he can, but he's more of a geologist than anything. Na and Pulen have been doing the write-ups, and Bon illustrates—"

"Wait, stop," I said, waving my hands, "what the heck are you talking about? Ingulf I know, but the others…who? *What* are you lot doing?"

"I'm working on a comprehensive map and field guide to the realm with five of your nieces and nephews," Joey said slowly. "Ingulf's our logistics guy and best muscle, Na's a self-taught biologist, Pulen's a botanist, Bon's a jack-of-all-trades naturalist because *everything* fascinates him, and Frances draws the maps. I handle the aerial photography because Georgie still likes me, and because Aiden keeps adding cameras to my gear. So…surprise?"

"How the devil did you organize *that*?"

"Talk to Mina," he said, grinning. "She's got stories. Those five get bored and start poking at things, so when I suggested we make this an organized effort, they joined up pretty quickly. They're all half fae," he said, turning back to his maps, "so we work well together. Mind you, they walk into trees, but they're mostly harmless."

"A rousing endorsement," I muttered. "What spurred this little project?"

Joey grimaced. "There are things out in the bush I'd *really* have liked to know about before I stumbled onto them. Anyway, the piq settlement is here," he said, stubbing his finger against the map. "To put it in context, there's a larger map on page seventeen…"

I flipped through the folio, trying to tally the hours that had been spent in its compilation. "Joey," I murmured after passing the fifteenth map of a remote lake I'd certainly never seen, "this is incredible."

"It's nowhere near finished—"

"It's fantastic." I looked up and caught the flush rising from his neck. "I need to leave you to your own devices more often, don't I?"

He shrugged. "Just giving you a reason to keep me

around, boss."

"I don't need a reason," I replied, pausing on a map that showed the piq lands in relation to the palace. "A little bird told me about certain giant spiders."

"Please don't remind me. I told Na she's on her own for that entry." He rose and nodded to Lailu, who stood on the table to better study the folio. "Unless there's something else I can show you, I'll leave you to it…"

I cut my eyes to the wall clock. "Going out?"

"Helen's birthday is Sunday. She's swamped with finals and stuff all weekend, so I thought I'd surprise her with breakfast today, and I've got to pick up a few things first."

I looked at him in disbelief. "It's what, three-thirty over there?"

"She's been getting up at four lately. If she's going to spend her birthday weekend with a paper and a lab report, the least I can do I make waffles, right?"

"Just one more moment," I told him, taking up my cane. "Lailu, if you would excuse us?" She motioned me on, and I followed Joey into the hallway. When the door closed, I quietly asked him, "Were you planning on staying here post-nuptials?"

Joey hesitated. "Well…Helen's going to be moving back to the silo after graduation, and I should probably be there at least part of the time, but I can't bring Georgie to Montana. If you'd rather I not stick around because of the Arcanum thing, I totally understand—"

"I want you here, Arcanum be damned. Could you split your time?"

The relief on his face was unmistakable. "Sure, boss. And hey, there's not a lot of competition to worry about. I don't think the Arcanum is exactly hiring…"

"Should they change their mind, I'll double whatever they offer."

Joey started to laugh, but he paused when he saw my expression. "I'm not trying to jump ship," he said, sounding concerned. "If you've still got a use for me—"

I gripped his shoulder, surprising him into silence. "You're welcome here. Always. Thank you for everything. Last year…the map project…all of it. Thank you."

"I didn't do anything special—"

"You kept Aiden alive, for starters. I owe you far more than a paycheck for that alone." I released him and stepped back, and cleared my throat to stall. "Look, about this wedding…"

Joey waited, and when I left the matter hanging, he guessed, "You're opposed?"

"No. If you're happy, go with my blessing. But…I don't mean to be crass, but these things are expensive, yes? Do you, uh…need anything?"

He patted my arm. "Appreciate it, but Aiden's been paying the bills. We've got everything booked—since Helen told me to stand back and show up when directed, everything's in order. All I had to do was line up counseling with Father Paul, and he gave us the *special* version, since Helen isn't converting any time soon."

"You're such a bad Catholic."

"Probably a good thing I left seminary, huh?" He leaned against the wall and shoved his hands in his pockets. "Anyway, we're all set for April except for this one little wizard ceremony, but thanks."

"What are the wizards going to make you do, jump a broom or something?"

"Comments like that will get you smacked around in the silo," he replied with a snort. "It's this traditional thing—Helen says they make sure you're not too closely related before you get married. I guess that could be a problem for old-blood families, but given my awe-inspiring lack of magical ability, I don't think there's much chance that I'm Helen's long-lost cousin. But if it makes the Council happy, I'm game. They're not sold on me, so the least I can do is prove that Helen and I won't be inbreeding, right?" He straightened and shrugged. "And on that romantic note, I need to shower and buy waffle mix."

"At this time of night?"

"There's a twenty-four-hour place near her apartment. The security bars add to the charm." He started down the corridor, but turned and spoke as he walked backward. "I'm putting your RSVP down as a yes, all right?"

"I'll think about it," I called after him.

"What was that?" he asked, cupping his hand around his ear. "'Yes, Joey, of course I'll be there'? Perfect."

I waved him away, and Joey jogged off to make himself presentable.

When I returned to my office, I found Lailu standing on the middle of the map. "I can show you with this," she said, waiting while I limped to the table. "The picture helps." She pointed to the photograph on the facing page, which mostly showed leafy treetops. "He is a clever boy, isn't he?"

"Joey?" I said, sliding onto the couch. "Yes, I think so."

"And you're fond of him."

"I am."

"The Lady is, too. And she is uncertain about the marriage."

"Last I checked, it wasn't any of her business."

"That may be," she said with a shrug, "but when has she ever kept her opinion to herself? Now, to work. Watch closely—I will walk our borders. You may wish to note them," she added, and smiled when I produced a pencil.

CHAPTER 4

The piq horde left that night, sped on their way by a gate. "Believe me," Aiden said once the last had passed through, "I offered to let them use a shortcut to get here, but Lailu insisted on doing it the hard way. I think she wanted to show Kuni the escape route."

As for the new envoy, he had set up camp in the barn once he realized that Georgie was out there. By the time I checked on him, he'd killed a rat, built a fire in the dirt, and was picking bits of blackened rodent out of his teeth. I offered him less rustic accommodations, but he declined and flew off to a hay bale, where he settled down like a living nightlight.

I woke late the next day, groggy but feeling whole enough to toss aside the embarrassing cane. After another gut-busting meal, I informed Val that Aiden and I would be going to Durham that evening. Though he fretted, he stood aside that night, tight-lipped but acquiescent, as I opened a gate onto a deserted alley.

Aiden poked his head through the hole, glanced around, then retreated and looked at me suspiciously. "Is this anywhere near the address I gave you?"

"Not exactly," I admitted, producing a wool overcoat against the wet wind blowing through the gate. "It's as close as I could get."

He sighed and considered the plastic trash bins shoved against the wall of the restaurant ahead of us, all three scuffed and rimed. "December," he muttered, then removed his canvas messenger bag and closed his eyes. In an instant, his T-shirt was covered by a thin black sweater, barely visible beneath a coordinating windbreaker. A black ski cap materialized over his light hair, hiding the top but doing nothing to disguise the ponytail. He slung his bag over his chest as the flap sprouted a set of crooked patches—flags, a few names I recognized as bands, and other mysterious logos—then reached inside and pulled out a set of fingerless black gloves. "Ready, then?" he asked, sliding a pair of headphones around his neck.

I stepped back and took him in, from cap and sunglasses to tight jeans and dirt-stained sneakers. "What's the disguise supposed to be?"

"I'm seventeen. May as well look the part."

My conservative overcoat seemed stuffy by comparison. "Should I change into something like—"

"No. *God*, no," he muttered, then jumped through the hole before I could press him further.

I followed him and closed the gate behind us. By the time I had my bearings, however, Aiden had already pulled a telephone from his bag, plugged the headphones into it, and was poking at the screen and mumbling under his breath. "Problem?" I asked, calling a scarf into being.

"Just waiting for—okay, good, we've got GPS. And now…"

"What are you—"

"Figuring out how we need to get across town. And…we're routing. This way," he said, striding out of the alley.

I paused to take in the city around us—we'd landed in a shopping area, I noticed, a well-populated strip of sidewalk even with the discouraging weather. The bulk of the traffic was heading *that* way, which meant the river was…

And I'd already lost my brother. Scanning the crowd for his hat, I spotted him and jogged through a flock of pigeons to catch up. "Aiden, wait," I puffed, already worn out from the unaccustomed running, "if we go—"

He thrust the phone toward me, revealing a street map and a blinking indicator. "About a fifteen-minute trek if we don't dawdle," he said, then nodded toward the approaching clump of pedestrians, all of whom were bundled in coats and scarves against the wind. "Try to blend," he said in quiet English.

My legs complained as we hurried up the sidewalk, skirting old women pulling folding shopping bags and teenagers too engrossed in their conversation or their phones to notice the patches of ice in their way. Dodging a couple on promenade with a stroller, I managed to grab Aiden's shoulder and pull him to a halt. "What's the rush? We know where we're going—there's no need to turn this into a death march."

He frowned impatiently and tugged me along. "She's on a schedule—I've watched her for two days, and she was back at the office this morning. She'll break for lunch at twelve-thirty, and I want to be in the restaurant ahead of her."

"Or we could confront her at her office."

"Or we could do this my way and lessen our chances of getting incinerated." He dug in his bag and produced his tablet computer. "Here," he said after a few taps, and handed me the screen. "Her dossier. She's spent the best part of the last two days in the university's history department, so she's probably a professor."

I looked over the document in my hands. "These names?"

"History faculty. Anything jump out at you? And watch your step," he said, shoving me out of the way of the Pomeranian squatting in the middle of the sidewalk. The dog ducked behind its owner's legs to whimper as we neared, and Aiden hurried onward. When we were a safe block away, he mumbled, "They *know*. That's been tough, staying under the radar in a strange city when everyone's dog wants to either maul you or run away." He checked his bag's clasp and sighed to himself. "I used to be good with dogs. Not anymore."

"It comes with the territory," I murmured as I leaned toward him. "And if the owners had half the sense of their pets, they'd do the same thing."

"Yeah, that's not making me feel any better. Done with that?" He took the tablet from me and stowed it away. "Anyway, back to Eleanor. If the pattern holds, she'll be breaking for a kebab momentarily, so we need to hurry."

"How momentarily?" I followed him through a crosswalk against the light, trusting that no one driving around us was in the mood for vehicular homicide.

He checked his phone. "About twenty minutes. If we—"

"Stop. Where's the river?"

After consulting the map, he pointed to the left, and I led him down a winding alley until the water—and our destination neighborhood on the opposite shore—appeared. I checked for witnesses, then clamped my hand around his wrist, muttered, "Hold on," and visualized the far bank.

It took only a fraction of a second to warp space around us, and Aiden jerked in shock when he found himself across the river. "The hell—"

"I'll teach you when you're older. Which way?"

He scowled at his confused phone, then pointed up the street. "Top of the road, hang a right. Why the heck has no one mentioned *that* trick?"

I elbowed him and set off, stepping over graying piles of refrozen snow. "Because there are certain skills that only come with age, kid. Try that now, and you probably wouldn't like the result. And kebabs, you said?"

"Yeah, it's a kebab shop. They didn't have a website, but I found good reviews on a student page."

"I'm going to pretend I understood that," I said, turning out of the side street, and spotted the walls of Durham Cathedral ahead. A line of miserable tourists passed, led by an overly cheery woman with a red umbrella, and I rubbed my gloves together against the chill. "Where to?"

"There," said Aiden, pointing down the street to the yellow sign jutting out of a line of nondescript stone buildings. "Come on, let's grab a table."

A bell jangled as Aiden pushed the door open with his shoulder, and my arm tingled in warning at the steel plate as I followed him into the warm restaurant. The place was tiny, a hole in the wall with plastic tables and mismatched chairs, weakly lit by the pale sun and the sole surviving fluorescent bulb in the ceiling, but the smells of meat and spices made my overactive stomach rumble. A few patrons, almost all of them toting backpacks or bags like Aiden's, occupied most of the available tables, but the young man behind the counter seemed unstressed by the moderate crowd. "Dine in or takeaway?" he asked us, looking up from his phone.

"I'll handle this," Aiden told me, and I squatted at a table in the back of the room while he put in the order and made small talk with the proprietor. He seemed at ease, I noticed, far more confident than I'd recalled. Then I thought about Aiden's spreadsheet and the one hundred ninety-four contenders he'd eliminated without my help, and my brother's nonchalance suddenly made sense. This was old hat to him—the preparation, the stake-out, the cover story, the clothing, everything planned and timed and sorted. I wondered how many of these jaunts he had made alone, striking out each time in hopes of uncovering someone with power as great as his. It was dangerous work for someone with experience, but *Aiden*…

My musings ended abruptly when he brought two filled pitas to the table. "Eat quickly, she's probably on her way," he whispered.

He didn't have to tell me twice. I dug in with gusto, and my stomach ached like it had never seen food before. Aiden chuckled at the state of my sandwich, but he attacked his own pita while keeping one eye on the door.

His stalking paid off. The clock on the wall was ticking the half hour when the doorbell rang again, and the clerk stood and smiled as a woman shouldered her way inside. "Hello, Dr. Richardson," he said, sliding the phone into his pocket. "The usual?"

She slid her brown leather gloves into the pockets of her overcoat and nodded. "Yes, thank you, Ferdi. How's your mum today, still feeling poorly?"

There was nothing remarkable about the woman. She was perhaps five and a half feet tall, softened and padded in the way of those ending late middle age. Her hair, short and neatly coiffed, was a flat shade of brown that could only have come from a box. Her cosmetics disguised some of the lines of her face, but they couldn't hide the bags under her eyes—green eyes, I noticed, the most striking feature in an otherwise ordinary composition. Though relatively handsome, she would never be featured in a pin-up calendar. Still, her polished tone was unmistakable, the aural mark of education and breeding. I could envision her in a lecture hall, commanding an audience's attention through inflection and well-timed glances over the top of her frameless glasses. Her camelhair coat and plaid scarf hid all but her sensible pumps, but I assumed the rest of her attire would be similarly conservative—or at least more appropriate for the climate than that of the idiot boy working on a laptop two tables down from us, who'd decided that cargo shorts counted as cold-weather gear.

As the woman and the clerk chatted, Aiden leaned toward me and muttered, "Let me do this my way, all right?" Before I could protest, he'd pulled a copy of the *Times* from beneath the table, pressed it into my hands, and was heading for his quarry.

And so I held my newspaper like a fool as Aiden stepped to the woman's left and cleared his throat. "Excuse me, Professor," he said quietly, "sorry to bother you, but I'm working on this project, and I was wondering if I could ask you a few questions."

She turned to him with an expression of polite interest and gave him a quick once-over. "You're not one of my freshers, are you?" she asked as her brow wrinkled.

He flashed a disarming smile. "No, ma'am, I'm not. My project is more of a poli-sci thing."

"Is that so?" She took a paper sack from the clerk and slid a few bills across the counter. "Well, my expertise is medieval Europe, so unless you're doing a deep retrospective, I'm not sure how helpful I can be. Who sent you my way?"

"Long story. Would it be possible to have a minute of your time? Somewhere a little more private, maybe?"

Watching as stealthily as possible from over my paper, I saw her give Aiden a look I'd witnessed countless times before: the subtle eye flickering of a faerie trying to read another person's thoughts. Aiden stood calmly beside her, letting her pry, and reached into his satchel while the blood drained from her face. "Something you wrote resonated with me," he said, pulling a hardback book the size of an unabridged dictionary from his previously flat bag. "I'm sure you're busy, but it won't take more than a few minutes. Promise."

She maintained her mask of composure. "I…suppose I have time. My office, then?" She glanced around the restaurant, and her eyes landed on me. "Ah. There you are," she said, raising her voice. "I assume you'd like a word with me as well?"

I folded the paper and dropped it on the table beside the remnants of my meal. "If this is a good time."

"Good as any," she muttered, shifting the paper bag to her hip. "Ferdi, you can keep the change."

Once we were back in the cold, she looked up at me, tight-lipped and taut as a bowstring. "I've done nothing to you," she murmured. "What are you doing here?"

"You know damn well what this is about."

She hesitated, reading my face for signs of a bluff, then sighed as her shoulders slumped. "You'd best come in, then," she said, turning back up the street. "Both of you. But I warn you, put one toe out of line, and I'll—"

"This isn't about intimidation."

"No? You bring an associate and ambush me, and it's not at all about intimidation?"

"I'm only tagging along. This has been his show for the last year. And he's my brother, by the way."

He jogged ahead of us and waved. "Aiden. Hi."

"Charmed," Eleanor muttered.

We finished the short walk in silence, and she led us through one of the nondescript doors that popped at uneven intervals from the row of stone buildings. Up two flights of creaking stairs and down a short hallway, she stopped outside an old wooden door and put her gloves back on. Once protected, she fished a ring of keys from her pocket and admitted us to a modest office, a tidy room dominated by the window behind the desk and paneled with filled bookcases. "A moment," she said, then opened an inner door to the adjoining office. "Walt? I brought your lunch."

The door swung open far enough to reveal a paper-covered desk, a cluttered bookcase, and what appeared to be a quintessential English professor of advanced years, complete with receding hairline, gold-rimmed glasses, and tweed coat, sitting in a swivel chair. There was no window, but he'd compensated with a pair of standing lamps and plunked a green-shaded light beside his laptop. "Thanks, love," he said, beaming up at her over his computer and half-dozen notepads. "How's the weather?"

"Warmer. Step out while there's still daylight," she said, unpacking the paper bag, then squeezed his meal into the one clean space left on his desk. "Fresh air would do you good."

He pulled his glasses off, closed his eyes, and rubbed the bridge of his nose. "No time, I'm afraid. This article won't write itself."

"You always say that." She leaned over the desk and

kissed his wrinkled forehead. "Don't work too hard, dear. It isn't worth it."

He looked back at her with a smile as he returned his glasses to their place, then noticed Aiden and me in the other office. "Hello, there. Company?"

"Nothing to worry about. I'll be in here if you need me," she assured him, and gently closed the door between the offices.

When I heard him begin to unwrap his food, I took one of the pair of wooden chairs in front of Eleanor's desk and watched as she stripped off her outerwear and sank into her own leather seat. "You're close to your colleagues?" I asked, switching into quiet Fae.

She didn't smile. "Walter is my husband," she replied in kind, though her Fae was accented almost to the point of incomprehensibility. "Touch him and I'll kill you, Coileán."

"Your husband?" I echoed as Aiden took the vacant chair. "I was wondering why you were looking so feminine these days."

Her lips pursed. "That's not actually far off."

Aiden dropped his bag to the thin rug and pointed to the inner door. "Does he…*know*?"

"Most of it," she replied, unwrapping her pita. "You'll excuse me, but I'm on my lunch break."

"It's Saturday."

"That doesn't seem to matter to my stomach." She took a bite, then jabbed the sandwich toward him. "And you can drop the glamour now."

"I'm not using any."

"You…" She put her food down, peered at him, and shook her head. "You showed me what happened to my darling brother in Vienna. I know you're not a child."

"Actually," I cut in, wondering anew what Aiden had been up to in my absence, "he is. Realm let him sub for me while I was indisposed."

Aiden grinned, then dug in his bag and extracted a

plastic-capped tube. "Amazing what you can do with one of these babies," he said, pulling the top off to reveal a thin Phillips-head screwdriver. "For the record, he started it."

"That doesn't surprise me in the slightest," she muttered. "Put it away."

He shrugged and recapped his weapon. "Got a flamethrower in there, too?" I asked, peering into his bag.

"Nah. Rope, bear mace, couple of knives, a decent machete...you never know. What?" he asked, looking up to find our wide eyes on him. "Do you have any idea how many of your siblings live in the middle of the damn *jungle*?" he said to Eleanor. "Or up a mountain? Or on a fortified island in the middle of a lake? Look, I've been learning all of this by trial and error, and sometimes, when there's a giant snake bearing down on me, I say to hell with magic and reach for the ready-made explosives."

Eleanor blinked, then reached behind her glasses and rubbed her eyes. "No, that's not at all concerning. Try not to burn the building down, won't you? And as for you," she continued, turning to me, "I've done nothing to warrant an interrogation."

I folded my arms and leaned back in the chair. "You know your father's dead, don't you?"

"If you came to offer your condolences, that's unnecessary."

"Hardly. If you were close to him, you'd probably be dead now, too. Aiden finished him off," I added, thumbing my hand at my brother.

Eleanor's eyebrow rose. "Throwing the boy under the proverbial bus?"

"If I thought you were going to be upset, I wouldn't have told you. So, you know what happens now."

"I can't imagine," she replied, propping her chin on her fist as she took another bite.

"Let's cut to the chase, then. You're the new queen. What are you going to do about it?"

She chewed in silence for a long moment, then dabbed her rouged lips with a paper napkin. "I have no idea what you're talking about."

"Bullshit."

"I don't—"

I held up one hand to stop the lie. "Aiden's paid a visit to all but three of you. The other two aren't nearly old enough, and you, if I'm not mistaken, remember the Plantagenets. Robin was born when, 1300 or so? There was about a century between us—"

"Close," she mumbled. "1307. He was two years older than me."

Having detected the strain of defeat in her voice, I continued to probe. "It came on you, didn't it? The boost?"

"Last December," she grudgingly admitted. "I was marking essays, and…well, I thought I was having a heart attack. Walt wanted to call the paramedics, but I stopped glowing eventually, and he put the phone down. The poor dear worries." Seeing Aiden's confusion, she explained, "Walt knows what I am. He doesn't know who sired me, nor need he ever know."

"That must have been an interesting conversation," he replied.

She shrugged. "He's a witch. We made our peace." She took another bite, but her eyes kept drifting toward the inner door.

"Running a home for wayward witches?" I asked. "Charitable of you."

It should be noted that looks *can* kill when a faerie is old and angry enough, but Eleanor settled for a non-lethal glower. "I can't see how my marriage is any of your concern," she said, then pushed her sandwich away and folded her hands on the desk. "All right, I suppose I'm the eldest left. What do you want?"

I leaned toward her and lowered my voice. "I want you to undo what your father did. Take the throne properly and bring your court back to Faerie."

She laughed so loudly that I was sure Walt would appear to check on her. "Not on your life."

"They've been trying to go home for centuries—"

"So let them in. No one's stopping you."

"They're *your* court—"

"Take them. I don't want them." Her head swiveled, but she kept her eyes locked on mine. "I'm serious, you can have the lot of them. Do what you like over there— I'm not going."

I exhaled slowly, willing myself to be calm. "They won't follow me, and you know it."

"And that's your problem, isn't it?"

"We need to get them out of this realm. Nothing good comes of leaving faeries up to their own devices."

"Excuse me?" she snapped.

"You heard me. You and I are living proof of it. Or did your mother knowingly jump into Oberon's arms?"

She bristled. "I think I've done a fair bit of good in my time."

"Then you're the exception." I stood and planted my palms on the desk, the better to lean over her. "They're your responsibility. The realm isn't going to let you abdicate."

"She's sentient," Aiden offered. "Opinionated. You know, the voice in your head?"

Eleanor frowned. "What voice?"

"You'll hear her over there," I explained. "But you need to corral the court and bring them back. There's plenty of room, we can settle any disputes—"

She held up her hands to silence me. "You expect me to leave my life and everything I care about in order to...to play referee in Bedlam? And I'll get to talk to myself, too? Are you *mad?*" she shouted, rising from her chair. "I didn't ask for this, and I am *certainly* not obligated to go over there because Oberon is out of the picture. This is my life. You don't get to dictate it. The damn realm doesn't get to dictate it. And *he* doesn't get to dictate it, posthumously or otherwise."

Eleanor and I remained in our angry tableau for a long moment, each trying to out-muscle the other, until Aiden asked, "How old is Walt? Seventy? Seventy-five?"

"Seventy-two," Eleanor muttered. "What does that—"

"You can save him." He began to dig in his bag as her eyes bored into him. "How many good years does he have left? How many years, period? Sure, you can extend life to a point. The Arcanum knows every trick in the book on that. Ah, here it is." He looked back at her far more calmly than anyone staring down an angry faerie queen had a right to do. "I've seen wizards well over a hundred years old because there are some incredible casters in Montana. But they still drop dead eventually."

Seeing where he was going, I jumped in. "Bring Walt to Faerie. As long as he's there, he won't age a day. Give him a touch of youth back—he might still feel his years, but there's no reason that he can't look like he did in his prime." I saw the first shadow of doubt cross her face and chanced my luck. "He doesn't have to die, Eleanor. It's up to you."

Her fists balled, and the long breath she drew did little to stop the tremor in them. "You bastards," she whispered.

"I'm not trying to be cruel," said Aiden, "just pointing out that you have an option."

"Oh, sure," she spat, "we'll drop everything we've worked for and go *there*. I don't suppose he'd be able to leave, would he? He would adore being a prisoner."

The inner door squeaked on its hinges, and Eleanor turned in alarm as Walt poked his head into the room. "Darling? Is everything all right?" he asked, looking at Aiden and me with heightened suspicion. "You were shouting, and it sounded...um..." I kept my face blank, and Walt looked for answers in his wife's. "What's going on, Ellie?"

"We should be going," I said, motioning for Aiden to stand. "Think about it," I told her, and headed for the exit.

But Aiden lingered to press a small plastic oblong into Eleanor's palm. "Here, for you. Be careful."

She and Walt frowned at the gift, and she flipped it over in her hand as she asked, "What's on here?"

"That's a list of all your siblings," he replied, slinging his bag over his head. "The copy on that thumb drive isn't going to keep updating, but that's everyone's location as of today."

Eleanor put it on her desk. "I don't associate with my siblings. If any of them are looking for me, I hope you've been discreet."

"I haven't said a word." He tapped the plastic thing and slowly met Eleanor and Walt's eyes. "One of them might want a certain gift that you've been given. Do you have any children?"

"No," said Walt, "none…"

"Then should something happen to you," he said to Eleanor, "that gift would pass to the next of them." He touched the plastic thing again, driving the point home, and turned away. "Be careful."

She gingerly picked it up. "And the price for this knowledge?"

"A gift. Purely a gift." Aiden nodded, pulled down his ski cap, and brushed past me into the hallway.

Once the door had closed, I opened a gate to my office in the middle of the corridor and nudged him through. "Disappointed?" I asked, tossing my coat onto a couch.

"That's not the worst trip I've had," he said, flopping onto the other couch as he dropped his bag. "I don't need medical attention. Nice change of pace."

"I can't believe Val let you get away with—" I began, but paused at a knock on the door. "Yes?"

An aide slipped inside and straightened his shirt. "Your pardon, my lord, but you have visitors."

I glanced at the starlit sky out my window. "*Tonight?*"

He nodded. "We would have made them comfortable until morning, but they brought a prisoner."

CHAPTER 5

As I ripped open a gate to the throne room, my guts threatened to return with interest the pita I'd loaned them. My mind blanked, but my heart insisted that the only prisoner who would be brought to me in such a fashion was Moyna.

Val had informed me in excruciating detail of the part my daughter played in Oberon's plan. The truth shook me to my core. How desperate to kill me must Moyna have been for her to trust *Oberon*? Grivam had used her as a pawn, and she knew it—why would she have again trusted someone promising to put her in power, especially someone who could have killed her without a second thought? Had she believed that Oberon's word was good, or was she so eager for vengeance that was willing to sacrifice herself in the process?

As I stepped through the gate, I steeled myself to see her—the blonde locks so much like Mother's, the permanent scowl beneath my Meggy's blue eyes—but when my vision adjusted to the candlelight and shadows, Moyna was nowhere to be found.

To say that I was unprepared for what awaited me would be a gross understatement, but I ascended the dais and tried to pretend I was undisturbed to find a naked young brunette kneeling in the middle of the runner, flanked by a pair of faeries—full-blooded ones, two of Mother's old favorites. They smiled, and one kicked the girl in the ribs, earning a grunt and a snarl from his captive.

I cleared my throat, buying time. "What's the meaning

of this?"

The taller of the pair stepped forward in a sweep of crimson robes and bowed. "My lord, we found the beast wandering across our lands. A spy."

His companion nodded fervently. "It wouldn't tell us its business, so we brought it to you."

I considered the silent woman, then her captors. "What beast?"

The shorter man chuckled. "It had taken the form of a wolf when we found it. Easy enough to hold the beast at bay, my lord."

"Damn it," I groaned, then caught movement from the corner of my eye as Aiden wandered in. He stopped in his tracks and gaped, and I shook my head when his mouth opened. "Not now," I told him, and turned back to the waiting hunters. "Is she a shifter, yes or no?"

"Yes, my lord," she first replied. "A spy."

"We would have killed her and saved you the trouble," said the other, "but the queen preferred to play with them first."

I could imagine the tortures my mother had inflicted on her captives, but I tried not to let the others see my disgust. "And she won't speak?"

"Oh, she *speaks*," said the shorter, "just nothing intelligible."

"She's been yapping for the last three days," his fellow added. "I suppose she didn't like her accommodations."

The two laughed at their own joke, and I stood to silence them. "So she does speak? And neither of you thought to…oh, I don't know, *learn the language*?"

They shrank at my outburst. "She's a spy, my lord," the shorter protested, suddenly uncertain of his footing. "And a beast. Why should we—"

"Go. Leave her."

They looked at each other, saw the anger I was barely holding in, and escaped into the night. When the doors slammed behind them, I sank back onto my throne and sighed. "Let's see…miss," I began, switching to English as a starting point, "do you understand me?"

"Yeah," she snapped, climbing to her feet, "I do. And you've got some *nerve*, asshole."

When she stood, I could see the athletic curves of her body—tanned runner's legs, a narrow waist, and a pair of small breasts that had yet to lose their bounce. "Stop gawking, Aiden," I muttered, then beckoned the woman forward. "I'm sorry for the mistreatment. They told me you were spying."

She rolled her brown eyes and huffed. "I was trying to get here as quickly as I could. If I were spying, do you think I'd run around shifted? I'm *noticeable*."

"Your business, then?"

She planted her hands on her hips. "Poppy Kane, on behalf of the Dark Company. Spare a few minutes?"

"Yes, of course. I assume they bound you?"

"He's blind," Aiden interrupted, heading for her. "Allow me." He flicked his fingers, and Poppy rubbed her wrists as if she'd been freed from invisible shackles. "I think that's it," he said, squinting at her body, "unless there's something deep—"

"I think you got it," she muttered, then looked back at me. "Your goons took my bag. If you two have ogled enough, some clothes would be nice."

Mumbling another apology, I imagined her into a pair of jeans and a sweater—something sufficiently shapeless by way of atonement. She considered her new ensemble, pushed up her sleeves, and strode toward the throne. "So, Daddy-o, let's talk about your kid."

My dealings with the Dark Company had been few, not least because neither side trusted the other. They'd cultivated a well-earned reputation as the mortal realm's foremost spymasters over the last millennium, loyal only to themselves but willing to undertake jobs for the right price.

The organization was comprised of shifters—a people mostly human, but with a touch of ancestry out of the Gray Lands. Though unskilled with magic, dark or otherwise, they were formidable when crossed, and their group vengeance was swift. Kill a member of the Company, and you were liable to wind up dead of unknown causes. Few rooms are perfectly sealed, after all, and a trained martial artist who can shift into an ant can easily sneak in undetected and wait until his target is asleep. I'd made it my practice to avoid them, and as we each had reputations that preceded us, they'd extended me the same courtesy. That said, I was unsurprised to learn that they knew a way into Faerie, but to find one of their number presenting herself to me in the open was troubling.

I escorted Poppy back to my office for privacy, and Aiden followed on our heels. If he'd learned to recognize the signals that his presence was unneeded, he chose to ignore them. He took a seat on the couch beside Poppy as I closed the gate, then asked her, "Hungry? Thirs—"

"Burger and a Sprite. Medium-rare. Garlic fries." She arched her eyebrow at me in challenge, but I let it slide. The food appeared, and she tucked in ravenously while we waited.

Three-quarters of a burger later, she stifled a belch and came up for air. "Needed that. Cretins gave me a bucket of offal. I've got gastronomic standards."

"Again, my apologies—"

She waved it off with her glass before taking a long drink. "Not bad," she told Aiden as she shoveled the last of the burger in her mouth. "Another."

He obliged without comment, but he cut his eyes to me as Poppy gorged herself. I shook my head, hoping he'd get the hint, and we watched her in silence until she had licked her fingers clean of garlic salt and beef juice. Before she could attack the plate, I ventured, "Dare I ask how you got in?"

She leaned back into the cushions with a sigh of satiated happiness, then wiped her mouth on her fist. "Boynton gate."

"The canyon leap? How on earth did you know where to—"

"Old Arcanum map. Just curious, but how does one go back through that gate?"

"Unless you can levitate, I wouldn't recommend it." Sedona's red rock canyon was lovely, but the gate hung several stories in the air, accessible only by climbing the cliffs and making a leap of faith. Traversing the gate from the wrong direction could end in a high-speed encounter with the unforgiving canyon floor. "I'll send you back by a safer route if you'll tell me what you're doing here."

"Anything to avoid the vortex tourists," she muttered, crossing her legs. "As I was saying, I'm here about your daughter."

"You've found her?" I asked, and chided myself for the eagerness I failed to mask.

"Nope. She found *us*. She's keeping her base a secret, but she's been skulking around."

I frowned at the news. "She wants intel?"

"Muscle. The damn weres are all over her."

At that, Aiden perked up and peered at Poppy. "Were…*wolves*?"

"Yeah," she grunted. "Stupid little shits are buying what she's selling."

His brow scrunched. "But…aren't you a were—"

Before he could finish, she grabbed him by the throat and pinned him to the arm of the couch. "Aren't I a *what*, punk?"

My temper flared, and I threw Poppy to the other end of the couch with a flash of force. As Aiden coughed and massaged his neck, I told her, "He's young, and he doesn't understand the terminology. I appreciate that you've had a difficult few days, but try that again, and I'll return you to the Company in an urn. Understood?"

The look she shot me was baleful, but she slid back to the seat she'd vacated and sipped her drink in sullen silence.

I rubbed my temples and turned to my brother. "*Shifters*," I told him, cutting my eyes to Poppy as I emphasized the word, "come in all varieties. 'Werewolf' is a term of strong derision—"

"Fighting words," Poppy muttered, twirling her straw.

"—even if a shifter takes a lupine form. Is that accurate, Ms. Kane?"

"More or less. The weres—they're the idiots in the 'pack' movement," she said to Aiden in a softer tone. "Follow an alpha, fight for rank, all of that bullshit."

He hesitated, trying to be judicious with his words. "I'm sorry, but…I thought…"

"He was raised Arcanum," I interrupted for Poppy's benefit, "and much of what he knows is self-taught. I'm working on it."

"Ah." She snorted and tucked her feet beneath her. "The popular conception more accurately describes weres," she explained to him. "They think of themselves as beasts with a human side. The majority of us think the opposite—human, but enhanced. If you're Arcanum, you should get that," she muttered, and swirled the ice in her glass. "The weres' beliefs are antithetical to everything the Company stands for. We're an equal-opportunity organization—sometimes the job calls for a wolf, and sometimes it calls for a shifter whose other form has more finesse."

"Is Jeanine still heading things?" I cut in.

"Yeah. Perfect example," she told Aiden. "My boss's shifted form is a rat. She's *brilliant*, but as far as the weres are concerned, she's prey. See where the friction comes from?"

"And speaking of your boss," I said, trying to steer the conversation back to my daughter, "does she know you're here?"

Poppy smiled grimly. "Who'd you think sent me? They've got her under surveillance, or she would have come herself. She sends her regards, by the way. You'll forgive me for the delay in conveying that—starvation and naked marching make me forget my manners."

"Understandable. But what of Moyna?"

She rubbed her shoulder and flinched at a sore spot. "Well, my notes were in my bag, but I'll tell you what I remember."

"I could retrieve it from—"

"Don't bother, they burned it. She's been coming around, making inroads with the weres. Calls herself the queen in exile."

My blood pressure began to rise. "She has a court, then?"

"What we've seen of it doesn't look too impressive by court standards, but in any case, we're dealing with a pack of faeries. Jeanine doesn't want to let this fester."

"Wise of her."

"Mm-hmm. I don't have numbers for you—we haven't found her base yet. The problem is that she's been making promises to the weres. Mutual back-scratching."

I created a glass of scotch and stared into its amber depths for a moment before slugging it down. "If she's coming to your people for assistance, then her forces can't be strong."

"Bingo, but try telling that to the weres." Poppy switched shoulders and groaned. "Sorry, that cage was hell. Anyway, Jeanine wants you to do something about this."

"Does she?"

"Boss is offering any assistance the Company can provide to stop this now. And since this would be for our mutual benefit, she's willing to waive the usual fee."

I snorted. "A generous offer."

"She thought so." Poppy shrugged. "She also thought you wouldn't accept this proposal from a gofer, so she invites you to meet her Christmas Day in Vegas. If you accept, I'll come back with the pertinent details."

"I suppose I could clear my calendar. Why wait that long?"

Her lips curled toward a snarl. "The twenty-fifth is the full moon this month. The weres go off into the woods for group hunts at the full. 'Pack bonding.' If they're preoccupied, Jeanine has a better chance of going undetected. Game?"

"That's two weeks," Aiden murmured. "If we need to find her now…"

He let it hang, but I nodded to Poppy. "Christmas in Vegas it is, then." I stood and gestured, and a gate back to the predawn Arizona wilderness materialized beside my couch. "Can you find your way home from the trailhead?"

"Easy," she said, pushing herself to her feet. "And to reach you between now and then? I'd rather not take another delightful romp through Faerie."

A black flip phone appeared on the coffee table. "My direct line. I've been told that no one will steal that."

She picked it up by its stubby antenna, made a face, and shoved it into her pocket. "Wow. Can I at least play Snake on that?"

"I'll expect word from Jeanine within three days," I said, ignoring the jab. "Don't keep me waiting."

Poppy smirked and slid past Aiden, ruffling his hair as she passed. "Cranky, isn't he?" she said to him, then slipped through the gate before I could counter.

We watched her walk off until the darkness swallowed her, and I closed the gate with a sigh. "Did that sound cranky to you?"

He stood and straightened his mussed ponytail. "I don't know, maybe a little."

"*Out*," I muttered, and he snickered as he left me to my thoughts.

I didn't know what information the Dark Company was

keeping from me, so I decided to undertake a little sleuthing on my own. Or, more precisely, I decided to employ Toula's services.

"I'm up to my ass in alligators here," she said when I called her the next morning. "My *freezing* ass. If you want to chat, you'll have to come to me—I'm in the trailer park. And bring coffee, okay?"

Ten minutes later, I found her standing in a snowdrift in front of the rusty trailer that disguised the opening to the Arcanum silo, muttering and waving her mittens like she was conducting an inaudible orchestra. "Dark roast, full strength," I said, extending to her an oversized thermos. "And what *are* you doing?"

"Hold that thought," she mumbled, then continued to swat at nothing for another thirty seconds until she stepped back and leaned over her knees, exhausted and sweating in the cold. "Coffee."

I passed her the thermos and watched her shiver as she chugged. "Here," I said, producing a hand towel, "you're dripping."

She snapped the straw back into the lid and wiped her face dry. A few clumps of dark, sweat-plastered hair peeked out from beneath her red knit cap, which, in combination with her flushed face, gave her the unfortunate air of a rot-spotted tomato. "Montana," she grumbled, draping the towel around her neck. "They had to buy a silo in friggin' *Montana*. Could have built somewhere temperate, but no…"

I shoved my hands in my pockets against the biting afternoon wind. Across the road, the Arcanum's cattle huddled for warmth. "And you're standing out here because…"

"Because Greg wants this re-warding finished ASAP, and I'm the best he's got. Lucky me." She finished her coffee, and the thermos disintegrated. "Thanks for that. With the work I'm doing right now, I'm not sure I have enough left in me to make my own."

I flicked my finger, and her thin overcoat puffed out into a down-filled marshmallow. "Or keep your temperature up. You're shaking."

She grinned. "Didn't know you cared, Gramps. And nice to see you again. How was our beauty sleep?"

"Too long." I considered the invisible wards around the trailer, smelling the burned citronella scent of active magic on the cold air but unable to pinpoint its source. "What does he want done? You're not rebuilding the network on your own, are you?"

"Almost as bad." She high-stepped out of the snow bank and brushed the clinging mess from her coat and calves. "You may have noticed that the Arcanum's defensive wards are somewhat porous."

"Those impenetrable wards that let me open gates straight into Greg's office? Hadn't noticed."

"I know!" She feigned wide-eyed shock. "For some reason, he wants the wards tightened. No more gating in and out from the hole."

"Ah. What about certain individuals who might need to slip back and forth on a semi-regular basis?"

"And that's why *I'm* out here instead of a bunch of wand jockeys. Hey, hit me again, would you?" A fresh thermos hovered before her, and she flipped the lid open with a look of silent gratitude. "The trick," she said after a long gulp, "is to make the wards selectively permeable, which means building well-defined exceptions into their architecture. Greg, Carver, and I get passes, and I'm preemptively writing Joey into this because I do *not* want to repeat this mess in the spring. And no, I'm not giving you a key through the wards."

I turned away to look at the miserable cattle, then murmured, "Supposing an emergency arose and I needed to get in. What then?"

"They'll be modifiable, but only from the inside. No sulking, now—you'd do the same thing, and you know it," she said, punching me in the shoulder. "So what do you need?"

"A back door into the silo."

"*Colin.*"

"Worth a shot, right?" Toula flashed a look of exasperation, and I shrugged. "Fine. Help me find Moyna."

She glanced over her shoulder at the silo entrance, then tugged my sleeve and pulled me down the circular drive and into one of the decoy trailers, an uninhabited shell with mildewed linoleum and an uncomfortable number of steel landscaping implements. "Security cameras," she murmured. "No one's bugged the tool shed, as far as I know, but stay quiet. Now, what's the rush? Aiden's been putting it off…"

I decided forthrightness was the best option. "She's mixing herself up with the Dark Company. They tell me they don't know where she's hiding, but if they *do* know, I don't want to be the last one to find out. That thing you did with Aiden's maps for Oberon, can you do it for her?"

"Technically, it'd be for you. Blood magic, ancestors and descendants, you know the drill. But yes, it would find her."

"What would it take?"

She scrunched up her face and examined the water-stained ceiling. "Give me a couple of days to construct the spell—I've got to finish Greg's ward project, and I'll need to do yours on the down low. I'll also need at least a few ounces of blood."

The thought of leaving that much blood with someone skilled in blood magic gave me pause. A practitioner sufficiently studied in certain restricted books could do a number of unpleasant things with the right amount of bodily fluids. While I suspected that I was strong enough to withstand most blood-crafted attacks, the fact that I was practically handing Toula ammunition sat ill with me. Then again, this was Toula. If I couldn't trust Mab's daughter, the quasi-matricidal, overly powered witch-blood, who *could* I trust?

"Just…keep it secure," I muttered.

"Fort Knox. And the spell will take every drop. This stuff ain't easy. Speaking of which…" She tossed her head toward the door and led the way back out into the chilly afternoon. "Love to catch up, but it's taking a lot of concentration to hold the wards together, so let's chat another time, okay?"

I followed her down the creaking steps and onto the frozen gravel road. "Sorry, I didn't know—"

Toula whispered a word, and the trailer park exploded in green light. I shouted in surprise and threw my arm in front of my face, but when the blast wave failed to come, I realized she had merely triggered a visualization spell and gaped at the result.

The wardwork was beautiful in its neat complexity, a glowing filigree the likes of which I'd never be able to replicate. It pulsed as magic flowed into and through it, diverting and rechanneling the magic that powered it into a force greater than its base components would suggest. This was the work of master wizards, the product of years of planning and construction…and there was Toula, tethered to the matrix by a dozen green streamers as she prodded and tweaked and reshaped the wards. No wonder she hadn't tried to make her own coffee—I had no idea how she was focused enough to carry on a conversation with that much spellwork being held in stasis by her willpower alone.

"Yeah?" she said.

"Impressive. Be careful, Glinda," I mumbled, and the lights faded into afterimages against the sky and snow.

Before she could retort, the front door of the silo opened, and the grand magus, leaning on an ebony cane, limped onto the trailer's porch. "I take it Aiden's out of a job, then," he said as he shuffled toward the wooden railing. "Enjoy your vacation, old timer?"

"Have I mentioned the security cameras?" Toula

muttered before turning back to her work.

I snorted and folded my arms against the cold. "Who's beating you up these days, Greg? Is Helen that anxious for the position?"

"Arthritis," he called down. "Cold does a number on my joints. By all rights, I shouldn't be able to walk right now, but you know," he said with a shrug, "magic can make up for missing cartilage if applied appropriately."

"So why aren't you, then?" I countered as I mounted the porch stairs to join him. "That cane has to be hell on ice."

Greg smiled dourly. "Flu down below. Infirmary's overwhelmed, and since a little stiffness is neither contagious nor life-threatening...well, you see."

"I could probably—"

"No. Thank you, but no." He pointed a twisted finger at the door and inclined his head. "Spare a minute? Come out of the cold? My bar's overstocked since no one's been around to drain my good bottles."

"Eventually," I replied, holding the door open behind him, "Missy's going to catch on, and you'll have to stop blaming me."

That earned a wheezing chuckle, and I wondered if Greg shouldn't be on the infirmary's admit list as well. The grand magus was eighty, and his years, it seemed, had finally caught up with him.

"Missy can try, but she's not going to make a teetotaler out of me," he said as the door latched closed.

The entry trailer was another gutted model, a shell with whitewashed walls and thin industrial carpeting, empty but for the pair of black security cameras in the corners of the ceiling. The metal circuit breaker box across the room was a decoy—the cover opened to reveal a palm scanner, one of the Arcanum's few concessions to modern security. Once an arriving wizard was green-lit by the system, a trapdoor would open in the seamless floor, giving him access to the steep stairway down into the silo.

Considerations for the disabled had never been at the top of the Arcanum's list. I looked at Greg, who had paused halfway to the box, then at the floor. "You know, Toula's still working."

He hesitated a moment longer, torn between protocol and the ache in his legs, then muttered, "Screw it," and gestured in the air. A gate opened in the middle of the trailer, and I followed Greg straight into his office.

"Take a load off," I said, making a beeline for the bar. "I'll pour. Single or double?"

He dropped onto the nearest couch with a little *oof*. "I'm fine—"

"Single or double? Or let me fix the pain—your call."

Greg sighed. "Single, then. And if you'd be so kind as to hand me the tube on my desk, I'd be much obliged."

I poured two glasses of scotch, Greg's single and a triple for myself, then levitated them to the coffee table and plucked the tube of Tiger Balm from the top of a stack of leather-bound books. "You're still using this stuff?"

"It helps. More or less." He lifted his glass in brief salute and sipped, and I handed him his ointment. "Now," he said as I made myself comfortable across from him, "I'm sure you've heard about the upcoming nuptials."

"As a matter of fact, I've received my invitation."

He drank again, regarding me over the crystal rim of the tumbler. "You know this isn't going to go down smoothly, yes?"

"I'd expect nothing less from your people. Cheers."

Greg's mouth twitched disapprovingly when I put my drained glass on the table. "Not *my* people—Council. The installation heads are on board with it, but the local magi have been strongly suggesting that Helen reconsider her life choices if she wants to keep her position."

"Am I right to assume that my name has come up in these discussions?"

"It's been frequently mentioned."

His tone was matter-of-fact, but I thought I detected a hint of unease. "What, exactly, does the Council think Joey does for me? Yes, I'm fond of the boy. Yes, he's been helpful. But I'm not going to...I don't know," I floundered, "force him to kill Helen in her sleep or something ridiculous like that. He's not my prisoner—he's just happy with his dragon."

"But you see the Council's position. I doubt there's anything nefarious here, but the Council—"

"Is paranoid."

"Is the Council, and they're past alarmed that the next grand magus is about to get herself hitched to a mundane who's chummy with you."

I considered Greg in silence, then enchanted myself a refill and lifted the glass again. "These new wards..."

"The Council doesn't know about the exceptions Toula's building in."

"Thought not." I drank, cringing at the burn, and returned the glass to its coaster. "She told me she's making one for Joey. Were you planning on giving him something to let him open gates? Got an amulet or some such hiding around here?"

"I'm working on it. Until then..."

"We'll continue as before." I pulled myself off the couch and looked down at Greg, who continued to savor his drink in tiny sips. "If the Council gets any noisier, you'll inform me, won't you?"

In that moment, Greg's hooded eyes looked as old and tired as I'd ever seen them. "Don't think I have a better option," he murmured, and watched me take my leave until I closed the gate between us.

CHAPTER 6

Though Kuni was fascinated by Georgie, she found the little guy unnerving. *He's everywhere*, she complained when I came out to check on him a few days after his arrival. Even with Lailu's assurances, I didn't quite trust the newcomer.

"You can't tell me he's cramping your space," I said to the dragon, who sulked in the back of the barn like an overgrown cat, an unhappy black ball of scales and teeth. "Surely sharing with someone that small isn't a grave inconvenience."

Her red eyes narrowed. *It's not his size that bothers me. He's everywhere, he's always moving, and he—*

The thought ended abruptly as Joey strode in from the practice yard, sword sheathed at his side and Kuni riding on his shoulder. "You missed it!" he called, pulling a towel and water bottle off of a stack of bales as his voice echoed in the cavernous barn.

"Missed what?" I asked.

He squeegeed his face dry. "Oh, nothing. I totally kicked Mina's—"

Before he could finish, Joey was tossed across the room into a pile of hay. Kuni, who had taken wing in the nick of time, squeaked and flew toward him as Georgie set off a psychic alarm. I turned and found Mina glowering in the doorway, her arms crossed and her brown curls limp with sweat. "What was that, boy?" she yelled as Joey dazedly sat up. "I couldn't hear you over that spectacular crash. Try to shield—oh, wait, you *can't*. And sit down,

Georgie, he's not hurt."

I'll be the judge of that, she snapped, lumbering to Joey's side to inspect the damage.

I gave my niece a hard look, ignoring the minor matter that she had been one of Mother's guards long before I was born, and thus was probably uncowed by my displeasure. "Was that necessary?"

"No, but satisfying." She helped herself to Joey's water as Georgie nudged him to his feet. "Boy needs to learn respect."

"It's all right," Joey said, stumbling toward us. "She's sore that I kicked her ass."

"Hardly," Mina retorted.

"I had you on the ground."

"I *tripped*."

"It counts. And I'll take that," he said, yanking the bottle from her hands.

I anticipated a messy reprisal, but Mina seemed amused by his antics. "You wouldn't be so brave if *he* weren't standing there," she countered, cocking her thumb at me. "And the next time we spar, I won't go easy on you."

He kneaded his shoulder while he drank. "That was supposed to be easy?"

"Because I didn't incinerate you from across the yard? Yes." A shadow fell over Mina, and she glanced up to see Georgie's teeth. "I'm *kidding*," she protested, sloughing off her practice padding. "I'm not going to fry him. Stand down."

Better not, Georgie thought, curling up on the floor again. Kuni flittered around her head like a firefly on speed, and with a well-aimed snort, she sent him tumbling into her water trough. *You see?* she told me, rolling her eyes—an un-draconic behavior I assumed she'd picked up from Joey. *He won't light anywhere.*

Kuni broke the surface and gasped between hacking coughs, then paddled for the side of the trough and let loose a high-pitched tirade. Georgie turned to Joey, who listened, nodded, and translated. "He says you did that on purpose. He didn't need a bath. And"—Joey paused as Kuni started tossing pieces of tiny, sodden clothes over the side of the trough—"and he'd appreciate it if you didn't try to drown him."

"That's actually what he said?" I muttered, impressed by Joey's ability to parse squeaks into speech.

"The clean version. Piq profanity is in a league of its own." He brought his sweat towel to Kuni, who fluttered into his hand and angrily dried himself with a semi-damp corner. "I'll make it up to you," he told the red-faced piq. "Still want to go out with us today?"

Georgie snorted again, but Kuni chattered back at Joey, appeased if still moist. With a promise to be back shortly, Joey carried him upstairs to his loft apartment, a suite that had more in common those days with a condo than a barn. When the door slammed behind them, Mina willed herself clean and shook her head. "He's good," she murmured. "He's *very* good. And if it goes to his head, it'll be the death of him."

"He understands that—"

"Does he? You and Aiden can say you're protecting him all you want, but if he antagonizes the wrong person…"

"He's not stupid, Mina."

"He's *young*. I worry about him. And now that you're back, I worry about Aiden as well. He doesn't know his own weakness."

"Val looks out for them."

"He can't be everywhere at once, and those two go where they will. If I were you, Uncle, I'd put some restrictions on them. Aiden, perhaps, can fend for himself, but Joey…" The wrinkle between her eyebrows deepened. "He relies too heavily on his steel."

Though I was troubled by her earnestness, I tried to mask it. "I'll have a talk with him. Remind him of what's out there—"

He knows more about what's out there than you do.

I squinted at Georgie. "Oh?"

The field guide. Who do you think has been carrying him around? We've been off the map, and he's written new bits in. Stop worrying so much, I'll take care of him.

"Ah, yes," Mina countered, "you with your great skill in magic."

Georgie opened her mouth in an approximation of a smile, which offered little warmth and many sharp teeth. *Magic isn't always the solution. I have ways of keeping Joey safe.*

I patted Mina's shoulder and headed out of the barn. "I'll have a word with him. And since we could have a situation with the Arcanum if he were hurt, how about not tossing him across the room? Let's try to keep all major bones intact."

Mina produced a sigh that spoke of long suffering. "You're no fun, and it's good for him."

"At least let him get through his wedding without crutches," I said, and stepped into the late morning sunlight, confident that I had the rest of the day well in hand. My schedule seemed clear, there were no fires on the horizon, and Poppy had called shortly after breakfast with the name of a casino and a meeting time. I was feeling almost like myself again, and as Toula was still working on the spell to find my daughter, I thought I might steal the afternoon and attack the dusty pile of novels I'd been meaning to read. And so I strolled through the roses back to my palace, confident that I had nothing more pressing to decide than whether I should opt for the couch or the recliner to accompany my paperback and bourbon.

Sometimes I'm an optimistic idiot like that.

The palace was quiet as I wound through the stone halls toward the library. A few guards nodded in passing, but with no audiences scheduled, I'd given most of them and my aides a well-needed day off. The staff had been on high alert during Aiden's regency, and they were finally getting a chance to breathe. The least I could do was offer a little vacation.

I'd just rounded the corner to the kitchen, hoping against reason to smell Astrid's pastries, when the realm began to scream in my head.

A shout of joy, I realized once the worst of the shock had passed and I'd found a wall against which to steady myself. Faerie was inordinately pleased about *something*, but the last time she had been so vocal had been when Oberon first returned...

"Where?" I grunted over the ringing in my ears. "Where is she?"

In my mind's eye, I watched in spinning panorama as a redhead knelt at the top of the palace steps, clutching her ears and rocking. With a location pinpointed, I opened a gate and staggered through, and squinted in the sudden light. "Hold on, Eleanor," I yelled, "she'll calm down in a minute..."

The redhead looked up at the sound of my shout, and my heart clenched. The sensible periwinkle twinset and trousers she wore surely belonged to the matronly professor, but the professor herself was gone, the glamour stripped away by Eleanor's passage into the realm. Before me was a slim, taut beauty, her face unlined and pale but for the twin spots of crimson on her cheeks, her hair long and full and a startling shade of red. The remarkable green eyes she'd sported before were truly hers, but as quickly as I noticed them, they squeezed closed in pain. I'd seen her expression before, but in a face with blue eyes, beneath soft red curls.

The resemblance between Eleanor and her sister was uncanny, and for a second, I entertained the wild fantasy that my Meggy had returned to me, alive and whole. But the notion passed as quickly as it came, speeded along by the surge of hatred that creased Eleanor's features and the twin yellow fireballs that appeared in her palms.

"*Where is he?*" she bellowed in English, scrambling to her feet as the realm's shouting subsided. "What did you do to him?"

I dropped to a crouch as the fireballs whizzed over my head. "To whom?" I cried, throwing up a shield as Eleanor readied another volley. "What are you talking—"

"*Walt!*" My shield trembled with the blast of canary flame. "Give him *back!*"

I winced as the fiery rain increased in tempo. "I haven't touched Walt!" I finally managed to shout above her wordless battle screams.

"*Liar!*"

The air between us shimmered with the discharge of magic. "I don't know anything about him! Damn it, stop shooting and talk to me!"

The barrage suddenly ceased as Eleanor cried out and fell. Behind her stood Val in a pugilist's stance, his fists primed to strike again if she rose. "Coileán," he began, "are you—"

"Stand down," I ordered in Fae, and the world around me flickered as I appeared between him and Eleanor. "*That's* Oberon's heir. No sudden moves."

He grunted, and from the corner of my eye, I saw his hands open and ignite in preparation while Eleanor coughed and tried to stand. After a moment, she picked herself up and wheeled on us, red-faced and furious. "I'm going to ask you one more time," she growled. "Where. Is. *Walt?*"

"And I'll tell you again, I don't know where he is," I replied in English, keeping my shield down to placate her. "I've not seen him since we left you."

"Then who of yours has?"

"No one, as far as I know. Check if you don't believe me," I offered, tilting my head toward her in invitation.

The light pressure between my temples came instantly, lingered for a heartbeat, and ebbed. When it passed, Eleanor frowned and folded her arms, then fixed me with an unblinking stare. "No tricks?"

"None. What's happened?"

Her grip on herself tightened, and I detected the sheen of panic in her eyes. Before I could press her again, Eleanor reached into her pocket and thrust a folded piece of paper at me. "Explain this."

Val twitched at the sudden movement, but I shook my head and took the paper. The page was thick as cardstock, unlined, and the color of weak white tea, creased twice in a messy double fold that left the rough edges unevenly matched.

"Someone taped it to the letterbox overnight," said Eleanor as I unfolded it. "I cut the sellotape off, thinking there might be fingerprints, but…"

Her voice trailed away, and I read the short note in my hands:

Good morning, Eleanor,

If you want to see your friend again, you'll be a good girl and do as I say. Surrender your court and let me bind you, and you may live out your days in peace. Defy me, and I will destroy you and everything you hold dear.

You have until sunset.

Coilan

"This isn't my hand," I said, passing it back to Eleanor. A shadow of doubt lingered in her eyes, and I tapped the page. "First, it's far too round. I'll be happy to give you exemplars if you doubt me. Second, if I were going to officially threaten you, I'd do it in Fae, not English."

"Protocol," Val offered.

Startled at the commentary and at the realization that my conversation with Eleanor wasn't private, I looked up sharply. "When did you—"

"Some months past," he replied, his English strongly accented but intelligible. "The boys kept having side conversations. Security measure."

"Do *they* know?"

He smirked. "They figured it out eventually."

"Clever," I muttered, and turned back to Eleanor. "One other thing: whoever wrote that misspelled my name." I stepped to her side and reread the letter, then gave her rumpled ensemble a second look. "This was left on your mailbox last night?"

She nodded, still bowstring-tight but suddenly weary. "I tried to sleep at two. Didn't work. I thought I heard the neighbor's cats in my bin at half-past three, and I found this waiting for me. Snipped the tape, found my shoes again, and came over...*here*."

By then, the realm's voice had subsided to an excited murmur, but I rubbed my temple at the recent memory. "It's not always that loud. Faerie was happy to see you."

"I noticed," she mumbled, folding the paper back into a square. "Does it ever shut up?"

"Eventually." I hesitated, then produced a mug of tea and offered it to her. "Look, I don't know what's going on, but why don't we go inside, and you can fill me in."

She eyed the mug with suspicion, then took it, sniffed, and gave it a test sip that ended in a brief grimace. "This is the best you can do for tea?"

"I'm much better at whisky."

"I'm sure." The mug shifted into a bone-china teacup filled with a brew far more fragrant than mine. "Lead on, then," she said after a long sip, and nodded toward the palace doors. "I doubt the fingerprints will be of any use at this point." She drank again, carefully balancing the cup on the saucer that had appeared with a thought. "And, ehm...sorry about the fireballs."

"Long night?" I asked as Val pushed the doors open.

"That's not the half of it," she said with a sigh, and followed us through.

When Aiden and I visited Durham, Walt had been putting the finishing touches on a presentation to be given in Edinburgh at a conference the following week. "Medieval warfare," Eleanor said, refilling her teacup on the couch opposite me. "The dear does love a good siege story. He's written three books, you know, he's…sorry," she muttered, catching our blank looks. "I'm sorry, I'm not usually this scattered, but—"

"But you have not slept," Val offered from his post by the door, keeping the conversation in the foreign tongue. "Take your time."

She flashed a brief smile of gratitude before burying her nose in her teacup again.

Eleanor had been a shaken mess after Aiden and I left, but she'd tried not to let on. By dinner, however, when Walt had emerged from his office to find her sitting in the dark in front of her computer, scrolling through the spreadsheet Aiden had given her, she'd had to confess. She'd told him about everything: her father and Titania and Mab and me, the court she had inherited a year ago, her one hundred ninety-six siblings and their potentially murderous proclivities. He'd sat beside her, watching her face in the glow of the screen while she'd spilled every secret she had kept from him. And when she'd finished, he'd taken her hands and told her he'd go beyond the edge of the universe if that was what it took to keep her safe.

"We talked it over," she murmured. "He said I should take the throne, get whatever guards I needed, pull the court out of the mortal realm. I told him that…that he could live forever. With me. And he said yes. But he wanted to go to his conference." She stared miserably at Val and me. "He'd promised months ago, and he didn't want to let anyone down…"

On Sunday afternoon, after brunch at their favorite spot, Eleanor had driven Walt to the train station to catch the two-eighteen to Edinburgh. "Don't worry about a thing," he'd told Eleanor with his goodbye hug. "We'll pack when I return, yes?" With a promise to call from the hotel and a last kiss, he'd wheeled his bag toward the waiting train and joined the boarding queue. Eleanor had watched as a young man lifted Walt's suitcase into the car, and then she'd waved as the train pulled out into the gray afternoon.

"It's two hours to Edinburgh," she said, staring at the space above the coffee table. "A little less if everything's on schedule. He was staying on the Royal Mile. Even if he'd walked, it wouldn't have taken him twenty minutes. But he never called." Her grip on her cup tightened. "I waited until six, and then I rang the hotel, and they told me he hadn't checked in."

Eleanor had spent Sunday evening on the phone, calling the train station, National Rail, the hotel again, and finally, as the clock ticked over into Monday, the police. She'd called the conference organizer and every panelist she knew, hoping someone had waylaid her husband, but no one had seen Walt. "He vanished somewhere between Durham and Edinburgh," she said. "And then that bloody note came this morning."

I did the math. "He's been gone about thirty-six hours, then?"

She nodded. "Before you say it, he wouldn't have run away from me."

Her tone warned against disagreement, and I erred on the side of safety. "Let's assume that someone took him, then. Who are your enemies?"

"You've seen the spreadsheet?" She considered her empty cup, which refilled. "Any of them could be behind this. The one who stands to gain the most from my removal is Iriella, but she would have to have been stalking me, and I'm *careful*."

"Not to be an ass, but Aiden found you easily enough."

"Only through blood magic," Val countered. "Spellcraft. Unless your sister had a wizard's assistance," he told Eleanor, "she could not track you in that fashion."

"Fine," she sighed into her tea. "Assume that Iriella or one of the others has been watching me. Someone has Walt. *Someone* was in Edinburgh on Sunday." She drank, paused, then looked at Val. "This blood spell—it shows where I am?"

"You and all of Oberon's descendants," he explained. "It was built from his blood."

"Well, that's simply delightful. Can it show where we've *been*?"

"No clue," I said, pulling my phone from my pocket. "I'll call the expert."

The others watched me until the line clicked open. "Still working, Gramps, and you shouldn't rush me," said Toula.

The muffled noise behind her suggested a television in the vicinity. "Working during the commercial breaks, are you?"

"I'm entitled to my holiday programming. And what's so important that it can't wait for business hours?"

"Missing person. That blood trace you set up for Aiden—can you rewind it?"

Her tone shifted from peeved to concerned. "Yeah, sure. On my way."

Before I had time to hang up, a gate ripped open in my office, and Toula, clad in ratty navy sweats and fuzzy slippers, strode through with her phone in her hand. I braced at the sight of her, expecting to hear the realm's protestations, but Faerie was strangely quiet at the intrusion. My surprise showed in my expression, and Toula smirked while she tucked her phone into her pocket. "Aiden cleared the air. *She* and I are cool," she explained, cutting her eyes to the ceiling. "Carver's been getting a pass of late, too. What's—"

Toula froze as she noticed Eleanor. "Whoa," she murmured a second later, "sorry, thought you'd taken up necromancy for a moment, there. Hi, weird lighting in here," she continued, switching into her oddly accented

Fae as she headed for Eleanor with her hand outstretched. "Toula Pavli. Who's gone missing, and how can I help?"

Eleanor's smile was too brittle to last, and it cracked into sniffles while she clasped Toula's hand. "Eleanor Richardson. Pleased to make your acquaintance, I…"

Without missing a beat, Toula produced a box of tissues and slid onto the couch beside her. "Hey, now," she soothed, "none of that. I've got a few tricks up my sleeve, okay? You need me to tweak the trace spell?"

She nodded and wadded her damp tissues into a ball. "My husband's been kidnapped, he's been gone a day and a half, they left a note, and his blood pressure's terrible, he needs his pills…"

As she spoke, Eleanor segued once more into her usual tongue. Toula listened for a moment without interrupting the rapid flow, then patted Eleanor's knee and leaned closer. "He's mortal?" she asked, following Eleanor's linguistic lead.

"Yes, and he's…he's not entirely healthy, he's seventy-two, and—"

"It's okay." She gave Eleanor's tissue-filled hand a squeeze and looked at me. "You think one of Oberon's took him?"

"Well," I replied, giving Eleanor a pointed glance, "*that's* his heir, and whoever took Walt tried to frame me for it, so that's our working assumption."

If it concerned her to find herself in proximity to a distraught queen, Toula didn't let on. "Worth a shot," she said, then glanced around the office until she spotted the pile of atlases by my desk. "Give me five minutes, guys. Eleanor, what's his last known location?" she asked, rising from the couch. "And when did you last seem him? Help me narrow this down."

A few minutes later, as Toula twitched her fingers in deep concentration over a map of northern England, Eleanor murmured to me, "You're awfully friendly with a wizard."

I glanced toward the door at Val, who offered a curt nod. "Witch-blood," I told her. "The one in a million who can enchant and cast, and she's *good* at what she does."

From the other side of the room, Toula called, "Didn't know you cared."

"And she has good hearing."

Toula didn't look up from her work. "I tend to listen harder when everyone gets quiet around me. But yeah, witch-blood." She paused, scowled at the map, and resumed her gesticulation with greater fervency.

Eleanor studied her for a few seconds, then turned back to me. "Your court?"

"Ha," Toula muttered.

"Officially, Ms. Pavli is Arcanum," I explained. "Unofficially, she's Mab's youngest. Does that answer that?"

She stiffened in her seat. "*Mab's*? How on earth—"

"Remember a couple of years ago when Faerie temporarily sealed off?" Toula interrupted. "Colin and I teamed up. And that was your brother's fault, by the way."

"So I'd heard. Ehm…your mother—"

"Only met her once."

"Ah." Eleanor frowned into her cup. "How many of them are left, do you suppose?" she asked me. "Mab's children. If that court ever tried to strengthen…"

I felt Val's eyes on me and cleared my throat. "As far as we know, there are two."

"Hmm. You're monitoring her sibling, I trust?" she asked, tilting her head toward Toula. "Given your intrusion into my affairs, I assume you're poking your nose into all of the courts."

I turned to look at Val in earnest, and his shoulders twitched in a subtle shrug. Deciding not to out him as Mab's unwilling heir, I told Eleanor, "The situation is in hand. Toula's sibling has no intention of rebuilding that court, and I respect his or her wishes."

Before she could press me for details, Toula

announced, "I've got some bad news." I cleared the coffee table for the atlas, and she took the vacant seat beside Eleanor and pointed to the train line. "I rewound it to the time you gave me, and I checked it twice. The only person of Oberon's blood who was anywhere near that train was you."

Eleanor's face crumbled. "He couldn't have just *vanished*..."

"The spell doesn't track every member of his—*your* court," she said, passing Eleanor the tissues again, "but now we know who wasn't directly involved. And that includes Moyna," she added, looking at me.

To my surprise, Eleanor's face registered familiarity with the name. "*Her?* She's been gone nearly a year. The last time she was seen, she was working with Oberon. Why would she be involved in this?"

Toula grimaced and concentrated on the map, and I knew that Val wasn't about to bail me out. With a sigh, I told Eleanor, "Moyna's alliances, her loyalties...to be honest, I don't know where they lie. She's my daughter."

Her jaw dropped. "*Your* daughter? I thought she was part of Mab's remnant. That business in Montana last year—"

"She'd like to kill me. And I have no idea where she is, but Toula's working on it."

"What did you *do* to the girl?"

I opened my mouth, floundered, and was still struggling when Toula stepped into the breach. "Titania stole her and raised her from a baby," she said, closing the atlas. "Moyna blames Colin for her death. And then he bound her and gave her a set of false memories so her actual mother could try to raise her, but that failed. Moyna tried to kill Megs, Colin tried to kill Moyna, Megs jumped between them. Little darling's been on her own ever since."

"Good heavens, I...wait, back up," said Eleanor, "you said she didn't take Walt, and no one of Oberon's blood was involved. But if she's yours..." The realization hit, and Eleanor stared at me in disbelief. "Oh, you *didn't*. You sired her on one of his daughters?"

"I didn't know," I protested, "Meggy was bound, *she* didn't know—"

"Cross-court relations never work out!" She folded her arms and regarded me with tight-lipped disapproval. "And which of my sisters spawned her?"

"Your youngest," Toula murmured. "Who was a dear friend of mine."

The edge in her voice gave Eleanor pause, and her tone shifted. "My apologies," she said, twisting a fresh tissue, "I don't know what's wrong with me..."

"Well, I can think of something," she replied, not unkindly. "Let's focus on—Walt, was it? Let's focus on Walt now, and you can critique Colin's life choices later. Does he have any children?" Eleanor shook her head, and Toula grunted. "And if he's in his seventies, we're not going to get a blood trace going from his parents. Crap." She cracked her knuckles and stared up at the ceiling fresco. "A blood trace is the quickest option, but I can work with other bits. It just takes longer to get the spell in place—there's nothing with the thaumaturgic properties of blood. Do you have his hairbrush? Fingernail clippings? Bodily fluids, anything."

"A hairbrush, yes," said Eleanor. "How long—"

"Days. Time we may not have. Come on," she said, going back to her feet, "take me to your place. I'll get the spell going there, but it's going to take a while to get it running."

I pushed myself off the couch. "What about Greg?"

"I'll call from...Durham, right?" Eleanor nodded, and Toula patted the phone in her pocket. "And I'm sorry," she told me, "but I can't run Moyna's tracker long-distance if I'm trying to do a rush job here..."

I shook my head. "Do what you need to do."

She flashed a thumbs-up and stepped toward the gate

Eleanor had opened. "Hey, you two come with us. Make sure I'm not overlooking anything."

Before I could follow, however, Val caught my shoulder. "You do know that's not Lady Meghan," he said softly.

I nodded, and with a brisk pat on the arm, Val led the way.

CHAPTER 7

We stepped through the gate into darkness, and my nose twitched. Eleanor's home smelled like December: the ghost of an extinguished fire, notes of vanilla and cinnamon, and an omnipresent scent of pine, finished with the crisp dryness of a drafty window. When the lights switched on, I found myself facing a photo-ready Christmas tree bedecked with crystal baubles and papier-mâché balls, surrounded by a spread of beautifully wrapped boxes. A glance at the mantle revealed a pair of stockings, each decorated with a needlepoint skating scene. The only clue that I hadn't stumbled into a holiday catalogue was the sickly white poinsettia squatting by the fireplace, which seemed to be weathering the season under protest.

I turned toward the sofa, a stunning piece whose back and cushions formed a pastoral tapestry—Louis XIV in style, and certainly not a reproduction—and caught Val gawking as he took it all in. "Check out the rug," I murmured as Eleanor and Toula disappeared down the hallway. "They've got more money on the floor than most people in this city will see in a year."

He considered the room-spanning silk carpet. "Interesting. One of them has a taste for gardening," he added, gesturing to the tree.

"It's short-term decoration. I'll explain later." With the initial surprise of its décor worn off, the parlor seemed mocking in its promise of cheer, and I folded my arms as I surveyed the rest of the antique furnishings. The grandfather clock in the dining room ticked insistently, the aural cousin of a dripping faucet, and I stepped over to check the time. Not quite five in the morning, and the house was still cooling toward the dawn.

"Any thoughts as to a plan?" Val asked.

I shook my head. "Suppose it couldn't hurt to start a fire."

By the time Toula shooed Eleanor from the bedroom where she'd begun the complex spell, I'd produced a proper blaze, and Val and I perched on the spindly armchairs flanking the fireplace. "I've reinforced the joints," Eleanor said when she spotted us. "You're not going to break them." She sank onto the tapestry sofa and rested her forehead on her fingertips.

"Does Toula need anything?" I ventured.

"No." Her voice betrayed the deep weariness lurking beneath her fear. "Just time. Possibly tea," she said, straightening as the thought hit her. "I should—"

Val stood and motioned her down as he headed for the hallway. "Coffee. Under control."

"She's going to be coasting on fumes soon," I cautioned when his footsteps faded. "Came over from the silo. The time difference…"

Eleanor squeezed her eyes shut and groaned. "I didn't think…of course the child needs coffee, she'll be dead on her feet soon enough."

"Maybe not. I don't know her limits, but she'll go as long as she can before she crashes."

That seemed to satisfy Eleanor, but her eyes darted around the room as if she expected to catch Walt jumping out from the shadows. "Look," I said, "you're a wreck, she's got to work, and there's little we can do without a lead. Why don't you take a nap?"

Eleanor snorted. "You expect me to leave you unsupervised in *my* house?"

"No tricks, I swear. Get some rest." I hesitated only a second before playing my ace. "You know Walt would want you to."

"He can chide me about sleep all he likes once he's home." She straightened on the sofa and crossed her legs. "So."

"So."

A log cracked like a gunshot, shooting a spray of embers to die on the white-tiled hearth.

"You've decided to take the throne, then?" I asked.

Her eyes widened in disbelief. "Bloody *hell*, Coileán!"

"It's important."

"Yes. No. I suppose," she huffed. "But I'm not making any decisions until Walt is safe." She rose to contemplate her too-perfect Christmas tree. "He loves this time of year. The parties, the carolers, the lights—he's like a little boy sometimes," she added, smiling wistfully at a tiny wooden sled. "I suppose you were wondering about the decoration."

"Not really." Eleanor glanced at me, puzzled, and I shrugged. "You've spent your whole life on this island, haven't you? I'd be surprised if it weren't in your blood by now."

"It's changed," she murmured, tweaking a glass snowman. "All of this, the trees and things…it wasn't always like this."

"I know. I was there."

"Here?"

"Ireland, mostly. Well, until the colonies opened up. Wanted to see what the fuss was about."

"And you still went back to…that place."

Her words were an accusation, but I let it go. "Faerie's not actually a bad choice as long as you're holding the reins. There's ample room for two courts."

She considered the tree in silence, and I was about to renew my efforts to coax her across the border when she said, "You got a child on my sister, yes?"

"Yes," I admitted.

"And she's deceased? This sister of mine?" I nodded, and Eleanor caught the motion out of the corner of her eye. "Your doing, Ironhand?"

Once more, I forced myself to nod.

She studied me with an expression so much like Meggy's that I could have sworn I was in the presence of a ghost until she spoke again. "You had feelings for her." I stared up at Eleanor while the logs snapped and popped, and she glanced away and slunk back to her sofa. "You think Moyna might have had something to do with Walt's disappearance."

"She wasn't there, you heard Toula say that, but…I'm not ruling it out."

We brooded in the fire's glow until Val returned with an empty carafe in hand. He gave us both hard looks, then settled into his creaking chair, held out his palm, and passed me a neat triple of bourbon.

There was no television in Eleanor's parlor, and sleep caught up with us all eventually. With the warmth of the fire, the numbing drink, and the hypnotizing ticking, I wasn't surprised to catch myself napping twice while we waited for sunrise. I watched Val through the quiet hours as he paced, and by six-thirty, our hostess had curled into a ball on the sofa and surrendered to sleep in spite of herself.

The sky beyond the Christmas tree finally lightened through indigo and cobalt to the sodden blue-gray of morning rain. As the clock chimed eight forty-five, I left Eleanor to sleep and joined Val in his circuit of the dining room. "Maybe we should go," I began, but he held up a finger to stay me and ducked behind the heavy curtains.

"Visitor," he muttered, cutting his eyes to the window, and I sneaked closer to the glass to look out on the drizzle. Eleanor's front yard was ringed with a low wooden fence, and a broad-shouldered, middle-aged woman in a tan mackintosh was latching the gate behind her. Her only memorable feature was her hair: chin-length and black but for a white streak over her left eye. She carried nothing to reveal her purpose as she started up the path—no purse, no umbrella, no package—but her raincoat was short enough to reveal dark dress trousers beneath it, as well as a pair of nondescript black boots.

I grimaced. "Police."

Val nodded curtly and headed for the back of the house to warn Toula. As he walked, his clothing shifted into a copy of my Oxford and jeans, down to the rolled sleeves and faded knees, and the bronze blade at his hip vanished. I threw a sweatshirt on so as not to give the officer pause, should she see us together, and then, after a second's hesitation, I shook Eleanor's shoulder. "You've got company," I said once her eyes popped open. "Better put your face on."

In one smooth motion, Eleanor sat upright and aged several decades. She stood and straightened her sweater, patted her dull brown hair into place, and gave me a warning look as she fluffed the flattened decorative pillows.

When the doorbell rang, she was poised. With a rapid step that barely betrayed her unease, she crossed the room and threw open the front door, then greeted the visitor with a tight smile. "Detective Parsons, good morning. Come in," she said, stepping aside. "It's raining again, isn't it? May I take your coat?"

The woman hurried into the warmth of the foyer, and Eleanor shut out the damp chill. As the newcomer dripped onto the hardwood, she glanced about her and noticed me standing by the antique sofa. "One of my postgrads," Eleanor lied, catching the direction of the detective's stare. "A few of them came over last night to keep me company, the dears."

The fib held water for the moment, and the detective

extended her hand. "Detective Inspector Parsons."

After a check for dangerous jewelry, I met her firm grip. "Colin Leffee, ma'am."

Her thin eyebrow quirked. "American?"

"Guilty."

That earned a fleeting half-smile, but she sobered and turned back to Eleanor. "Dr. Richardson, I'm sorry for the early call—"

"Oh, no trouble at all," Eleanor interrupted, waving to the sofa. "I was dozing. Cup of tea?"

"Thank you, no. Ehm…" The detective gave me an uneasy look, then shoved one hand into her coat pocket. "If I might speak to you in private…"

"Of course. Excuse us, Colin," said Eleanor, and guided the detective into the kitchen.

I waited for a moment, wondering whether I should join Toula and Val, but before I could investigate the rear bedroom, an anguished cry broke the quiet of the house. I froze, listening for further information, but nothing was forthcoming until Detective Parsons emerged a few minutes later, alone. Spotting me on the threshold of the parlor, she came close and murmured, "I know this isn't your responsibility, but if you hear her say anything *concerning*, call me." With that, she pressed a business card into my hand, turned up her collar, and let herself out into the rain.

When the door latched, I slipped the card into my pocket and headed for the kitchen. "Eleanor?" I called as I rounded the corner. "What is it? What happ—"

She crouched and leaned against the cheery red cabinets with her hands over her mouth, perhaps holding the screaming back through manual force alone. "Eleanor," I said, hurrying to her side, "are you all right? What did she say?"

The distant clock ticked off a full minute before Eleanor seemed to notice my presence. Her green eyes rose, breaking her thousand-yard stare, and started to fill.

"They found Walt," she whispered.

"They did?"

"They think so. In the…in…" She paused, took a long breath, and forced down the sob that threatened to break loose. "A body washed up last night. Leith. Hadn't been in long, she said…"

"Shit," I muttered, kneeling to join her. "They identified—"

"Not yet. No head, see. Bit of a problem. Taking prints. Can't exactly do dental." Eleanor giggled, then clamped her hands over her mouth in shock.

"Moon and stars, I'm so sorry. Maybe it's not Walt, you don't know yet…"

But the tears were already spilling down her wrinkled cheeks, and she shook her head. "Still had his wedding ring."

"Lots of rings look the same. You don't know—"

"'Amor vincit omnia' and our anniversary. They checked that first. He designed them." She raised her hand and showed me the gold band around her finger, a simple piece inlaid with a trio of diamonds, then pulled it off and held it so the overhead light caught the script inside. "See? They're almost twins."

Words deserted me, and Eleanor kissed the ring and slid it back over her knuckle in silence. She sighed and closed her eyes until her tears slowed, then stood. I rose as well, trying to think of the proper response to the situation, but Toula beat me to it.

"Hey," she said as she came into the kitchen, "what's go—oh, *no,*" she murmured, brushing past me to wrap her arms around Eleanor. "Oh, I'm sorry…"

The fragile control Eleanor had managed to regain cracked under that hug, and I looked away as she wept in the embrace, wailing as Toula rubbed her back. Val poked his head into the room, took one look at the tableau, then beckoned me into the safety of the hall.

There was no point in continuing the spell she'd begun, so Toula, punctuating every third sentence with a yawn, explained that she was going back to Montana to catch a few hours of sleep. "I'll pick up with Moyna in the morning," she told me. "Need a little shut-eye first."

Given the work she'd been doing of late for Greg, I wondered how Toula was still on her feet. "It can wait—"

"No, it can't." Her face hardened, and she glanced pointedly at Eleanor, who was slumped on the sofa with an untouched cup of tea. "Take her home with you. She doesn't need to be alone."

"I doubt she has any desire for my company."

But Toula was having none of it. "Take her with you. If not for her sake, then for the safety of the rest of this city. Okay?"

"I can't *force* her…"

While I was still making my excuses, Toula marched across the parlor and around the sofa, then rested her hand on Eleanor's shoulder until she looked up from her lap. "Hey, Ellie," she murmured. "That's what you go by, right? Ellie?" Eleanor dipped her head, and Toula slid beside her on the embroidered cushion and took her hands. "I want you to do me a big favor and go hang out with the boys. Can you do that? In case whoever went after Walt comes after you, I want you to be safe. Let Colin and Val worry about security. You need a hot bath and bed."

Eleanor blinked slowly as she made sense of Toula's words, then looked down at her pocket. "My phone, if they call me—"

"They'll be able to reach you. Come on," she coaxed, standing to pull Eleanor to her feet. "Colin's not going to mess with you. Go home with them for now, yeah?" Eleanor's brow furrowed, and Toula added, "Either you go with them or I stay here with you. I'm not leaving you alone."

"You needn't worry, child." She sighed. "I'll be all

right."

"Maybe, but I'm going to worry anyway. *Please.*"

Eleanor regarded her for a long moment, then squeezed Toula's hands and released her. "I'm no concern of yours."

"Now you are. I've made you my concern. Tough."

She smiled sadly, closed her eyes, and nodded as her chin began to tremble. "I…fine, I…I'll go."

Toula hugged her again, but she traded glances with me over Eleanor's shoulder, giving me a look that told me all too clearly what she thought of my people skills. I shrugged, and Toula rolled her eyes. "Let me give you my number," she said as she broke her hold on Eleanor. "Just in case those two decide to be idiots."

Eleanor walked as if dazed, but she followed me through the gate onto the front lawn of my palace. If she noticed her glamour dissolve into youth, she gave no sign. She shielded her eyes and squinted at her surroundings—the sun was declining, but it was still brighter than the wet gloom we'd left behind—and I swung my arm toward the building. "You're welcome to come in," I offered as Val closed the rift behind us. "I mean, you don't have to—if you want to set up your own place, be my guest. I don't think Oberon left anything here, but there's room to build…a nice sea view if you head west…"

She shook her head. "Not today. I…I don't have it in me."

"Sure, sure," I said too quickly, and cringed inside. "Uh…come in, then?"

"Perhaps—"

Before she could finish her though, the realm sounded its alarm, and Eleanor cried out and covered her ears. "Won't do any good!" I shouted over the voice in my head. "Internal! Hang on, it'll stop in a minute!"

Rubbing her temples, she stared at the sky as if

expecting to find the source of the noise above us. "Does this happen often?"

"Not like this!" The psychic shrieking crescendoed, and a split-second later, I saw what was bothering Faerie. "Intruder!"

"What?"

"Intruder! Listen to the voice!" I glanced at Val, who, to my surprise, was also holding his head. "She's yelling at you, too?" I asked him.

He nodded vigorously, then held up one hand for quiet and stared into the distance. "Where?"

Deep forest, came the reply. *Deep and far.*

"How many?"

One. Moving quickly.

His brow furrowed as he considered this information. "Who's closest?"

Joey.

"And is he aware?"

He knows.

"Taking precautions?" When that garnered no response, Val muttered, "Damn it, boy," and opened a gate into a stone-walled room. He ducked through the rift, and after trading looks with each other, Eleanor and I followed.

Aside from a slit of a window in the far wall, the room in which I found myself was lit entirely by a bank of four oversized monitors mounted above a long desk. Two showed static images of green foliage and one a video of the same, but the fourth was a collage of graphs and scrolling text—feedback, I realized, spotting a heart monitor in the bottom corner. In front of the array sat Aiden in a swivel chair, shouting at the microphone in his headset. "I've got your 20, you're on the map, but barely," he said as a red grid overlaid the video stream. "She showed me the new gate—it's maybe ten miles to the northeast. I'm shooting you the terrain map"—his fingers flew over the keyboard—"but it's low-res, we don't have enough data for anything better. You're going to have to get under the canopy for visual confir—"

Val yanked the headset off him, shoved it in place, and planted his palms on the desktop. "Unknown faerie. Do *not* engage," he barked. "That's an order, Joey. Do you hear me?"

Aiden tapped a button on the keyboard, and Joey's staticky voice echoed around the room. "Map's up, and yeah, I got you, Aid. Scan cams are running—should have enough to fill out the map next time. And hey, Val. Hang tight."

"*Joey.*"

"Yes? Realm's not happy. I'm going to get a look—"

"Negative. Stay high and out of range. Come back."

I could almost hear him bristle. "We're *fine*. Let me see what we're dealing with."

"That is an *order*."

"It's under control."

Aiden grimaced, then picked up a second microphone and muttered, "Dude, if it's a rogue faerie out there, hold back. You can get the flyover pass later. And you're down to nine miles. Still on course for encounter."

"Look," Joey snapped, "we're the only ones out here, and I'm the guy with the dragon, remember? We'll be fine."

"Yes, the dragon who can't breathe fire right now," Val retorted. "Abort."

"Which is why I'm packing the nail gun."

Val ripped the headset off, spun around, and shot me an impatient glare as he thrust the equipment in my direction. I slipped it on and approached the screens. "Listen to Val, kid. Turn the lizard around and let someone else deal with this."

"I'm telling you, it's under control!" he protested.

"Eight miles," Aiden muttered.

"This isn't a request, Joey," I replied, watching the trees rush past through his helmet's camera. "Get out of there."

His voice rose with his frustration. "I know what I'm doing! This isn't the first bogie I've found in the bush!"

"It's not a *bogie*, it's fae, and the realm is concerned. This isn't up for debate."

"If the realm's concerned, then you need to see what's out here. I'll have it in a matter of minutes—I'm going to dip low enough to get the visual."

"You'll be an easy target. Turn around."

I waited, but the video showed no sign of a sudden banking. "He's not turning, is he?" I asked Aiden, covering my microphone.

Aiden shook his head. "Joey's pretty stubborn when he runs across something dangerous out there. He can handle it."

"Not if his target starts throwing lightning," said Val. "He's going to kill himself."

By then, Eleanor had joined us in contemplation of the monitors, and she reached over Aiden's head to tap the video stream. "How is he traveling?"

"Dragonback," said Aiden, arching an eyebrow as he noticed who was standing behind him. "Georgie's tough, but she's not indestructible. If she gets in the way of a volley from the ground—"

"He can't shield his mount?"

"He's *mortal*," Val interjected. "Useless with magic."

Eleanor's eyes widened. "Oh, dear. Pull him out of there." She paused, frowned at the screen, then turned back to me. "Did he say he has a *nail* gun?"

"Modified and effective," I replied, then uncovered my mic. "Joey, everyone with an ounce of sanity thinks this is a bad idea."

"Have a little faith, huh?" he pleaded. "I'm not helpless!"

I rubbed my face and tried to find the right angle, since Joey obviously hadn't accepted the notion of a chain of command. "No one thinks you're helpless. No one wants to deliver your remains to Helen, either. If she were here, she would agree with us, and you know it."

Aiden turned around and whispered, "Want me to get her?"

I mulled that over, weighing the likelihood of Helen's success against her displeasure at being pulled from bed at an unfortunate hour, but before I could tell Aiden to summon his sister, Eleanor stepped back, turned to the empty room, and said, "Take me to the intruder."

I looked over my shoulder in time to see a gate open into the primeval woods of uninhabited Faerie, and Eleanor marched through without a second's pause. *He's coming your way*, said the voice of the realm. *Arrival is imminent.*

"Come on, then." I sighed and waved to the others. "Before Joey gets there. Pity to spoil his fun."

Muttering curses, Val strode past me into the trees, and Aiden hurried after him with a green fireball primed in each hand. I came last, closed the gate, and located the path as a figure appeared from the shadows.

The intruder was male, tall and lean and pale, and his translucent excuse for a tunic did little to hide the muscle beneath. He wore his dark hair long and tied back, and the tail bobbed when he spotted Eleanor and came to an abrupt halt. She marched toward him, straightening her twinset as she crossed the litter of dead leaves. "You come uninvited. Your name?"

He smirked and folded his arms. "My, my. This must be the little Lady Eleanor. And she comes with…friends?" he added, glancing at the rest of us. "Valerius. Never thought I would see you standing with one of Oberon's brood."

Val shrugged dismissively. "Times change, Sevim. You look well," he continued, giving the newcomer a quick appraisal. "Life outside the Gray Lands seems to suit you. Where did you land?"

Sevim only smiled. "My lady sends me with a message for the little girl who would be queen," he said, turning his attention back to Eleanor. "She's left a gift for you at your abode. A trifle for you in your time of grief."

Eleanor stood with her back to me, but her shoulders didn't so much as twitch. "How thoughtful of her. And who, pray tell, is your lady?"

He straightened under her gaze. "I serve the one true queen of Faerie. She sends you her condolences, child…and a warning."

The trees began to rustle overhead, and I picked up on the distinctive thump of dragon wings.

"Oh?" said Eleanor. "And what would that be?"

The smile he wore seemed less a reassurance than a threat. "Surrender. This war is not yours. This land is not meant for you. Return to your little life and be safe." He paused, letting that sink in, then gestured to Aiden and me. "You were happy before *they* thrust themselves upon you, were you not? My lady wishes only that you be happy once again. Happy and safe and far from this place."

His tone was honey, but his words were barbed, and I waited for Eleanor to explode. Instead, she stood in silence for a long moment, then glanced behind her at the sound of heavy footsteps. From out of the trees strode Joey, helmeted, strapped, and ready for action. "A moment, please," she told Sevim, then hurried over to Joey and pointed at his smoked visor. "You! Are you the dragon rider?"

I couldn't see his face through the helmet, but he froze in his tracks when she wheeled on him. "*Meg?*" came his disbelieving reply through the helmet's speaker.

"No, and you have a lot of nerve, young man." With her back now to Sevim, Eleanor lifted her hands to her breast, and a pair of gardening gloves manifested around them. "Listen to your elders. And where's this bloody dragon, anyway?" Then, lowering her voice to a low murmur, she asked in English, "What's the pull weight on that gun of yours?"

Joey might have been flustered, but he could take a

hint. "About four pounds, ma'am."

"Steel, I trust?"

"Handle's wrapped in leather and packing tape, but you're going to need something covering your trigger finger."

"Understood." Without further warning, she pulled the nail gun from the holster at Joey's right hip, spun on her heel, and fired off a quick trio of shots toward Sevim. The first two missed their mark, but the third hit him in the groin, and he shrieked as his trousers began to smoke. "Closer to three and a half pounds, I'd say," Eleanor told Joey as she slipped the gun back into its place. "You could use a sight on that thing."

He tapped a button on the side of his helmet, and the visor retracted to reveal his wide eyes. "Uh...yeah. Sure?"

"Just a thought," she replied, then patted his shoulder and marched back to Sevim, who had fallen to his knees and was screaming with the pain. "Come, now," she said in Fae, "it's only a little iron burn." When that did nothing to silence his shouts, she delivered a well-placed kick to follow the nail and stepped aside, giving Sevim room to topple to the dirt and writhe. "Low-hanging fruit, perhaps," she said, catching the identical looks on our faces, "but it's *effective*." With that, she headed for me and tossed her head toward the casualty. "I'd rather not kill him outright while he might still prove useful. Might you have some facility where he could be accommodated? Temporarily, of course."

Too stunned to question her, I nodded, and Val hurried to bind Sevim.

"And now," she continued, turning to Joey, "if I recall correctly, you were going to do an overhead pass. Where's the dragon?"

He cocked his thumb over his shoulder. "Canopy's too thick to get her down. The channel went dead, and the realm told me you'd all be on the ground—"

"Take your helmet off." Shooting me an uneasy glance,

Joey obliged, revealing his sweat-dark hair and flushed face. Eleanor considered him briefly, then grabbed his ear and yanked his head down to her level. "Follow orders! Good God, child, there are easier ways to commit suicide! What sort of fool brings a gun to a magic fight?"

"It *works*," he protested, struggling in her grip.

Eleanor released him, shook her head, and flung him into a tree twenty yards away with a flick of her wrist. "Now you're out of range and dazed," she called as Joey picked himself up. "And sore, am I correct? And—oh, what is—"

Aiden darted between her and the streak of golden light headed toward her face, then snatched Kuni out of the air before the piq could attack. The little creature squeaked in protest and beat his free hand against Aiden's fingers, but he carried him away, muttering an explanation into his fist.

"That's Kuni," I told Eleanor, who stared at the glowing captive in shock. "He's piq. Also fond of those two, apparently," I added, pointing to my brother and Joey, "so let it go."

She blinked. "That...*that*...would be a—"

"Pixie, I know. They're native, too."

Eleanor crossed her arms and glared in exasperation as Val carried the unconscious Sevim through a fresh gate into my dungeon. "Well, that's distressing," she muttered, then looked up as a large shadow passed through the canopy. "Dragon?"

"Dragon," I replied, caught in a sudden rain of leaves as Georgie alighted on the trees above us. "Want me to make the introductions?"

Her mouth tightened to a fine line. "Perhaps later. I should see what this 'one true queen' has given me first." She opened a gate back into her house, then added, "I understand that the intruder is your prisoner, but should this gift displease me, will you allow me to return him to his mistress in an appropriate fashion?"

I didn't want to think about what Eleanor had in mind,

but the look in her eyes warned me against quibbling. "As you wish," I said, and followed her.

CHAPTER 8

Late morning outside of Durham was sodden, the sky dark as lead. As I closed the gate, Eleanor turned in place in her foyer, looking for anything out of the ordinary. Satisfied, she unlatched the front door and found a carton waiting on the welcome mat.

The box was perhaps a foot square, wrapped in brown paper, and tied with twine. Frowning, Eleanor picked it up and headed for the kitchen. "Heavy," she grunted as she dropped it on the counter.

As Eleanor donned an oven mitt and moved toward the knife block, I tried to push down the image that had arisen in my mind. A box of those dimensions, a *heavy* box, and Walt missing…

Armed and protected, Eleanor returned to the package but hesitated with her finger under the twine. "Something tells me this isn't a bowling ball," she murmured, giving voice to our shared fear.

"I'll do it. There's no need to put yourself through this."

"No. This is for me." She considered the box for a moment, breathed out a long sigh, then set to work.

If Eleanor had been expecting a booby trap, the package was a disappointment. The string fell away, the paper tore as usual, and then she was down to a sealed cardboard box. Pressing on despite the tremor in her hand, she neatly sliced through the packing tape, then put the knife and mitt aside, gripped the box flaps, and pulled them back. She hesitated for a second on the last flaps, but with a presumptive grimace and a little moan, she threw them open and bent to see her prize.

"*Walt!*" she screamed, tripping over her feet in shock. Her back hit the granite island, and she gripped it as she stared at the carton with an ashen face.

Something inside the box made a muffled sound.

Keeping my eyes on Eleanor in case she protested, I peeked into the box, expecting to find a head, probably something unpleasant and ripe.

I hadn't expected the eyes inside the head to *blink* at me.

"Moon and stars," I whispered, and then, ever so carefully, I pulled Walt's head free.

Someone had taped his mouth shut. Nestling the head in the crook of my arm, and trying not to look at the ragged stump where the neck should have been, I picked the tape off and tossed it aside. Walt opened his mouth, revealing the rags that had been shoved inside, and I pulled them out as quickly as I could. He moved his jaw experimentally, blinked in the brightness of the kitchen, then croaked, "Ellie?"

I looked at Eleanor, whose tears were already spilling, then back at Walt. "She's here," I told him, wondering whether I should put him down. There was no set etiquette for having a conversation with a severed head. "Just, uh…caught off guard."

Walt squinted up at me. "You're the man from the other day, aren't you? You and the boy, you gave Ellie that spreadsheet—"

"Yes. Um…"

"I thought so, but I'm blind without my glasses. You're a large blur. Is Ellie—"

"I'm here," she interrupted, pulling Walt from my grasp, then cupped him in her palms and held him close to her face. "It's me, love, it's Ellie…"

He smiled weakly. "Your hair's gone red again. I'm sure it's lovely."

"Oh, *Walt*," she breathed, pulling him against her. "Who did this? I'll kill him. Tell me who did this to you..."

His dark eyes rolled, searching for hers in his myopic fog. "Some men, I never got a good look. Ambushed me on the train and broke my glasses, and the next thing I knew...well." Somehow, despite his missing anatomy, he managed to sigh. "I've no idea where they took me."

"They found the rest of you in the Firth this morning. The detective came round to tell me you...oh," she said through a sob, "I thought I'd never see you again." She clung to him so tightly that I was sure he could hear her heartbeat. "I love you, darling," she whispered into his thin hair. "We'll make this right. You're going to be fine, everything is going to be fine..."

Ignoring the ghastliness of the tableau, I stooped until I was on Walt's eye level. "Did you hear anything unusual? Names, places?"

Walt's forehead furrowed in thought. "I didn't recognize any voices, but a few names were repeated. Ellie's, of course. Someone called Ironhand—"

"That's me. Anyone else?"

"Ehm...yes, there was one other. Lady Moyna, I believe. Wasn't she the one in Montana last year?"

My stomach clenched. "So I'm told. I swear, Eleanor, I had nothing to do with this—"

"Understood," she said, cutting my denial short, and closed her eyes as she held Walt. "I'm going to find her," she murmured. "I will find her, and she will pay. *Dearly.*"

As I watched her hold her husband's head and kiss his balding spot, I realized the full implications of Moyna's deed. A major enchantment, the sort my daughter couldn't have produced on her own, was the only thing keeping Walt alive. Eleanor couldn't take him into Faerie—passing into the realm broke all enchantments on living things. But if Walt couldn't go, he would surely die within a decade or two—unless the enchantment on him stopped the aging process as well. Eleanor would have her Walt, but he would forever be either only a head or some cobbled-together construct held intact by magic.

In any case, he'd be an easy target for Moyna or anyone else who wanted to take a crack at Eleanor, the biggest chink in her armor. With Walt stuck in the mortal realm, Eleanor would never take Oberon's throne—and if Moyna applied enough pressure, perhaps Eleanor would stand against me. Moyna wasn't a queen while I lived, but if she could draw a queen into her forces…

As I mulled this over, Eleanor released Walt from her death grip and held him up to her face. "Are you in pain, dear?"

He grimaced. "It's a phantom pain, I suppose. Everything below the neck hurts, but I don't suppose I can do anything about that."

She closed her eyes and concentrated, and a look of relief crossed his face. "Better?"

"Much. Thank you, dearest, I…" Tears began to roll down his face. "I'm sorry, I'm a silly old fool, I should have been more careful—"

"Shh, stop that. It's not your fault, and I'm going to make it right." She kissed his lips, then gave him a tiny smile—a weary smile, but one tinged with hope. "Come on, love, I'm going to take you somewhere safe while I figure this out."

And with that, Eleanor opened a gate.

"No, *stop!*" I cried, realizing what she had in mind, but Eleanor was on a mission to save the man she loved. A freight train wouldn't have stopped her as she carried Walt between the realms, back into the relative protection of Faerie.

"You'll be safe…" she told Walt, then turned on me in alarm. "What—"

"The crossing breaks enchantments," I said slowly, watching her from the other side. "You didn't know?"

She looked down at the motionless flesh in her arms,

and as she understood what she had done, Eleanor fell to her knees and screamed.

The sky had purpled before I convinced Eleanor to come inside. She pushed me away when I tried to pull her from the grass, but after much coaxing, I led her the few feet through a fresh gate into a spare bedroom. She sank into an armchair by the window, staring at nothing, and I created a few lamps and a pot of tea before making my cautious approach. "Ellie," I said, squatting before her in the gloom, "let me have it."

She shook her head and tightened her grip on the little that remained of her husband.

"He's gone," I murmured. "That's not Walt anymore. You know it." The severed head's face had begun to take on an odd color as the afternoon waned, and I didn't know if Eleanor had the presence of mind to stop the rot. "I'll take care of it. It'll be waiting when you wake up, as good as...now," I finished lamely, wondering whether she would notice if I glamoured up the head to look livelier. "But you need to rest. Go to sleep. Want a drink?" I stood and produced a teacup. "Something warm? Brandy?"

She closed her eyes and held the head, and I was nearly convinced that she'd fallen asleep in front of me when she whispered, "Him."

"Pardon?"

"Not *it*. Him."

"I'll take care of him, I promise." Ever so slowly, she relaxed her grip, and I pried the head out of her arms. "Sleep," I told her, trying to touch as little of the head as possible without showing Eleanor how distasteful I found the endeavor. "Try to rest. I'll send someone around to check on you later, all right?"

She gave no reply, and I carried Walt back to my office for safekeeping, enchanting away the decay as I went. Once upstairs, I paused under a wall sconce to examine my work, then wished I hadn't. He wasn't leaking, at least, but his eyes hadn't quite closed in death, and with his odd complexion and his gaping mouth, he had the air of a man coming down from a long, hard bender. Suppressing a shudder, I bound his mouth and eyes shut, put a splotch of pink back into his cheeks, and proceeded with my unpleasant burden.

To my surprise, I found Val waiting on a stool outside my office. He stood when he spotted me and sent his seat back into the ether, then did a double-take. "What are you—"

"Moyna sent Eleanor a little something special," I interrupted, brushing past him into the room, then wedged Walt out of the way on my bookshelf and called a clean shirt into being. "He was still alive when she unwrapped him."

Val swore softly. "What happened?"

"Seems no one ever told her about Faerie's enchantment-stripping powers."

"You mean—"

I nodded and motioned the fire to life. "Carried him over herself. She's in the north wing, so if you could set a guard to ensure she's not disturbed…"

"Of course." He paused at the door. "I assume we'll not be seeing her for the immediate future."

"Probably not," I muttered, sinking onto the couch as a glass of gin materialized in my hand. "I know the feeling, Val."

"Ten days is the time to beat," he replied, and shrugged at the look I shot him. "She can mourn later. Moyna's active—every day you wait is another day she has to build her forces."

"I'm well aware. And please tell me you haven't killed Joey for his stunt."

He smirked in the firelight. "Eleanor gave him a few cracked ribs and a nice set of bruises. I told him I'd patch him up once the barn's clean."

"Ouch."

"He must learn. Now, I can't guarantee that Aiden hasn't visited in my absence to start the healing."

"That *is* the risk inherent in leaving them unsupervised."

"Mm." Val leaned against the doorframe and shook his head. "Joey is fighting limitations that he simply can't surmount. He's a natural with a blade, he takes instruction well, but…"

"But he can't defend himself against magic. I know."

He hesitated. "The Arcanum—I've heard they make weapons for their…'duds' is the term, yes?"

"Yeah, charge-storing rods. Slim has one, but it probably doesn't hold more than ten shots. I could be wrong, but I don't think it's a long-term solution to Joey's handicap."

The captain watched as I finished my drink. "Could one of these rods be modified? Instead of shooting, could it shield?"

"You'd have to ask Slim."

He mulled that over, then nodded curtly. "If Joey's to remain here, something needs to be done. For the boy's sake, ask him. You must do *something*," he pressed. "He chafes when I hold him back, and he's going to kill himself trying to prove me wrong. Either find a crutch for him or…" Val grimaced. "If it's the only way to save him from himself…send him home."

"Send him home to die, you mean," I retorted as my glass disintegrated.

"Surely fifty or sixty years with Helen would be preferable to ten here and a messy end."

I pushed myself off the couch and paced to control the anger bubbling up. "I'll talk to Slim tomorrow."

"And if there's nothing he can do for Joey?"

When I turned on Val, I saw him through the haze of the shield he had created, already primed for my outburst. I realized my upraised hand had begun to spark with blue flame and forced it, and my temper, down. "Point taken."

"What if it had been Joey who provoked you instead of me?"

"You made your point," I snapped, and Val left me with Walt's head to stew in silence.

My plans for the rest of the night had included brooding by the fire, drinking too much, and doing everything in my power not to think of Meggy. But three drinks in, I acknowledged that I wasn't going to do anything *but* think of Meggy if I sat alone until dawn, and so created a bit of camouflage around the head as a security measure and took myself to Slim's.

After spending much of the day going back and forth to Durham, I was momentarily surprised to pop out in the alley beside the bar and see pale light in the eastern sky. More surprising still were the concrete planters someone had arranged outside the bar, long box gardens of stubby, light-strung holly bushes. Glancing down the street, I spotted similar planters at regular intervals—perhaps the mayor's idea of a flourish on the downtown rebuilding project, or at least a way to finish off the federal funds brought in after Rigby's brush with the Gray Lands. Still, the little else I could see in the cold predawn was familiar: the trash cans out for pickup; the grit on the sidewalks from an early snow's sanding; the disquieting juxtaposition of a seagull nestled in the bank's oversized Christmas wreath, a garish green ornament viewed best under cover of darkness. A rusty pickup truck rumbled down the street, belching a white cloud from its exhaust pipe, and I shivered.

Though last call was long behind us, I was worn out and getting colder, so I chanced knocking on the bar door. A moment later, I heard someone pull back the bolt, and the door cracked open on the barkeep himself, puffy-eyed and armed with a push broom. "Hey, stranger," he said, opening the door wider. "Wards are off. Come in."

I slipped inside and waited while Slim reengaged his Arcanum-built security system. The bar, at least, seemed unchanged—vinyl stools, dirty windows, warped floorboards, and all—which gave me a sense of comfort with the world until I noticed the odd configuration of tables near the low stage. Someone had jammed the mismatched squares and rectangles into a unified mass, at the center of which sat a glass bowl of plastic fruit atop a cheap red velvet swag. Ringing the table was a detritus of stemware, papers, and what looked suspiciously like paintbrushes.

"Art night," Slim explained, divining the object of my interest as he leaned the broom against the bar. "Got a group of ladies that come in on the regular. They can't paint for shit, but they drink all night long. Liquid inspiration, I think." With a snort, he picked up a plastic bin and lugged it over to the *artistes'* table to load it with wine-stained glasses. "Got to keep up with the trends."

"Say it ain't so, Slim," I replied, pulling out my old stool. "That's what the tiki bar is for."

He dropped a pair of stems into the bucket with a grunt. "Idiots remodeled. They've replaced the beachfront wall with a glorified garage door. Nice to open the place up in the summer, but now? That thing is *not* insulated."

"Stopped in to spy, did you?"

"It's not espionage if you're paying to drink. And good to see you again," he added over the clinking of shifting glasses. "Feeling better?"

"I was." I considered Slim's top shelf for a moment, then slapped a fifty on the bar, let myself behind it, and selected my prize and a chipped tumbler. "Need your help."

He had the decency not to mention the hour or his liquor license. "That depends," he called over his shoulder as he carried the bin toward the kitchen's batwing doors. I drank while the industrial dishwasher roared to life and the microwave beeped, and Slim returned with a mug in hand. "It's getting to be past my bedtime," he explained, and hefted himself onto the stool beside me. "Coffee? It's gone cold, but it reheats well enough."

I lifted my glass and shook my head.

"Suit yourself." He sipped and forced the bitter brew down. "What's up, Colin?"

"Joey," I muttered. "Kid labors under the delusion that he's invincible."

Slim nodded. "Sounds about right. He'll grow out of it."

"Not if it kills him first. What are the odds that I could get my hands on a Dud Defender?"

He chose his words carefully when he broke the silence. "Your odds would depend on the crafter you approached and whether he could make one without the silo finding out."

"Understood. And could a Defender be modified? Maybe a defensive rod instead of an offensive weapon?"

Sipping his coffee, Slim stared out the grimy window at the morning, then barely nodded. "A shielding spell can be stored in the rod matrix. There's a spell on the rod itself that holds the others at the point of release. Simple enough to charge if you've got the knowhow, but a pain in the ass to make. Now, this isn't something a crafter could do alone—you'd need a wizard to do the spellwork."

"Let's assume I could procure one of sufficient skill."

"Pavli could do it."

"I was thinking Carver, actually."

He pursed his lips in thought. "Ballsy, but since this is for her fiancé…yeah, Carver's got the chops, but could you get her here?"

"So you'll do it?"

"Yeah, man, but this ain't an overnight job," he cautioned, running his pudgy fingers through his thinning hair. "And the wood I'll need is ensorcelled before I ever lay hands on it. This isn't going to be cheap."

I shrugged, and a fat stack of twenties appeared on the bar between us. "Your price?"

"Let's barter. I want something I can't buy."

My eyebrows rose. "Are you asking for a *favor*, Slim?"

He chuckled and swirled his coffee. "Come on, I'm not that stupid. I need dragonscale. Supplies have been low for ages."

"How much do you want?" I asked, wondering how best to approach the idea with Georgie. "A pound? Ten pounds?"

"God, no, nothing so drastic. I don't want to hurt the poor girl. Five medium scales would do me for at least the next few years. Have Joey collect them when they fall out, then pay me when you've got it."

I finished my drink and deposited the glass in the collection bin. "You're a good one, Rick."

"Debatable." He grinned. "I'll tell you when I'm ready for Carver."

"I'll let her know. And keep the cash. I probably still owe you for a drink or two." As I slid off the stool, a thought pierced the warm whisky haze like an icicle to my gut. "One other thing. No reason to panic, but keep your wards up. Moyna—"

To his credit, Slim didn't flinch. "Shown her face?"

"Yeah." I looked around the bar—the warded, yet otherwise undefended bar—then back at Slim. "Keep the wards in order. And maybe buy a gun."

I'd already opened a gate when he said, "How bad is it? Give it to me straight, Colin."

"I'm not sure, but this might be a good time to start circling the wagons. Spread the word."

"Understood," he said, and as the gate closed behind me, I heard him add, "Be careful."

I fell into uneasy dreams, a surrealist parade that left a vague sense of dread on waking. Shortly before dawn, I gave up on restful sleep and dragged myself to my favorite dining room. I passed the north wing on the way, but the guard shook his head in reply to my unspoken question. I hadn't *expected* to see Eleanor again so quickly, but still, the waiting left me unsettled.

Astrid, my head cook, sent out a platter of eggs and potatoes, then carried a pot of coffee to the table. "How strong do you need this to be, my lord?"

Suppressing a yawn, I reached for the carafe. "I'm not hungover."

"Very good. And your...guest? Will she be dining this morning?"

"Unlikely." I held my warm cup close as if I could osmotically receive a pick-me-up through the porcelain. "Should she appear and request something, please do what you can for her, but...she just lost her husband."

Astrid's blue eyes softened. "Oh, no, the poor dear—"

"You've been told who she is?"

She nodded vigorously. "Word spreads, my lord."

"Good. Take whatever precautions you think necessary, but try not to let on, hmm?"

Before she could reply, she turned at the sound of boots on the stone outside the dining room, and Joey popped his head around the door. "Hi, boss," he mumbled. "Morning, Astrid."

She chewed her lip and stepped aside as I beckoned him into the room. After a few seconds' hesitation, he complied, albeit stiffly. "How's the barn?" I asked.

"Cleaner." He paused halfway down the table. "Still working on the dump pile. I guess I'd forgotten how much of a mess Georgie can make." He reached for his neck, then winced and lowered his arm.

"Val didn't fix the ribs?"

"It's no big deal. I told him it's not bad."

"And Aiden?"

"He's cleaning up the map data. Got a backlog to work on."

The kid looked miserable, and I rose with a sigh. "Come here, Joey," I ordered, then rested my hands on his ribcage until his face relaxed. "Val wanted you to learn a lesson, not become a martyr. Hungry?"

Satisfied that I wasn't about to incinerate him, Joey followed me back down the table and helped himself to Astrid's offerings. "He's *pissed*," he muttered between mouthfuls of potatoes.

"Because he cares, as does Aiden, as do *I*. What's gotten into you? You're a smart kid, Joey—why risk it all for nothing?" He kept chewing, so I tried another approach. "Is this about Helen? I hate to break it to you, but she's always going to outclass you in magic."

"I know," he said quietly after a swig of coffee.

"So you're going to tell me this isn't all some stupid attempt to run with the big dogs in order to impress a girl? It's been tried, seldom with any success."

He continued to eat in silence, then put his fork down and stared at the wall, avoiding my eyes. "I'm not helpless, okay? I've held it together now for two years. But all I hear of late is, 'Don't do that,' and, 'Be careful of this,' and…I mean, I *know*," he said, agitated. "Okay, I get it, magic's never going to be my strong suit. But I'm not *useless*. I'm good for more than handling questionable metals."

I waited and drank, and shortly, Joey gave in and looked at me. "The last person who thought you might be useless was Robin," I told him. "Now, which one of you is still living? You're a remarkable young man, Joey. Everything you've done with Georgie—everything you've done for Aiden and me—that's not to be discounted. Helen chose well. That said, I'd like to ensure your continued safety. There are some walls that you aren't going to be able to punch through, no matter how much you practice. So with that in mind, I'm working on getting a Dud Defender for you. It's going to take time, but—"

"*Seriously?*" he yelped. "Like…fireballs?"

"Shields," I replied, and his sudden excitement dulled a

degree. "I don't know how strong they'll be or how many a rod can store, but seeing as you're going to be spending so much time around a certain grand magus, I'm sure she wouldn't mind recharging as needed." His face creased in a genuine smile, and I grinned into my coffee. "Let me break the news to Helen, all right? This is being done strictly off the Arcanum books."

"Thanks, boss."

I nodded. "Rather you didn't spend too much time in a body cast. And for heaven's sake, listen to Val," I added, jabbing my dirty fork at him. "Yes?"

"Yes," he mumbled.

"Good. Eat up. I'll take care of the disposal issues at the barn after—"

That was as far as I got before Toula marched into the dining room. "*There* you are," she said, pushing up the sleeves of her paint-flecked sweatshirt. "We've got a problem."

"What sort of problem?" I asked. "Did the Council wise up to the holes in the silo wards?"

"Nope. This." She reached into the pocket of her jeans and extracted a glass vial on a gold chain. The vial held a red liquid near its tip, and my stomach clenched in anticipation of Toula's news. When she pinched the chain between finger and thumb, the vial rose and pointed at me like the tip of a divining rod. "Spell's running. Totally functional," she said, walking around the table as a demonstration of how steadfastly the bloody vial sought out its object.

"And Moyna?"

Toula returned her toy to its hiding place and shook her head. "Can't find her. It goes in circles."

Joey's brow furrowed. "Surely she's not in the Gray Lands."

"Well, she's not back home, and I assume she's not here. Process of elimination," Toula replied with a shrug. "But that would mean—"

"Nath is aware," I interrupted. "And so the Gray Lands is supporting her. *Shit.*"

My companions kept their silence as I mulled over these tidings, but when I continued to glower at my cooling eggs, Toula cleared her throat and asked, "So…how's Ellie?"

CHAPTER 9

The morning passed without a sign of Eleanor, though the guards kept their quiet watch. Astrid left a covered plate of breakfast for her with a little knock to announce the delivery, but the food remained untouched, the door latched.

Meanwhile, alone in my office, I tried to decide what was to be done about Moyna. If she were truly in the Gray Lands, I wouldn't be able to touch her without great risk. If she weren't, then she'd found a way to hide herself from the Arcanum. I was to rendezvous with Jeanine Nadel in nine days' time, but until then, I had no leads on my daughter, and that worried me to my core. By midday, having grown sick of waiting, I reasoned that Moyna could have slipped up and left a clue to her whereabouts at Eleanor's house. Opting not to inform Eleanor of my outing, I collected my thoughts and opened a gate…

…and leapt back as the flames on the other side flared through the rift.

"*Shit!*" I yelped, beating the fire out of my clothes, and slammed the gate shut as I caught my breath. Fire. There was fire. My shirt had sprung a fine set of blackened holes, but I seemed to be intact…

Eleanor's house is on fire.

Forgetting my stupid shirt, I tried to recall what little I'd seen of Eleanor's street from her front windows, then aimed and opened a pinhole-sized gate over the sidewalk. Pressing my eye to the crack between the realms, I peered out and found chaos in the neighborhood.

A heavy rain was falling over the city, but Eleanor's house was an inferno, the center of a mass of firemen and concerned neighbors in their nightclothes and overcoats. Two hoses blasted, sirens wailed as reinforcements neared, and every dog in a half-mile radius howled. Spotting a deserted driveway, I steered my tiny gate into the shadows and expanded it enough to slip through, then made my way toward the burning house, another rubbernecker in the throng.

The place was little more than a blackening shell, and broken glass from the exploded windows twinkled in the smoldering grass. No one noticed my presence, or if they did, they were too concerned for their own homes to worry about me. I paused a few yards beyond Eleanor's fence and sniffed deeply, trying to pick up on any trace of dark magic. All I got for my trouble was a chest full of smoke and a coughing fit, however, and as I bent over to hack it out, someone thumped me between the shoulder blades.

Whipping around, I saw a familiar face, a woman with an upturned mackintosh collar and a white streak in her hair. "All right, then?" she asked, folding her arms.

I wiped the rain from my eyes and managed to nod. "Detective Parsons," I croaked, and coughed again. "Hi."

"Mr. Leffee, wasn't it?" She gave me a hard look, then pointed down the street to a parked police car. "Want to get out of the wet?"

"Thanks, I'm fine—"

"Don't make a scene," she said, lowering her voice. "It's only half five, and it's been a long morning already."

I met her stare and held it. "Shotgun or back seat?"

"You can sit up front for now." She marched off, and deciding that I needed to cooperate to maintain Eleanor's cover, I hurried after her. By the time I caught up, the detective had unlocked the car and was holding the passenger door open. "Go on," she said, and waited while I folded myself into the tight quarters before taking her own seat. Before I could question her, she wiped her face on her soaking sleeve, cranked the ignition, and pulled off into the wet predawn.

"Um," I ventured a few blocks later, when the fire had receded into a bright spot in the rearview mirror, "are we heading back to the city?"

"No. We need to talk." She pulled up at an intersection and proceeded after a rolling stop. "What do you know about Dr. Richardson's whereabouts?"

"I'm sorry, Detective, I haven't—"

"In Fringe circles, my code name is Badger."

I froze, replaying what I'd heard. "You know who I am."

"I've a decent memory for faces, and you weren't exactly disguised." At the next light, she slowed only enough to avoid flipping the car when she turned. "Hannah Parsons."

"Colin. Coileán. Whatever's easier."

The detective grunted an affirmation and swerved around a driver who had the audacity to keep to the speed limit. "Dr. Drummond's disappearance—well, his murder—is my case. Twenty-four hours after he washes up, his house burns down, and his widow's MIA."

"You don't really think Eleanor would torch her own place."

Hannah shrugged. "I've seen a lot of weird shit. The preliminary assessment on the Drummond–Richardson property is a lightning strike."

I glanced out the rain-streaked window at the distorted streetlights. "Sounds plausible."

"Perhaps, but this isn't a thunderstorm, and a bolt from the blue is terribly convenient."

She waited, letting me sit in the uncomfortable silence deployed by all good interrogators, and I finally gave in. "What do you want me to say? Yes, it sounds fishy as hell. I didn't do it."

"Did Dr. Richardson?"

"No."

"Quick answer." She risked a glance at me as she ran a red light. "How do you know her? What were you doing with her yesterday?"

I've terrorized my share of passengers with my lead foot, but I was getting paid back with interest as Hannah put her car through its paces. "Want to slow down?"

"There's no traffic yet. How do you know Dr. Richardson?"

"You're aware of the courts, yes?"

"Sure."

"Oberon kicked off a year ago. Eleanor's his heir."

The car screeched to a halt as a semi crossed the intersection ahead. "She's *what?*" Hannah demanded.

"She's a queen. Whether she decides to act like one is another matter, but technically, she's got a court to command."

The detective blinked a few times, then slammed her head back against the seat and groaned. "I could have checked, there are sensitives—"

"Why would you have suspected she's fae?" I asked, breaking into her self-castigation. "She's good at passing—she's been at this game for a while."

Hannah massaged her forehead. "Charger married a faerie. No wonder he kept to himself."

"Charger?"

"Dr. Drummond. Charger to the Fringe. I've known him by correspondence for years…"

The light turned, but the car remained stopped through the next cycle. When it flipped to green for a second time, Hannah remembered that she was supposed to be driving and took off at roughly NASCAR speed. "He's not the target, *she* is. He's a means to an end."

I gripped the door handle against the force of the little car's acceleration. "That's the working theory, yeah."

"So who's after her?" When I gave no immediate reply, the detective said, "Look, I need to know whether I'm going to be able to find Charger's killer without trying to weasel a favor out of the Arcanum."

"Probably not. And for your own well-being, put this investigation on ice."

Hannah contemplated this as she performed another half-dozen road maneuvers that would have cost anyone else his license, then pulled onto the motorway and picked up speed. "This wouldn't have anything to do with the alert Slim sent out yesterday, would it?

If the detective's stunt driving was a ploy to unnerve me, it was succeeding masterfully. "What did he say?"

"That your little girl might be out for blood again. Ready the jump bags."

"Yeah. That's, uh…yeah."

"So what are you doing about it?"

"I'm working on it, and are you going to tell me where the hell we're going?"

"Edinburgh. I was supposed to be up there at seven for a meeting—might still make it if these idiots will get out of my way." She switched lanes and shot a rude gesture out of the other driver's vision. "Still no sign of the head, but I think the fingerprint comparison should be finished—"

"The head's at my place. Someone delivered it after you left yesterday."

Her jaw dropped. "Fucking hell, did she see—"

"She unwrapped the box. He was still alive…kind of."

"*Kind of*?"

"Heavy enchantment on the head. Eleanor…"

The detective tried to follow my unspoken thought. "Put him out of his misery?"

"Accidentally. She, uh…she's not in a good place right now."

"Jesus," she whispered. "Poor old girl."

We drove in silence as Hannah fit this new information into her mental case file. After a time, she muttered, "I need to tell her about her house."

"I'll handle it," I offered. "You've borne enough bad

news for one week, don't you think?"

"Appreciated, but she's my victim. Where's she staying?"

"My place, which is why—"

"Don't tell me you left her with the bloody head!" She almost ran into the guard rail when she turned to glare. "For crying out loud, you didn't—"

I raised my hands in pacification. "I separated them! Please drive!"

Though unconvinced, Hannah put her eyes back on the road. "So she's in Faerie?"

"Last I checked." I willed my heartbeat to slow. "Haven't heard otherwise today."

"Hmm. That complicates matters." She hesitated, then asked, "I don't suppose you'd let me have a word with her?"

I shrugged. "I'll take you over, but I don't think she's seeing anyone right now."

Hannah considered this. "You would guarantee my safe return?"

"No, but I'd offer a ninety-nine percent chance of success."

"Close enough. And this return would be at a time of my choosing, in conditions conducive to my safety?"

She couldn't see me roll my eyes in the darkness. "Do you guys have little laminated cards or something? A list of loopholes to close?"

"That's not a bad idea. Well?"

I sighed. "Detective Parsons, I assure you that I will keep you as safe as possible while in Faerie, and if you don't take too long, I'll get you to Edinburgh for your appointment. Good enough?"

"Deal."

"Pull over, then. The breakdown lane will suffice."

She did as instructed, and I opened a car-sized gate directly ahead. "I don't mean to be rude," she said over the squealing of tires—I couldn't blame the other drivers, given that there was suddenly a hole of blazing sunlight on the side of the road—"but there are certain precautions one takes when dealing with the fae. You understand."

"Better go before you cause a wreck," I said, and Hannah gunned it through the rift before anyone could double back to investigate. I sealed it behind us, and she pulled to a stop on my front lawn as she squinted in the afternoon sun. "No driveway. Don't worry about the grass," I added, letting myself out of her death trap, and she followed suit. The headlights flashed and the horn beeped as her door slammed, and I snorted as she straightened her damp coat. "Why bother locking it? There are maybe two guys in this realm who'd get within ten feet of your car."

"Police property. Nice shack you've got," she said, nodding to the palace as we approached.

"It's oversized for a bachelor pad, but it works. And here, let me," I said, willing her clothes dry.

Hannah smiled when her shoes stopped squelching. "Much appreciated." As she climbed the front steps, she opened her coat, reached into the breast pocket, and extracted a spiral-bound notebook and a stubby golf pencil. Flipping to a clean page, she caught my questioning look and explained, "This investigation's still live. And I suppose I'll need to keep two sets of notes now," she mused. Can't bloody well tell my super that I interviewed the victim's widow in *Faerie*."

I waved the heavy doors open as we approached. "What's the official line, then? Where was Eleanor during the fire?"

"I'm still working on it," she replied, tucking the pencil behind her ear, then sighed, muttered, "Let's get this over with," and followed me in.

Mina stiffened when she saw the detective, but I nodded reassurance, and she let us pass without protest. Despite

Hannah's no-nonsense demeanor, I noticed that she sidled closer to me as my niece gave her a second look. "You're safe," I murmured. "She works for me."

"Yes, I gathered that," she said, but her darting eyes betrayed her anxiety.

I led her to the door at the end of the quiet hallway and paused. "Give it a shot. You don't have to, but as long as you're here…"

She took a deep breath, stepped around the cold breakfast tray, and rapped on the wooden door. "Dr. Richardson! It's DI Parsons from the Constabulary! Might I have a word with you?" She paused, then looked at me uncertainly.

"Might be asleep."

Frowning, Hannah began to knock again, but she stepped back at the sound of footfalls on the other side of the door. To my surprise, it opened a crack, revealing Eleanor's mussed hair and puffy eyes. "Detective?" she mumbled. "What…how…"

The detective gave her a quick but careful examination while Eleanor stuttered out a greeting. "Dr. Richardson?"

"How on earth—"

She pointed to me, then stuffed her notebook into her pocket. "I'm sorry to bother you, ma'am, but there's…well, there's been a fire," she said in a rush. "Your home caught fire overnight. Looks like a total loss…"

Her voice trailed off as Eleanor stepped back and sank onto the side of the unused bed. "My house?" she asked plaintively. "What happened to my house?"

Hannah hesitated on the threshold, then followed Eleanor into the suite and stood by the door. "The early indicators suggest a lightning strike, but I think that's nonsense. Whoever was after your husband probably torched your home."

Eleanor gave no indication that she'd heard Hannah until she looked up and noticed me waiting outside. "Moyna did this."

"That would be my guess," I replied. "Unfortunately, Toula can't find her—she may well be hiding out in the Gray Lands."

Hannah grimaced, then plucked her pencil free and pulled out the notepad again. "I know you've had a difficult few days, Dr. Richardson, but there's bound to be an inquest sooner or later. It's going to look suspicious if you disappear during this investigation. We need a cover story to explain why you weren't home last night, and you'll need to give a statement."

By then, Eleanor was resting her head in her palms. "I don't care. Do what you need to do. Walt's gone, our *home* is gone, and the little demon's playing games with me. Whatever you think best, Detective."

She put away her tools and folded her arms. "What if you died in the fire?"

Eleanor raised her head and frowned. "Come again?"

"Well, obviously, you've been playing a role for some time. What if Eleanor Richardson died? You could go after Dr. Drummond's killer without worrying about blowing your cover."

"I…I suppose, but I don't have another identity ready yet…"

"Just a thought, but aren't you a queen now? Do you still need a secret identity?"

Eleanor's eyes began to well. "I love teaching," she replied, and sniffed.

As the tears fell, Hannah extracted a crumpled packet of tissues from her coat and pressed it into Eleanor's hand. "Go on, take what you need. I've got loads in the car."

She dried her eyes and blew her nose, then worried the damp ball in her hands as she looked up at us. "I don't have anything left in Durham. Just my job. My students. But…" She paused to honk again into a fresh tissue. "I must do the right thing for Walt. Whatever that entails. I owe him justice, and…and now there are certain things *I* can do that a history professor cannot."

I nodded. "You're taking the throne?"

"For Walt's sake." She stood and tugged at her wrinkled sweater. "Perhaps for mine as well." Keeping her eyes on me, she said, "I'm going to destroy Moyna. One way or another, I will have vengeance."

Eleanor passed judgment simply, without emotion, and I bowed my head in acknowledgement. "Understood."

"Will you try to thwart me, Coileán?"

I still saw much of the professor I'd first met in Eleanor's true face, but I found Meggy's shadow hiding in her features. Taunting me. Condemning me.

"I'll help you," I replied.

And Hannah, who formed the third point of our uneasy triangle, whistled softly and rubbed her arm. "Ordinarily, I'd say it's unwise to plot murder in front of a police officer, but this is outside my jurisdiction. So how are we going to stage this?"

I offered to handle the dirty work, but Eleanor insisted on seeing the damage for herself. After dropping Hannah off on a lonely stretch of road outside Edinburgh, Eleanor and I returned to Durham and watched at a safe distance as the fire crew continued to hose down the ruins. Much of the exterior walls remained, but the roof and all the windows and doors were casualties of the blaze. Eleanor clung to her umbrella against the drizzle, shoved her free hand in the pocket of the navy anorak she'd conjured up, and sighed. "Our home. Everything I had left of Walt…"

"I'm sorry," I murmured.

She sniffled again. "I can't even give him a proper burial. If I disappear, they'll never release the body, and…you know…it's not attached to the rest of him."

"We'll get it back," I promised, seeing the tears threaten again. "Look, we've got an in with Hannah. You'll take care of Walt."

Her head bobbed. "You…saw to him?"

"My office. Whenever you want him."

"Thank you." She pulled up her hood, hiding her vibrant hair as the wet skies tried to lighten. "Aren't you and I supposed to be working at cross-purposes? Or am I missing something?"

I shrugged and tilted my umbrella against the shifting wind. "Your father and I never saw eye to eye. No offense, but he was an ass."

"Yes, well, you're preaching to the choir on that count."

"Good. I didn't think you two were close, but—"

"He sired me. I've had nothing to do with him since."

"Sounds familiar. You know, I'm not my mother, you're not Oberon, so there's no reason that we can't avoid some of the, uh…animosity."

Eleanor studied my face with a measure of care. Her eyes narrowed, and then, before I could block it, I felt the light touch of her consciousness on my thoughts, there and gone like a half-heard whisper in my mind. When she retreated, her expression softened to pity, and she laid her hand on my arm to stop me before I could protest the intrusion. "I'm not my sister, either," she murmured. "Whoever she may have been, whatever connection the two of you may have had—"

"I know," I said too quickly.

"As long as we're clear on that point. But you've shown me kindness, Coileán, and I appreciate it." Releasing her hold on me, she switched her grip on the umbrella and stuck her newly-freed hand in her pocket to warm it. "What was her name, again?"

"Meghan," I mumbled, avoiding Eleanor's eyes. "Meggy to me."

"And you…recently lost her?"

Without looking into her thoughts, I couldn't tell whether Eleanor was still trying to pry or being polite. "About two years ago. It's still fresh."

"I understand. Walt isn't the first spouse I've buried.

The grieving can take time."

"Yeah, but I, uh…I lost a year. Recuperating. That's why Aiden was terrorizing your siblings instead of me. It's been two years, but it hasn't *been* two years, you see?"

She nodded, and we watched while the firemen called to each other. The crowd thinned as the sun rose behind the wall of clouds, and Eleanor quietly sighed again. "I think most of them are out of the house," she said, jutting her chin toward the knot of firemen. "Let's see how well I can do this from a distance."

With that, she closed her eyes and breathed slowly. I watched her eyes move beneath their lids and wondered what she was envisioning until she murmured, "How blackened should I go on the bones? Broiled or ash?"

"Recognizably human," I replied, and kept a watch out for curious neighbors as Eleanor worked her grisly enchantment. A few seconds later, she took a long breath. "And it's finished," she said, then pointed to a pair of firemen heading into the house. "We'll find out how well I did soon enough."

It didn't take long for the two to reappear, and if their hurried chat with their supervisor revealed little about what they had seen, the sudden appearance of a white sheet from the truck told us what we needed to know. "Come on," said Eleanor, turning away from the house as the crew covered her false remains. "Help me move a few things from my office before anyone notices I'm dead."

As Eleanor toted the last armful of books into my library, she glanced over her shoulder at the empty bookshelves of her office, then turned away and nodded. I closed the gate, and her shoulders slumped as she dropped her burden on the nearest table beside her good leather briefcase, a stack of framed photographs, and her white laptop computer. "I do hope that's not going to give Detective Parsons a headache," she said, brushing bits of decaying paper off her palms. "Looks suspicious, doesn't it? My house burns, my office is ransacked…"

"Then again," I replied, "you're dead."

"True." Glancing about her, Eleanor took in the scope of the library my mother had begun—or rather, the collection I was arranging into some vague notion of order—and craned her neck to peer at the mismatched chandeliers hanging from the vaulted ceiling. "Is that a Waterford?" she asked, pointing to the delicate crystal array above us.

"Not sure about that one. It looks best at midmorning, when the light's at a good angle."

"Well, let's have a peek, anyway." She took a seat cross-legged in a convenient overstuffed armchair, which rose toward the chandelier and hovered within reach. Eleanor turned over a few of the pieces until she found what she was looking for, then called down, "Genuine!"

"Dusty?" I yelled back.

"Filthy." She waved one hand at the chandelier, and the dirt that had blanketed it blew off in a gray cloud before vanishing. Her chair sank again, and Eleanor slipped out of her seat. "Much better. Your mother had taste. It's a shame to see a piece like that locked up and forgotten."

"Would you like it?" I asked her, then kicked myself. Eleanor was going through emotional hell, she knew my feelings about Meggy…

To my surprise, she grinned. "Really?"

"Housewarming," I suggested, thinking quickly. "For your new—"

I stopped mid-thought, but Eleanor filled the silence. "My new house. Go on, say it. You're not going to make the situation in Durham any worse by acknowledging it."

"I'm sorry, it slipped out—"

She held up her hands to cut off the apology. "I appreciate it. Thank you. And once I have a new place, I'm sure that chandelier will be exquisite." Seeing me flounder, Eleanor shook her head and turned her attention to her office haul. "I can't stop to think too much right now," she explained as she nestled the computer and its accessories into her briefcase. "You saw what happened yesterday. If I stop, I'm lost."

I slipped around the table and caught her wrist before she could close the bag. "You're entitled to mourn, you know."

"And I will, eventually. But as the poet said, I've got miles to go before I sleep. Sitting in your guestroom, having a come-apart, isn't taking me where I need to go." Her stomach suddenly rumbled, and Eleanor blushed. "I should tend to that, shouldn't I?"

"My cook brought you breakfast," I told her, sliding her a chair while a stuffed baguette manifested in Eleanor's hands.

"I know." She sat, bit into the sandwich, and rolled her eyes with pleasure. "Smelled good," she mumbled around bread and ham.

"I'm sure it was. Astrid's brilliant."

"Do you think I could offer her a more competitive benefits package?"

"You're already taking my decoration. Don't push your luck, Eleanor."

With a wicked smirk, she continued her attack on her long-delayed meal.

The afternoon had reached that comfortable sweet spot between the heat of the day and twilight when Eleanor and I stepped to the edge of the bluff and gazed out at the empty sea. She squinted, shading her eyes with her hand as she looked west, then frowned at her wristwatch. "What time…"

"About four," I guessed, considering the cloudless sky. "But you'll probably want to give up the watch—days vary around here."

She replied with a consternated grunt but otherwise

seemed content with her surroundings. "I'd almost forgotten what proper daylight looks like. Winter's a trying season," she said, and tucked her loose hair behind her ear. The wind immediately tugged it loose again, but Eleanor paid it no heed. "This is the place?" she asked, turning in a slow circle to take in the grassy headland.

We'd spent a quiet hour in my office, poring over Aiden and Joey's map book while Eleanor chose a homestead of her own. The location she selected was isolated—framed by the sea on three sides and perhaps fifty miles to the southwest of my palace—but we agreed that it was best for her not to start a turf battle with my court if the situation could be avoided, which meant settling at a distance from the outlying estates.

"Yeah," I said, "this is it. Suitable?"

She completed her rotation, and the breeze turned her hair into a flashing fire behind her. I looked away, but not before the longing hit with an intensity I'd not felt since the first weeks after Meggy's death. *This* wasn't my Meggy—she carried herself with age-forged confidence, and her features held an angularity that Meggy's had lacked—but when I caught her from the corner of my eye, the hopeful part of my mind insisted I was seeing Meggy, alive and whole. But the vision faded all too quickly, and my internal realist pointed out that Eleanor's hair was more auburn and far too straight, her eyes bright green instead of Meggy's pale blue, her breasts fuller, her fingers thinner, her eyebrows slightly unkempt gold smudges. And that periwinkle twinset—Meggy would never have been caught dead in something so sensible. But despite all logic, I couldn't quite erase Meggy from my field of vision.

Eleanor nodded at the waves. "Suitable. Here, join me," she said, beckoning me to her side at the top of the bluff. "I *think* I can do this, but in case I'm wrong, best not to stand in the line of fire." I made my way through the calf-high grass, and when the area was clear, Eleanor closed her eyes and stretched out her palms.

In the span of five seconds, the meadow gave way to a three-story Tudor-esque mansion of limestone and white marble. An avenue of mature oaks rose from the suddenly manicured lawn and traced the paved path that unrolled from Eleanor's feet, while a longer double line of trees stretched in the opposite direction, heading east until they were matchsticks on the horizon, then splitting and growing into a living wall. A lake bubbled forth within Eleanor's garden, complete with a sextet of white swans, and a delicate gazebo rose on its bank. The gazebo's twin sprouted beside us, as seamless as if it had been carved from a single tree. Eleanor patted its railing and nodded to herself as a trio of climbing roses snaked their way up the trellised back. "What do you think?"

"I think you're missing a Bennet sister, but other than that…wow."

She flashed a smug smile and started down the path toward the house. "The inside's empty, but I'll take care of it."

"You've been planning to build for a while?" I asked, trailing after her.

"Not in Durham, naturally, but one does pick up bits and pieces along the way. You know how it goes. And speaking of going"—she turned and stopped me with a hand to my chest—"it's time I was alone."

"Alone? But wouldn't you'd feel better if—"

"Believe me, I know my own mind. I've found work to do, and I'll have a think. This is when you leave me."

"Are you sure?"

Her expression, a mask of polite blankness over stone, told me in definite terms that my presence was no longer required and would not be suffered.

"Okay," I muttered, "I get it." I backed up a few steps and opened a gate in the middle of the path. "If you, uh…if you need something, or if you get lonely—"

"Have a nice evening, Coileán."

A flush raced up my neck. "Yeah. Sure. Um…

goodbye," I said in a rush, then slipped through the gate and shut it before I could make an even bigger fool of myself.

Safe in my office, I put a dot on the map to mark Eleanor's claim, then closed the book and plopped onto the couch. My eyes wandered to my bookshelves and lighted upon Walt's head. Eleanor would come back eventually, I reasoned. She *had* to come back, as long as I was babysitting Walt. The thought reassured me, and I tried to convince myself that I wasn't a monster for anticipating another sight of the grieving widow's face.

CHAPTER 10

Though Aiden had done well in my absence, I had a backlog of correspondence to review. At least the general nature of the court's grievances hadn't changed. My people wasted their energy in petty squabbles: boundary disputes, exclusion from a guest list, a questionable facial expression, or a greeting that, if one listened to every third word, was clearly a vile insult. One complaint triggered reciprocation, a back-and-forth litany of wrongs that could stretch centuries into the past. Still, even if the aggrieved could remember every cross word they'd exchanged in the last five hundred years, their memories varied when it came to recalling how my mother had settled their previous disputes. Without fail, every petitioner was sure she had seen things his way.

Mother, of course, kept no record of her arbitration, and I'd largely shot from the hip, but Aiden had taken careful notes concerning his decisions in case he had to explain himself. When I approached him at breakfast about obtaining a copy of those notes, he brought me back to his screen-filled control room and opened a laptop. "Here you go," he said after a few pokes and clicks. "I put everything in a database. Searchable by party, nature of dispute, resolution, date, and keyword." When I asked if I could have the information in printed format, he hung his head and sighed in the manner peculiar to the put-upon adolescent. "Do you have any idea how many pages that would take? And you'd lose all of the functionality I built into this thing."

"So…no?"

Aiden brows lowered. "This is the twenty-first century. The magic light-up box isn't going to bite you."

"But it's *not* magic. That's the problem with the damn thing."

"*Coileán.*" He turned away and began clearing the debris from the counter. "Almost everything of importance is digitized these days. Even the Arcanum's scanning and logging. Hell," he said, glancing over his shoulder, "how do you think the Fringe works as well as they do? They've got their own software, fantastic encryption, and a team of hackers."

"Your point?"

"My point is that if a bunch of witches and quasi-fae can build a secure worldwide network, then you can figure out how to use a database." He pulled up a swivel chair and plunked the laptop on the counter. "Sit."

Over the next hour, he guided me through the basics: turning the computer on, taking notes, using his database, and accessing the map project. He'd even taken a census in the last year and labeled estates with their inhabitants. "No need to charge the computer," he concluded. "Call me if you get stuck—oh, and don't touch the ports," he said, catching my wrist. "They're steel. No way around it."

I carefully tucked the laptop under my arm and made my exit before my brother could decide that I needed an e-mail address. Back in the safety of my office, I set the computer aside, far from anything flammable. Turning to the stack of letters on my desk—all reassuringly crafted from actual paper and ink—I made slow progress through the morning, taking notes and scribbling responses as necessary. And then, when the mound of broken seals grew too high and the complaints began to run together, I gave in, opened the laptop, and followed Aiden's instructions.

After fifteen minutes of reading his heavily cross-referenced notes, I actually understood what I'd been trying to piece together letter by letter over the last hours. I wrote out decisions that made sense—I even updated the database—and when Val knocked at noon, I had a set of letters ready to be delivered.

He chuckled when he saw the machine sitting on my blotter. "Boy got to you, did he?"

"You knew this was coming?" I asked as he collected the outgoing mail.

"I knew he planned to give it to you, but whether you would *take* it was still a variable." He frowned as he considered the letters in his arms. "More disputes of late."

"Not particularly. I've let these pile up since I woke—"

"This came in the last days," he interrupted, plucking a letter from the discard pile. "As did this one." Putting the delivery stack aside, he riffled through the letters I'd opened and scanned their headings. "These are fresh but for the last two. Aiden kept the backlog small in your absence."

I sighed and rubbed my temples. "A welcome-back present from the court, eh?"

Val's dark eyes were troubled. "Coileán...may I offer you counsel?" I waved toward the chair opposite my desk, and he sat stiffly. "Have you looked at all of Aiden's records?"

"Not yet, I imagine," I said, pulling the laptop into position. "What do I need to see?"

He took the top letter off the discard stack and read the name. "Oliriar. What do the notes say?"

Slowly, I found the proper keys and pulled up the record. "His last recorded issue was five months ago. That's not bad for him."

"What's the final entry?"

"Aside from today? Let's see..." Sounding out Aiden's Latinized phonetic rendering of Fae took a moment's work. "*Boundary fixed, W given.* What's 'W'?"

He rose and joined me behind the screen, puzzling over the notation until the answer clicked. "Slipped into the wrong language. *Warning*."

"What warning?"

After a moment's hesitation, Val said, "Aiden needed to prove himself. When he first began to hear complaints, he did so much as you had done, albeit with better records. But the number rose, and he needed time—he was running about in search of the heir, and the Arcanum kept asking to meet about Moyna. So I advised him to approach this more as your mother had."

I bristled. "What's that supposed to mean? A reign of terror?"

He backed off a few paces. "No. Will you hear me, or should I start shielding first?"

"Go ahead," I muttered, keeping my twitching hands under the desk.

Val retreated to his chair but waited to sit until he was sure I wasn't about to throw fireballs. "Titania ruled through force. They all did."

"Was that supposed to come as news to me?"

He folded his arms and stared until I mumbled something approaching an apology. "Perhaps their tactics weren't perfect or always fair, but they kept the peace. They also kept complaints to a minimum."

"People were too frightened to come to court?"

"No. They understood what they risked by doing so. Titania might settle a quarrel, or she might punish both parties for bothering her. There was no way of knowing." Val spread his hands. "It's amazing how many conflicts could be resolved without involving the queen. Now, I realize you've taken a different approach. You've tried to be reasonable. I admire the attempt, but your system isn't sustainable in the long term."

When I didn't interrupt, Val continued. "Aiden tried to do things as you had done, but it was overwhelming him, and I made a few suggestions. The warning was his idea."

"Dare I ask?"

"When a new complaint arrived, he brought the parties

in, heard the problem, and settled it as usual—and then, he told them that they next time they raised a frivolous issue, he'd throw them into a cell with each other for company until you woke up. The complaints dropped off dramatically."

I frowned. "He didn't have to follow through with it?"

"No need. Everyone knew what he'd done to the prisoners—Aiden proved himself a force to be respected within a few months." He shifted in his chair and crossed his legs. "Now that you're back, the complaints are starting again. I appreciate what you've done, Coileán, and were you ruling over anyone but faeries, your strategy might work. But for your continued sanity, and especially if there's any chance that Eleanor will try to bring her court home…"

There was no need for him to spell out the direction of his thoughts. "I hear what you're saying," I murmured, "but I'm not my mother."

"I never suggested that."

"I'm not ready to be a despot, Val."

Nodding, he rose and collected the letters. "Understood. I'll see that these go out," he said, sounding resigned, and took his leave.

Disconcerted by our conversation, I glanced at the bookcase across the room, where Walt silently judged me. "What do you know?" I muttered at the head, then enchanted myself a sandwich and bent back to my work.

I was wrapping up my lunch when my phone rang, and I glared at the readout. "VIVIAN" was all it said, but that was enough to set me on edge, as the clock showed it was barely two a.m. in Virginia. I liked Vivi—a competent Fringe coordinator-in-training who was also the barely talented baby sister to a dozen half-fae brothers—but calls at that hour seldom portended anything good. Still, as I doubted the kid was drunk-dialing me, I flipped the phone open. "Ms. Stowe?"

"Hey, Chief," came the familiar voice, though I detected the clipped tones of disquietude. "And it's actually 'Mrs. Perryman' these days. Hal and I made it official while you were napping. Anyway, I've got a little problem."

"Figured this wasn't a social call. How did you know—"

"That you were up? Rick filled me in. Feeling better?"

"Until now."

She sniggered. "Okay, here's the sitch. I'm running tech tonight for Colonial Paranormal. You've met."

"Damn it, Vivi," I groaned.

"Come on, they're mostly harmless. They mean well." She lowered her voice. "We're out in Spring Crossing. Our supposed poltergeist growls at us in Fae, and my spider sense tingles like hell. If you've got time, I could use some help."

"You're *asking*?" I said in disbelief. "You didn't just run off the cliff first?"

"Well, it was either call you or Father J, and I figured I'd cut out the middleman."

"Good choice. I'm, uh…I'm proud of you, Vivi."

"I'm totally trainable, and am I hallucinating, or did you just say something nice?"

"I'll deny it if questioned. Did anyone ask his name?"

"Oh, sure. He started with 'Legion,' but he seems stuck on 'Zuul' now. Sound familiar?"

"I've got an idea," I muttered. "Side note, but how much coffee have you had this evening?"

"All of it," she chirped. "So, you want the address?"

"Where are you, again?" I asked, tucking the phone against my shoulder as I dug through Aiden's map stack for the U.S. atlas.

"Spring Crossing. It's about an hour from Richmond. Grocery store, gas station, and the requisite cannon pointing north. The house is two blocks east of the post office…"

I flipped to the Virginia page and hunted down the hamlet. "Don't know the area well enough to pop through."

"I'd send you a photo, but I doubt your dinky little phone even handles them," she said. "How do you feel about summoners?"

"Who entrusted you with a *summoner*?"

"Arcanum made a few for Rick. Emergency use only, you know the drill, whatever. You mind?"

"No, but…"

"But what?"

"Vivi," I said slowly, trying to pierce her caffeine haze, "what are your friends going to say if I materialize?"

"Nothing good, but at this point, I'd rather no one got killed. They're in there now trying to cleanse the house with sage, and you can imagine how well that's going."

"Vividly, but whatever happened to keeping mundanes in the dark?"

She sighed. "Under ordinary circumstances, I'd be all about it, but these guys want to help people, and they can't be dissuaded away from jobs they shouldn't be taking. If giving them a peek behind the curtain keeps them from killing themselves, then I'm willing to pull it back."

"As you like," I said, opening my bottom desk drawer to find my old kit, a black plastic box full of nasty surprises and props. Gear in hand, I walked to the middle of my office, a clear space for the summoning. "Whenever you're ready."

"Gotcha."

The phone clicked off, and I tucked it into my pocket as a glowing circle appeared in the stone floor. Recognizing the unscratchable-itch sensation of a summoning spell, I braced myself and stepped into the light. A few seconds of freezing fire later, I found myself on the front lawn of a well-maintained Victorian home, a few yards away from the paranormal investigators' black, windowless tech van. I gave my limbs an experimental pat, then noticed the scorched grass around my shoes.

"Don't worry, we'll find a way to explain that," said Vivi, who tossed the spent summoning sphere from hand to hand like a metal ping-pong ball. The greenish light from inside the van reflected off the fingerprint smudges on her usual black-framed glasses, but she had forgone the pigtails that night in favor of a single dark braid. A purple windbreaker was her one concession to the chill. "Hiya, Chief," she said with a grin, her breath puffing in the cold. "Okay, there?"

"I seem to be," I replied, creating a jacket for myself. And, um…congratulations?"

Her smile widened, and she held up her left hand to show off the jewelry. "After all that, he still put a ring on it."

"Where is Hal, anyway?" I asked, heading for the house.

She fell in step beside me. "School function, a talent show fundraiser thingy. The coaches have a lip-synch routine to 'Material Girl,' but as much as I'd like to watch my husband strut around in heels, this gig came up."

I quickly suppressed the resulting mental image of poor Hal. "Shall we get this over with, or would you rather break your team in gently?"

"Nah. They're less likely to make a fuss if they're scared. By the way, I've cut the recording feeds off, but if you could avoid frying all of the equipment this time, that would be swell."

"I'll do what I can," I replied, then jogged up the short brick staircase and dropped my toolbox on the porch. Unlatching the lid, I found my reliable leather gloves where I'd left them and slipped them on. Beneath the top tray of odds and ends was the real weapon, an iron bar I kept for only one purpose. I felt the warning tingle even through my gloves, but the leather did its job, and I gripped the bar tightly as I entered the house.

The high-ceilinged foyer was dark, lit only by a camping lantern, and I paused to check the floor for trip hazards. Within seconds, the sounds of shattering glass and shrieking echoed down the hallway, and Vivi muttered, "You want to go first, or should I?"

I called up a ball of blue fire in my free hand, and the shadows danced in time with its flickering—an eerie effect when coupled with the panicked cries. Trying not to creep myself out, I used the fireball as a flashlight and cleared my throat. "If this goes south, don't be a hero."

"Understood," said Vivi, reaching into her jacket's deep pocket. "But I'll try to have your back."

"What do you—"

The faint light showed the contours of a slingshot in her fist. "The first rule of having brothers," she explained, digging in her jacket, "is that you have to learn self-defense. And believe me, there's nothing as effective as a well-aimed steel ball. See?" She flashed half a dozen marble-sized projectiles. "These hurt like hell, or so I've been told."

My eyes widened. "Your parents *bought* you steel ammo?"

She fit one to the sling. "Of course not. I had sticky fingers as a kid. Ready?"

I nodded and followed the sound of breaking china.

A plate whizzed by my ear as we neared the end of the hall, and Vivi yelped as she ducked. My temper rose as I marched into the rear parlor, and the fireball showed the terrified investigators huddled against the walls, backed into the corner against an onslaught of flying knickknacks. Two wore night-vision goggles, but the others crouched and covered their heads, waiting for the attack to subside.

Unsurprisingly, none of them seemed overjoyed to see me.

"*Benatin*, you little beast!" I snarled in Fae, letting the fire flare. "Show yourself!"

The ceramic statue hovering in midair crashed to the

floor, and footsteps ran for the window. With a flick of my wrist, the fireball followed the noise and hit its target, and Benatin popped into view as he screamed, revealing a towheaded boy for only an instant before the glamour dissolved into his true adult form. He wailed and beat at the flames, rolling on the rug in an effort to put out the unquenchable fire.

I watched with grim satisfaction while Benatin writhed and flailed, but then, perhaps half a minute later, Vivi tugged my sleeve. "Hey, Chief? You got him."

Startled from my trance and suddenly cognizant of what I'd done, I let the fire die. Benatin curled up and cried with his burns, and the first rush of guilt swept over me. "Stand down," I told Vivi, putting my bar in my pocket, and flipped the light switch. The frightened kids scrunched their eyes with the sudden illumination, but I ignored them as I approached my sobbing victim to inspect the damage. His hair had burned away, as had most of his clothing, and raw welts oozed across his bare and blackening skin.

I could have killed him, I mused. It would have been simple—I'd caught him off guard, and he hadn't had time to shield. I could still do it...

But then I got a whiff of the smell of burned flesh and froze.

No. That was *Mother*, not me. I wouldn't...

I saw Robin again in my mind's eye, set aflame by our mother, melting and blackening as he tried to put out the fire and begging for death even as he screamed.

Ignoring the breaking wave of self-loathing, I bent to touch the least charred portion of Benatin's arm and started the healing enchantment. His cries subsided as the pain dulled, but he stared up at me in fear. "What have I told you?" I murmured. "How many times, Benatin?"

His chest heaved. "My...my lord, I...wasn't—"

"I saw the whole thing. Never again." I straightened, the better to glower down at him. "But I'm feeling merciful today. We can finish this, or I'll take you to your queen and let her decide what to do. I should warn you that she's not in the best frame of mind right now."

The peanut gallery began to murmur, and I heard Vivi move between us—whether to keep them calm or keep me at bay, I couldn't tell.

Benatin's breathing quickened as he realized his predicament. "I have information for you. Let me live, and I'll tell you what I know."

"About what?"

"Moyna."

He whimpered as I squatted beside him again and grabbed his arm. "What do you know about her?" I growled. "Tell me *everything*, dog."

He nodded frantically. "I hear things. I haven't seen her, my lord, but I hear many things, reports—"

"Stop babbling and tell me what you know."

Benatin paused, took a deep breath, and winced at the stress on his burned skin. "Mab's people have no leader. The ones left aren't going to follow the witch-blood. Some died at the silo last year. Lord Oberon was supposed to bring them back to Faerie, but he failed. Some of them cling to Moyna. The shadow court."

"Why?"

"Best hope. If you're gone, she's queen, and they follow her home."

I lowered my face to his, trying not to show my disgust at his injuries. "Tell me where she is."

"I don't know—"

"What do the rumors say?"

He gasped when I tightened my grip, but he managed not to scream. "I hear two stories, my lord. Two."

"Tell me."

Even with the enchantment at work, his eyes watered. "Some say she's in the Gray Lands. That Nath protects her."

"Why would Nath do that?"

"I don't know, my lord, I don't know anything…"

I waited until his desperate denials wound down. "The other story?"

"A wizard. There's a wizard who helps her. He has friends. A shadow arcanum for the shadow court."

I shook my head. "That makes even less sense. Moon and stars, do you take me for a fool?"

"Please, no, these are things I hear!" he cried, flinching away from me. "I don't know, I haven't seen her, that's all I know!"

By then, Benatin was crying in earnest, and I let my mind scan his thoughts: pain, terror, desperation…but no deceit. However ridiculous his story seemed, he reported it faithfully, and I released him and rose. "Go lick your wounds, and don't mistake my mercy for weakness."

Slowly, cringing like a beaten dog, he pulled himself together and stood. "Thank you, my lord," he sniveled, cradling the arm I'd squeezed. "Never again, I promise, I won't—"

"No, you won't, because I'm going to tell your queen all about you. She's half fae, you know. Rather like me." His eyes widened in alarm, and I felt my lips curl. "Oh, yes. Lady Eleanor's been in this realm a *long* time. When I tell her how you've been amusing yourself"—I pointed to the cowering investigators and the shards of porcelain and glass at their feet—"she'll be cross. Do you understand?"

He nodded miserably, then limped off into the night.

The front door slammed, and I slowly released the breath I'd been holding. "All right, Vivi?" I asked, changing tongues.

"All right," she replied, but she couldn't hide the unease in her voice.

I turned to give the quaking team a proper look and spread my empty hands. "Problem solved. That wasn't a poltergeist. You can go home and get some sleep."

Their leader, identifiable by the way the others kept shooting him panicked glances, took a slow step forward and nervously adjusted his baseball cap. His goggles shifted against his T-shirt as he sidled toward me, and he looked like he was on the verge of needing new trousers. "I remember you," he said, his voice cracking. "You busted our cameras."

I shrugged. "Gave you fair warning, didn't I?"

"Man, those were expensive!"

"Too bad. Magic and electronics don't always play nicely."

One of the girls—I recognized her as the team's psychic by her coke-bottle glasses and flowing skirt—stepped forward. "*Black* magick? I'll have you know I'm a witch—"

I groaned and cut my eyes to Vivi. "Seriously?"

"Hey," Vivi said, raising her hands, "I just do the tech work."

"Granted, but you're the one with the spider sense." I pointed to the ersatz psychic. "Is she or isn't she?"

Vivi grimaced. "Not in the slightest. I'm sorry, Angie," she told the girl, "you don't actually have any magical talent. It's nothing you're doing wrong—"

She crossed her arms and glared at Vivi. "What would *you* know about magick? You…you're the *camera girl*. What the hell do you know of the spirits or the energies or—"

"My parents are fae," Vivi murmured, and Angie, startled, fell silent. "My brothers are fae. Technically, I suppose I'm fae, but I didn't get the power. I didn't get the immortality and the eternal youth and all that jazz. So I got good with computers," she continued, addressing the rest of the team. "And I keep an eye on people like you to make sure you don't do anything stupid. Don't put *my* guys in danger. Last time you saw him," she said, jabbing her finger at me, "it was because that guy he just crisped up was messing with us. I thought I could fix the problem on my own." She shrugged. "I've been schooled since then. And when our 'poltergeist' tonight started making lewd jokes in Fae—that wasn't Aramaic," she told Angie—"I knew we needed backup. So I asked Lord Coileán for assistance."

Their leader's brow furrowed. "Lord…"

"'Colin' also works," I told him. "Hi."

Vivi folded her arms. "He's one of the most powerful magically gifted people alive. So you would all do very well to go home and not talk about what you saw. Don't forget it, now," she continued, looking them all in the eye. "But don't talk about it. No one would believe you, but more importantly, *he* might be annoyed if you run your mouths." The kids nodded—a few seemed on the brink of tears— and Vivi pointed to the door. "Pack up. Investigation's over. We'll tell the clients that the house blessing worked and leave it at that."

One by one, they scurried for safety until only Angie was left with us. "I *am* a witch," she insisted, balling her fists as she glared at Vivi. "You can't walk in here and tell me I'm not."

"She's not trying to be cruel," I interrupted, and Angie twitched like she'd been goosed. "Wizards are born, not made. You either have the talent or you don't, and no amount of mystic candles and charm bracelets will change that. Trust me," I said, shoving my hand in my pocket. "I've known a lot of wizards, kid."

"I'm not a kid," she retorted with a withering sneer. "I'm twenty-eight, and I've been a witch for ten years now. Trained, recognized, and certified by the Mid-Atlantic Circle. I have a webcast with—"

"That's cute. As long as you want a pissing contest, I'm eight hundred and change. Been fae all that time. Actually know a few things about magic," I continued, and called up a fireball in my free hand. "Now, do you want to have this fight, right here, right now? Think about it. *Kid.*"

Angie's mouth flapped open and closed, and then, with a dramatic sniff, she swept out of the room…and ran for the exit.

When the front door slammed behind her, Vivi sighed

and shook her head. "I'll deal with the cleanup. Thanks."

I doused the fire and flipped on the rest of the lights in the house with a little surge of will, the better to survey the damage, and patted her shoulder. "Go get your sage. I'll put the breakables back together and patch the paint."

"You don't have to—"

"Go on."

She turned to go but looked back at me before she left the room. "Um…quick question."

"Shoot," I replied, leaning against the wall.

Vivi gave me a hard stare. "If I hadn't said something, would you have killed Benatin?"

I sought the truth in my thoughts, then nodded. "Probably."

"Why didn't you?"

"Concentration broke. And I remembered who I'm supposed to be." I considered the blackened rug, then swallowed hard, tasting bile. "Hurry it up with the sage. This place smells too much like a barbeque."

Vivi slipped out, and I knelt behind the sofa by the broken statues and plates, letting myself shake once I was alone.

When we finished, the house stank of burned herbs and flambéed faerie, a combination disturbingly close to Thanksgiving dinner. I saw Vivi off—the team had left their tech van and half their equipment in their rush to escape—then took myself home to think and drink heavily. But when I returned to my office, I found a note waiting for me on the coffee table, a folded piece of cream-colored stationery marked with a short message in a flowing hand:

> *My apologies for coming uninvited, but I was told you were away. I reclaimed my belongings from the library. Thank you again for the chandelier.*

Your captain told me where to find Walt. I am better prepared now to face the inevitable, and so I've taken him with me. You have my gratitude.

The prisoner you were holding for me is no longer a concern.

I would be most appreciative if you would respect my privacy at this time.

E

I read the note twice, then searched the bookcase, but the head had disappeared. Eleanor had come and gone—and killed Moyna's messenger—and I'd missed her. And plainly, she wanted nothing to do with me.

I conjured up a generous double of scotch and sat in front of the cold fireplace in the waning afternoon glow. After the day's events, the thought of setting something else ablaze was nearly enough to turn my stomach.

The room felt emptier without Walt's silent presence. But this was how it was supposed to be, wasn't it? I couldn't even be trusted around the people I loved, never mind those who drove me into a rage. Solitude was safest. If I remained alone, I wouldn't do anything like…

Robin's face rose again behind my closed eyes, burning, twisting in agony.

Meggy was in my arms, bleeding out from the wounds I'd given her.

Eunice smiled at me, then crumpled to the ground and shuddered her last.

And other faces flashed as well, the ones I'd pushed to the back of my mind. Faces of those I'd killed in anger, in fear, in self-defense. Faces of those I'd killed in mercy, bewildered old faces half-blind with the sudden degeneration of once-deferred years paid in full. Áedán gurgling as I pulled the dagger from his throat. Áed collapsing at Mother's feet before he had time to register the fatal blow. Mab, defiant to the last as I moved in to destroy her.

And Moyna, the lost child weeping on my kitchen floor, desperate to find her way home. Joyful as she'd run back to Titania. Horrified as Toula's stroke hit home. Enraged as Geheret fell. Smugly satisfied as I cradled Meggy in her dying moments.

The child who craved nothing more than revenge.

The child I'd promised Eleanor to help kill.

My child.

I slammed my glass into the fireplace and buried my head in my hands.

CHAPTER 11

If my aides thought of checking on me around the dinner hour, they gave no sign. Then again, I'd removed my office door, a strong hint that I was in no mood for company. I turned my phone off, sprawled across a couch, and stared at the ceiling until the light purpled and faded. Eventually, I dozed for a time, then woke with a crick in my neck, lit a candle, and checked the wall clock. Five past ten in Virginia—and judging by the stars outside my window, I surmised it was midmorning there.

Surely Paul worked on Fridays.

I called an unwrinkled shirt into being and opened a gate into the parking lot behind Sacred Heart's parish office. Shivering with the sudden cold, I hurried past the cars and shouldered open the heavy door to the church's business annex.

The receptionist looked up from her crossword at the sound, then leapt from her chair with far more grace than any woman of her years and spherical build should have managed. Her sweater, across which pink flamingoes in Santa hats paraded, shifted to reveal a flash of the coordinating turtleneck tucked into her denim skirt. "You," she managed, extending a shaking finger toward me, "*you*...you stay back, you hear?"

"Good morning, Doris," I muttered as I slunk past her desk. "Is he in?"

"I'm warning you..."

I glanced at her in time to see that she'd armed herself with a box of paperclips. Her fist exploded with an overhand volley of metal, and I threw up a shield before she could finish her war cry. "*Really?*" I sighed as the paperclips tinkled against the floor. "At least try the stapler first. And what's in your other—" The generous splash of holy water she threw at my face ran down the shield and dripped onto the stone. "Feel better?" I said. "Look, it's been a long day. Cease fire?"

"What the—oh, for heaven's sake, Doris," snapped a familiar voice, and I turned to find Paul scowling at the receptionist. It's difficult to look intimidating in full vestments, but he was giving it his best shot. "He's with me. Honestly," he muttered, and beckoned me down the hallway toward his office. "Sorry about that, Colin. Come in."

I slid past the steel knob as the priest held the door open. "Thanks. You're looking festive."

He glanced down at his robes, several embroidered layers of cotton and polyester that stank of mothballs. "The bishop's coming on Sunday, and they're letting me dress out for the occasion. Thought I'd air the good duds ahead of time." His deep wrinkles creased when he grinned, but the twinkle in his eyes took a few years off his face. "And we've got an ecumenical Evensong, to boot— us, the Methodists, and the J.V. Squad."

I didn't have to ask for clarification. Sacred Heart had a longstanding rivalry with the Methodist church across town, thanks to the youth basketball league, and Paul's mild disdain for St. Luke's, the little Episcopal church two blocks over, was nothing new. "They're making you go, are they?"

"It was strongly encouraged." He opened his closet and began stripping off his outerwear. "I was wondering when you'd stop by."

"Slim told you?"

"Sure did. And Vivi called early this morning, so I assumed you'd be in today." He shrugged at my surprise. "You burn a man half to death, who else are you going to visit? Have a seat." I settled into one of Paul's old armchairs and watched as he removed his vestments. "Now, did you wake up feeling homicidal, or is there something we need to discuss?" he asked.

I massaged my head. "You're not even going to ask if Benatin's okay?"

"Speaking as a priest, I hope he makes a speedy recovery. Speaking as myself, the little bugger probably had it coming. What's troubling you?"

Paul's eyes were kind, concerned if not overly worried. Then again, he'd spent much of his career listening to my litany of sins. I'd come to him more times than I liked to admit with blood on my hands.

"Short version?" I mumbled. "I'm infatuated with Meggy's sister, Moyna ordered the hit on her husband, and I told her I'd help her kill Moyna."

"Sounds like another day in paradise."

"I can't *look* at her without thinking of Meggy, Paul. It's driving me nuts."

He closed the wardrobe and settled into the other armchair. "Is she interested?"

"Seeing as her husband's been dead less than a week and she took his head out of my office earlier today, I would think not."

"Jesus, what were you doing with the *head*?"

"Keeping it safe for her. Long story."

Paul crossed his legs and rested his chin on his fist. "Uh-huh. And does the lady have a name?"

"Eleanor."

"Does she at least have a three-digit age?" He seemed unfazed by my glare. "I've seen your track record, it's a fair question."

"Yes," I grumbled.

"And she must resemble Meggy, or else you wouldn't be such a mess. Do you want my advice?"

"I'm here, aren't I?"

"Yes," he replied with a little smirk, "and once more,

you've come to the one avowedly celibate man in your life with girl trouble. Take this for what it's worth." He waited until I met his eyes. "She's grieving. Don't be an ass, Leffee."

"Right," I sighed.

"Does she know about you and Meggy?" I nodded, and Paul shrugged again. "Then this is doubly sticky. Back off and try to get acquainted. If she's interested someday, I'm sure you'll know. But she's been widowed, and you had a child with her sister. Those aren't optimal conditions." He watched me try to formulate a response. "How'd you two meet, anyway?"

"She's Oberon's heir."

Paul closed his eyes and groaned. "*Abort.*" I began to protest, but he continued over me. "No excuses. She's the nearest thing you've got to a colleague. You do *not* need to be mixing your libido up in this."

"But—"

"The last time a king and queen got together, they made the Puck, yeah?"

"That was different—"

"Different how? Those two weren't even talking by the end, were they? How'd that work out for the larger magical community? Come on, you're old enough to know when you shouldn't act on a crush." He held up his bony hands. "Then again, I'm just the priest. That's my advice. Do with it what you will."

After a moment of grudging contemplation, I replied, "You know you're more than just the priest."

"Then listen to your friend. I've known you too long, Colin. I watched that debacle with Meggy unfold and did nothing to stop it. Let me be your better angel this time around."

I looked back at Paul—the ever-thicker glasses, the ever-thinning gray hair, the paunch that had steadily grown since he hit forty-five—and realized with a pang that I'd slept through his seventieth birthday. My friend. For many years, my only friend. And now he was seventy and arthritic, and probably had questionable cholesterol.

Divining my train of thought, Paul reached for my hand. "I'm still hanging in there," he said with a faint smile. "Let me help you."

My throat had tightened, and I coughed to clear it. "Paul...my offer stands. If you ever want to retire..."

He nodded and released me. "My place is here, but thank you anyway." With that, he rose, crossed to the sideboard, and held up two mismatched ceramic mugs. "There might still be some coffee down the hall, but it's generally cold by this time of the morning."

I took the hint, and the mugs filled. Grinning, Paul carried them back and handed me one as he took his seat. "Now, tell me about Moyna. What's the situation?"

I collected my thoughts while I finished my coffee—which, unlike Paul's, had a generous splash of Irish thrown in. "I don't know what to do," I finally admitted. "She may be in the Gray Lands, or she may be lurking somewhere in this realm, but she's thwarting the blood trace Toula put on her."

"In other words, you have no idea where she is."

"Bingo. As I said, she had Eleanor's husband killed, and she's been making nice with the remains of Mab's court and an offshoot of the Dark Company. I'm meeting with the Company's leader next week to discuss it."

Paul frowned. "The werewolves?"

"How did you—"

"The Fringe gave me credentials. I check up on the feeds, and there's been chatter."

"Lovely. So Eleanor wants Moyna dead, and I...told her I'd help. Sounds bad, doesn't it?"

"Abhorrent," he agreed. "Well, abhorrent under ordinary circumstances. Here, now..."

I watched him drink in silence. "Am I to understand," I ventured once his mug was drained, "that you're not entirely opposed to this plan?"

He eyed me, then carried our mugs back to the sideboard. "I like to think I'm a man of God," he finally replied, though he addressed the box of sugar packets. "Murder is a sin. But there are situations in which homicide is justifiable. Maybe not *right*, certainly not good, but justifiable. Do you understand?"

"I think so."

Paul turned to me and spread his hands. "If she's not a psychopath, she's flirting with the idea. Don't take this the wrong way, but I think she got the worst bits of both of you, and Titania didn't do anything to smooth her out." He sighed as he returned to his chair. "You control psychopaths through might. Now, I think we both realize that Moyna is never going to give in. We can debate the ethics of how you treated her, but that's water under the bridge. So the way I see it, you have three choices." He held up one finger. "You can let her continue to harry you until she tires of it, but God knows how much damage she'll do in the meantime. People died in Montana last time."

"And in Faerie. I was told."

"All right." He held up another finger. "Or you can catch her and contain her. Not ideal, but it'd keep her from hurting anyone."

I hesitated. "Or."

The third finger rose. "Or." He put his hand down and shook his head. "I can't make that call for you, Colin. I'm sorry."

"I wouldn't ask it of you."

A rapid knock interrupted our conversation, and Paul frowned as he stood. "Yes?" he called. "Come in!"

The door cracked open, and a portly young man in a black shirt and clerical collar stuck his head into the room. "You wanted to see me, Father?"

"Ah—Isaac. Yes. Good morning. Sorry, absent-minded," he mumbled, and headed for his wardrobe. "I was going to ask if you had the proper attire for Sunday's big shebang. If not, something in here should fit you—"

"Thank you, but Father Richard took care of that. Was there anything else?"

Paul presented the young priest with a polite smile. "No, nothing."

"Thanks, then," Isaac replied, and saw himself out.

I waited until his footsteps faded, then cocked an eyebrow at Paul. "My successor," he murmured. "Hand-picked by the bishop. I've had nothing to do with his training."

"No?"

"I had one strike already with Mr. Bolin," he said, regarding me over the back of his armchair, "and once the bishop met you…"

"They know who I am! I've probably got a file in the Vatican's secret archives."

"And I'm sure it's a thick one. Knowing you exist is one thing, but seeing magic happen can take some getting used to. Nick never did. So he found himself a promising boy fresh out of seminary, and he's been training him as the replacement exorcist."

"What does the damn bishop know about exorcism?" I scoffed. "Do they make a Cliff's Notes version these days?"

"He's the bishop. His call. And right now, the call is pretending you don't exist."

I smirked as I stood. "No one let Doris in on that."

"Doris is a force of nature," he replied, "and I don't think that even the Holy Father would be able to sway her. You may have noticed that she doesn't like you."

I considered this, then pointed to an empty space in the office. "Might it be a good idea if I didn't run the paperclip gauntlet again, then?"

"It might." He stood aside and waited while I ripped open a gate, then squeezed my shoulder. "Hang in there. You know where to find me."

"Likewise," I said, and paused with one foot in the

other realm. "And Merry Christmas, Paul."

He smiled. "Nollaig shona dhuit."

There are few things sadder than a casino on Christmas morning. Commercials soliciting donations for doe-eyed orphans and abused puppies, perhaps, but it's a close call.

Jeanine had chosen a nicer casino for our meeting place, a relatively new complex of smudge-free glass and spotless chrome. I heard the telltale chirps and clangs of a room full of slot machines the instant I passed through the sliding doors into the air-conditioned lobby. The light was disorienting—not the hypnotically flashing lights around me, but daylight itself—and I kept my sunglasses in place as I moved through the glass-ceilinged concourse. Faerie was completely off-sync with Las Vegas at the time, and though locally it was five minutes before ten, my head insisted it was closing on midnight. I'd strapped on a homemade watch out of caution, anticipating the general lack of clocks inside the casino. What use is a clock, after all, when your business model hinges on time standing still?

The artificial Christmas trees were fooling no one. Scattered along the main corridors at regular intervals, decorated with colored balls and too much tinsel, they squatted like silent reminders of how wrong the whole scene was. But this was Jeanine's show, so I bit my tongue and followed the signs past the saltwater aquarium and the smoky blackjack tables to the buffet. Twenty-five dollars later, having acquired a plate of questionable crab legs, I wound through the sea of red and green tablecloths toward the rear of the dining room, where I spotted Jeanine waiting at a quiet four-top in the corner. Beside her sat Poppy, sawing through a double portion of prime rib like she hadn't seen meat in a month. The younger shifter might have been engrossed with her meal, but Jeanine ate mechanically, keeping her eyes in a constant sweep of the room. It didn't take a genius to understand why she'd chosen the seat that put her back to the wall.

I was still four tables away when she noticed my approach, and she gestured to the empty chairs in invitation. Foregoing the pleasantries, I pulled up a seat, removed my shades, and regarded her carefully. I'd seen her before—the magical community is small, after all—but not in some time. Her thick salt-and-pepper hair fell in a bob to her rounded chin, while her wide-set hazel eyes examined me in turn. She'd painted her lips a glossy peach, but all of her cosmetics couldn't hide the progression of age. Jeanine had to be approaching sixty, and while she had never been a knock-out, the years and the stress of her job were wearing her down.

"Ms. Nadel," I said, breaking a crab leg in two. "You wanted to see me?"

Her mouth moved into a shadow of a smile. "I trust you won't be offended if my associate joins us, Mr. Leffee. You've made Ms. Kane's acquaintance, yes?"

Poppy looked up from her plate, swallowed a mouthful of overdone meat, and flicked her head in acknowledgement.

"No offense taken," I said, and Poppy resumed her attack on the steak. "You have information for me?"

Jeanine's thin brow arched. "The Company has information. Whether I share it with you has yet to be determined."

"Fair enough." I continued to rip my platter of legs apart. "Then I'll go first. You're losing control of your organization. The young kids—the *strong* kids—aren't listening to you because you're past your prime, and rats aren't impressive. Moyna's recruiting, and your werewolf imbeciles are too stupid to realize that nothing's more dangerous than a desperate faerie. They'll follow her because she makes promises beyond their wildest dreams." I glanced up to find her staring at me and pressed on. "You haven't slept easily in weeks because you're too worried that they're going to come for you one night. It won't be subtle—the weres don't have any respect for finesse. You'll be sitting there in your bed, looking out at those eyes. Nowhere to run, nowhere to hide—"

"I get the picture."

"So you drag me into this, because you sure as hell can't take down Moyna on your own. Not with your muscle going feral." I popped a piece of crab into my mouth and smiled. "Our interests may have aligned, and if that's the case, I might be willing to assist you. Now, what do you know?"

If I'd unnerved Jeanine, I couldn't tell. The woman had the composure of an Arctic lake at midwinter. "She's hiding in this realm," she replied. "We laid eyes on her in the last week. She doesn't stay in one place for long, but she's definitely here. Not in Faerie, not in the Gray Lands."

"How do you know? And where did you see her?"

"*Where* is information I hold on a strict need-to-know basis, and you don't have that clearance yet. As for how we know she's not traipsing back and forth, we've dealt with the Arcanum's crafters over the years," she said, spearing a bite of salad. "There are ways of detecting elevated concentrations of dark magic. Got a tracker close to her with the right tools, and voila. We haven't seen anything residual on her or her people."

"All that means is that you haven't caught her going across. Nath could be—"

"Nath wants nothing to do with her. You're going to have to trust me on that—I don't divulge sources."

I knew better than to press the issue. If there were denizens of the Gray Lands roaming the mortal realm, the Dark Company might know of them, but getting that information out of Jeanine would be impossible. Shifters made excellent spies for several reasons, among them the quirk in their makeup that prevented unwanted mental intrusions. With enough enchantment, I could look into almost anyone's thoughts, but the only way into a shifter's head without his consent was to smash his skull open, and a fat lot of good *that* did you if you wanted more than gray matter.

"All right," I said, pointing a leg at Jeanine. "Let's assume you're correct. How is she hiding from a blood trace?"

She smirked as she chewed. "Spellcraft can block spellcraft. Girl's made a friend."

"Could you be less vague?"

Jeanine scanned the room again, then leaned toward me and lowered her voice to a murmur. "She's got a wizard in her back pocket. He's male, but that's all we've been able to find on him."

"Have you seen him?" I replied, moving close enough to Jeanine that I could feel her breath on my face.

"Not personally. Some of our number may have, but for reasons of which you seem to be aware, they're not discussing the matter with me. This is the best I can give you." She pulled a phone from her purse and began scrolling through her pictures. "Look here. We know he's male from the chatter—the weres have been dropping pronouns, at least. But you see the problem, right?"

The image was dark and grainy, but I could spot my daughter's face in the crowd. She was growing to look more like her grandmother, a blonde beauty with high cheeks, a delicate chin, and a slight upward turn to her nose. It could have been glamour, I reminded myself, but something told me that Moyna wasn't playing dress-up with Titania's face. Standing beside her was a silhouette in a hooded black robe, a garment akin to a cheap Grim Reaper costume. The figure's hands were gloved in black, and he wore a black mask—a balaclava, perhaps—beneath his hood, obscuring his features. Knowing Moyna's height, I estimated that he was maybe an inch or two south of six feet tall, but that did little to narrow the candidates. Hell, even Greg was five-ten.

"That one," said Jeanine, holding her finger above the screen. "That's the rogue wizard. See the identification problem? He takes precautions."

"What about his voice?"

"Never the same twice. Our first thought was that there were multiple guys under the hood, but we ran the recordings through a computer and compared them. His speech patterns are constant—he modulates the pitch. He's not stupid, whoever he is."

"And the others in the picture?"

"My problem children." She returned the phone to her purse, then resumed eating her salad. "This is the situation as I see it," she said between bites. "Your daughter is rebuilding, and she has an unknown number of faeries on her side. A small but significant group of shifters finds her rhetoric appealing. And she has at least one wizard on the payroll—someone with enough skill to hide her from a blood trace. We're not dealing with a novice, obviously. That said, what are you prepared to do about this?"

"I'm hamstrung until I locate her. How about letting me know where you saw her?"

Jeanine offered a slight shrug. "That picture was taken near Leavenworth in Washington, but the camp's been deserted for two weeks. They've moved on. I have theories, but we haven't been able to get anyone close of late. The shifters working with her frequently go wolf, and you can imagine what their noses are like."

"But you do have theories," I pressed.

"A few. Yet to be investigated."

"Understood. Investigate, then, do whatever you need to do. Find Moyna, keep her in one place long enough for me to get there, and…I'll deal with it."

Her head tilted. "Oh?"

"Yes."

"Suppose I could put a mole among the weres instead of trying to hide a spy…someone who could infiltrate, gain their trust, and report?"

We both looked at Poppy, who continued to eat as if she hadn't heard us.

"Is she willing?" I asked Jeanine.

"She is. It won't be easy, and this could take time, but it's our best shot of getting you to Moyna. That would solve both of our problems, I imagine."

"Understood." With a glance at the wreckage of my crab legs, I pushed back from the table and rose. "How's the prime rib, Ms. Kane? The seafood is disappointing."

Poppy shrugged and stood. "Not bad. I'll hit the buffet again with you. Jeanine, refill?"

Jeanine shook her head, and the two of us marched through the long dining room single-file, passing tables of disoriented gamblers whose stomachs had finally won out. When we slipped behind a partition and reached the back of the serving line, I stood close to Poppy and muttered, "You sure about this?"

She hesitated. "I'm sure something needs to be done. There aren't many candidates who can do it." Catching my frown, she said, "Way too many of us—the ones like me," she said, keeping it vague in light of the diners around us, "have gone wild. The ones who haven't are mostly the older ones. I'm young, I'm strong…no sense in pushing this off onto someone less qualified."

"Just checking."

She snorted. "Appreciate the concern."

We picked up plates, and I held two folded cloth napkins together as a makeshift potholder. "Metal tongs," I explained when Poppy gave me a questioning look. "Just pretend I'm germaphobic and move on."

"If you were germaphobic, you wouldn't be eating at a buffet."

"This story doesn't have to withstand much scrutiny, so don't be difficult. It's late, this whole place smells like cigarettes—"

That was as far as I got before the dining room let out a collective scream.

Dropping our plates, Poppy and I pushed out of the buffet aisle and ran into the dining room in time to see four oversized wolves make a running beeline for the back corner. I saw Jeanine's face for only an instant before she vanished. Her clothes fell into her chair, and I knew she'd shifted, the better to hide. But two seconds later, as the shrieking patrons fled, the pack leapt upon her table. The lead wolf, a brown-pelted beast of nightmarish proportions, snaked and dove around the furniture, then threw his head back like he was trying to swallow a pill. As it went down, I saw that the string-like object dangling from his teeth was a twitching rat tail.

"*Jeanine!*" Poppy cried.

Her scream morphed into a keening howl, a sound that could never come from a human throat, and I acted on instinct. In the blink of an eye, Poppy was gone, and I threw myself onto the back of the massive gray wolf that stood in the middle of her shredded clothing. "Oh, no, you don't," I said through clenched teeth, holding on as she tried to buck me, then opened a gate in the floor beneath us. Poppy and I tumbled between the realms into my office, and by the time she rose and shook herself off, I'd sealed the rift and put distance between us.

Seeing a room around her that was definitely not the restaurant, Poppy growled and bared her fangs, and I wondered if I'd backed up far enough.

"You can't help her." I held up my hands to stop her before she leapt for my throat. "We both saw what happened. I'm not going to let you kill yourself. If they didn't get you, security will be there any minute, and they'll be armed."

She growled for a moment longer, fixing me with her golden eyes, but as I held my breath, the wolf melted away, and the girl reappeared—naked, crouching on my rug, and trembling. She howled again as the last of the wolf vanished, and her cry dissolved into wracking sobs. Poppy hugged her knees, lowered her head, and wept.

And that was how Eleanor found us two minutes later when she knocked and let herself in.

"I can explain," I hastily told her as she wheeled on me. "Her boss was just eaten."

Eleanor's jaw dropped. "But why the hell is she *naked?*"

I pointed to the rags around us, the bits of Poppy's ruined clothing that had fallen through the gate. "Shifter."

"Oh, for heaven's sake," she snapped, marching across the room, "*move.*" Shoving me out of the way, she produced a fleece blanket and wrapped it around Poppy's shaking shoulders. "It's all right, dear," she murmured. "I know it hurts. Deep breath, now." Poppy managed a shuddering gasp, then uncurled as Eleanor pulled her into her embrace. "Let it out," she soothed, stroking Poppy's dark hair. "That's my girl. Try to breathe." When the worst of Poppy's fit had past, Eleanor helped her to her feet, and a fluffy bathrobe materialized around her. Eleanor led her over to the couches, then gave me a reproving look. "Tea, if you please."

Chastised, I created the necessary cups and brew, and Eleanor continued her monologue of comfort as she fixed a cup for Poppy. By the time the girl calmed enough to drink, Eleanor had pulled the necessary details from me. "So which do we tackle first," she asked, "the Dark Company or the Arcanum?"

My eyebrows rose. "*Tackle?*"

"It sounds like Moyna's receiving help from both. So which would you rather investigate first, the pack of werewolves or this rogue wizard or wizards?"

"I'll talk with the grand magus in the morning—"

"No, you'll talk with him *now.* Or I will."

"Eleanor," I muttered, rubbing my head as if I could wipe out the memory of the rat tail's last spasms, "it's Christmas Day, and it's not even noon in Montana. He's not going to appreciate the interruption."

"Jeanine Nadel is dead. His dinner can wait." She waved a gate open, and I peeked at the wood-paneled, painting-lined corridor on the other side. "Go. I'm taking her home and putting her to bed," she said, keeping a protective arm around Poppy.

The shifter glanced up in confusion. "No, I need to get back, I've got to—"

"You're not going anywhere over there until it's safer than suicidal," Eleanor interrupted. "Let us handle this for now." She looked back at me, her mouth a tight line. "Talk to the grand magus. And if you're feeling so inclined, Coileán, you can tell him that I'm calling my court tomorrow."

I nodded. "You mean—"

"I mean to prepare myself. Sooner or later, I'm going to war."

CHAPTER 12

What was I doing, I asked myself as I stomped up the silo's gravel driveway. Twenty minutes ago, I'd had the situation well in hand. I had a plan, a potential ally...I was in *control*. And now, my ally was dead, my plan was kaput, and Eleanor had yanked the reins out of my hands. She was back in Faerie, tending to my shell-shocked shifter, and I was marching through the cold on her order. Who did she think she was, locking herself away for days, then dropping in, uninvited and unannounced, and presuming to boss me around? In *my* office, no less?

I didn't need to wonder how she'd gotten in. The realm liked Eleanor at least as much as it liked me, and I doubted that she'd had any difficulty making a gate straight into my palace. Even if she had sauntered in the front door, my two best guards were occupied. While Joey took Helen home to Virginia to spend Christmas with his parents, Toula had organized her own celebration, and she, Val, Aiden, and Mina had slipped off to Aiden's suite to watch an all-day movie marathon and eat Chinese takeout. I'd been stumped as to Mina's presence in the planned foursome until Val took me aside and explained that while I'd been asleep, Toula had briefly tried out one of my other guards, Cyrus, before turning her attention to my niece. The two of them had been quietly spending time together for months, and they seemed to be having fun.

At least someone was having a merry Christmas. As for me, I was about to ruin Greg's.

Since the Arcanum had a mole in its midst, I decided to

exercise caution. After a quick search of the trailer park, I located the un-bugged tool shed and walked around the building until I found shelter from the wind. I enchanted an overcoat into existence as I slogged through the snow drifts, but gloves would have to wait until I made the call.

To my surprise, it only took three rings to reach Greg. "Hey, there," he said, sounding far cheerier and warmer than I felt. "What's new?"

"I'm topside," I replied, keeping my voice low. "How quickly can you come up?"

Silence stretched on the line, and then I heard the telltale sound of a latching door. "Emergency?" he muttered.

"Yeah. Sorry to drag you out, but—"

"I'm on my way. Stay put, I'll find you. And is this going to take long? The kids got in an hour ago, and the great-grands are unwrapping their gifts…"

"Not long, but I assumed you'd rather I not walk in on the festivities down below."

"Appreciated." The phone clicked off.

I pulled up my collar, created a thick pair of gloves for my numb fingers, and leaned against the trailer. Briefly, I considered taking more drastic measures against the cold, but considering the Arcanum's vast network of protective spellcraft, I decided against it. I didn't like to think of what Toula would do if I ruined her work in progress.

Five minutes later, a gate opened in the middle of the trailer park. Out limped Greg, swamped in a larger man's trench coat and leaning on his cane, with his wife following a step behind. Missy had opted for bedroom slippers in lieu of appropriate footwear, and her quick slip on an icy patch in the driveway did nothing to improve her mood. Spotting me, she led the way through the hard-packed drifts toward my trailer, scowling like I'd loaded her car with kittens and driven it into a burning house.

"Make it quick," she snapped as Greg puffed along in her wake. "The babies are finishing Christmas, and I do *not* want to miss—"

"I didn't call you," I interrupted before her rant could fully flower. "Go on, we won't be long."

"Like hell." She crossed her arms and glared up at me through her thick glasses, her single concession to her years. She had hidden her wrinkles behind makeup and rouged her lips, and if I wasn't mistaken, she was sporting false eyelashes for the holiday. Though she had forgone the wigs and heavy extensions of late, her short hair was now raven-black, a color it hadn't naturally been since the eighties. "Well?" she said. "Spit it out, we're waiting."

Greg planted his cane on a patch of cleared ground and nodded. "What's the trouble?"

After sparing a reciprocal glare for Missy, I turned my attention to him. "Jeanine Nadel is dead. Murdered less than an hour ago. I thought you'd want to know before the rumors begin."

He gaped, and even Missy had the grace to look less than annoyed. "Dear God," he said, "what happened?"

"We were meeting. She didn't realize she'd been followed, and by the time she figured it out, a pack of werewolves was on her."

Greg turned aside and covered his mouth, and Missy gripped his shoulder as he shook his head. "Broad daylight?" he finally managed.

I nodded. "And in public. She shifted, but she wasn't fast enough to hide."

"You mean—"

"Yeah. Wolf versus rat. Wasn't much of a contest."

I created a bench behind Greg before his knees could buckle, and he sat without speaking. Missy, however, was another matter. "You didn't try to help her?" she demanded. "You let her get *eaten*? And what, pray tell, were *you* doing with a shifter?"

Even Missy's dark skin and pancake makeup couldn't hide her angry flush, and I resisted the impulse to shield. "Anything's possible if the price is right or the shit's deep enough. Jeanine was worried about the weres."

"*Shifters.* The term—"

"I'm well aware of the terminology, and if you knew anything about the Company's situation at the moment, you'd understand me. Isn't that right, Greg?" I asked, leaning around Missy to the slumped grand magus.

He nodded and stared at the dirty snow. "I've heard rumblings about trouble with some of the lupine shifters. Jeanine and I were going to chat about it next week, but...goddamn it," he muttered. "Want to tell me why she'd gone to you, too?"

"The weres are working with Moyna and whatever's left of Mab's court. Jeanine was going to help me find her before this gets out of hand."

Greg looked pained. "And you couldn't save her."

"It was over in a matter of seconds! I got the other shifter out of there, but that was the best I—"

"Poppy Kane?"

"You know her?"

"Jeanine's personal assistant. Her muscle, I guess." He pushed himself to his feet, unable to hide his wincing, and joined his wife. "She's safe?"

"For now. She's—"

But Greg held up one hand. "Don't tell me. If the Company comes calling, I don't want any part of this circus."

I couldn't hide my surprise at that. "You said you were meeting Jeanine. If you weren't planning to get involved, then—"

"Professional courtesy, nothing more. We don't get involved in court politics, and the same goes for Company matters," he said as Missy nodded silently beside him.

"Actually, this time, you don't have a choice. You've got a spy."

Missy's thin eyebrow quirked. "Says who?"

"Jeanine. She had a picture, too, but that was on her camera, which is in her purse, which is probably in an evidence bag. Male, maybe your size," I said to Greg, "and talented enough to thwart a blood trace."

It was Greg's turn to look peeved. "Is Toula—"

"She's done nothing to hurt the Arcanum, and she's trying to help me find Moyna before the kid screws up her courage again," I snapped. "Remember what happened the last time my daughter got a brilliant plan? Something about a siege, or was I misinformed?"

Greg regarded me as he mulled that over. "I'll handle this alleged spy my way. *Quietly*. But I'm not dragging my people into someone else's war."

"Damn it, Greg," I started, but cut the thought short as a tall, stocky young man rounded the corner of the trailer with a little girl perched on his shoulders. The man wore only a Saints sweatshirt over plaid flannel pants, though the child was swaddled in a puffy brown coat and ski cap. Sizing him up beside Greg, I realized where the grand magus had found his new oversized outerwear.

"Hey, there," the newcomer drawled, looking back and forth between the Harrisons and me with bemusement. "Lilly wanted to know when Memaw and Pop-Pop were going to come play Legos. Also, Abby said to tell you the appetizers are almost out." Greg and Missy shot each other uncertain glances, but the young man, oblivious to their distress, stuck out his mittened hand. "Chris Tomlin," he said, grinning as I met his firm grip.

"Colin Leffee. You're—"

"Cora's husband. And since it's, like, minus a hundred degrees out here, how about we move this party inside? I don't know about y'all, but I plan to be there when the crab dip hits the table. You coming to dinner?"

"No," I said as Missy opened her mouth, "just passing through."

Chris glanced around—looking for a car that wasn't there, I suspected—and Missy seized the opportunity to take the situation back in hand. "Baby, you come with Memaw," she said, pulling the bundle of child and clothing from Chris's shoulders. "You're going to freeze out here! And *where* is your coat, young man?" she demanded of Chris as she steered then back toward the main trailer.

"Pop-Pop borrowed it—"

"Inside before you get pneumonia. March."

He glanced over his shoulder, waved, and had time only to call, "Merry Christmas!" before Missy had dragged him around the building and out of view.

Greg and I waited until we heard the distant slamming of the trailer door. "My granddaughter's husband," he murmured. "Lilly's our eldest great-grandbaby. Does that clear it up?"

The idea that Greg had great-grandchildren was still sinking in, as my mind had frozen his daughters, Cindy and Abby, at about ten years old. Then again, I'd never had occasion to interact with his children—I'd caught a glimpse of their picture in Greg's wallet once, but I'd not met any of his family beyond Missy, who wouldn't have shed a tear if I'd dropped dead at her feet. "How many—"

"Four granddaughters and a grandson, three great-granddaughters and a great-grandson. It's tough for us boys," he said with a mirthless smile.

Something else niggled at my thoughts. "Chris has no idea who am I, does he?"

Greg shook his head. "Mundane."

"You let *mundanes* in the silo? Whatever happened to secrecy?"

He sank back onto the new bench and shrugged. "Only way to see my girls. They both married mundane."

"*What?*"

"Yep. Don't get me wrong, they're good men, but they're as mundane as they come." He rubbed his face with his cold-stiffened fingers. "It's the usual story—the girls went off to school and fell in love, and there wasn't a damn thing we could do about it. They take after their mother, you know. Hardheaded."

I took a seat beside him, and Greg slid toward the end

of the bench to make room. "What happened? You showed them the clubhouse? Threatened to turn them into toads if they broke your daughters' hearts?"

"Thankfully, I didn't have to go that far. They're sworn to secrecy. Guess they love my girls, eh?" He shoved his hands into the pockets of his appropriated coat and turned to face me. "Council wasn't happy about it, but I knew the girls weren't going to let their husbands run their mouths. Well, that, and who would have believed them? Wizards in a missile silo? Come on. But still…you know what the Council's like. Once was bad, but I thought I was going to have a mutiny when I had to do it again."

"But the girls are happy, yes? And you did get grandchildren out of the deal."

"Yes on both counts," he said, but sighed. "Five grandkids, and only two witches among them. Other three are duds. The grands that have married went with mundanes, too. *All* the greats are mundane."

"Shit," I muttered.

"Yeah. Cindy's clan's based in New Orleans, and Abby's bunch ended up around LA. You can probably imagine why they don't make it up here that often." He snorted. "Not like the Council's ever given my girls a shot at magus. But no, Chris wouldn't know you from Adam's housecat. Best to keep it that way, understood?"

I saw in Greg's eyes what he wasn't saying aloud. The embarrassment that a magus's child—let alone the *grand* magus's child—would abandon the Arcanum for life with a mundane spouse and live somewhere that wasn't several stories belowground. The humiliation that both of his daughters had turned their backs on magic and its politics. The deep shame that the greatest wizard of his time had no one to carry on his name and dynasty—just his renegade daughters, a couple of witches, and a family of duds. *Duds*.

And I saw what else was hiding in Greg's tense stare: fear. This was all about to happen again—another fight with the Council, another mundane in the silo, another powerful wizard whose children might all be duds, thanks to their inept father. Perhaps it was touchy when Greg's daughters made their choice and left, but for the *grand magus* to wed a mundane...well, Helen wasn't grand magus yet. If the Council pushed her out, the succession would be in chaos—and the specter of the Great War's embattled arcana loomed in the back of Greg's thoughts.

But at that moment, Helen and Joey's matrimonial plans were the least of my worries. "Going back to Jeanine—"

"We're not getting involved."

"What if you don't get a choice? What if the fighting comes to your doorstep again? Help me find Moyna, and—"

"Yeah, the fight came to us. We lost nine, and it wasn't even our fight. I'm not dragging us into another one, Coileán. Not this time."

I had to count to five before I muttered, "Look, I'm not asking you to take up arms. Not now, anyway. But Jeanine was worried enough to contact you *and* me. She's gone, so God knows what's going to happen to the Company. Moyna's planning *something*, Greg. Help me find her and stop her. It's in everyone's best interest. Hell, Oberon's daughter wants Moyna found, too. If she and I can work together, then surely you could help with intel."

Greg pushed his glasses down his nose. "There's a new queen?"

"Eleanor. I'll make the introductions, if you like."

"Not today." He readied his cane and stood. "I'm going back to my family. We're going to have a nice meal, and the babies are going to play with their toys, and I'm not going to think about any of this court and Company nonsense. I said I'll deal with the spy," he added before I could jump in. "But not today."

He limped off, opening a gate into the hallway outside his apartment as he hobbled down the road. Watching him, I thought about the family waiting inside the silo, those wizards and witches and duds and mundanes he called his own. Of course Greg didn't want to fight—he had too much to lose. And as long as he was preaching isolationism, the Council would back him with glad hearts.

I sat in the cold for a moment longer, imagining the party somewhere below my feet, the smiles and the laughter and the hot crab dip, and then I dissolved the bench I'd made and took myself home to sleep.

My ringing phone jolted me from my glorified nap, and as I fumbled on the nightstand for the accursed thing, my eyes tried to focus on the darkness outside my windows. By the time I'd flipped the phone open, my brain had caught up with the situation: it wasn't yet morning, and having planned on a much longer rest, I labored to move with the weight of my exhaustion. "Yes?" I grunted into the handset, not bothering with the ID. "Problem?"

"Hello to you, too," said a familiar female voice in poorly accented Fae. "Bad time?"

"Helen?" I mumbled. "What're you—"

"Greg called to tell me about Jeanine Nadel. Want to give me the real story?"

I sat up in bed and ran a hand through my mussed hair. "How graphic do you want this? And I thought you were with Joey."

"I'm up in the guest room—he's chopping firewood with his dad, and his mom's getting dinner finished. I'm allegedly calling my grandmother, so play along if this conversation gets weird." Springs creaked, and Helen's voice grew quieter as she settled onto her borrowed bed. "Here's the long and short of what I got: Jeanine's been killed by her own people, Moyna may or may not be involved, and we're not getting our hands dirty. What else do I need to know?"

"You're about to eat dinner."

"*Talk.*"

"Your stomach, not mine," I muttered, resting my head on my propped hand. "She wasn't killed—she was eaten alive by a werewolf. In rat form," I clarified, "so it was quick, but still, it was a nasty way to go."

"Shit," she whispered.

"Yeah. Her associate is over here for her own protection. Last I saw, she was with Eleanor—"

"The new queen?"

"Greg told you about that, too, did he?"

"No, Joey told me the day after she moved in. Why wait for Greg to give me the censored version when I can get it directly?"

"Smart girl." I rose and crossed to the open window, letting the cool night air rouse me. "Here's what I can tell Magus Carver: Greg has the final say in the silo, so calm down and wait for instructions from him."

"Uh-huh. What can you tell *me?*"

"I think this is going to get messy sooner rather than later. And when it does, Greg may find himself in the crosshairs he's so desperately trying to dodge."

I stood in the silent room and waited while Helen mulled that over. After a moment, she quietly asked, "What can I do to help?"

"Nothing."

"Come on, don't be difficult. Tell me what you need."

"What I need and what you can do are two different matters," I replied, leaning against the windowsill. "Greg's made up his mind for now. You're not going to be able to operate behind his back, kid."

"Want to bet?"

I appreciated the bravado, especially considering our positions. Helen owed me nothing—she was Aiden's blood, not mine—and the fact that she was willing to jump in when her boss hesitated told me what I needed to know about the incoming grand magus. Still, attitude alone wasn't going to be sufficient that time. "I'm sure you have your ways, but you're not losing the grand magus gig on my account, which is *exactly* what will happen if the Council finds out you're calling me in the middle of the night and plotting ways to circumvent Greg."

"Ooh...we're still off-sync, aren't we? Sorry," she mumbled.

"Forget the time. I don't want you sabotaging your career for nothing."

Helen huffed into the phone. "I survived an Arcanum warrant. The Council doesn't scare me."

"Just do me a favor and play it safe until your name's on the office door, yes?"

"But I—"

"Hear me, Helen. I *want* you to become grand magus. I can work with you, and I think you can work with me. We'll see about Eleanor together," I muttered. "So let's not ruin your chances. Do as Greg says, and I'll tell Joey to continue giving you full reports."

"If he doesn't, Aid will," she replied, sounding moderately mollified.

"Of that, I have no doubt. What about a consolation prize?" I offered. "Eleanor's planning to call her court together tomorrow and officially take the throne. I'll make an appearance, and it might be a nice gesture if someone from the Arcanum were to show up."

"Might be. Would Eleanor be offended if said wizard weren't there as an official representative?"

The breeze picked up against my bare back, and I shivered. "Tell you what, ask Greg. If he balks, come over anyway, and you can ask forgiveness later. Deal?"

"Deal," she agreed, but hesitated. "I'm taking the job in January, you know. Marrying in April, and I'll walk at graduation in May if I'm not too swamped. It's going to be a busy year."

"I got the invitation. Thank you."

"Glad you're coming. It means a lot to Joey."

"Eh, I wanted to see you in a poufy dress."

"Jerk," she muttered, but sounded pleased. "Listen…when I take the helm, some things are going to change."

I enchanted a robe around me to block the worst of the wind. "Such as?"

"Well, for one, I'm not going to sit on my hands and wait to see how the Council feels about my every move. I don't mind working with the courts if it's to our mutual benefit. I mean, you know, I think I've cultivated a halfway decent relationship with yours."

I chuckled. "You do realize that Aiden's not running the show any longer, yes?"

"So I'd heard. Welcome back, belatedly. You were, um…missed."

"For all the wrong reasons, I'm sure." I straightened and headed to my rumpled bed. "By the way, congratulations on finishing your degree. See you soon, Helen."

"Thanks, and y—no, the weather's perfect," she said, suddenly switching to English. "You have a good holiday, Grandma."

I ended the call and left Helen to her playacting. Surely, I decided as I burrowed beneath the blankets, she could handle Joey's parents without my assistance.

As I drifted toward the border between waking and sleeping, a thought occurred to me: what, exactly, had Joey told them about his fiancée's career plans? The kid was a fine dragon rider but a lousy liar. Trying to imagine the looks on his mundane, Catholic parents' faces if he so much as mentioned the Arcanum, I let myself sleep.

The summons went out at dawn. I woke to feel Faerie thrumming with the message, which seemed to reverberate from the realm's foundation as it sounded.

Come. Your queen commands it.

Realizing I wasn't going to get any rest while the realm

was broadcasting, I rose, dressed, and went to my preferred dining room. As I waited for Astrid to surprise me, I checked my phone and found a note from Aiden: *The subwoofer blocks the worst of it. Join us.* I'd begun to consider the invitation when the realm suddenly fell silent, and Astrid rubbed her ear as she appeared from the kitchen with a platter. "The queen's emerged, my lord?" she asked as the smell of bacon filled the room.

"Apparently. Thank you." I tucked in while she fetched the rest of my breakfast and kept toying with the phone, watching to see if another message would come. But when half an hour passed with no further word from my brother, I grew impatient and called him to say that the movie marathon was over for at least Val and Mina.

Shortly thereafter, the four of them, looking somewhere between haggard and strung-out, staggered into the dining room. "Have fun?" I asked.

"Sick of popcorn, but coffee will fix that," Toula replied, marching straight to the carafe. "And how are your shifter buddies?"

"One's dead, one's hiding over here. Help yourself."

She froze with her hand over the pot. "*Shit*, Gramps. Why didn't you tell us sooner?"

"You couldn't have changed anything. Drink up. This could turn into a long day, and"—I looked at the glazed faces ringing the table—"I take it no one has slept?"

"We weren't scheduled to be on duty today," Val pointed out.

"I know, and I'm sorry. I'll make it up to you, but—"

"This is an emergency, we understand." An oversized mug of coffee manifested in his hands, and Mina took her cue from her boss. "Has anyone heard from Joey? It would be safest if he stayed away today."

I shook my head. "I filled Helen in last night. Wouldn't be surprised if he turns up early."

Though he looked displeased, Val drank in silence.

Having consumed roughly a gallon of soda overnight, Aiden was perky enough to make himself presentable and accompany me to Eleanor's mansion. He whistled as he stepped through the gate onto the far end of her lush, immaculate grounds. "Nice place," he murmured, and pointed to the little knots of people climbing the wide front steps. "You think she's going to want extra visitors?"

"Honestly, I don't care. Protocol is protocol," I replied, setting off down the tree-lined avenue, "and she has something of mine."

"Yeah?" He jogged to catch up. "What's that?"

"Poppy, the shifter. I brought her back with me, and Eleanor...*commandeered* her, for lack of a better term. The girl's my responsibility."

Aiden frowned and tugged at his ponytail to tighten it. "You think she's going to hurt Poppy?"

"Probably not. It's the principle of the thing. This is twice now that Eleanor's waltzed into my office uninvited. If she gives me any trouble today, I'm going to have to put my foot down."

"Meaning?"

"A show of force, if need be. She's new, she's figuring things out, I get it, but...you know," I said, pulling him to a stop in a patch of shade, "I can't afford to look weak. Neither of us can. We need to strike a balance if this is to work."

"Uh-huh. And how's that going to happen if you're mooning over her?"

"I am not *mooning* over anyone," I said stiffly, hearing the lie in my voice. "Anyway, she's made her feelings perfectly clear. Ours is to be a professional relationship, nothing more."

My brother's expression spoke volumes, but he held his tongue and set off for the house, shaking his head.

Eleanor had been busy, I mused, turning about in the

grand foyer to take in the pastoral reliefs, the white marble floor, and the extravagant marble-and-gold double staircase that spun on itself before reaching the second floor some twenty feet above. Hanging over the center of the foyer from an ornate gold medallion was the Waterford she'd fancied, its electric bulbs replaced with perfect white flames that threw rainbow prisms on all below.

There's no requirement that the inside and outside of a building correspond in any way if it's faerie-made, but even I was taken aback at how little restraint Eleanor had exhibited in her architectural choices. The mansion's stately façade hid a designer's fantasy—a far cry from the modest home she had chosen in Durham.

Following the gawking stream of newcomers, most of whom gave Aiden and me a wide berth, I passed through more marble-floored corridors and paused to admire the scenes carved in the walls, bits of Romantic landscapes she'd lifted from canvas and copied in stone. Soft light filtered through tall windows draped in white gauze, and every corner revealed some new point of interest: a mahogany table beneath a massive spray of pale pink roses, a pair of golden cherubs flanking the door to a circular library ringed in shelves of polished wood and brass, a black baby grand sitting unattended in a salon, playing a piece I thought I recognized as Mozart. As we approached the heart of the house, Aiden leaned close and muttered, "Compensating much?"

"Maybe a little," I agreed, "but I don't have room to talk."

He snorted. "You borrowed the grand magus's office. Slightly less ostentatious."

"Yeah, but I also lifted from Notre Dame de Paris." I ran my fingers along the curve of a marble shepherdess's face. "She knows what she's doing. The better the show, the fewer awkward questions."

"Granted," he said, raising his voice over the thunder

of falling water, "but I still think it's overkill."

He had a point, I concurred, as I followed him into Eleanor's throne room. Design-wise, she'd opted for more of the same, plenty of marble and golden accents, but here, the ceiling rose to a dome with a skylight directly above her throne. Behind the gilded seat, a curtain of water fell from midair into a basin that formed a moat around the dais. A single bridge laid with a gold runner connected the throne with the rest of the room.

"It's beautiful," I said, watching a pair of songbirds swoop and dive through the sourceless waterfall.

"Too showy." He wrinkled his nose. "I mean, yeah, it's *pretty*, but think about how much she's going to regret that waterfall after a few hours of court."

"What do you mean?"

Aiden's brow arched. "Constantly running water—that's going to make for an uncomfortable day if she has anything to drink."

Before he could drag me further down that road, Eleanor swept toward us in a trailing confection of blue silk and diamonds. "Coileán, Aiden," she said, lifting a flute of sparkling rosé. "I didn't think I'd invited you."

"Sorry to crash the party," I replied, conscious of the cautious, hostile eyes on us. "This won't take long. A moment?"

"Certainly." She gestured toward a door set in the far wall, then nodded to Aiden and said, "Make yourself comfortable, child. Coileán, my office?"

CHAPTER 13

I followed Eleanor across the room, skirting the rippling basin, then passed through the wooden door and into a marble-walled antechamber furnished with plush sofas and a koi pond. Another door waited at the far end, and I anticipated something suitably grandiose for her personal suite.

What I found, however, was only a step up from her office in Durham. True, the view was fantastic, a floor-to-ceiling window facing the sparkling sea, but the sturdy bookshelves, institutional desk, and wooden chairs seemed to have been copied from memory.

Eleanor pulled out her chair and sank in a cloud of skirts. "You understand," she mumbled, glancing about the room.

"Completely." I sat and steepled my fingers. "Nice shindig."

"I'm doing the best I can on my own. Thought it might be rude of me to ask to borrow your cook. How'd you find her, if I may enquire?"

"Astrid came with the job, but I wouldn't worry. You're about to find that people are willing to do *anything* to get in your good graces, and that includes making the tea."

"Oh? What's in it for them?"

"I look after my own—as, I assume, will you." Feeling uncomfortably empty-handed, I produced a flute to match Eleanor's and raised it. "To keeping the peace."

"Hear, hear." She downed her glass, then dabbed a

drop of wine from her lips with her fingertip. "So, what brings you here? I take it you're not joining my court."

"Poppy. Where is she?"

"Asleep, poor thing. I stayed with her until dawn, and then I put her under. She needed the rest, and I can only control so many fires at once." Eleanor watched her empty glass as it refilled. "She's comfortable here, but if you'd rather have her now, that can be arranged."

I frowned and sipped my wine. "You're not going to fight me over her?"

"No. Were you expecting a fight?"

"Considering how you swooped in last night—"

"She was traumatized, and you were in over your head. I was trying to improve the situation." She paused to examine my expression, then said, "I don't want a turf war. If you can wait until evening, I'll lift the enchantment and bring her back to you myself."

My eyes drifted to the bookshelf beside her desk as a flush crept up my neck. "I suppose I misinterpreted your actions," I mumbled. "My apologies."

Eleanor massaged her forehead. "The way I see it, there's no need for us to work at cross-purposes. We're both relatively rational adults, aren't we? If our people are to coexist, it might behoove us to put up a unified front. Establish some common rules, punish those who break them equally. That way, they'll have a baseline to use when they're deciding whether it's worth it to attack each other."

I nodded. "Sounds fair."

"Tomorrow, perhaps? You, me, hours of tedium?"

"When you put it like that," I replied, chuckling. "But yes—unless Poppy's still a mess. And I've yet to make contact with the Dark Company. Greg was useless. Helen might be willing to help, but I'd rather she not sabotage herself before she can actually make the Arcanum play ball."

Eleanor's brow puckered. "Helen…"

"Carver. Grand-magus-to-be come the new year, and

incidentally, Aiden's sister, so for my sake, try to be civil, won't you? She'll probably be by today to introduce herself." I swirled my wine and sipped. "You've already met her fiancé, Joey—you threw him headfirst into a tree, remember?"

"The dragon rider, yes." She nodded vigorously. "Is he…"

"Hard-headed. No lasting damage"

"Good. I feel terrible about that, but—"

"Walt. I know."

"Exactly. *God*," she sighed, closing her eyes. "I keep expecting to find him by my side when I wake."

"I know."

She breathed deeply, tightening her grip on herself before the crack could widen, then gave me a stiff smile. "I'm beginning to think I misjudged you, Coileán."

I shrugged and rose. "As you said, we're both relatively rational adults. Let Poppy sleep—I'll check on her tomorrow. The rest might do her good." My glass vanished as I finished its contents, and I gestured toward the door. "Better go find my brother before he makes trouble. I don't know everything that happened last year, but if what I *have* heard is a fair indication, then some of your siblings have bones to pick with him."

She followed me out of her office and stopped me in the antechamber. "You don't have to leave right away. If this Helen is coming, I'm sure she'd be more comfortable seeing a familiar face or two."

I laughed incredulously and pointed to myself. "*This* is a familiar face to the vast majority of your court, and it's not one anyone out there wants to see."

"My court, my rules. Stay. The more you see firsthand, the less I'll need to regurgitate tomorrow."

To my surprise, her expression was serious. "If you're sure."

"I am. But I *will* have to ask that you refrain from killing anyone in my house."

"I suppose that's fair," I said, then offered her my arm. "May I? A lady shouldn't be forced to make an entrance alone."

"Thank you, but this lady is most capable of managing." She glided past me to the door and smirked. "Besides, what would people say if they knew I didn't loathe you?"

Eleanor threw open the door, head high and gown shimmering, and I followed a few paces behind, reddening in spite of myself. Something less than loathing was, at least, a start.

Even with the room steadily filling, it didn't take me long to locate Aiden, who was engaged in animated conversation with a black-haired man in a tweed coat and corduroy trousers. I puzzled over the situation until I picked the man's face out of my memory: Rufus Stowe, one of Vivi's dozen brothers. Our only meeting had been brief, but Val had told me of his assistance during my incapacitation. Judging by his and Aiden's laughter, the two had been friendly for some time.

I cleared my throat to interrupt, and my brother waved me closer. "Coileán, come here, do you know Rufus?" he said, throwing his arm around the man's shoulders. "This guy's great."

Rufus grinned at him, then stuck out his hand. "We've been introduced, my lord, but it's been a time."

I matched his firm grip. "Mr. Stowe, I believe I owe you more than thanks."

He shrugged awkwardly. "Just doing what needed to be done. This one and Joey did the heavy lifting," he added, cutting his eyes to Aiden. "I had a little Montana vacation."

"A vacation from hell," Aiden chimed in. "And it's *Dr.* Stowe."

"My apologies," I said. "Medical?"

"Ph.D.," he replied, reddening. "American history. I've been teaching for the last few decades, nothing special."

Aiden flashed a mischievous grin. "Rufus takes me to college bars."

I chuckled as his eyebrows waggled. "Educational experience, huh?"

"Nothing too intense," Rufus hastened to assure me, then paused and considered me closely. "Not to pry, my lord, but what brings you two here today?"

"Heard the summons and stopped by to see how things were going. Maybe get some interior design tips."

He cracked a smile. "Might be a *little* overdone for my taste, but…"

Rufus's voice trailed off, and I followed the direction of his stare to find Eleanor approaching. "Amazing," she said. "Am I imagining things, or has the Ironhand found someone in this court that he isn't desperate to stab?"

"Very funny," I muttered. "Dr. Stowe here was saying how much he admired the—"

"Dr. Stowe?" she echoed, then leaned toward him, gasped, and beamed. "Rufus! It's me, dear, it's Ellie Richardson."

"*Ellie!*" Slipping past me, he grabbed her bare shoulders and laughed aloud. "I thought you were *dead!* We heard about the fire—"

"I'm sorry to have disappeared like that, but…my goodness, I had no idea you're—"

"You, either! You know what this means, right?" he teased. "Our glamour is *superb.*"

"Or we should probably be more observant," she countered, but her smile widened. "Oh, Rufus, I'm so glad to see you. Dr. Stowe is brilliant," she said to me. "Wonderful writer, superb presenter. How many times have we gotten drunk at a Society for Military History conference," she asked him, "sixteen? Seventeen?"

"At least," he replied. "Which reminds me, are you two coming to Calgary next month? I was on the planning committee, and there are a bunch of papers that will be right up Walt's alley." He glanced around, then frowned at Eleanor. "Is he here? I'm sorry, but with everyone's glamour off..."

She shook her head, and her smile dimmed to the polite expression of the pained.

Rufus watched her struggle for a few seconds before the realization hit. "*No,*" he murmured, wrapping her in a tight embrace. "Ellie, I'm so sorry. If there's anything I can do..."

She sniffed and pulled away, still smiling but glassy-eyed. "Thank you, dear. Walt was looking forward to Calgary. I understand the two of you were considering an edited volume on the history of siege warfare."

"We'd started e-mailing, but that's it. My sincere condolences, Ellie. He was a gentle soul. I'm very grateful that you're still with us, but—"

Eleanor hugged him in turn. "Thank you. That means more than you know."

Rufus looked down at her as she broke her hold again. "So, what now? Starting over? No pressure, but if you're feeling up to Calgary, I'd be happy to pass you off as one of my promising young advisees."

She paused, and I caught a flash of teeth as she nibbled her lip. "Well, you see..." Eleanor hesitated. "I'm going to be out of academia for a while. I inherited a position, you might say. Ehm..."

Seeing her struggle, I stepped into the breach. "Rufus," I muttered, "I see you've met Lady Eleanor."

"Oh, yes, we've been acquainted for—" He paled as the tumblers fell. "My lady," he said slowly, backing off a respectful few paces. "Forgive the impudence, I didn't—"

"Stop that nonsense, Rufus, it's *me,*" she said in consternation. "You know me better than anyone here. What could there possibly be to forgive?" Seeing the trepidation in his eyes, she clasped his hands. "You've been my colleague and my friend. Nothing's changed. I took a new job, that's all."

"Bit of a promotion, wouldn't you say?" he ventured.

"Maybe. Ask me in another month, and we'll see." She shook her head, gave his hands a squeeze, and released him. "Thank you for coming."

He shrugged, still visibly shaken but trying to play it off. "You rang, we ran. May I ask what this is about?"

Eleanor glanced at the milling crowd, many of whom had taken interest in our little knot, then drew closer to him and lowered her voice. "I'm opening the border. If I'm going to be in residence, then the rest of this sorry lot may as well come with me."

Rufus nodded slowly. "In that case, am I to understand that I won't be going to Calgary, either?"

She frowned, surprised. "Gracious, no. If you're willing to risk a blizzard, then I won't stand in your way. Go, have a good time. Have a beer for Walt, if you think of it."

"This isn't a mandatory move, then?"

"Not for you. Not for many. I'll make exceptions—Coileán, I'm sure you have suggestions," she added with a smirk. "But no, Rufus, I'm not trying to force you out of Alaska. Now," she said, folding her arms, "that said, we need to have a talk about your plans. You're going to be pushing the envelope if you try to stretch your current identity another five years. How old are you, ninety?"

"Ninety-two," he said, rubbing his neck. "I've been thinking about laying the groundwork for a new one, but it's such a hassle—"

"Believe me, I understand. Come talk to me when you find the time—you've clearly never forged your credentials before."

"Is it that obvious?"

Eleanor patted his cheek. "You're still so young. I insist that you allow me to help you transition. It'd be my pleasure." Stepping back, she cast another glance at her curious court. "Did you come alone?"

Rufus pointed to a clump of men on the other side of

the waterfall. "Most of my brothers are here, and our parents. One is running behind, but I could fetch him now—"

"I'm in no rush," she said, waving the offer aside, then gave the pack of Stowes a second look. "Goodness, how many of you *are* there?"

"Twelve boys and…uh…"

He fell silent, and I cut my eyes to Aiden, who remained mum.

"*Uh?*" Eleanor echoed, looking at the three of us in turn. "Something I should know?"

When Aiden and I didn't rush to fill the silence, Rufus cleared his throat and hid his hands in his pockets. "We have a sister. I doubt that she attends." Seeing Eleanor's arched brow, he explained, "Vivi's Fringe. Do you—"

"I know what the Fringe is," she said softly. "Your sister lacks talent?"

"That's an understatement. I've been checking my phone," he said, pulling it from his jacket as proof, "but she hasn't asked for a lift yet."

Eleanor considered this in silence, then seemed to reach a decision. "Might I speak with her?" she asked. Rufus blanched again, and she hastily added, "I mean her no harm. Just a word, if that would be possible."

I saw the panic in his eyes, but thwarting Eleanor on her own turf struck me as a remarkably stupid idea, and Aiden appeared to have drawn the same conclusion. Finding no help from us, Rufus reluctantly tapped his phone's screen. "I'll give her a call," he mumbled, then held the phone to his ear and said with false calm, "Hey, Princess. Are you up?"

While he made small talk with his sister, Eleanor pulled him into the quiet of her office, then beckoned for Aiden and me to join them. I shut the door in time to hear Rufus say, "There's someone who wants to talk to you. Is that…okay, here you go."

Eleanor took the phone from him and pecked at it until

it went to speaker mode. "Hello, Vivi?"

"Yup," came the response, her voice weary with the late hour in Virginia. "Who's this?"

"Ellie Richardson. I'm a friend of your brother's—you know how incestuous academia is, yes?"

Vivi hesitated. "Sorry, which of my brothers did you say you know?"

"Rufus."

I understood Vivi's uncharacteristic quiet. Anyone who knew Rufus professionally would know him as an old man, and Vivi, on her best day, barely sounded twenty. "Hey, kid, it's Coileán," I cut in, stepping toward the phone. "Your brother's not the only faerie with tenure."

"*Ah*," she sighed, sounding relieved. "Gotcha, Chief. And, uh…it's Ellie, right? What can I do for you?"

Eleanor pulled the phone closer to her face. "Did you get the summons today?"

"What summons?"

"A few hours ago," Rufus interjected. "The, uh"—his eyes flicked nervously toward Eleanor—"the new queen ordered everyone into Faerie."

I could almost hear Vivi stiffen. "Nope. Missed that memo."

"The boys are here, and I'd be happy to pick you up—"

"Thanks, but no. I'm not going where I'm not invited. Tell everyone hi for me, won't you?"

Rufus looked helplessly at Eleanor, who shook her head and leaned toward the phone. "You're invited, dear. Please come. There are canapés to spare."

"Appreciate it, but I'm not going to get on the queen's bad side by crashing the party."

"It's not crashing if you're invited. And anyway, Coileán and Aiden have already crashed the event—your presence would be far less objectionable."

She snorted her disagreement. "Right, because this queen of yours is going to want a Fringer lurking in the back."

"Actually, I'd like that very much."

The phone went silent for a few seconds until Vivi managed to squeak, "Come again?"

"My late husband was Fringe," said Eleanor. "Walt Drummond. He went by Charger."

Vivi began to sputter as the missing pieces fell into place. "You're...but you said you know Rufe—"

"We've been colleagues for a while. I never thought I'd be making this sort of career shift, to be honest."

"But Charger was a *witch*."

"Not a particularly good one, the poor man."

"But...but *you're*—"

"He knew what he needed to know about me, and he showed me what the Fringe does. Not everything, but I know enough about the organization to respect its work." She paused. "You obviously were acquainted with Walt. If I may ask..."

"Monkey," Vivi murmured. "Most folks in there know me as Monkey."

Eleanor's eyes widened. "*Monkey*? You were at the center of that business in Montana, weren't you? Walt read the feeds—"

"Yeah, I was there. So was Rufe. I, uh...I heard that Walt passed away not too long ago. No details, but the news made the rounds. I'm sorry."

"Thank you." Eleanor cleared her throat and held the phone closer. "As I said, I already have party crashers, and I understand that someone from the Arcanum is probably on her way. I'd be honored to have a Fringer present. If your brother were to bring you, would that be acceptable?"

"Well...uh..." Vivi stammered, then said with a hint of exasperation, "Can you give me ten minutes? I mean, flannel pajamas are sexy as hell, but I wouldn't want to be overdressed."

"Take your time." She chuckled and handed the phone back to Rufus, who muttered goodbye. "I know *exactly* what your sister did in Montana," she told him as he put the phone away. "Half of the messages coming out of there had her name on them. Walt said Monkey was young, but I had no idea she was *that* young."

"Vivi's never done things by halves," he replied, and opened a gate into a darkened kitchen. "I'll go over and wait for her. She'll want to chew me out, I'm sure."

We lingered in the office until Rufus returned with Vivi, who had traded her loungewear for black pants, a tank top, and a coat of mascara. By the time we emerged again, the throne room had reached three-quarters capacity. Eleanor's mouth scrunched in thought, and the walls retreated a few yards in all directions, giving the assembled elbow room. The gesture wasn't purely for their comfort. Oberon's court had been scattered, and though many of them hadn't seen each other in some time, a faerie's grudges are nearly impossible to extinguish. Preventing flare-ups before Eleanor's people had time to cultivate a proper fear of her was key.

"There they are," said Aiden, and pointed across the room.

Following his finger, I saw the rest of the Stowe clan, now with two additions: Helen, who had forgone her ceremonial robes in favor of a conservative purple dress, and Joey, who stood at her side in his well-worn flying duster and silently scanned the room. From the way his hands kept creeping toward his hips, I assumed he'd come with concealed weapons. Touching Eleanor's shoulder, I whispered, "Carver's arrived. Joey's with her, and he's armed."

She nodded, picking them out of the crowd. "All things considered, I wouldn't be surprised if he'd left the dragon out back. Shall we?"

Rufus and Vivi had spotted their family, and we followed them closely through the crowd, which had a convenient tendency to thin every time we were noticed. As Vivi hugged her parents, Helen left the security of the huddle and nodded to us. "Lady Eleanor," she began, clasping her hands in front of her. "I apologize for coming uninvited, but Lord Coileán suggested I attend. If my presence is unwanted—"

"It's lovely to meet you, Magus," Eleanor smoothly interrupted. "Be welcome. You've come from Montana, I assume?"

"Virginia. I would have been here sooner, but in light of my current accommodations, I had to delay my arrival."

"What she means," said Joey as he joined us, "is that we had to wait until my parents went to bed to sneak out of the house."

Eleanor chuckled and motioned him closer as Vivi and Helen waved at each other. "Young man," she murmured, "I owe you an apology."

"What, the thing with the tree? Don't worry about it, I get worse than that all the time. No permanent damage."

She patted his arm. "You *have* been here too long, haven't you?"

"I've had some excellent teachers, but they consider it their duty to keep me humble. A bump on the head is par for the course."

Smiling, she turned back to Helen. "I should like to speak with you at length, but not today, considering our mutual scheduling constraints. Next week, perhaps? Or in the new year?"

"Next week would be best," said Helen, cutting her eyes to Joey, who nodded. "I'm supposed to take over in Montana on the fifteenth, but Joey and I have a few matters to take care of between now and then."

Aiden snorted. "Mom still wants you to wear her wedding dress?"

"No, *that's* been put to rest. There will be no recycling of the puffball."

"The puffball?" Eleanor echoed.

Helen grimaced. "Imagine the worst fashion choices of the eighties, all in one gown. The only thing that dress has going for it is that it's not in a neon color." Eleanor winced in sympathy, and Helen turned back to Aiden. "No, we've got to get through the Unveiling."

"Seriously?" he muttered. "Why waste the time?"

"I don't know, tradition? Keeping the Council appeased? In any case, the ceremony shouldn't take an hour, and then they'll probably swear Joey to secrecy if they can't talk us out of the wedding, but that's all. It just means another day or two of dealing with Mom and Dad. Speaking of which—"

"Oh, no, you don't," said Aiden, holding up his hands to ward her off. "I'm not getting involved in this mess."

"But it's my *wedding*, Aid," she faux-pouted.

"You can get through the Unveiling without me."

"Excuse my ignorance," Eleanor cut in, "but what unveiling?"

My brother rolled his eyes. "It's the Arcanum's pre-wedding ceremony. Basically, they check that no one is being coerced into the marriage, and then they make sure you're not too closely related. Even the old-blooded wizards look down on inbreeding."

"Which is why it's ridiculous that Joey and I are having to go through this," Helen explained. "I'm old-blooded, and he's mundane. The chances of too much overlap are infinitesimal. But since keeping the Council happy is the end-all, do-all of the grand magus gig, apparently…" She crossed her arms and looked at Aiden. "You're coming. You can stand for Joey if you want, but you're coming."

"*Hel.*"

"You, too," she told me, ignoring his whine. "Someone has to vouch for Joey, and you've known him long enough."

"Vouch in what capacity?" I asked.

"That the person being tested isn't actually a glamoured or transformed stand-in. Can you handle that?"

I smirked. "Sure you don't want to let Ma and Pa Bolin do the honors?"

Joey shook his head. "The fact that we sneaked out tonight should tell you how much they know about Helen, boss."

Her interest piqued, Eleanor leaned in and lowered her voice. "I know this is none of my business, but what *have* you told your parents? The Arcanum's a nuisance—no offense, dear," she said to Helen—"but Walt was far enough removed from it that I never had to hide it from anyone. What's the protocol these days?"

The couple looked at each other for a long moment. "Well, uh," Joey mumbled, "there's no set script, so we've been improvising. Um…"

"Mission trips," Helen offered as he reddened. "The Bolins think he's been building houses in Honduras since he left seminary, and we hit it off when I came down on a short stint."

Much as I hated to embarrass Joey, my laugher welled up without warning, unstoppable as a tidal wave. By the time I'd dried my eyes and dragged my cackling under control, Joey's face glowed with his flush. "Sorry," I gasped, "I'm sorry, but…*Honduras?* They think you've been—"

"What do you want me to do, tell them the truth?" he protested. "They'd throw me in the loony bin."

"I know, I'm sorry. If I need to work up a tan for you the next time you go back, say the word."

"Thanks, but I told them I'm transferring to Montana with Helen. Guess that's not entirely a fib…"

Helen wrapped her arm around his waist and turned to Eleanor. "Excuse us, this wasn't supposed to devolve into—"

"No, that's quite all right," she replied, flashing me a look of reprimand. "Make yourself comfortable. If you're thirsty…" She gestured toward the flute-laden side tables, then paused and frowned. "Virginia, you said?"

"Yes, ma'am."

"Mm. In that case," said Eleanor, producing a pair of mugs, "and since you're sneaking about in the middle of the night, how do you take your coffee?"

By noon, Eleanor had expanded the throne room three times, yet the crowd continued to swell. I lingered on its edges with the other unexpected guests, keeping to myself so as not to cause trouble. Vivi, Rufus, and a few of their brothers wandered by on occasion, but all had the sense to keep our interactions brief—nothing good would come of the Stowes blatantly fraternizing with the enemy. Joey stayed vigilant through a cocktail of adrenaline and caffeine, but Helen managed to catnap on his shoulder off and on as the morning progressed. Aiden, who slumped against the wall beside them, knocked back an alarming number of espresso shots as his cinematic all-nighter caught up with him, and I kept finding reasons to lock eyes with Eleanor, trying to prod her into getting to the main event. Still, she continued to delay until a tiny golden light zipped through the main doors and landed on her outstretched palm. Squinting, I recognized Kuni and nudged the others as Eleanor carried him over to us.

"I can't understand him," she apologized, looking at Aiden and Joey for a hint.

Kuni squeaked for a moment, and Aiden nodded. "He says that no one gave him a time to be here, and he's peeved that I left without him. Sorry, bud," he told the piq, who folded his wings and sat in Eleanor's hand.

"Ah. Would, ehm…" She glanced meaningfully at her occupied hand, and Aiden cupped his below it as she coaxed Kuni out of his seat with her fingertip.

He squeaked again at the disturbance, and as she departed, Aiden muttered, "I'm not translating that."

"I think I got the gist," I replied, and watched Eleanor approach the bridge across the basin.

The cacophony of the crowd softened as people noticed and shushed their neighbors. By the time Eleanor mounted the dais and sat, the room was silent but for the splash of the waterfall. She smoothed her skirts, then placed her fingers at the hollow of her throat. "My people," she began, her voice magically amplified around the room. "Honored guests. Thank you for making the journey. I am Eleanor."

She paused, examining the sea of watching eyes on the far side of the moat. "My name and face are as unfamiliar to many of you as are yours to mine. This morning, in fact, I've met a score of my siblings." I watched her nod to a few of the audience nearest the moat. "I barely knew my father, and I can't explain his decisions. I don't know why he left Faerie. I don't know why he chose to return in the manner he did. What I *do* know is that last year's assault on this realm and the Arcanum was an unnecessary waste of resources and lives."

Eleanor waited, letting the rumbling subside, and drummed her fingers on her armrests. "Some of you may have been involved in that campaign. I don't know, nor do I wish to know. Perhaps you were anxious to come home, or perhaps you were following your king. I'm not sitting in judgment today. The others suffered casualties, this court suffered casualties, and Oberon paid with his life. Such...*stupidity* will not be tolerated again," she said with distaste.

"This is not a role I accept lightly," she continued, silencing the few grumblers with her stare. "It's not a role I've ever sought. The opposite, in fact. I rejected this responsibility for a year, hoping it would go away if I paid it no heed. The realm, as you see, had other plans." She hesitated, then sat up straighter and lowered her voice, forcing the crowd to listen closely. "I waited, and my reluctance cost me someone dear to me. You see, while my father lost his life, his protégée—or perhaps Titania's protégée, *Mab's* protégée—endures. She's angry, and she will seek to destroy anyone who opposes her. Reports suggest that she leads the tattered remnants of Mab's court. I refuse to allow her to destroy mine."

She gestured toward our overly caffeinated knot. "Lord Coileán has been of great assistance to me in these last days. With his cooperation, I intend to restore this realm to what it was before Oberon chose to go on walkabout. My people"—she spread her hands and smiled—"welcome home."

The crowd's roar of joy overpowered even the waterfall as it reverberated from the dome. Catching Joey's look, I pulled out my phone and pressed an oft-used button. "Val? Hi," I shouted to be heard with the jubilation. "Triple the guard, please."

CHAPTER 14

Eleanor worked the room long into the evening. A few hours after sunset, as I was catching up on correspondence in an effort to avoid thinking about the Dark Company, I heard a knock and looked up to find her head poking around the door. "Bad time?" she asked. I waved her in, and she flopped onto the sofa with a sigh. "What a day. I'm exhausted. And we have to talk land before war breaks out. Have you got a decent map?"

Sunrise caught us bent over the homemade atlas, surrounded by the night's detritus of empty cups and bowls. Eleanor had exchanged the gown for pajamas and a bathrobe, and I'd followed suit with sweatpants. She'd pulled her hair into a sloppy bun with a pair of pens, and a faint set of dark circles had manifested beneath her eyes. I looked away from my stolen glance while my mind replayed a slideshow of Meggy's inventory all-nighters. Sensing movement, Eleanor glanced up from her notes and frowned. "All right, then?"

"All right," I mumbled, staring at my jottings to avoid her eyes.

By lunchtime, we'd hammered out boundary lines, complete with a buffering no-man's land. As Astrid delivered our meal, Eleanor flashed a smug grin. "Found a cook."

"Did you?" I asked, salivating at the smell of roast chicken. "Already?"

"And by luck. One of Rufus's brothers is a chef in Honolulu. He gave me the quick résumé, but I didn't care once I heard 'Cordon Bleu' and 'Michelin.' Lucian, I think he was called."

I reached for my fork. "Trying to make me jealous already?"

Her Mona Lisa smile said it all.

After a long afternoon of political nitpicking, I returned with Eleanor to her palace to check on Poppy. The enchantment holding her unconscious had lifted at nightfall, and she seemed rested, if frustrated. "I've got to get back there," she said between rapid bites of the Stowe boy's perfect sirloin. "If the weres take power, a ton of us are going to be in danger."

"If you go back now, you're dead," Eleanor pointed out. "Give us time to scout."

"But I—"

"You can't protect them if you're a corpse," I interjected. "Just a few days, Poppy."

She growled her frustration but acquiesced.

In the end, I left her where she was, deciding that one guest suite was as good as another. But as I stretched out that night, I couldn't quiet my mind. Resigning myself to insomnia, I rose in the small hours and padded to my cold office and the stack of complaints demanding my attention. It had grown during my absence, I noted glumly as I started a fire. Helping myself to a little bourbon, I carried the bundle of complaints to the coffee table and opened the computer, intending to either drink or bore myself to sleep before dawn.

Ten minutes later, a soft knock drew my attention from the latest squabble, and I looked up as Val poked his head inside. "Coileán? Is everything all right?"

"Can't sleep. It was either work or stare at the ceiling."

His gaze landed on the letters beside my computer. "You've seen the newest, I trust?"

I held the letter in my hand toward the fire, the better

to read it. "Someone was overserved at a dinner party and mouthed off, and now I'm supposed to treat it like a war crime. The usual."

He began to speak but converted the thought to a sigh. "I'll see that you aren't disturbed, my lord."

"Say it, Val. What's troubling you?"

He waited while I finished my drink, then glanced at the complaints. "Brace yourself. Intra-court disputes are one thing, but inter-court mean blood. Remember what I told you," he added, and saw himself out.

I sat in silence, mulling over Val's concerns as the blazing logs popped, and then I realized the soft muttering I was hearing wasn't in my head. Rather, it was coming from the bookshelf, and I carried my refilling bourbon across the room to peer through Aiden's tiny gate into Stuart's apartment. All that met my eye was blackness, however, and I widened the gate enough to admit an exploratory finger. The hole, it seemed, was covered by butcher paper—the back of a framed picture. Carefully, I opened the gate enough to fit my hand through, then silently slid the picture out of the way.

Stuart sat on his sofa, surrounded by cats, and read aloud from a paper on the table. "*Gracious ladies, Goddess three, send my lover back to me*," he said to himself, rubbing the nearest cat's back. "*Fill his heart with love and pity…*"

"'Or my outlook's pretty shitty'?" I ventured.

He shrieked and leapt up, scattering cats, papers, and pencils as he scrambled for the baseball bat in the corner.

I spread the gate enough to cross through. "It's *me*, Stuart. Who else would be in the wall?"

Panting, he dropped the bat and glared at me. "Would knocking be such a burden?"

"Sorry. Heard the poetry session."

"It's not *poetry*." He eased back onto the sofa as he calmed. "I'm writing new spells. Valentine's Day is coming—love charms are a hot commodity this time of year, you know."

I leaned against the wall and smirked. "You know those things are worthless."

"If the caster has enough faith—"

"*Stuart.*"

He grunted and picked up his pencil. "I'm a firm believer in the power of positive thinking, and nothing you say is going to change that. Now, since you're here, can you think of any rhymes for 'pity'?"

"I gave you my best attempt, and real spells don't come as rhyming quatrains. Whatever a wizard says is only to help him focus."

Stuart gave me a look of long suffering. "*You* know that, and *I* know that, but the average customer expects a certain level of—"

"Poetry?"

"Yes. At which I, unfortunately, do not excel." He tapped the pencil against the table and frowned. "Seriously, any suggestion?"

I flicked a finger, and a well-worn rhyming dictionary appeared beside him. "Had that one for a while. Good for writing quasi-witty seasonal signage."

"Thanks," he said as I turned to go. "Hey, Colin?"

"Yeah?" I asked, pausing with one leg between realms.

"Satisfy my curiosity. A real working love spell—what would that look like?"

I shrugged wearily. "Lust is easy to create, but I've yet to meet anyone who could magically induce *love*. And if you ensorcelled someone into loving you, would that be love at all?"

He held up the unfinished spell. "Point taken, but that doesn't mean people won't *try*."

"Just don't offer any money-back guarantees," I told him, and slipped home in search of sleep.

The next morning, Helen sneaked over for brunch with Eleanor. "Perfectly civilized," she reported to me on her way back to Virginia. "She's got sixty varieties of tea on hand, did you know that?"

"She *is* English," I replied.

"Says the Irishman with the office bar." She opened a gate and grinned. "By the way, the Unveiling is Saturday at noon. See you then."

If the progressively better situation with Eleanor had improved my outlook, the circumstances with the Dark Company were the fly in the ointment. The question of how to proceed left me flummoxed. I didn't know the location of the Company's current headquarters, let alone how best to infiltrate it, and something told me that Poppy would be cagey if I pressed her for details. Still, having failed to come up with a brilliant plan by New Year's Eve, I was on the cusp of interrogating her when my phone rang. Glancing at the readout, I wandered to the window, grateful for an excuse to look at my roses instead of the papers covering my desk. "Afternoon, Vivi. Ghost hunting again?"

"Morning, you mean," she croaked. "We're still off-sync."

I checked the clock, saw that it was barely four in Virginia, and grimaced. "Trouble?"

"Maybe. Got a voicemail from an unknown number—someone wanted to send you a message. Called himself 'Alpha.' It doesn't give me the warm fuzzies that someone outside the Fringe has my contact info, but hey, at least he made himself easy to trace. Want the short version?"

"Sure."

"Turn over the shifter you're hiding. You know, the one who was there when Jeanine Nadel got whacked. Kane, right?"

"How did you know about—"

"Nadel? Chatter's been heavy—we've got ears in Company and Arcanum lines. Is there some reason you hadn't mentioned this to us yet?"

"I was getting around to it."

"Uh-huh. You got word to the silo, and then nothing. Look," she said over the sound of pouring coffee, "we've circulated the security footage from the casino. There are Fringers who probably know the events better than you do. I've been authorized to offer our assistance."

I slid into my desk chair and leaned back. "Nice to know."

"I was authorized four days ago."

The silence hung between us, broken only by her slurping sips and the squeak of my chair, until I took the bait. "Why wait to tell me?"

"Figured you didn't want it, seeing as how you didn't even tell us Nadel was dead."

"Vivi, I—"

"Don't sell us short. We're not useless, okay?"

"I never said you were."

"Yeah, well, actions speak, too, damn it." She paused, then sighed. "Coffee's kicking in, I'm going to be grumpy until it does. Hang on, I'll pull up what I was able to find on this Alpha—"

"I'm sorry."

"No, I snapped, I'm—"

"*Stop*. You're right, I should have said something, and the Fringe's input is appreciated. I'm sorry."

She took a noisy slurp. "Okay."

"Are we all right?"

"Uh-huh." Hearing the sound of typing, I assumed she'd put me on speaker. "My notes are up. Would you do me a favor?"

I grabbed a notepad and pen and cleared a spot on the blotter. "Within reason. What did you have in mind?'

"Data first. The call came from a cellular number registered to Sarah Knott, fifty-nine, in Boise. Her family members include a son, Bradley. He's thirty-two, and he has a Facebook page that's wide open. Lists his residence as Coeur d'Alene. Favors the shirtless selfie. You think this guy is Company?"

"I think he's a were."

"Sounds like it, but…"

My pen tapped against the pad as I waited for her to finish. "But?"

"But if he's Company, then why is his security so shitty? They're spies, but he's got an electronic footprint the size of an elephant's."

I considered that. "What if the information you found is a decoy?"

"Could be, but…okay," she murmured after another shot of caffeine, "let's say all of this is legit. 'Alpha' is a thirty-something bro out in Idaho who's spent too much on self-tanner. Assume he's not the brightest."

"Go on."

"He's big, he's built. If he's a were, then he's also a big, built *wolf*. He and his buddies aren't going to get far in the Company, but this pack gives them a place to belong. And now you've got a bunch of jacked-up werewolves of moderate intelligence—"

"And Moyna and her wizard friend come to play. So they pick off Jeanine. Try to force the Company to see their side of things."

"Something tells me she won't be the last one. Give me a little time to finish my homework. We've got boots on the ground all over the northwest, and I'll see what we can dredge up on him. Yeah?"

"Much appreciated. And what was that favor you wanted, anyway?"

She sounded sheepish. "Don't tell my folks that I gave you lip, okay? Mom's worried enough about me as it stands."

I could have avoided the Unveiling. Helen had guilted Aiden into attending, and he knew Joey well enough to vouch that he wasn't an imposter. Heck, it would have been impossible to replicate Joey's expression, a nauseated smile that spoke equally of love, excitement, and sheer terror. Beyond that, I had no desire to socialize with the Inner Council—it's difficult to be cordial to people who wish you were dead. But Joey was my friend, and I wasn't going to leave him at the mercy of a roomful of wizards.

If Joey appeared green, Helen was resplendent, a dark-haired beauty in a violet dress and matching pumps. She sat beside him before the grand magus's desk, holding his hand and beaming reassurance.

"I don't know why I'm nervous," he'd confided earlier when I'd popped into the barn. He'd stood before the dresser mirror with one end of his tie in either fist, squinting at the glass like he'd never heard of a knot. "We're not related. There's no way in hell we're consanguineous. And I know my lines…"

Seeing the tremor in his hands, I'd taken the tie from him and executed a half-Windsor. "You're not going to mess this up. And if you flub a line, so what?"

"This means a lot to her, and…and I want this to be perfect."

I'd clapped him on the shoulders. "You're going to be fine, and should any of those bastards complain, Aiden and I will be there to shut them up." Stepping back a few paces, I'd given his attire a critical look—navy blazer and chinos, the uniform of the young—and stuffed a pocket square into his jacket. "Come on, let's not keep her waiting."

Not knowing if Toula's wards were operational, we three had braved the freezing wind and entered the silo the long way, accompanied by a pair of dour guards. The Council and the Carvers were already assembled around the walls when we arrived, and several magi—the installation heads, assumedly—had intercepted Joey to express their congratulations.

While the Council fixated on the couple, Rachel Carver

slipped from her husband's side and made her way to Aiden, who stood beside me, watching his sister work the room. Squeezing his arm, she murmured, "Don't you think it's time for a haircut?"

"Hi, Mom," he whispered, and let her melt into the throng.

Before I had a chance to concur, Greg called the proceedings to order, and the magi found their places. Greg sat behind his desk and scanned the room, nodding at us and at the Carvers. As his face creased into an irked frown, the door opened, and Toula hurried inside. "Sorry," she mumbled, shedding her overcoat to reveal a black suit, its professional luster dimmed only slightly by the gelled spikes atop her head. A few of the magi looked at her askance, but she grinned at Aiden and me as she hurried to the chair beside Greg's desk.

Greg cleared his throat and spread his hands. "We come together today for the Unveiling of the prospective bride and groom. Magus Prescott, are you prepared?" he asked the white-haired man monopolizing the coffee table.

The magus nodded and held his pen over a fat ledger. "Ready, Grand Magus."

Turning back to the candidates, Greg asked, "Who comes before me this day?"

Helen released Joey's hand with a final squeeze and stood. "Helen Isadora Carver, a wizard of the old blood, a woman grown, a magus by election of the Council. I come of my own free will and without deceit," she concluded, and exchanged grins with Joey as she sat.

Magus Prescott's pen scratched in the book, and Greg gave him a moment to catch up before turning to Joey. "Who else comes before me this day?"

He stood, straightened his jacket, and took a steadying breath. "Joseph Percival Bolin. I...I'm not of the blood, but I'm a man grown. I come of my own free will and without deceit." Joey sat and once more found Helen's waiting hand.

Greg's eyes twinkled behind his glasses, and I wondered if he was remembering his own turn before the Council with Missy at his side. "Who will vouch for this woman? Who can attest that she comes unveiled?"

At that, the Carvers stepped forward together. "I do," said Howard, uncomfortably cutting his eyes to the magi. "Howard Carver, a wizard of the old blood, a man grown. Helen is my daughter."

"And I do," Rachel chimed in, looking tense but less grim than Howard. "Rachel Voss Carver, a wizard of the old blood. Helen is my daughter."

Greg nodded to them both, then gestured to Aiden. My brother's eyebrows rose in question, but Greg beckoned him forward. As a few of the magi muttered, he looked at Helen, then back at Greg. "Aiden Carver," he said slowly, "born of the old blood and the old queen, a high lord of Faerie. Helen is my sister."

The scribe continued his slow work, and I examined Aiden's face as he returned to his spot on the wall. Howard seemed, by turns, ready to lunge at him and to shrink into the corner, but if his father's reaction bothered Aiden, he gave no sign.

When the pen came to rest, Greg asked, "Who will vouch for this man? Who can attest that he comes unveiled?"

Aiden's mouth quirked, and I stepped forward. "Coileán," I said to Greg, "king of Faerie by blood and right. Joseph is my friend."

That little declaration wasn't going to win Joey any points with the annoyed magi, but to my surprise, Toula rose as well. "Fotoula Pavli, born of the new blood and…uh…"—she glanced at Aiden, and they shrugged together—"and the other old queen, a woman grown. Joseph is my friend as well."

Far across the room, someone muttered, "Mongrel."

Toula's shoulders clenched, and as Aiden's face darkened like a thunderhead, I grabbed his shoulder to restrain him. Fortunately, Greg stepped in before the matter could escalate and pointed to a middle-aged man who stood with his arms folded. "Magus Mulligan, another outburst like that, and I *will* have your chain. Do you understand me?"

The offending magus bobbed his chin, and I realized he had to be kin to my brother's former tormentor. Aiden's expression hadn't softened with the man's acquiescence, but to my relief, he didn't start throwing fire when I released him.

Greg gave Magus Mulligan another hard look, then resumed the ceremony. "You who vouch for this woman and this man, I charge you to speak if they answer falsely," he said, and focused on the couple. "Do you swear that you are not now bound in marriage to another?"

"We do," they replied.

"Do you swear that you suffer no infirmity that would prevent you from freely entering into marriage?"

"We do."

"And do you swear that you come today willingly and with no motive other than the love you bear one another?"

They glanced at each other and smiled. "We do."

"Then I'm satisfied." Greg motioned for Toula to rise. "Unless this marriage is prohibited by blood, you'll have the Council's approval. Ms. Pavli, if you'd be so kind."

Toula moved into the space between Greg's desk and the pair of chairs, and stopped in front of Helen. "Don't worry, this doesn't hurt," she murmured, then held out her hand and began to mutter. As she cast the spell, a glowing orb manifested above her palm, solidifying in seconds into a brilliant green lattice. The orb rotated, and its tendrils pulsed with energy. "Wizard," Toula announced. "*Definitely* a wizard." A few of the magi chuckled, and she flicked her fingers. Helen's aural orb flattened and split over and over until sixteen green orbs hung between the two women. "To the fifth generation. A wizard of the old blood. Now, let's compare."

She took a step to her right, winked at Joey, and extended her other hand. "Not that we're going to see overlap," she murmured, eliciting grins from the couple before she began the incantation. As the room watched, Joey's orb shimmered into being, a spherical white mist that coalesced and began to solidify into a lattice. The orb shifted to blue, the color of all mundane lines…

But.

Deep within the lattice, like blood swirled into moving water, was a bright streak of red.

"Oh, no," Aiden whispered. "No, that's…oh, *shit.*"

The magi began to shout in protest as Joey turned frantically in his chair, looking for an explanation. As the cries crescendoed, Greg stood, raised his hands, and bellowed, "Quiet! I *will* have quiet!" It took a full twenty seconds for the voices to subside, and still Joey glanced around for a clue. Toula looked stricken, and Helen, frozen behind her green orbs, bit her lip. When the last of the magi fell silent, Greg caught Joey's attention and pointed to his orb. "Do you know what you're seeing?"

Joey shook his head. "I thought for sure we wouldn't overlap—"

"You don't." Greg's voice wasn't unkind, but I detected something hard below the surface. "Green in an aural orb denotes wizard blood, old or new. Blue denotes mundane." He pointed to Joey's, then quietly explained, "Red's the mark of fae blood."

The boy stared at him, then shook his head vehemently. "No. No *way*. I'm not—"

"It's less than a quarter, but still."

"For God's sake," Joey shouted, "I joust! In full *plate*!" He laughed, but the sound betrayed his rising fear. "You can't be serious, this is some sort of *joke*—"

"Toula," Greg murmured.

She flattened and split Joey's orb into sixteenths—fifteen blue, and one blazing red. "A great-great-grandparent," she said, avoiding Joey's darting eyes.

"Hardly enough to make a difference, Grand Magus."

But he pressed his lips together. "Helen, Joey...I'm sorry." He sighed. "I wish I could tell you otherwise, but there's nothing I can do."

"What do you mean?" Joey demanded, going to his feet. "I don't understand—"

"I can't sanction this marriage. I'm sorry, son, but...no. You, uh..." He made a face. "'Tainted' is such a strong word, but it's the truth. There's no getting around *that*," he said, gesturing to the red orb.

I had never seen Joey in a full-blown panic. His chest heaved, and he stared down at Helen, who watched with stunned confusion. "No," he whispered.

As the magi's voices rose again, purple-faced Howard pushed his way out of the press and jabbed his finger toward Joey. "If you so much as touch my daughter again, then so help me, I'll—"

"Shut up, Dad!" Aiden yelled, joining the cacophonous chorus. "You're not helping!"

"*You* don't tell me what to do!"

"Prove it," he growled, storming across the office through scattering magi.

I had only an instant to wonder about exactly what Aiden had gotten up to in my absence when I saw Helen reach for her fiancé. "Joey, I don't...I...please..."

Judging by the look on his face, he didn't even see her in that moment. Pale, shaking, and breathing like a sprinter, Joey turned about madly, but he was met on all sides by windowless bunker walls and hostile magi. "Got to get out of here," he whispered. "Got to get out, got to get out..."

Suddenly, a gate ripped open in the middle of the room, inches from where Aiden and his father were poised to come to blows. I jerked and looked at Toula, but she seemed as surprised as I was. Before either of us could investigate, however, Joey ran through the rift, and the gate sealed behind him.

"*Joey!*" Helen cried, leaping to her feet.

Toula, who'd had a head-on view of the gate, raised her voice over the clamoring wizards. "Looked like your place," she told me, then broke the spell and dissolved the orbs. "You want to—"

But that was all the hint Helen needed to create her own gate and jump through, and I beckoned to Toula. "Let's try to intercept. You can fight later, damn it," I added, grabbing Aiden's collar, and half-dragged him back to Faerie.

With her head start, Helen had disappeared around the bend in the corridor by the time the three of us arrived and closed the gate. I motioned for silence and listened, then pointed down the hallway. "Footsteps, that way. Come on."

When we found her, she had her forehead pressed against a section of unbroken wall. "Please come out," she said. "*Please*, Joey. Talk to me."

Toula gave us a warning look, then sidled closer to her. "What gives?" she murmured.

"Locked himself in. I got here in time to see the door vanish. Joey, please," she continued, raising her voice to be heard through the wall, "you've got to talk to me." That garnered no response, and Helen's face began to work. "Joey!" she cried, slapping the stone. "I'm not leaving. You can't hide from me all day."

"Night," Toula muttered, glancing at the nearest window, then took Helen's arm. "Come on, Carver, let's sit down for a second."

But Helen was unmoved. "*Joey!*" she begged. "Just talk to me." She hit the wall again, then closed her eyes and listened to the stillness around us. "I love you. Come back to me."

And then, muffled by the thick stone, we heard his faint voice: "Helen?"

She let out the breath she'd been holding. "I'm right here, sweetie. Will you come out?"

"I...I can't find the door," he said, sounding dazed. "I think it's gone. It's dark in here, and I can't feel the knob."

I willed the door back into being. After a few seconds of fumbling, Joey stumbled into Helen's embrace. "It's going to be okay," she murmured, rubbing his back. "Everything's going to be okay, I promise."

When he lifted his head from her shoulder, his eyes were red-rimmed. "I didn't know. I swear I had no idea, I didn't know—"

"It doesn't matter."

"But the grand magus said—"

"I know what he said. And I'm telling you, I don't care. Do you hear me, Joey Bolin? *I don't care.*"

As they held each other, I caught a gate opening from the corner of my eye and whirled around to find Eleanor hurrying down the hall in her nightclothes. "Realm's agitated," she explained. "Said the problem was here—what did I miss?"

Toula beckoned her closer. "Apparently, Joey's a touch fae. The Council flipped out."

A brow rose. "Do tell."

"All I know is he's one-sixteenth fae. Pretty much the definition of 'lesser blood,' but Greg's being stubborn."

Eleanor folded her arms over her bathrobe. "Who's that sixteenth, then?"

"You know, that's probably not the most important issue to address right now. Greg put the kibosh on the Arcanum-sanctioned wedding, Carver's dad's up in arms"—she glared at Aiden—"and little bro almost lost it, those two need some time to—"

"Daig," Joey mumbled.

Aiden looked at him sharply. "Huh?"

"Daig," he repeated. "Remember what Lailu said when we met her? Realm told her to expect a pair of daig. We thought she was confused, but then you—"

His eyes grew round. "*Shit*, man. The realm knew all along."

"No wonder she's never given me any trouble," said Joey, weakly shaking his head. "Of course she wouldn't. Not if I'm…"

My thoughts flashed back to a morning two years before, when the realm's petite avatar had yanked me from my isolation of grief. She'd smiled when I'd asked about keeping Joey around.

I welcome my own.

"Well," I said to Joey as Val and half a dozen guards jogged toward us, "since Faerie tolerates you, we can eliminate one court. But there's no reason to worry about this now. You two rest, talk this out…"

But Joey shook his head. "I need to know. Give me the worst, and let's get it over with." He paused, frowning. "Assuming you know something, I mean."

"I didn't get a chance to take a good look at the orbs," Toula told him, "but if you want…I can't make any guarantees, but I can check it against what I've got on file."

He met Helen's eyes, then nodded.

CHAPTER 15

As Toula gave Val and his team a quick rundown of the situation, I located a suitable sitting room and ushered Eleanor, Joey, Helen, and Aiden inside. Catching two of the guards before they could disperse, I murmured, "If you see anyone from the Arcanum try to break in, stop them. Use nonlethal force if possible, but if they fight back…" They nodded and took up positions outside the room, and Val followed me in.

The others pulled the furniture into a circle, and Joey and Helen landed on a green leather settee. His shoulders hunched, and his hands clenched over his knees, but Helen kept her arm around him and watched the room as if expecting an ambush. Once I'd locked the door and found a chair, Toula muttered, "Okay, take two," then started tapping on her quartz ring. As Joey's orb was projected above her hand, she gave him a reassuring smile. "I made the ring into a storage drive for these things. It's how I've been doing the court census for Aiden. Now, to isolate the faerie…"

The orb began its series of splits, but the blue halves disappeared each time, leaving only the red lattice to consider. She flattened it and peered at the swirls. "This could take a few minutes. Ellie, while I have you here, mind if I grab a reference sample?"

Eleanor cocked her head. "I suppose not, but I've never had children."

"Satisfy my curiosity, then." She held out her free hand and began her muttering anew. When Eleanor's red and blue orb crystallized, Toula split it, then tapped her ring until the image of a stored red one appeared and flattened. The two red lattices overlapped perfectly, and Toula nodded as she flicked Eleanor's away. "Well, that answers that. Megs was your sister."

Eleanor looked at the remaining red lattice with distaste. "Then that one belongs to—"

"Oberon. I got a full set for the Three by pulling from their kids." She frowned at the lattice, then slid Joey's closer for inspection. "Hang on," she muttered, tapping at her ring, and a series of red and green orbs flashed and dissolved until only a third red orb remained. As before, she flattened the orb and pulled it close to Oberon's, then focused on Joey's and gestured with two fingers. His remaining lattice split in half, and she moved the pieces atop the other projected signatures. "Match," she said, meeting Joey's worried eyes.

He sat stiffly, but I could see the blood draining from his face. "Who?"

A pair of lattices landed above each of Toula's upraised palms. "The match isn't to the unknown contributor in your aura. It's to our mystery man's parents."

Joey cocked his head. "*Man?* How do you know—"

"Because there's only one person it could be. Oberon, Titania," she said, lifting each hand. "Their child is your genetic donor."

"Their chi—" He froze mid-word.

"Yeah." The lattices disappeared, and Toula gestured to Eleanor, Aiden, and me. "Uh, folks…meet your nephew. Well, distant nephew, but—"

"*Robin?*" Joey yelped. "He was my…" Groaning, he buried his face in his hands and rocked on the sofa.

"It's all right," Helen soothed over his muttering, "it's okay, Joey, I'm right here…"

After a moment, he pulled himself together long enough to raise his head and look at her. "We're screwed. Once Greg finds out, he's never going to let us get married."

She cupped his chin in her palms and held on until he stopped rocking. "Hear me, and hear me well. Greg doesn't get a vote in this."

"But he said—"

"All that...*bullshit* means is that the Council's not going to support the marriage. There's not a damn thing they can do if we elope."

Joey's eyes welled, and he blinked to hide it. "You're a magus, Helen. You can't throw your career away."

"First, it's *my* career, so let me worry about it. And second, I'm not throwing anything away. You know what I want?" She pulled his face to hers and kissed him deeply, lingering long enough that Eleanor cleared her throat. "I love you, you crazy goober," Helen told Joey. "And I don't care what the Council thinks."

At a loss for a better plan, I opted to let the couple be and tried to sleep for a few hours. But even in dreams, I couldn't get the matter out of my mind, and so I rose before dawn and set off for the barn, assuming I'd find the lovebirds in the loft.

As I approached the sheep pen, I heard Joey's voice on the night wind, soft but unmistakable. Applying a touch of glamour to blend into the shadows, I slipped around the barn, then peeked inside to find Joey sitting with Val on a hay bale in the light of a solitary lantern. Georgie slept beside them, her snores a subwoofer rumble that rattled the storage canisters on the shelves. Across the well-trampled practice yard, a sheep bleat as it split in two.

"You're the same man now that you were yesterday," said Val as Joey picked a piece of straw loose and twisted it in his fingers. "Nothing's different. Whatever piece of the Puck you carry has always been part of you." He paused, watching Joey shred the straw. "I knew him when he was a child. Impulsive to a fault, but often clever. He simply failed to think matters through before acting."

"He was an asshole," Joey muttered.

"You just described most faeries."

Joey's mouth twitched, and he leaned back on his elbows. "Been trying to figure out where he fits into my family tree for the last hour."

"He was the grandfather to one of your grandparents, was he not?"

"Yeah, but pinpointing which one is the trick." Joey gazed at the shadow-shrouded rafters. "My dad's family is documented for generations. I pulled up my copy of the family tree when Helen dozed off, and my second-great-grandfathers are all accounted for: two farmers, a fisherman, and a blacksmith. About as mundane as you get."

"Unless one of them wasn't actually your blood," said Val. "You've eliminated the possibility of a dalliance?"

"No, and I was worried about that until I got to thinking about my mom's family." He sat up and began counting on his fingers. "Mom's an only child. Grandma and Granddad Murray were normal, as far as I know, but I never knew them well. Grandma died when I was six, and Granddad...he died two years later."

"Took his own life?" he asked.

"Close enough—drunk-drove himself straight into a tree. He never got over Grandma's death," Joey explained. "Mom said Granddad always had some issues—his mother ran out on him when he was a kid, and his father raised him alone. Buck and Ducky, everyone called them. Granddad couldn't pronounce 'Douglas' for a while."

Val's head tilted as he considered this. "What became of Ducky's mother?"

"See, that's the problem—no one knows. She ran off one day. Left a note, said she loved everyone but had to go. They never found a trace of her." His fingers chose a new piece of straw to worry. "And there was no sign that she'd run off with anyone. Liza," he said, folding and unfolding the straw. "Liza Bell, that was her name."

"Robin's child would be half fae," said Val. "At some point, this person would have realized there was something wrong with him."

"The iron allergy wouldn't have spontaneously popped up one day."

"That wasn't what I had in mind." He tucked his leg onto the bale and squinted at the lantern. "Some half-breeds raised in that realm come to magic early, instinctively. Others of us discover it by accident. I'm in that camp, and it wouldn't surprise me if your great-grandparent was, too. What do you know of Liza's upbringing?"

Joey made a face. "Not much. The Bells came from Baltimore, and I think her father—her presumed father—was a banker. Probably pretty ordinary."

"Very well. Assume that she grew up without any idea of what she was. She has a particularly bad allergy, but that's no reason to suspect anything magical, is it?"

"In turn-of-the-century Baltimore? Nope."

"So she marries Buck, has a son…and something happens. Something triggers it. Maybe she falls and stops herself, maybe she sets the house on fire, maybe she lashes out and hurts someone." Val leaned toward Joey as the dragon snuffled in her sleep. "Or perhaps she realized she'd stopped aging. That might have made her flee, if she thought she was putting her family in danger by staying."

Joey mulled that over. "She could still be out there. Or here already—Robin's children would be in Eleanor's court, right?" He paused. "Shit, what does that mean for me?"

"Court affiliation?" Val leaned against the wall and chuckled. "I chose my own. If you wanted to swear fealty to Eleanor, that would be your right, but I suspect Coileán would protest if she tried to poach you. He's quite fond of you. And he should do a better job of disguising himself if he wants to spy," he added, raising his voice above the snoring dragon.

Startled, Joey turned to the doorway, and I revealed myself. "Hi," I muttered. "Passing through."

Val rolled his eyes. "*Really*, my lord."

Joey slid down the bale, and I took a seat on the far end. "It would probably be for the best if we tracked down Robin's child," I told him, not bothering to pretend that I hadn't been eavesdropping. "Toula can run a blood trace on you—that would pinpoint any surviving great-grandparents easily enough."

"Okay. What about my parents?"

"What about them?"

Joey grabbed a fistful of straw from our makeshift bench. "The gate that opened today, right when I wanted it—Helen said she didn't make it. Did any of you?" I shook my head, and he wadded the straw into a messy ball. "So a gate spontaneously appears, right back to your place, and I happen to find a perfect room to get away from everyone. So perfect, in fact, that the door vanishes."

I looked past him to Val, who patted Joey's shoulder. "For those who come to magic later," he said, "there's usually something that pushes them over the edge. Magic's a last defense."

"But I don't have any talent," Joey protested.

He shrugged. "This may have been building. You've been here more than two years."

"So?"

"So prolonged exposure to a high concentration of magic, coupled with a spark of talent—do you see what I mean? I've known mundane changelings who developed a bit of skill when they'd been here long enough. But you, now, you aren't mundane. You just needed a push."

He tossed the straw ball into the darkness. "You think this is going to happen again?"

"Quite possibly."

"That means I've got to tell my folks." Catching our expressions, he explained, "I freaked out and flared. One of my parents is twice as fae as I am. Someone's got to warn them."

"If they remain in that realm," Val pointed out, "nothing may ever happen."

"But it *might*. And if it does, I don't want that hanging over my head."

"Another thing," I said. "The Fringe."

"What about it?"

"You qualify. Your quasi-fae parent qualifies, and the other would share the benefits. In case something should happen, it couldn't hurt to have Fringe contacts."

"I guess," he said, and smirked at me. "Trying to get rid of me, boss? Foist me off onto the Fringe and be done with it?"

I punched him in the arm. "Perish the thought. I've yet to settle on a favorite nephew—you may be in the running."

"Try great-great-grandnephew."

"Close enough." I slid off the bale and brushed down my trousers. "Shall we deliver the news in the morning? Your parents are in Virginia, aren't they?"

Joey nodded. "Today's still Saturday, right? They'll go to Mass tonight and work around the house tomorrow. Mom's making costumes for a few people before the Ren Faire season kicks off, and Dad...uh..." He hesitated as he met our enquiring looks. "How do we feel about smithies?"

The Bolin homestead was a modest farmhouse with white siding and blue shutters, a weather-faded mailbox, and an RV parked under a metal shed. A wide, winter-brown lawn rolled down to the dirt road fronting it, and a skeletal oak stood sentinel by the garage, a black-fingered victim of the season. Ringing the property on the other three sides was a patchy forest—nothing old-growth, not in the fertile Shenandoah Valley, but sufficiently dense with pines and hardwoods to give the place privacy. A distant hawk cried in the quiet of the late morning—and then, worryingly, I heard the ring of steel on steel.

Walking up the road beside me, bundled in a gray peacoat and cashmere scarf, Eleanor cocked her ear toward the sound and pursed her lips. "A smithy, you said?"

"Joey said he does custom work," I replied. "Armor, swords, what have you."

"Fantastic," she sighed.

I glanced at the rest of our pack as she prepared for the meeting. We made a motley crew: Joey in well-worn boots and his flying duster, a look straight off the cover of a post-apocalyptic Western; Helen on his arm, wrapped in a plaid shawl; Aiden keeping pace with them in a brown windbreaker and matching ski cap, his blond ponytail swaying with every step; and Toula and Val bringing up the rear, he in an overcoat largely appropriated from me, she in a puffy green jacket, pulling him along when he stopped to gawk at a passing plane. I hadn't intended for our party to be so unwieldy, but word spread, and no one with a plausible reason to take the field trip would be denied. Most framed their desire to accompany Joey as offering moral support, but I suspected that deep down, we all wanted to see the Ren Faire fanatics who had spawned him.

As we turned up the driveway, Joey pointed to the substantial brick outbuilding behind the house. "Dad's back there, I hear him. Guess that's as a good a place as any to start, right?"

"Whatever you think best," I said, glancing at the smoke curling from the smithy's chimney. "Though if we disturb him at his work—"

"I'll go first. Stay back until he puts the hammer down."

A short walk through the grass later, he paused outside the smithy's door and took a deep breath. "Ready?" I murmured.

"Nope," he said, squeezing Helen's hand. "But let's get this over with." With that, he squared his shoulders and cracked the door open, releasing a blast of heat. "Dad? Hey, Dad?"

I loitered close enough to catch the expression of the gray-haired man standing over a worktable inside, peering at the glowing piece of steel on his anvil. "Joey?" he said, blinking behind his bifocals, then broke into a wide smile. "*Joey!* What are you—Helen, sweetie!" he cried, abandoning his work to crush them in a sweaty hug. "What are y'all doing here? I thought your plane left Friday!"

Though he'd feigned confidence well only thirty seconds before, Joey began to hem and haw. "I, uh...different flight," he managed, rubbing his neck. "Um..."

"It's okay," Helen told him as he stammered. "Tell him."

The elder Bolin—Peter, I recalled—looked at her curiously, then at his son. "What's wrong, JoJo?"

Joey glanced away for a second, regaining his composure, then faced his father. "Dad...I need to talk to you. And Mom. It's, uh...something's come up."

"What's going—oh. Uh, hello?" said Peter, finally noticing the rest of us crowded near the door. "Are these your friends from the mission, Joey?"

"Something like that," I replied while Joey searched for the best lie. "Mr. Bolin, why don't we step inside the house?"

Though he shot Joey a worried frown, Peter sloughed off his gloves and apron and led us through the patio door into the kitchen. "Rebecca?" he called. "Joey and Helen are back! They brought friends!"

A moment later, a short blonde in sweatpants ran into the room, still sporting a pincushion on her wrist. "*Joey!*" she exclaimed, and the hugging resumed. "Sweetheart, aren't you supposed to be in Honduras?"

When he managed to break away, he turned to give us one last uncertain look, then faced his concerned parents. "There's something I need to tell you," he said quietly, and pulled his phone from his duster pocket. "This is going to take a few minutes."

Rebecca clasped his free hand. "What's wrong, sweetie? Has something happened to the mission site? Did your visa get messed up?"

Joey sighed. "Honestly…there *is* no mission. And I want to show you something," he said before they could interject. "It's not a big album, but have a look." He handed his phone to his mother and waited, watching over her shoulder as she scrolled. "That's Georgie. She's my bud. Well, more than that, but it's hard to explain," he said in a rush. "I raised her from a hatchling. There, that one— that's one of her baby pictures. Gosh, I forget how small she was…"

Rebecca frowned at the phone, and Peter looked over her other shoulder as she flipped through the pictures. "Is this CGI?" she finally asked. "You're…doing graphics work?"

"No. No trick photography, no editing. That's my dragon."

His mother's expression was bemused, but I spotted little tells of fear in her face. "I don't understand, Joey. What…what are you showing me?"

His Adam's apple bobbed as he took his phone back. "Magic is real. And there's something you need to know."

Over the next thirty minutes, Joey made a full confession in the sunny kitchen. As he spoke, his parents' expressions shifted through worry, alarm, and disbelief. When he told them of the Arcanum, they stared at him in incredulity, then gawked at Helen, who stood by with her arms folded. And then, once he'd recounted the disastrous Unveiling, he fell silent and waited. Watching them struggle, he turned to me and asked, "Do you suppose you could swing a demonstration, boss? Nothing huge, just something to let my folks know I'm not crazy?"

"That's still up for debate," I replied, but held out my palm. The Bolins stared with saucer eyes as a globe of blue fire appeared. "Here," I told them, lobbing it into the air, and they scrambled backwards as it floated in their direction. When it came to rest, Rebecca hesitated, then slowly approached the hovering fireball. "I wouldn't do that," I cautioned as her finger stretched toward the fire. She retracted her hand like a sprung trap, and the fire disappeared without a trace of smoke. "Harmless to the one who makes it, nasty if it hits anyone else. A simple bit of enchantment, but effective nonetheless. And no one here intends you ill," I said as she shrunk toward the table, "so you needn't worry. No one's getting turned into a toad."

She swallowed. "That's...a possibility?"

"Technically, yes," said Eleanor, "but that's messy and pointless. Do be seated, dear, your legs are wobbling." Peter pulled out a chair, and as Rebecca sank down, he stood guard behind her, gripping her shoulder. When neither gave any indication of imminent fainting, Eleanor clasped her hands together. "I fear this has been disconcerting—"

"Disconcerting? Shit, they're *terrified*," Toula interrupted, and flipped a flopped spike of hair from her forehead. "Hi, I'm Toula, and I'm definitely not the scariest person in the room, so relax." The Bolins nodded weakly. "The original plan was to keep you out of the loop. Most mundanes get twitchy when they see behind the curtain, and the Arcanum gets even twitchier when non-wizards get wind of its existence. But in light of what we've learned about Joey, you needed to be clued in. It's a matter of safety."

"Safety?" Peter echoed, clutching the steadying edge of

the table.

"Yeah, safety. Here's the deal." Toula cut her eyes to Helen. "The Council hasn't liked Joey from the get-go, partly because he's been hanging out with Coileán, but mostly because he's not good enough for their precious snowflake."

"*Hey*," Helen snapped.

Toula brushed her off. "He's not. Carver's the best wizard born in decades, and wizards tend to marry other wizards. There's less to explain that way, but there's also a better chance of having kids who are wizards instead of witches or duds."

"Weak wizards or those born without any talent," Helen clarified.

"Bingo. Now, the Council would like nothing better than for Carver to marry another strong wizard and have lots of kids, so Joey was already close to the bottom of their list of matrimonial candidates as a mundane. He and Helen *could* have a litter of wizards, but the odds aren't as good. And then we got this new wrinkle."

Toula cocked her thumb at Aiden. "Rapunzel over there and I are witch-bloods—witch-blooded fae if you're being technical, mongrels if you're an ass. Faerie-wizard cross, a fifty-fifty split. Most of the time, witch-bloods have close to zero talent, but I'm a freak of nature, and he's a special case. That said, we don't have a lot of data on what happens when you cross a wizard and a lesser blood. Joey's fae content is low enough that he and Helen might still have talented kids, but no one can say for certain."

"Couple that with the Arcanum's hatred of anything coming out of Faerie, and you see the problem," my brother added. "And it's Aiden, actually, not Rapunzel."

"Says the boy with the flowing locks," Toula muttered.

"Says the *porcupine*."

"Children, please," Helen sighed, then offered the Bolins an uneasy smile. "Rebecca, Peter...the thing is, I love Joey." She rested her hand on his shoulder, and he reached back to clasp it. "They can't stop us from getting married. But knowing who—and now *what*—he is, we're concerned that they might try to put pressure on you."

"You need to know what's going on before a gang of wizards shows up on the front step," said Joey, and shuddered. "Trust me, that doesn't end well."

"With your permission," Helen continued, "we'd like to hook you up with the Fringe—the techie folks Joey mentioned, yeah? One of you qualifies for membership— we're not sure which, but it's simple enough to find out. The other gets spousal protection. The Fringers take care of their own, and it wouldn't hurt to have them on speed dial."

"They also run a support group," I offered. "A fellow in Rigby is one of the higher-ups. He's probably seen most of the permutations on the spectrum by now."

The Bolins looked at each other, and Peter tightened his grip on his wife's shoulder. "You're saying that one of us is…uh…"

"Slightly fae," said Toula. "One-eighth, to be exact."

He frowned. "But, like…that fire trick. Nothing like that has ever happened to us."

"It wouldn't." I shrugged. "In terms of ability, there's no difference between full faeries and half fae. But once you get a lower percentage than that…"

"I've known of four quarter fae," Eleanor added. "Three aged normally, and one made it to one hundred twenty before the inevitable. Their power wasn't at all reliable. Someone at an eighth could have no apparent talent."

Suddenly, Val slipped from his place by the door and looked at Rebecca. "Something is troubling you."

"What *isn't* troubling right now?" Peter countered. "Y'all told us—"

But Rebecca shook her head, and he fell into a confused silence. "My daddy," she murmured, looking back at Val. "He…" She took a long breath, then turned to Joey. "There are some things you don't know about Granddad. You were little when he died, and…I guess there was no reason for it to come up."

Joey clasped his mother's hand. "Go on."

"My daddy," she said, glancing at the rest of us, "was one of the kindest people I've ever known. Good man, worshipped the ground my mother walked on. But…" She hesitated. "Daddy had a temper. He didn't lose it often, but when he did, he would *rage*. I only saw it a few times, because whenever he blew his stack, Mom would make him go out to the woodshed until he calmed down. I didn't know why until I was ten."

Rebecca's expression was inscrutable. "We were in a cold snap one weekend, and the power company had cut us off—a clerical error, but nothing we could fix until Monday. Daddy called from the neighbors' farm, but he couldn't get anyone to help us. By the time he got home, he was fit to be tied. Angry, embarrassed, chilled to the bone…and he started yelling about the power man. He was going into a fit, and Mom told him to go outside, but the wind was howling, and it had started to snow. I was hiding on the stairs, waiting for him to calm down, when the glass started shattering. Mom screamed, and Daddy got quiet, and I came in to see…"

She stared into space. "Every window in the kitchen was gone, and snow was blowing in over the sink and the table. The glass front of the china hutch, all of her crystal goblets…well, Mom was standing there in the middle of the room with her hands over her mouth, and Daddy looked so guilty. He got a broom and swept everything, boarded up the windows, fixed all the glass when the storm was over, and Mom forgave him, but I understood the woodshed then.

"He was careful after that, but…you know, no one's perfect. It happened twice more—when you temporarily dumped me for Wendy Pugh," she said, looking at Peter, "and after Mom's funeral. You'd taken Joey back to the motel after supper, and I was cleaning the dishes, and he'd been drinking all afternoon—"

"Baby," Peter whispered, crouching beside her chair, "why didn't you tell me? God Almighty, I wouldn't have left you there alone with—"

"Because I did it, too." She looked into his eyes as hers began to water. "Just once. You were out of town, and Joey was colicky, and I was so tired…"

Her voice faded, and Peter's jaw dropped. "The TV?"

"There was no power surge. Just…me. I'm so sorry…"

He wrapped his arms around her, holding her as she quietly cried. I considered stepping outside to give her a minute, but Toula, wasting no time, extended both palms and began muttering. As the Bolins watched, a pair of spheres manifested: a solid blue orb by Peter, and one with a telltale streak of red by Rebecca. "Aural analysis," Toula explained before they could ask. "Congratulations, Peter, you're as mundane as they come. As for you, Rebecca…well…" She tossed her head toward the rest of us. "Meet your kin."

A few tense minutes later, Joey coaxed his parents onto the couch in the adjoining den, and Eleanor pulled a lacy handkerchief from midair and offered it to Rebecca. She stared dumbly at the cloth, and Eleanor began, "I know this must come as a shock—"

"How…" she interrupted, looking from the handkerchief to Eleanor. "That…but how…"

"Magic. When in doubt, that's almost certainly the answer."

"But…but that can't…" Flabbergasted, she peered at Eleanor, then at the rest of us, and finally managed, "Y'all can *all* do that?" We nodded, and Rebecca slowly exhaled. "Okay. O…*kay*," she mumbled, and turned to Peter, who seemed as baffled as she was. "Magic. That's…that's magic. *Real* magic." Wheeling back on us, she prodded herself in the breast, then demanded, "And I—*me*—I'm…"

"Somewhat fae," said Toula.

Rebecca blinked as if clearing a mirage, then reached for Peter's arm and took a few deep breaths. When she seemed to have retreated from the brink of panic, I slowly approached under her husband's watchful eye. "There's something else we wanted to tell you. Joey thought about it, and he's guessing that Ducky's mother was our niece. Ducky was your father, right?"

Her eyes, though still wide, were once again beginning to focus. "Yeah."

"And his mother, Liza—no one knows what became of her?"

"That's right."

Given the Bolins' state at that moment, I tried to choose my words carefully. "If Liza is who we think she is, then she's, uh…like us," I said, pointing to Eleanor and Val. "And that means she may still be out there. If so, we need to find her."

Rebecca's expression grew troubled. "How?"

"A blood trace can take care of it," Toula explained. "I'll get Joey to give me a sample and set one up this afternoon."

"The concern is that Liza may be unaware of her full abilities," said Eleanor. "She may need instruction to ensure she's not a danger to herself."

Rebecca mulled that over, then bit her lip and looked up at me. "So…my grandmother may still be alive? And you're going to find her?"

"That's the idea, yes."

"Well…in that case, can I come, too?"

CHAPTER 16

As the morning was drawing to a close and neither of the elder Bolins was in any shape to consider lunch, Toula produced a stack of pizzas and several bottles of soda. "I'm going to apologize in advance for the drinks," she said as a sleeve of plastic cups appeared beside her. "My Coke always tastes flat, and the others are either going to be too sweet or not sweet enough."

Peter gingerly prodded one of the bottles, which was cold enough to sweat. "Considering that those popped out of midair, you probably shouldn't be too tough on yourself."

When Rebecca's back was turned, I muttered to him, "Need something harder?"

Relief flickered in his eyes. "You've got a flask in that coat?"

"No, but pick your poison."

Peter poured himself half a glass of Toula's off-brand cola and whispered, "Rum?" The liquid level rose by two inches, and as Peter took a test sip, his eyes flew open wide. "*Whoa.*"

"Too strong?"

"No, it's fantastic. What am I drinking?"

"The original came from Barbados," I said, peering into the nearest pizza box. "Moderately aged. A friend of an associate was a connoisseur, and I might have pilfered the bottle from his stores. He didn't miss it. Old boy used to buy his liquor by the barrel."

Peter swirled his drink and sipped again. "Expensive

taste."

"Yes, but I believe his uncle had a plantation down there." I pulled a couple of meat-topped slices free and added my own olives. "But all of this was in about 1745, I think, so the details have gone fuzzy."

He goggled, then drank too deeply and sent a generous swig down his windpipe.

"All right?" I asked, thumping him on the back as he coughed.

"Fine," he gasped. When he'd caught his breath again, he wiped his eyes, drank properly, and said, "I'm guessing this is old hat to Joey, huh?"

"He adapted quickly," I mumbled, following his gaze to his son, who was sitting beside Rebecca in the next room. "Sorry…is it too much, too soon?"

But Peter shook his head and kept drinking. "It's a lot, but I'm not running for the hills yet." He looked me in the eye and lowered his voice. "Be honest with me—is my family in danger?"

"Maybe. It's too early to say one way or another, but…maybe."

"Then tell me how to protect them."

I sighed and put my laden plate down. "Joey's usually with one of us or with Helen, and odds are decent that if he's in Faerie, that dragon he showed you is within shouting distance. She's *highly* protective of him. Rebecca, though…do you have a mobile phone?"

"Of course." He frowned, pulling one from his pants pocket. "Why?"

I flipped mine open and found Slim's number. "This is for Rick Matherson in Rigby. I'll tell him to expect your call. He runs a bar, though, so if you want to stay on his good side, don't call in the middle of the day."

Peter punched the number into his phone. "This is that Fringe thing y'all were going on about?"

"Exactly. They'll send warning if something comes up. Other than that…" I paused, making sure that Rebecca was still occupied, then muttered, "How's your aim?"

"I've had a Winchester and a compound bow for the last thirty years, if that's what you're asking."

"Good. Keep them in working order. Helen figured out some steel ammunition once for Joey—ask her to do the same for you. If possible, keep something iron-based and pointy on hand. A switchblade, even a pocketknife. A sword might be overkill," I added, glancing out the window at the smithy, "but you get the gist."

Putting his empty cup aside, Peter dug in another pocket and extracted a three-inch folding knife. "Like this?"

"Open it." I held my hand close to the nicked blade and felt the warning tingle. "Yeah, that'll do. Severe contact allergy," I explained. "Iron and silver, but iron's better in a fight."

Recognition creased his features. "Cold iron. That's real?"

"*Painfully* real. If a faerie comes after you, reach for that. If it's a wizard…well, a slug in the chest is a slug in the chest." Seeing his unease, I added, "Tell you what, I'll ask Toula to set up early-warning wards around your property."

"Wards?"

"Think of it as a magical fence. It'll keep unwanted visitors out, or at least slow them down."

Peter smiled wryly. "Give me time to get my gun?"

"And to call me," I said, pecking at my phone again. "Here, my direct line."

He copied the number. "Thank you, uh…"

"Colin's fine."

"Colin. Thank you." He finished his drink, then looked me in the eye a second time. "You promise me you're taking care of my boy?"

"As well as I can. He's helped Aiden and me far more than I'm comfortable admitting. You, uh…you raised a good one, Peter. I'm sorry if you had your heart set on him becoming a priest—"

"*Lord*, no. Glad he got that out of his system. I mean, it's a fine calling, but Rebecca and I were hoping for grandkids."

"Would you take little wizard grandkids?" I asked.

He turned his attention to the pizza. "I'll love them, whatever they are. One more question, eh?"

I bit into my first slice, which, to my dismay, was approaching room temperature. "Go ahead."

Peter smirked. "I'm guessing we shouldn't call the Carvers and try to work out a pre-wedding get-together, should we?"

When the pizzas were gone, Eleanor noticed the half-finished costume Rebecca had been sewing when we barged in. Holding the parti-colored hose to the light, she nodded approval and neatly folded them. "Nice work. You do all your stitching by hand?"

"Some," said Rebecca, who was calmer after her own stealthy rum and Coke. "That's for one of the boys Joey used to ride with—Mark Gorey," she added, turning to her son. "He needed something that wasn't polyester."

Joey made a face and shook his head. "He can have it. No hose for me."

"They look authentic," Eleanor replied, carefully holding the matching woolen tunic to avoid the pins. "And this is lovely. Why are you so opposed? I had a pair of hose like those once."

His brows rose. "That's supposed to make me feel better about strutting around in them?"

"I was passing as a man at the time," she said with a shrug, "so yes. They were fashionable."

"She's right," I added. "Come on, hose is more comfortable than armor, isn't it?"

"It's a different kind of uncomfortable," said Joey. "And I'll bite: why the cross-dressing?"

Eleanor put the tunic aside. "When I was a girl, shortly before I was to be married, I met my first wizard. He tried to kill me, and I went on the run. Easier to hide in plain sight as a man."

"God," Rebecca murmured, "that's horrible—"

"Oh, it was for the best. My intended much preferred the company of men. Of *boys*, actually." Her lips tightened to a disapproving line. "Anyway, this being about 1325, it made sense to go as a man. Not a difficult task—I grew up with six brothers." Peter and Rebecca stared at her in stunned silence, and Eleanor rubbed her arm. "Ehm…something I said?"

"*What* year?" Rebecca whispered.

Before she could answer, Joey intervened. "Remember when I said they stop aging, Mom?"

"Well, yes, but…I didn't think…"

"You're trying so hard to be polite and not ask me my age," Eleanor interrupted. "I'm long past the point of caring. Born the fourth of April 1309, if you're keeping score."

Her eyes flicked back and forth as she made the quick computation. "You're…*seven hundred and six*?"

"Seven this spring." She flicked her hand toward Val and me. "Those two are older. The others are babes."

"Thirty-seven is slightly beyond 'babe,'" Toula protested, earning a pat on the head from her brother. "What? I'm legal. More than Rapunzel can say."

"Dang it, *stop*," Aiden griped.

"If you complain about the nickname, she's going to keep it up," I warned him, and turned to Joey. "Daylight's burning, kid, so roll up your sleeve. Time to make a donation."

He let Toula draw a pint with barely a flinch while his unnerved parents looked on. While he went out to the RV to filch their atlas, she explained, "I've had practice with this spell, and given that I'm only expecting to see a handful of hits, this shouldn't take many hours. That said, this isn't an immediate process, and I'm going to need privacy to concentrate. Could I set up around here? Got a spare room I could borrow?"

They looked at each other, silently communicating in the subtle physical language of the long-married, and Peter nodded. "Sure, not a problem. I think we're going to take it easy for the rest of the day. Uh, where were all y'all planning to stay?" he asked the rest of us. "There's a motel back in town—"

"Thank you," said Eleanor, "but I'm going back. Boys, Helen, why don't we give them some space, hmm?"

"We'll be in the loft," said Helen, and muttered a gate into existence. "Toula, come get me if you need relief."

Joey hugged his dumbstruck parents and followed her, and Aiden and Eleanor quickly took their leave. "I'll be fine," Toula assured Val and me as we lingered near the open gate. "How much trouble could I possibly get into?"

But Val was unmoved. "You can't cast and protect yourself simultaneously."

"I'm fine."

"*Fotoula.*"

"*Valerius.*" She pointed to Peter and said, "That nice man has a sword collection, and I'm sure he knows how to use it."

Unconvinced, he shook his head. "If something disturbs you—"

"I'll come running. Go home, mi frater."

Val sighed in resignation, then kissed her forehead and slipped away. I followed, but before my gate closed, I heard Toula tell the Bolins, "Big brother, over-protective. Do you have a coffeemaker?"

The sun was on the ascent by the time I fell into bed, and I blacked the windows to let myself rest. Having not had a good night's sleep in several days, I collapsed and trusted that the realm could look after itself for a few hours.

Exhaustion is its own sort of magic, and I knew nothing until Val nudged me awake that afternoon. "Toula says she's found the match," he began while I groaned into the pillow. "Should we proceed without you?"

In minutes, we'd reassembled in the Bolins' kitchen, where Toula sat at the table, rubbing her head with one hand and clutching a stained mug with the other. She looked ragged after her night's work, but Peter and Rebecca appeared the worse for wear. Sporting sweats and slippers, both bore the telltale dark bags of a sleepless night, and each held a mug like Toula's. Then again, it had to be early yet—the house was cold, and there was no sunrise glow through the eastern windows.

"Morning," Toula muttered, and swung the mug over the open atlas. "Lucked out. Target's in the States."

"Where?" I asked, slipping past the huddled Bolins to read the map.

"Baltimore," she yawned. "Looks like Liza went home." I followed her finger to a side street a few blocks from the Inner Harbor, where a drop of blood marked the target's location. "The only other hits were here, so this has to be the one. She moved to her current spot about two hours ago."

"Out and about already? What time is it?"

"Closing on four, but she works at a donut place, so I'm not surprised."

Eleanor, who had joined us at the map, frowned at Toula's pronouncement. "How do you know?"

Though weary, Toula managed to smirk as she lifted her phone off the table. "Street View is a wonderful thing. A little cross-referencing, and *boom*. Sunrise Sweets opens in"—she tapped the phone on—"half an hour."

Duly chastised, Eleanor crossed her arms and muttered, "Silly question?"

"Uh-huh." She stretched and slurped her coffee. "I've been through Baltimore a few times, but if anyone else wants to do the gates, be my guest."

I considered the map again, then tapped a cross-street two blocks inland. "Close enough for you?"

"Yeah. Let me finish my breakfast."

Toula chugged the rest of her drink while the Bolins anxiously stood by. Catching his parents' expressions, Joey said, "This won't hurt, I promise. Done it a zillion times."

Peter still looked uneasy, but Toula set her mug aside, tucked the blood-dotted atlas under her arm, and gestured to the empty space by the kitchen island. "Hit it, Gramps. Daylight's burning."

"What daylight?" I grumped, but opened the gate onto an alley and slipped out behind a Dumpster.

The others quickly followed suit—all but the Bolins, who hesitated on the far side and stared at the predawn city. "Come on, Mom," said Joey, holding out his hand. "Trust me."

Rebecca gave him a measured look through the rift. "*Honduras.*"

"That wasn't a lie, that was a cover story. Totally different things."

"*Sure* they are." Still, she latched on to his hand and nodded. "Okay. Let's do this," she said as she closed her eyes, then tensed as if anticipating a blow and stepped through.

"It's over," Joey told her a few seconds later when she showed no sign of relaxing. "You made it. Mom? *Hey,*" he said, snapping in her face, "look at me."

She blinked, noted her surroundings with a relieved sigh, then beckoned to Peter, who still waited in Virginia. "Oh, that's *easy*. Hurry, Pete, you're holding up the parade."

He crossed on his own steam, and I closed the gate before they could have second thoughts and quickly exchanged their bedroom slippers for sneakers. "The harbor's that way," I said, pointing down the alley as the Bolins goggled at their feet. "Toula, you have the address?"

"*GPS* has the address," Aiden interrupted, holding his

phone out, "so let's go, I'm freezing. Say what you want about Oberon, but at least he had sense enough to move to the Keys."

Five minutes later, as the wet wind reminded us that January wasn't the ideal time to sightsee in Maryland, we reached a little storefront squeezed between a drug store and a sandwich shop. Warm yellow light spilled from its plate windows under striped awnings and puddled around the plastic tables and chairs on the sidewalk. I walked closer to inspect the logo on the door, half a sprinkle-topped donut peeking over the water like the rising sun, and motioned for the others to join me. "This is it, but they're not open…"

My voice trailed off when I saw a young woman emerge from the back, bearing a tray of muffins. She'd tucked her bright red ponytail under a baseball cap, but there was no denying her familiar features. She was perhaps half a foot shorter than he'd been and proportionally slimmer, but…

"Good heavens," Eleanor murmured beside me, "she looks just like Robin."

"I noticed."

"How is she going to…*ah.*"

The woman tripled her foodservice gloves before opening the steel door at the back of the glass-fronted counter. She slid the tray inside, straightened a placard, and closed the door—and then, perhaps feeling the eighteen eyes watching her, she looked at the window and jumped. Breaking into an embarrassed grin, she held up one finger, then flipped on the television mounted in the corner and hurried to the door to unlock it. "I'm so sorry, I'm not open yet," she said, "but it's too cold to stand out there. Come in, I'll be with you in a second. Coffee's almost up."

The scent of the well-heated store was glorious, a drool-inducing perfume of medium roast and warm sugar. I took a seat at a bistro table, keeping one eye on the CNN ticker while sneaking glances at the redheaded proprietress.

While Aiden made a beeline for the pastry case, Eleanor joined me, and I saw in her eyes the question that had come to my mind: what was the best way to go about this? *Hi, we think you're our niece* seemed too direct.

If she had any idea who we were, she'd shown no sign; her polite, flustered smile spoke of nothing but professional cordiality. Over the next few minutes, she lugged more trays of sugary delights from the kitchen, and as the coffeemaker clicked over to its warming setting, she mimed wiping her brow and took her place behind the waist-high counter. "Good morning, folks," she said with a little wave. "What can I get you?"

The moment had come, but before Eleanor and I could make our move, Rebecca slipped to the head of the line and stared into the woman's dark eyes. "I'm looking for Liza Bell," she murmured.

"That's me. Can I—"

In that instant, recognition registered on her face, and she retreated a step from the counter as her muscles tensed. Seeing her mood shift, Rebecca held out a hand to stay her. "Wait, please—I'm sorry, I…I'm Ducky's daughter, I'm—"

"Rebecca," Liza whispered, her cheeks draining to the color of whey.

"You know about me?" she asked, surprised, then reached across the counter to grab Liza's wrist. "Don't go. I know why you ran away—why you look like you do. Please, I just want to talk to you. These folks with me, they're here to help."

Her eyes widened in fright, and Toula hastily added, "We're not feds. No black vans, promise."

That seemed to calm her a degree, but Liza still breathed heavily as slipped free of Rebecca's grasp. "Wait there, I'll be back," she managed to say before disappearing into the kitchen. She returned with a battered wallet, reached into an inner pocket, and extracted a wad of yellowed newsprint. Her hands shook, and Rebecca helped her spread the clippings on the counter.

"Mom and Dad's wedding announcement," Rebecca whispered, smoothing one piece flat. As she bent down to read the next, she laughed incredulously. "This is—"

"Your birth announcement," said Liza. "I had to stop taking the paper after that, I'd moved too far away again…" Slowly, as if moving underwater, Liza reached across the counter and placed her trembling, gloved palm against Rebecca's cheek. "You look like him," she said as her eyes filled. "Like my little Ducky."

Rebecca covered Liza's hand with her own, then pointed across the room. "My son," she said, and Joey went to his feet. "He took after Dad, too."

Liza gasped as she noticed him, and the tears began to fall. "Oh, my God, he…"

She nodded as Liza covered her mouth. "I know, it's striking. Joey's our only child." She gently pulled Liza's hand from her face to clasp it between her palms. "And I was Dad's only child. I don't know if you…if you saw…it was almost twenty years ago…"

Liza sniffed. "I keep the obituaries at home. But…but how did you—"

"How did we find you?" Eleanor offered as she stood. "Magic, and I'm not being flippant." She looked out the windows at the empty sidewalk, then waved a couple of floor-to-ceiling shades into existence, giving us privacy from any passersby. "Joey, be a dear and lock the door," she said, and turned back to the counter to find Liza staring at the new shades in shock. "Don't be alarmed, Ms. Bell, but your uncle and I need a word with you."

We coaxed Liza into a chair, and while Rebecca went to the back to save some muffins from burning, I coaxed three quick shots of vodka down Liza's throat. "No fainting," I told her, pulling up another seat. "I'm sure you have questions. Oh, and don't worry, he'll pay for whatever he eats," I added as Aiden gloved up to raid the pastry case. "Now, let's talk about your father."

Toula poured Liza a cup of coffee, and she wrapped her hands around it and stared at nothing while Eleanor and I spoke. Twenty minutes later, we'd hit most of the salient points, and she sat shell-shocked in our little semicircle as Joey and Aiden continued their quest to sample one of everything in the store. As we wound down, Eleanor squeezed Liza's arm and said, "We're here to help you. The better you understand your talents, the less likely you'll be to have an accident with them. You've never tried to use magic before, have you?" Liza slowly shook her head, and Eleanor released her grip. "Come back with us, at least for a little while. You don't have to stay, but for your own safety, you need to understand who and what you are." She hesitated. "The day after Christmas, did you, ehm…*hear* anything? A summons?"

A sheen of panic glazed Liza's eyes. "I thought I was losing my mind. What was—"

"That was from me, and that does answer one question." Eleanor glanced my way. "Robin chose our father's court, I inherited it, and you, I suppose, were born into it. Of course, you have blood ties to Coileán and me, and I doubt Joey will ever be persuaded away from Coileán"—he looked up, his cheeks puffed with donut, and shook his head—"so if you want to distance yourself from Robin, I'll understand." She drummed her fingers on the tabletop and frowned. "You *did* know that your mother's husband wasn't your biological father, didn't you?"

Liza's chin dipped and rose. "I knew. I don't look anything like my father, and they told me eventually. When I was old enough to know why people were talking." We waited while she let out a slow breath. "My mother was raped."

"I'm so sorry," said Eleanor. "Truly. It's…" She struggled to choose her words. "Unfortunately, it's a common occurrence among our kind. Your conception, I imagine, was similar to mine." An edge crept into her voice. "Robin had much in common with our father."

"Mother was no better," I muttered. Seeing Liza's brows knit, I explained, "She had the power to do almost anything she wanted and no scruples to prevent her from doing so. For whatever reason, she decided to toy with my father, and..." I looked up, but my brother's attention was on the croissants. "She punished Aiden's. That's part of the reason why I've been eager to get as many faeries out of this realm as I can—if we can corral them over there, we can prevent...well, the incidents that led to *us*. But we're not trying to force you to relocate—half fae are a different matter. I assume you're mostly law-abiding, aside from whatever falsified ID you're holding."

Liza sighed and nodded. "No one looks like this at a hundred and eight."

"Oh, *child*," Eleanor replied with a snort. "We'll talk."

She stared into her untouched coffee. "I only returned to Baltimore a few years ago—when I was sure everyone who'd known my family was gone. I'd been a scandal, you see. Everyone but Father thought Mother had cheated on him. He was the only one who believed her about the red-haired man." Her jaw clenched. "And then I almost killed her in delivery. They couldn't have another child, so that was us—the cuckold, the whore, and the reminder. That son of a bitch ruined my parents' chances of having the family they wanted, and he never showed his face again."

The stacks of plates and mugs began to rattle, and Liza squeezed her eyes closed until the shaking ceased.

As the room fell silent, Joey choked down his latest bite and slipped back around the counter. "I met him," he told her. "We didn't know anything about the connection, but I did meet him. I was there when he died."

Liza's hands balled into tight fists. "Painfully, I hope."

"Burned alive."

She considered that, then sniffed. "Good. May he rot in hell."

I hesitated, then said, "If it makes you feel better, we

weren't fond of him, either. I think I dealt with him more than you did, Eleanor—"

"Lucky you," Eleanor muttered.

"He was usually insufferable," I told Liza. "Cruel when it suited him. I know you're not the only child he sired, but I can't say how many like you are out there."

"Actually, I know of two," offered Eleanor, "but they're both full-blooded, so there's no reason to rush that meeting unless you're curious."

"Here's the truth of the matter," I said, and waited until Liza's eyes met mine. "You obviously have a life here. If you're happy, great. We just want you to have the skills you need to take care of yourself in the long term. And, uh…I think Rebecca and Joey might want to get to know you."

"Absolutely," said Rebecca with a hopeful smile.

Liza gave her a long, searching look, then began to tear up. "I *abandoned* your father. Why would you want anything to do with me?"

Rebecca leaned toward her. "Because I understand. I saw what happened whenever Daddy got angry. I blew out a television and three windows when I was at my wits' end. I showered my baby in *glass*. I get it, you didn't want to hurt them. And you were scared, and you've lived your whole life knowing that deep down, there's something wrong with you." She took Liza's hands, then glanced over her shoulder at Peter. "God help me, I thought about running, too."

"But you didn't—"

"Trust me, I thought about it long and hard. I wouldn't have been able to live with myself if I'd hurt my family. It hasn't happened again, but I live with that nagging fear that one day, I'm going to lose control, and everything around me is going to *explode*." Lacing her fingers through Liza's, Rebecca murmured, "You would have had to disappear eventually. I get it now. And Daddy…I think he would have understood. He loved you. He kept hoping you'd come home, but…" She looked into Liza's welling eyes and nodded. "He would have forgiven you, Grandma. I forgive you."

The dam broke, and as Liza burst into tears, Rebecca embraced her and rubbed her shuddering shoulders. "I'm sorry," Liza sobbed. "I'm so sorry, I—"

"Shh. It's okay." She pulled back far enough to see Liza's streaming eyes. "You're not alone anymore. You've got a family…I mean, if you want one…"

Liza nodded as she wept. While she tried to stop the flood, Toula squatted beside her chair and said, "Just a thought, but maybe today would be great for a sick day, huh? Maybe all this week?"

She sniffed and swiped at her nose. "Vacation?"

"That's the spirit. So I'm going to go hang a sign in the window," she said as a piece of paper materialized in her hand. "Let's get you somewhere more comfortable. Hey, Ellie," she added as she headed for the front of the store, "how're you set for guest rooms?"

"I'd love to have you," Eleanor told Liza, then looked at me strangely and cut her eyes to Toula.

"Don't fight it," I whispered. "The girl's on a first-name basis with anyone she likes. But since she ignores protocol, you can get away with this." I raised my voice. "Hurry it up, Glinda! We don't have all day."

"Bite me," she retorted, conjuring up a strip of tape.

"Such a remarkable display of maturity," Eleanor muttered, and pulled Liza to her feet. "Come with me, dear, before the boys eat themselves sick."

Just then, my phone began its insistent fugue, and I puzzled at the readout as I flipped it open. "What are you doing awake at this hour?"

"By any chance, are you in Baltimore?" asked Vivi.

"Why?"

"Are Helen and Joey with you?"

"Yes, *why*? What's wrong?"

"Arcanum squad's on the way. Get out of there. Come

get me in about five minutes, I'll fill you in," she added, and the line went dead in my hand.

CHAPTER 17

I didn't know what Vivi's weekly caffeine consumption was, but something told me it would pain any cardiologist.

"So," she demanded, pacing a groove across Eleanor's throne room, "whose bright idea was it to not let us know about the brouhaha in the silo?"

Helen bristled. "I don't see how our personal affairs are any of the Fringe's business."

"Wrong," Vivi snapped. "Anything that gets the Council up in arms isn't your personal business anymore. This is *big*, Carver. Eighty percent of the Arcanum chatter in the last two days has been about this shit."

"How the hell would you know?"

"Because that's what we *do*. You morons don't tell us anything until it's too late."

"*Excuse* me?"

"You heard me! How hard is it to loop us in, huh? 'Oh, hey, guys,'" she minced, "'the junior grand magus is on the run because Joey's fae'—welcome to the club," she added, glancing at him, "'so if you hear anything about a worldwide manhunt, don't be alarmed.' Would that have been so difficult?"

"Seeing as you obviously know everything—"

"Because we pieced it together! *Jeez*, why are you being dense?" Vivi muttered, then noticed the wide-eyed Bolins and Liza. "Hi. Sorry. Been up for forty-two hours. Not a happy camper."

"We noticed," I replied, creating a chair along her path. "Sit down before you drop, kid."

Vivi scowled, but she did as directed. "They got the trace on Carver around midnight. Two squads are on standby to bring her in. I called as soon as I got word that they'd been given the go to hit Baltimore."

"Hit?" Liza echoed.

"Retrieval." She swiveled in her chair to follow Liza's voice. "What the hell were you doing in Baltimore?"

Liza lifted a finger. "I live there."

"And you are?"

"My great-grandmother," Joey interrupted, leaning over Vivi's chair, "who is none of your business. Got it?"

Though she seemed poised to protest, she caved when confronted with Joey's glare. "Okay, *okay*. Back off." He obliged, and her eyes darted among the rest of us in an agitated jig. "We're trying to help you. Treat us like an ally instead of an afterthought. The sooner we know what to expect, the better we can analyze what we see and hear." Turning to me, she added, "I've got some notes on Alpha for you, but I want to talk to Kane."

"Much appreciated," I replied, "but you need to sleep first."

"But—"

"Do you want me to call your mother?"

She grunted. "I'm twenty-five, not twelve."

"You didn't answer my question."

She rose from the chair. "Damn it, *fine*, I'll go crash. Happy? I warn you about a retrieval squad, and this is the thanks I get?"

I caught her by the shoulder. "I'm grateful, Vivi. But go home, your shift's over. I'll handle this with Greg."

A flash of panic swept across her face. "You're not going to tell him I—"

"Of course not. And why didn't you call me when the Arcanum started making noise? I would have told you what was going on, had you asked."

"I…" She frowned. "I…but you…I mean—"

"Sleep, kid," I ordered, opening a gate back to her

kitchen. Looking through the rift, I saw Hal slumped over a bowl of cereal. He peered up with mild curiosity when reality tore five feet away, then lifted a hand and returned to his soggy flakes. I nudged Vivi on her way home. "You've broken him in so nicely. Well done."

When I'd closed the gate, Peter cleared his throat. "We should probably get going, too—"

"Are you kidding?" Rebecca interrupted. "You heard her, there's a pack of wizards hunting for Helen. What if they decide to check on us?"

"How would they even *find* us?"

"Believe me," Helen interrupted, "we have our ways. You two are on the radar."

"Well, that's just dandy." Rebecca sighed and turned to Joey. "How about it, son? Got a futon you can spare until this blows over?"

"We can do better than that," I interjected. "Come with me, I'll find you a room—"

"What about Liza?" asked Peter. "Where's she going to stay?"

Eleanor and I regarded each other carefully, measuring our planned responses against each other's likely sentiments, until she broke the standoff. "Why don't all three of you go with Coileán?" she proposed. "Joey's apartment is there. In fact, Coileán, why don't you take Poppy as well? I suspect she's lonely here."

My eyebrows rose. "You're sure?"

"Certainly. And I've been neglecting my own problems of late, so—"

"What problems?"

She sighed and gestured toward the golden throne. "You would think no one had ever relocated before. If it's not a squabble over a boundary line, it's a fight between neighbors who remembered they're engaged in a blood feud and can't possibly dwell within a hundred miles of each other. Have you any idea how many hours I've spent up there in the last week?"

"May I suggest a cushion and a stiff drink?"

Her mouth tightened. "Give me a few more weeks like this one, and I'll stand a round. Go on, then. I'll send Poppy."

Back at my palace, I summoned a couple of aides and situated the newcomers in adjoining suites. When I finished with the necessary linguistic modification, they regarded me warily from the thresholds of their rooms. "Unfortunately, as you can tell," I began, pointing to the nearest window, "the time here is nowhere close to the one you left. Dinner will be around sundown, but if you'd rather not eat, you won't hurt my feelings. I'd advise you to remain on the grounds for now. Peter, you have my number, yes?" He nodded. "Share it with the others, call if you need something. Oh, and"—I unfolded the piece of paper Aiden had slipped me—"apparently, the Wi-Fi password is 'password,' so do with that what you will."

"Where did the kids go?" Rebecca asked, glancing past me down the hall.

"The barn. I think Joey was going to exercise Georgie," I replied, heading into her room with Liza on my heels, and pointed to the wide window. "See, it's that building out there, past the roses. Can't miss it."

Peter followed my finger and frowned. "That's a *barn*? Looks like a hangar to me."

"Maybe," I allowed, spotting a familiar head emerge from the main doors, "but Georgie needs room to stretch out." The others gasped as the dragon lumbered into the afternoon sun, and I tapped the glass. "See the bump at the base of her neck? That's Joey. Don't worry, he knows what he's doing."

With a flurry of beating wings, Georgie took three galloping steps and rose, climbing like a pillar of smoke above a wildfire. She banked over the gardens and sailed off toward the orchards and the rolling hills beyond my estate. Liza and the Bolins stared out the window, mouths agape, until the dragon disappeared over the horizon and broke their paralysis.

"Oh, my God," Rebecca whispered. "That…that's a—"

"Dragon," Liza finished. "Holy moly, it's *huge*."

I cut my eyes to Peter, whose face was wrinkling into an ear-to-ear grin. "That's what he rides these days," I said. "Not the same as a horse, but—"

"Can she hold two?" Peter asked in a rush. "Think she would? Does Joey take passengers? How's he controlling her? Can she breathe fire? And damn, what do you *feed* that thing?"

Behind him, Rebecca covered her eyes and sighed, and Liza patted her shoulder in sympathy.

Val was waiting when I escaped to my office. "I discovered where Joey gets it," I muttered, slumping onto a couch. "Good luck getting Peter out of the barn tonight."

He chuckled as he locked the door. "Hard to fault him. She's a magnificent specimen."

"And game for pony rides, I hope," I began, but paused when my phone rang. "Please tell me no one's dead already," I mumbled, then saw the readout. "Ah. About time." Val pointed to the door, but I shook my head and opened the line. "Greg?"

"Coileán," he replied quietly.

I enchanted myself a double of bourbon. "Something on your mind?"

"I seem to be missing a certain magus. Got any idea where she might be?"

Commending myself on the color of the drink, I knocked it back and winced. "You know I'm not going to answer that."

"You don't need to. I was asking as a formality. All part of the illusion of civility—I pretend that I don't know you're harboring Helen, you pretend that I won't see through the lie you give me. That's how this works, isn't it?"

"Ah, but I didn't lie to you. Does this mean the planned negotiations are doomed to break down? Pity—we were off to such a good start, too." I heard shuffling in the background, followed by a sound like loud radio static. "Hello? Greg?"

"Right here, old timer," he replied, his voice clear above the garbled hiss. "Got a couple of spells in play, and patience is key with these things. The one detecting eavesdroppers needed a minute to work. The distortion you're hearing right now is the other spell for privacy."

"Cone of silence, eh?"

"More like a sphere. Should keep the internal snoops in the dark for a bit, but since the Fringe is most definitely listening to every word we say, how about we do this mano a mano? Your place?"

"You're asking to come over," I said in disbelief. "Here. You."

"Seeing as how Vegas didn't work so well the last time you played at espionage…"

"Are Toula's wards operational yet?"

"Nope. Fire at will. I'm in my office."

Though unnerved, I opened a gate and stood back as he limped through. "Close it," he muttered. "In case someone's got a flow gauge in the vicinity, let's not stick me with a surge of magic to explain." While the realm protested Greg's arrival, I did as he bid, and he turned to take in his surroundings. "Should I ask why your office looks like mine?"

"Imitation, flattery, and a backlog of tasks more important than redecorating," I replied, and waved toward the copied couches.

Greg sat, then rubbed his temples and sighed deeply. "Right. What the hell are we going to do about the lovebirds?"

"I have no idea what you're talking about," I said, refilling my glass.

His eyes rolled. "Missy's got a trace going on Helen as we speak. Girl's gone off-map, so she's either dead or out of the realm, and my money's on Faerie. Want to prove me wrong?"

"And if she were here? In that purely hypothetical scenario, what would you have me do? Hand her over to your goon squad? What's your plan?"

"Officially? My job is to locate Magus Carver and bring her back to the silo for a chat with the Council."

"Unofficially?"

After giving silent Val a long look, Greg said, "I did tell you Missy's running the trace. You actually think it took my wife thirty-six hours to get a single-target blood trace going? Come on, Coileán, she's one heck of a magus."

"I don't follow."

He leaned back and folded his hands behind his head. "A few hours after the Unveiling went to hell, I got a call from Abby, who'd heard a rumor from an old friend who still lives in the silo. I told her what was going on, and I said the Council was getting together a retrieval team. Know what she told me?" He smirked. "If I didn't get those two to the altar, she'd never speak to me again. So I got off the phone with her, and five minutes later, who should call but Cindy? Same message. I gave up when Ashleigh and Cora told me they wouldn't bring the babies around if I didn't straighten up and fly right."

I drank deeply. "The great-grands, you mean?"

"Yep. The girls and the grands might have taken all of this business with Helen and her mundane-if-you-squint fiancé a little on the *personal* side."

I thought of genial, clueless Chris and little Lilly in the snow. While I mulled the matter over, I produced two cups of espresso, then beckoned to Val and added a third to the mix. He joined me on the couch as Greg slugged back his tiny drink. "You're right. They take after their mother," I finally said.

"Suppose they're better for it. Suppose I am, too. And

as long as we're talking about Joey…"

I nudged a refill toward him. "Yes?"

"Who does he belong to, you or Eleanor? Please, tell me not Mab. No offense," he added, cutting his eyes to Val, "but this PR campaign is going to be rough enough as it is."

"He's not Mab's," I replied.

"Good. Then whose?"

While I consulted the ceiling mosaic for guidance, Val came to my aid. "What sort of explanation do you want? How complicated should this be?"

Greg drained his cup and plunked it onto the table. "How complicated do you need to make this to tell me what I need to know?"

Val sipped his coffee. "The boy's last full-blooded sire was the Puck. Obviously, his allegiance is different than—"

"*Shit*, you're telling me he's a lord? Is that what I'm dealing with, guys?"

"Honestly? I'm not sure," I admitted. "There's no question that he's a lesser blood…"

Greg groaned and rubbed his forehead. "How far down the line do titles carry? Robin would have been a high lord, right? And his kids are lords and ladies?"

I nodded, making a mental note to break the news to Liza. In the rush to get out of Baltimore, the matter had escaped my attention. "Arcanum does its homework. I'm impressed."

"You don't want to see your file. But what about Robin's grandkids? Great-grandkids? When does the relation become too remote to sustain the title?"

Flummoxed, I turned to Val, but he seemed unruffled. "Distance does not matter," he told Greg. "A high lord or lady's descendants are lords and ladies as long as they're sufficiently fae. But Joey?" He shook his head and finished his drink. "As you said, he's mundane if you squint. Untitled, I would think."

"You're not saying that to make me feel better, are you?" Val chuckled, but Greg resumed his frustrated head massage. "The fact that I had to ask means this whole shebang is teetering on the edge of disaster. I've got to work around the damn *Puck*?"

I let Greg tend to his tension headache for a moment, then asked, "What are you proposing?"

He scowled. "Quickest way to put a stop to the talk about preventing the wedding is for the kids to elope."

"Won't the Council switch topics to divorce?"

"No. I mean, there's a possibility that someone will suggest it, but you know we don't favor the practice." Greg rubbed his white stubble, then seemed to reach a decision. "Here's what I can offer. Kids need a marriage license and someone to officiate. Last I checked, Missy hadn't told the retrieval teams that Baltimore was a bust. She could give the kids a brief distraction."

"Such as?" Val asked.

"Maybe an hour's cover. She could, you know, *see* Helen pop up in another city"—he mimed quotation marks—"which would give them time to get to a courthouse and at least get the paperwork. If they want a white wedding, do it here and fudge the form. You've got that priest on speed-dial, don't you? Wasn't he going to marry them anyway?"

"He probably wouldn't mind bumping the date up a few months," I replied. "How soon does this need to happen?"

Greg made a face. "Today. The sooner, the better."

Fortunately, Helen insisted on in-flight safety precautions, and Joey was easily recalled with a message to his helmet. Sounding remarkably composed for a man suddenly finding himself on his way to the altar, he and Helen made the arrangements with Father Paul, and Joey hurried back to freshen up.

At exactly six a.m. in Montana, Missy reported to the Arcanum squads that Helen had reappeared in Nashville. The retrieval teams thought they'd caught a break. While Nashville was no mere hamlet, Helen's college apartment was on file, and the list of other places she would hide in the city at that hour was short.

Five minutes after the wizards left the silo, Paul met the couple in the Sacred Heart parking lot and drove them downtown. They hurried out of the courthouse with their papers half an hour later, and Helen brought them over after a quick trip back to the parish office for Paul to retrieve his gear. When they arrived, however, they found Eleanor pacing in my office, anxiously awaiting their return. "*There* you are," she said, grabbing Helen's hand. "Come with me, we have work to do."

With the fugitives once more out of the mortal realm, Greg called his elder daughter, who called her mother to ask about a meatloaf recipe. Missy reminded her of the secret ingredient, then hung up and alerted the squads that despite their best efforts, Helen had slipped through the net yet again.

Upon arriving at Eleanor's place twenty minutes later, I saw what she'd been up to since I'd informed her of the change of plans that afternoon. The rose-covered gazebo she'd planted on the bluff had been bedecked with white ribbons, and a matching arch of roses had sprung up before it, the terminus of a petal-strewn path flanked by white chairs. Someone had coaxed Joey into putting on a tux and trimming his beard, and his parents and Liza, cleaned up and dressed appropriately for an evening ceremony, sat by at the ready. All three seemed overwhelmed, but whether that was due to the impromptu wedding, the revelations of the last day, or the dragon curled up nearby, I couldn't say. Greg had staked out a lonely chair on the bride's side, and after a moment's pause, Aiden joined him. The grand magus leaned over and whispered to him, then patted him on the shoulder as

Aiden nodded. Before I could ponder this development, I heard the realm's voice speak over my thoughts: *He asked if Aiden was all right.*

"Is he?" I muttered.

Yes. He is pleased.

Just then, Eleanor appeared beside me in a green satin skirt suit and pointed toward the glowing western horizon. "The sunset's progressing awfully slowly today. I thought we'd have lost the light by now"—she gestured toward the dozens of white orbs floating at the ready around the gazebo—"but it seems I was hasty."

"It seems you aren't the only one who likes weddings."

"The realm told me she's made her peace with Helen."

We stood aside and watched as Mina and my other nieces and nephews arrived in a chattering pack. "Your kin?" Eleanor asked.

"Some of the few remaining. Mina's in my guard"—I couldn't help but notice that she found a seat beside Toula—"and the other five are collaborating with Joey and Aiden on the map and field guide."

"Ah. Liza's cousins, then. Should you introduce them?"

I considered the redhead in the front row, whose stiff shoulders betrayed her unease. "Not today. One step at a time."

"Agreed. And there's the priest," she said, jutting her chin toward the figure in voluminous vestments picking his way up the path. "Want a seat?"

We found an open pair of chairs on the bride's side and watched Paul approach the rose-heavy trellis in the reddening light of sundown. When he reached his position, he started to shake Joey's hand, then converted the gesture into a long hug. A flash went off, and I noticed with surprise that both of Joey's parents had pulled out their phones as cameras. Another light, a familiar gold blur, zipped three laps around Aiden's head before Kuni settled on his shoulder for the duration.

And then, as the sun melted into a flaming puddle, a

blast of invisible trumpets echoed from the bluff in a fanfare. I stood and turned to see a gate open twenty yards away in the middle of the path. From the rift stepped Helen, polished and poised. Her dark hair cascaded in waves over her shoulders and down the back of a shimmering, long-trained gown. With every step she took, the thousand tiny diamonds woven into the dress caught the last rays of the sunset and reflected them in bright bursts, setting her gown a-twinkle. That effect was nothing new to Faerie, but Helen was radiant with joy. She carried red roses, a bouquet that captured the color of the sun just before it vanished.

I turned to the front in the nick of time and caught the expression on Joey's face, a broad smile that spoke of excitement, incredulity, and love.

Helen made the long walk unaccompanied, never faltering even when the sun finally sank and Eleanor's orbs rose into place like floating candelabra. When she reached the trellis, Joey took her arm, and the two turned to the priest with a shared smile.

Lacking a church, an altar, or any of the usual trappings of a Catholic wedding, Paul did the best he could and kept the ceremony brief.

He did. She did.

And as we clapped and cheered, the newlyweds embraced by starlight.

Three days later, having brought Slim over, I sat with Helen on a hay bale and watched Joey learn to use his new Dud Defender. "So," I said as Slim's rod threw another fireball at Joey's faltering shield, "you survived the inquest."

"Barely. Did Greg give you the rundown?"

"He hit the high points. What the hell did you talk about for twenty-one hours?"

She snorted. "*We* didn't talk. *They* harangued me, and

occasionally I got to say 'yes' or 'no.' Loads of fun. I'd give anything to get out of the silo for now, but that's not going to happen." She cupped her hands around her mouth and called, "*Focus*, Joey! The shield only holds as long as you concentrate!"

As Joey batted the latest flames out of his T-shirt, I said, "Good thing those rods are rechargeable."

"No kidding." She winced as Joey's shield flickered and died again. "That's not the easiest spell to start with. He doesn't have the discipline to hold a shield together…"

"Yet."

"Right. In the meantime, I hope Val's good with burns."

We watched as Joey and Slim went another brief round, which ended with Joey rolling in the dirt.

Softly, Helen asked, "What's going to happen to him?"

"What do you mean?"

"Two years in Faerie, and he can manage gates—"

"Once. He made *one* gate in a moment of panic. Same goes for the vanishing door. But that's the only thing he's done."

"Maybe because he hasn't tried."

"Oh, he's tried," I muttered. "He doesn't know that I know, but he's experimented. Nada."

"Okay, so he can't reliably use magic after two years. We both know there's something in him. What happens after five? Ten?"

"I can't tell you, Helen."

"But you can make an educated guess." She leaned over to look me in the face. "What are we in for?"

I shrugged. "The longer he's exposed, the greater the probability that he'll start to exhibit talent. If and when he does start to have flares with any regularity, we'll work with him to keep him from hurting himself, but that's all I can offer you now."

She sighed. "Greg didn't tell them about Robin. He said you two didn't know where Joey had come from and wouldn't be able to figure it out for some time, if ever."

"That was probably the wisest course of action."

"They asked me what I would do if he ever figures enchantment out. How I thought it would look if the grand magus were literally sleeping the enemy."

"What did you say?"

"I told them you'd bound him to be absolutely certain his incident wouldn't happen again."

"Mm." I waited while Slim emptied his rod at Joey's shield, which disintegrated four seconds into the barrage. "He's starting to get the hang of it," I said as Joey threw himself into the sheep's water trough. "And I'm not binding him, so don't even ask."

"I'm not. Just wanted you to be aware of the official line."

"Understood. Does this mean you still have post-graduation employment?"

"Through no fault of my own, apparently. The vote was tight—Greg won't tell me the tally, but I was probably within two votes of being out of a job." Helen picked at the pilling on the arm of her sweater. "The installation magi are still in my corner. I think I've lost the support of the silo crew, but I can work with the external half until the Inner Council comes around. I hope. Hang on, they need charging," she said, then slid off the bale and jogged across the yard to re-ensorcel the rods.

While Helen worked and the combatants took a water break, I compared what Helen was telling me with the report Greg had sent via Toula the day before.

Helen and Joey had only their wedding night to enjoy their new marriage. The next morning—which was still the previous evening in Montana—they had gone to Greg to turn themselves in, and he'd called the Council to break the news of their elopement. Missy acted peeved enough to escape suspicion, leaving the magi with the discomforting thought that their junior grand magus was sufficiently skilled to evade a blood trace.

Greg had done his best to spin even that worrisome fact in Helen's favor. Over the next hours, he'd pleaded her case before the Council, talking up her power and promise while talking down my influence on her new husband. As the meeting stretched into the morning, he'd reminded them of her brilliance, her skill, and his confidence in her ability to shepherd the Arcanum through the next decades, regardless of her spouse.

Still, the irate faction of the Council had seemed poised on the brink of an override until assistance arrived from an unanticipated source: Arnold Lowe, the most junior of the magi from Arcanum 2, a soft-spoken, prematurely gray Englishman. "I'd like to remind you of three things," he'd told the others. "First, Magus Carver is uniquely positioned to negotiate with the courts, which is an asset, not a liability. Second, the grand magus's choice of successor should be given utmost deference. If he believes that Magus Carver has not been compromised, then I'll respect his judgment. There's been much talk of divided loyalties, but I've yet to see proof. Surely I'm not the only one who remembers last June."

(At that point, seeing my bemusement, Toula had paused in the retelling. "Council asked Aiden to come in for a meeting about Moyna. Tempers flared, one of the magi said something stupid, Aiden got pissed and pins him against a wall, and Carver, I kid you not, stood up and said, 'Sit down, Aid, you're being an asshole.' And he did. She even got an apology.")

As the angrier faction of the Council had muttered, Magus Lowe had stood at the podium like a calm parent waiting for a tantrum to end. When they'd been embarrassed back into silence, he'd said, "Finally, I would remind you that Magus Carver came to our assistance with a warrant hanging over her head, a warrant *this body* issued. She worked with the Fringe *and* the courts to end the siege on Arc 1." He'd paused, letting that sink in. "She didn't have to come back. I dare say that most of us would have avoided this place. But she returned, and she did so with a highly fae army that left when the siege was broken. *That* is a grand magus," he'd said, meeting the eyes around the Council table. "And that is why I'm willing to overlook the horrifying fact that she married a man who's never done us any harm."

The rest of Arcanum 2 had sided with him, and the other satellites had fallen in line. When Helen's long examination limped to its conclusion, the factions had been nearly equal—and in the end, it had been one of the Inner Council who cast the deciding vote. "I'm trusting you, Greg," she'd warned as her light glowed green. "Don't fail us."

Now Greg had little to do but box up his office. Helen would take the reins of the divided Council in eight days' time, giving her a week to pack her Nashville apartment, move into her new suite in the silo, and make sense out of Greg's files. Joey planned to be with Helen through her inauguration for heavy lifting and moral support, but the two had postponed the scheduled packing of her old apartment when Slim called with the promised Dud Defender. He'd taken pains to camouflage the rod, outfitting it with a dagger handle and enough steel around the joint for it to pass as a blade when holstered. The design was anything but traditional, but then again, nothing about Joey's situation was by the book.

With the retrieval squads deactivated, the Bolins were able to return to Virginia. I sneaked them back in the middle of the night after prying Peter away from Georgie. He gave her a last wistful pat goodbye as he stepped into his kitchen, but before Rebecca crossed the border, she gripped my arm, looked me dead in the eye, and murmured, "You take care of my boy."

I was left then with only Liza and Poppy to host. Liza had stayed behind to come to terms with her own power, and Val and Mina, finding themselves without their usual punching bag while Joey was away, were happy to take on the challenge. I'd moved Poppy into the room beside Liza's, and the two women quickly took to each other, bonding as strangers in a strange land.

Recalling my to-do list, I brought Vivi over to talk with the shifter. Though Vivi could be persuasive when she set her mind to it, Poppy had been reluctant to share any Company information with the Fringe until Liza, who had no allegiance to either side, listened to both positions and coaxed Poppy into opening up. I was surprised to hear of her success—extracting intel from a member of the Company usually required force—but she shrugged it off as nothing. "They're reasonable people. Someone just needed to show Poppy that her organization's goals are in alignment with Vivi's," she said, then paused. "Well, for the moment. No two intelligence-gathering agencies are ever in agreement for long."

"You have experience in the field, do you?" I teased.

At that, Liza blushed crimson and folded her arms in defense. "I've watched a lot of Bond, okay?" she mumbled, then slipped off to train.

CHAPTER 18

Days passed with no sign of Joey, but I left him in peace, assuming that the last thing he wanted was additional interference. There was no way Helen would be able to break free of Montana for at least a couple of months, which meant that the last hectic days before the handover were the kids' only chance to be together, even if they spent most of that time with cardboard boxes, a tape gun, and the threat of lurking magi who wanted a word with the incoming boss.

I'd expected a lavish ceremony for Helen's inauguration, but that night, as she sprawled barefoot on one of my office couches with a glass of wine, she set the record straight. "Magus ceremonies are a big deal. You dress the part, you get your chain, everyone says nice things about you." She sipped and shrugged. "*Grand* magus ceremonies are little more than a handshake and a transfer of office keys. We had three grand magi in a row who couldn't be bothered with the pomp, and it became tradition. Besides, any day that I don't have to wear the wool robes is a good one. Those things are *heavy*."

From my bar, I considered the difference two and a half years could make: a court of my own, a queen I could work with, and a grand magus hanging out with a bottle of chardonnay while her husband took his dragon for a long ride. True, I needed to find my missing daughter before she tried to kill me again, and I needed to get to the bottom of the situation with the Dark Company, but that night, I felt more at peace than I had since waking five weeks before.

And in that moment of peace, I thought of Meggy.

My gut clenched as her face flashed behind my eyes. The moment passed as quickly as it had come upon me, but the ache lingered, the sting of remembered grief in the midst of happiness. I didn't know what had triggered it, but I gripped the edge of the bar until I could press my sorrow back into its abyss.

Helen took her leave shortly thereafter, recalled to the silo by the knowledge that she was already shirking her duties, and I sat on the window seat and stared at the stars. I'd intended to drink until I didn't hurt anymore, but before I could begin working on that night's liquid balm, the flash of a gate lit the rose garden, and I peered down to find Eleanor at the head of the path in jeans and a pink sweater. "Hello!" she called, waving up at me. "Lovely evening. Want to walk?"

She sounded strained, but I appeared beside her before I had time to change my mind. "Evening," I said, and pushed open the gate to the garden. "Shall we?"

She nodded and slipped past me onto the winding lane, which was hedged on both sides by night-black rosebushes as high as a man. "Nice variety," she said, pressing her nose into one of the blooms. "I might have to steal it."

"Be my guest." I latched the gate and set off on a slow stroll, and Eleanor plucked a thornless rose, tucked it behind her ear, and kept pace beside me.

She said nothing as we took one avenue after another, heading deeper into the maze I was designing as we went, until we reached the maze's heart, a rose-covered gazebo strung with white lights, where she laughed aloud. "Stealing from me, now, are you?"

"The first thing that came to mind," I admitted, then cocked my head and reimagined the space. The vine-covered scaffolding vanished, replaced by a pair of wooden chaise longues with a lit candelabra on the matching table between them. "Better?"

"Different, but I'll take it." Eleanor stretched out in one of the chairs and stared at the cloudless sky as I made myself comfortable beside her. "Beautiful night."

The candlelight revealed little of her face, but her voice betrayed her. "What's troubling you?"

I listened to the bleating of the nearby sheep with my eyes closed until I heard her sigh. "Tomorrow will be a month."

Her tone left no question as to the subject of the anniversary, and I wished I knew what to say. "You've made it through the worst part. And you've done so much since then—"

"The first month isn't the worst. The first month is when it's *sharpest*, but the dull pain lasts. And that's what I have to look forward to," she said, keeping her eyes on the heavens. "Missing him. Forever."

Before I could offer another lame attempt at comfort, she burst into tears—angry, ugly, wretched sobs that shook her thin body. She hugged herself and tucked her head, and her loose hair fell around her to shield her grief from my eyes. But I saw her anguish and self-recrimination in that moment, and I knew too well the place from whence it sprung.

I don't remember getting up, but suddenly, I was holding her as she cried on my shoulder. Her perfume, a blend of vanilla and jasmine, overpowered even the omnipresent smell of magic, and I was acutely, achingly aware of the way her body fit against mine. All I could see of her was her shaking back and her curtain of hair, which flickered like fire in the candlelight, and something within me cried out. "I'm sorry," I mumbled. "I'm sorry, forgive me, I'm so sorry."

Eleanor lifted her wet face and searched mine, trying to puzzle through my rambling before I admitted her to my thoughts. "*Oh*," she breathed, then rested her head against my chest and let me hold her as her breathing slowed.

Don't be an ass, Leffe, my conscience nagged, and I

desperately wished—not for the first time—that I could shut it up.

Walt was my officemate." Eleanor took a long drag of her cigarette, held the smoke, and blew it into a thin stream that curled in the night breeze. "The budget was tight, and we had to share space. Two professors to a suite, plus a shared vestibule for waiting students. Close quarters, you understand."

"I get the picture," I replied, swirling my needed scotch.

"Prison cells had more room. But I digress." She paused for a pull, then tapped the cigarette against the ashtray she'd created. "Walt was hired in '69, and since I was an old codger without a heavy teaching load, he was put in my spare room."

"You were still living as a man, yes? What was the alias, Richard—"

"Poole, and of course. Durham hired me that time in the thirties—they wouldn't have taken a female professor."

"True." I smirked at her over my glass. "Richard, Richardson—did we get a little stumped for names, Ellie?"

"No." She produced a glass of wine and took a sip. "My father was called Richard. I've used his name several times—a poor tribute, I suppose, but I'm his only child left, even if I wasn't his. None of my brothers lived to have children, so I'm all that remains." Eleanor drank again as she stared at the rose hedge around us, which I'd sealed off for a modicum of privacy. "My father was a good man. He loved to entertain, and he had this wonderfully booming laugh…" She sighed as she reached for her cigarette. "He deserved grandchildren. So did Mother. They would have been so happy with a score of brats underfoot."

I hesitated, uncertain of the solidity of the ground on which I was treading. "Richard thought you were his daughter?"

"If Mother ever told him the truth, it was after I fled. She told me when I was nine, but I suppose she had to— I'd been cross with the cook and set her dress on fire."

"You *what?*"

"We'd quarreled over something trivial. But yes, I set her on fire from across the room, and then I panicked and ran to Mother, and she told me everything. Raped by a redheaded stranger after a banquet, a man who vanished before her eyes." Eleanor smoked in silence, then stubbed the cigarette out and cleared her throat. "Did you tell me Titania tricked your father into bed?"

"Yeah," I mumbled, chasing the word with a long swig. "She was traveling as a man. He was a monk."

"*That's* unfortunate."

"It was Mother. You, uh…you've never…"

"Never what?" she asked, then divined the direction of my thoughts. "Oh, that. Yes, I've coupled as a man. It's not difficult. A little glamour, a bit of skill, and some familiarity with the terrain, and you can do a passable impression. But to fall pregnant that way—I've never even tried. The mechanics are distressingly complicated."

"Wouldn't have been my cup of tea," I said, trying to force from my mind's eye the visual that had flashed up in glorious Technicolor. "If I may ask…"

"Go ahead."

"How long *did* you pass, anyway?"

Eleanor tucked her free arm behind her head, cushioning it against the wooden slats. "I ran away when I was sixteen and about to be married and made my first male alias, and I kept one until 1971."

"That long? You prefer going male?"

"Not at all—it was safer. A man could do so much more, and no one looked at me askance if I was unmarried. I mean, I took a wife from time to time, but it wasn't something I craved. Walt was my first husband." Seeing my bemusement, she shrugged. "I pursued girls with no interest in men. When I needed to marry and I was certain of a girl's tastes, I'd tell her I could take care of myself and her services wouldn't be needed in the bedroom."

"That, uh…that's decent of you, Eleanor."

"Or at least mutually beneficial," she replied.

"Granted. You said you ran from a wizard before your first wedding, yes?"

Eleanor produced another cigarette, lit it with a flick of her thumb, and took a drag. "I haven't smoked in ages," she finally said. "Walt was asthmatic, and I didn't mind giving up the habit for his sake. But tonight…"

I lifted my tumbler in salute. "To vices."

"Cheers." She rested the smoldering cigarette in her ashtray and turned back to the stars. "So, my teenage wedding. Our family priest was growing feeble, and the bishop sent a young priest to assist him. An Arcanum plant, as it happened."

I snorted. "The clergy was lousy with them for a while."

"Oh, I dealt with my share. But I was only a girl then, and I gave myself away—I never drank from the chalice, and he caught on. Silver, you see. Shortly before my wedding, he asked to meet with me in private. When we were alone, he pulled a wand and started shooting, and I set his vestments ablaze and ran. I couldn't go home—not if my priest was trying to kill me—so I changed my name, changed my face, moved to a town several miles away, and started over."

Eleanor paused to smoke her cigarette down to the filter. "I returned to that church every so often once the wizard was gone. One by one, my parents buried my brothers, and then Mother buried Father. I paid for her Mass," she said quietly. "An anonymous donation, but I wanted her to have the proper rites. She did the best she could to protect me."

We sat beneath the stars, listening to the night around

us. After a time, I glanced at Eleanor to find her with a third cigarette pinched between her fingers. "You were telling me about Walt."

"I know."

"You don't have to—"

"No, it's fine," she said too quickly. "Walt was my suitemate. The ink on his doctoral diploma was still damp, so our department head gave him to me to mind until he found his feet. The placement was a bit of hazing, too— Walt was twenty-five and dashingly handsome, and the rumor was that I was an old poofter. I didn't deny it," she added, smirking. "But 'Richard' was also seventy-something, so no one thought Walt was in any danger from me."

Her eyes twinkled in the candlelight. "Naturally, I thought him a good-looking specimen. Hair like bootblack, and those big brown eyes…he wore glasses, but he was adorable." She sighed to herself, then took a drag. "I assumed he'd have a girl on his arm within the first week of the semester, but he was shy—he migrated among the office, the lecture hall, his terrible little flat, and his local. I coaxed him out for lunch a few times, but he kept his own company.

"And then the kettle seemed to break. It was mid-September, and the damn thing had been unreliable since the summer, but the department secretary always knew how to deal with it. Well, she was out that morning, and I was working with my door cracked, and I saw Walt trying to make his morning tea. Nothing worked. Finally, he stepped out of my line of sight, and I thought I heard him muttering, so I sneaked to the door to see what he was doing." She chuckled at the memory. "The dear was standing across the room from the kettle, holding a pencil like a wand and mumbling incantations at it."

"Did it work?"

"Heavens, no. But I saw the problem—the switch controlling that outlet was flipped off, so I took care of that for him while I was spying. Bless him, he thought he'd actually pulled off the spell when the water started simmering." Eleanor took another smoke break, then cocked her head at the sound of bleating. "I've been meaning to ask..."

"Georgie's flock."

"*Ah.*" She waited until the surprised bleating of the latest budding sheep had subsided, then continued. "So I was sharing an office with a witch. He was none the wiser, but to prevent any nasty surprises, I thought the only appropriate thing to do would be to give him an inkling of the truth. That way, he wouldn't have to worry that I'd see something I shouldn't, and if he couldn't bear the thought of being in proximity to me, we could find a way for one of us to transfer. I didn't want to make him miserable," she explained. "I'd begun to have feelings for him by then. We were spending so much time together, you see, and he had a devilish sense of humor."

I sipped my drink and waited for Eleanor to finish her latest cigarette.

"That afternoon," she said as the ashtray vanished, "since we were alone, I called him over to my room and told him I'd never heard of the Arcanum making wands with graphite cores. He went white, but I said he'd forgotten to flip the switch and not to worry about the kettle, and that was all we needed to discuss. He tripped over himself getting out of our suite, and I assumed I wouldn't see him for at least a day or two. But he rang my bell that night," she said, pulling the afghan up to her shoulders. "He was terrified, but he'd drunk enough courage at the pub to pay me a visit. So we sat at my kitchen table, I gave him tea to sober him up, and he asked me point-blank how much glamour I was wearing."

I chuckled at the notion: Eleanor as an old man, trying to explain herself to poor, tipsy Walt. "What did you tell him?"

"I said, 'A touch.' He sat there for a minute, thinking it

over, then asked me, 'What the bloody hell are you doing at Durham?' And I said, 'I've been teaching history since it was current events. Are we going to have a problem?' Well, he thought about that some more, drank his tea, then said, 'No, old chap, I guess you're all right.'"

She laughed to herself. "God, he was drunk. I talked him into sleeping it off on my couch and left him there to snore in peace. The next morning, I found him scrambling eggs. He was embarrassed, and he was trying to make it up to me with breakfast. I helped him with his hangover, he realized I wasn't out for blood, and we finally talked things out."

"How'd he take the news of your sex change?"

"Oh, I didn't tell him *everything*," said Eleanor. "He admitted he was a witch—raised in Glastonbury. His family are all wizards, and I think one of his aunts made magus before she died. But Walt didn't have it, and so he struck off for academia." She thought for a moment. "I won't say that he and I were bosom friends after that, but we had an understanding. Things were comfortable. And I helped him with an article he was writing, so we gradually became friends. We used to go to the pub," she said, leaning towards me as if she had a great secret, "and the rumors were *vicious*. Walt was straight as an arrow, but he was spending far too much time in my company for his own good."

"When did you make the big reveal, then?"

"Not for months." She folded herself into a plaid-wrapped ball. "Around the end of October, things started to become awkward between us, and I didn't know why. I thought Walt had finally got wind of the rumors, but he didn't start taking girls out, which would have been the next step to proving himself a 'man's man,' if you will. So then I thought that perhaps I'd caused offense, but he was as cordial as ever. He'd simply ceased to come near me unless the situation warranted face-to-face contact."

I shivered in the breeze, considered Eleanor's afghan,

and duplicated it for myself. "You poked around, didn't you?"

"Eventually. I was stumped," she protested. "There I was, infatuated with the man, and he was pulling away. What would you have done?"

"Much the same. What was the problem?"

"In short, he liked me a little too much, and it was deeply unsettling to him. Remember, aside from the basic problem of gender, 'Richard' looked old enough to be his grandfather—and I'd been upfront about my true age. Part of him wanted to be with me, part of him recoiled at the notion, and since he couldn't reconcile the two, he avoided me."

"What did you do about it?"

"Nothing," she said, shrugging under her blanket. "I was in a quandary as well. I wanted to pursue him, but I couldn't tell him the truth about myself, you—"

"Stop. You could tell him you were fae, but not that you were *female*?"

"I was his *colleague*. The only women working around us were the girls at their typewriters or the cleaners, and I didn't know what he would think. Sounds silly now, doesn't it?"

"In retrospect—"

"Don't answer that, Coileán."

I laughed at her embarrassment. "What changed your mind about your dark, unspeakable secret?"

Something yanked my afghan off and sent it sailing onto the rose hedge, and Eleanor grinned as I grunted and waved it back to me. "I didn't intend to out myself," she continued as I tucked the blanket into place. "The department was having a pub night, and after the third round, the conversation turned to the subject of women in higher education. That was when I discovered how truly chauvinistic most of my closest colleagues were. Women weren't as clever as men, they couldn't compete, they had no business mucking about in academia—you know the rest. I took all I could take and excused myself. I didn't see Walt follow me out."

She stared into space as her teeth worried a raw patch on her bottom lip. "I went back to the office to calm down. Walt came in two minutes behind me and asked what was wrong. He knew—the others were too much in their cups to recognize it, but he'd seen that I was upset. I asked him whether he agreed with what had been said around the table. He told me he didn't know, and I…" Her eyes drifted away from mine as she tried to give form to the memory. "I was furious and so hurt, and I remember asking him if he respected me. And he told me—I remember this clearly—he said, 'Of course I respect you, Richard. You're one of the finest historians I've ever met.' So I looked him square in the face, and I said, 'Richard was my father's name. My mother called me Eleanor.' And I dropped the glamour."

"Well played," I murmured. "Points for theatrics."

"At that moment, I was past caring about mature responses. Perhaps I should have handled myself differently, but I was *this* close to breaking something."

"How did Walt take it?"

She began to smile. "His mouth hung open like an imbecile's, and he blinked at me for a good minute before he found his voice. And then he exclaimed, 'Richard! Dear God, you're *beautiful!*'" Her eyes opened in feigned surprise as she replayed his reaction. "Well, I was still angry, and I snapped back, 'Yes, you dolt, I'm well aware of that.' Before Walt knew what had hit him, I pushed him out of my office and locked the door."

"That was certainly the adult response," I replied.

"It was either get him out of my face or shove his head through the wall, and I did have feelings for the boy. So I went home that night, took stock of what I had done, and had a minor panic attack—I'd come out to Walt in the worst way possible, and I'd have to face him the next morning."

"Let me guess, you took yourself on holiday."

"I thought about it, but then I remembered that he was in the wrong, and I wasn't going to pass up the opportunity to give him a well-deserved cold shoulder until he saw the error of his ways."

"As one does."

"Naturally," she muttered. "I was a regular joy that week, and Walt avoided me. He'd sneak into and out of his office, he did his marking at the pub, and he did everything he could to prevent himself from crossing my path short of calling in sick." Rolling onto her back to get the candles out of her face, she said, "By the next Monday, I'd mellowed, but I still didn't see so much as Walt's shadow until that Friday. I was marking late that evening, and he knocked on my office door with a bouquet of daisies, called himself an idiot, and asked if he could take me to dinner."

The subtle twitches of her facial musculature betrayed her valiant effort not to cry. "You let him?" I asked quietly.

She nodded. "It was terrifying, but I went as myself. We had a lovely evening," she said in a wobbling voice. "Dinner and dancing, and we talked about everything but work. I went home with him that night—I couldn't waltz past my neighbors looking like this—and before I made the gate back to my place, he took me by the hand and said, 'Thank you for the pleasure of your company. Can we discuss the edits you suggested to my article on Monday?'" She smiled despite the tremor in her jaw. "I knew he still respected me then. And I gave myself permission to learn to love him."

While Eleanor pulled herself together, I looked away and finished my latest drink to give her privacy. She cleared her throat when she was calm once more, and I cast my tumbler into oblivion. "You dated on the sly, then?" I asked.

"Not at first. We were both busy with the end of the semester, and then he went back to Glastonbury for a week at Christmas. The next time I saw him again as myself…" She grinned at the thought. "One of the deans had thrown a New Year's party, and Walt and I were in attendance. I played it cool with him all night, but shortly before midnight, I told him to come with me into the garden. When we reached the bushes, I dropped the glamour and dragged him behind a holly hedge. I was going to kiss him when the countdown ended, you see, but he pulled back, and I thought I'd been too forward until he said, 'I should warn you, I have fillings.' I told him I knew what I was doing, and that was that."

Eleanor smiled wistfully at the night. "I think we both knew it was only a matter of time after that. 'Richard' retired in 1971, but before he did, he went to the head of the department and stressed how much the university needed to hire this promising young woman who was graduating from Leeds and had already published two articles. It took planning, but I was able to implant enough memories in the right people's minds over there for my newest persona to get hired. And with Richard gone, they gave me his empty office, which came with a delightful colleague who was only too happy to show me the ropes."

"And other things, I'm sure."

A flash of wicked mirth flickered across her face. "You'd be amazed how much I taught him in that regard. *He* was."

"I'll remember that," I said, matching her grin. "But how did you work around his family situation?"

"Ah, that little matter of the Arcanum." She unkinked her legs and stretched, then curled up again with a sigh. "Bear in mind that he was a witch—the magi in Glastonbury knew better than to expect anything from him, so there was no objection to his marrying a mundane girl. He told his family that he had told me they were dead to prevent awkward questions about the Arcanum, and they fell for it. I never met them, and he 'sneaked off' to visit them every so often. They didn't even try to come to our wedding—September of '73, one week into the new term. We wanted to be certain that the rest of the department could attend." Eleanor fell silent for a moment. "Last year was our forty-second anniversary. We'd talked about spending the next one in Paris, but...well."

"I'm sorry, Eleanor."

"I know. Thank you." She sat up, swung her legs over the side of the chaise to face me, and wrapped the afghan around her shoulders like a cloak. "Coileán...I know you fancy me." I began to mumble denials, but she held up her hand to stop the fumbling lies. "Whether it's for me or for the memory of Meggy, I'm flattered. You...you're not the man I thought you were a month ago. Someday...*perhaps*...I'll be in a position to consider that sort of development in our relationship. But not now. Not anytime soon. I hope you understand."

I nodded, not trusting myself to speak.

"I love Walt," she continued with a sad smile. "He's gone, but I still love him. And you love Meggy, I know you do." She reached across the gap between us and took my hands. "I need to mourn him, you need to mourn her, and I'd want us to come together because we want each other, not because we're trying to fill a hole. But until such time..." She looked at our clasped hands, then into my eyes. "Thank you. I mean it."

With that, Eleanor released me and disappeared into the lonely night.

CHAPTER 19

Over the next few weeks, life returned to what passed for normal in my orbit. While Helen remained locked in meetings, Joey divided his time between realms, catching her when she was available but otherwise digging into the mapping project. As he and Georgie scouted, Aiden hunkered at the command base to keep them company, and my exploration-minded nieces and nephews checked in with notebooks and rucksacks. With the immediate problems solved, I could step back and take stock of the larger issues looming on the horizon. Three came to mind.

First—and most aggravating—was the growing inter-court friction. I received daily messages from the lower lords and ladies claiming that the newcomers had committed all manner of atrocities against them. Eleanor, who heard a similar litany on her side of the border, compared her scribblings to mine at night. Finding nothing of substance, we simply ordered the complainants to stay out of the buffer zone.

"They don't give up," Eleanor groaned one evening, and pushed a page of notes across the table. "This one, Jermian, claims that one Raingol is making hostile incursions onto her land and changing the terrain. Cross-reference that here"—she turned my laptop around and searched through Aiden's database, which I'd been updating under threat of adolescent scorn—"and *voila*. Raingol wrote you two days ago to complain that Jermian has been sneaking onto *her* land and undoing her landscaping. Do we have a map?"

I flipped through the homemade atlas until I found the proper pages. "The buffer passes between them," I said, tapping the dotted red lines that Frances the cartographer had drawn in. "They're squabbling over nothing."

"Hmm. Do you suppose boundary markers would cure this?"

"They probably wouldn't get the picture unless we erected a boundary wall topped with razor wire and laser cannons, and then they'd complain that it was blocking their view," I replied as I put the maps away.

"What if we made it sufficiently sparkly? I'm joking," she added as my expression shifted toward incredulity. "But I'd love to know how our predecessors handled nonsense like this."

Val, who had been standing guard at the door while we worked, coughed to draw her attention. "The Three took a more hands-off approach to dispute resolution, my lady. In general, these matters reached equilibrium on their own. The Three were seldom dragged into the fray."

"Why not?" she asked him.

"Because requesting adjudication usually ended in a solution more painful than the problem. If they were sufficiently irked, they'd throw the parties into solitary confinement for a few years, or worse."

Recalling the hours I'd spent on disputes that day, I met Eleanor's eyes and shrugged. "It's a thought."

"It's barbaric," she retorted. "Surely we can reason out a compromise—" She paused and glared as Val chuckled. "Come, now, the idea's not *that* ridiculous."

The second problem facing me was the most immediate: what was to be done about the Dark Company and Jeanine's murder? True, it wasn't my fight—or, strictly speaking, my business—but I couldn't do *nothing*. Poppy's presence was a constant reminder that I had unfinished business with the weres. At least she'd ceased to pester

Eleanor and me about returning—whatever Vivi had shared with her had quelled her impulse to run back to headquarters.

Of course, I wouldn't have had Poppy on hand if not for the third problem, the largest: Moyna. Toula kept the location spell running, but Moyna had yet to show herself. With Jeanine out of the picture, gone too was our best source of information on the weres running in Moyna's circle. Whatever she had known about their location had died with her—she hadn't shared it with her underlings, and so Poppy couldn't confirm that Alpha was one of the werewolves we were hunting. Her list of likely collaborators did me little good without people who could follow them to my daughter, but the Fringe had drawn a firm line when I broached the subject. "We can't," Slim explained. "It's too dangerous. What do you want to do, set a witch on the weres and hope he doesn't get noticed?"

Fresh out of options, I bided my time and hoped Poppy wouldn't get restless enough to sniff out a gate home. In truth, I was grateful for her presence for Liza's sake. Having ripped my niece from her life, I felt guilty about the limited assistance Eleanor and I had provided in helping her acclimate. But Liza proved more resilient than I'd anticipated, and during her first weeks in Faerie, I saw her most often in Poppy's company, sitting together in the garden. Mina had taken the lead in Liza's training, and she favored a more relaxed approach to education. "There's nothing to be gained by overwhelming Liza," Val explained. "She's an apt enough pupil, but she fears her power. This is delicate work, and it shouldn't be rushed."

"But she does have talent?" I asked.

He nodded. "Without question. She will be her father's daughter in time." My brow creased, and he said, "In power. Temperamentally, she's different. Robin had a malicious streak—"

"Pain was always entertaining."

"You realize that's not uncommon, Coileán," he said

with a hint of irritation. "Robin was no worse than many."

"Granted, but I don't have to like it. Liza lacks that charming character flaw?"

Val folded his arms. "As far as I can tell. She *is* somewhat impetuous—"

"What do you mean?"

"Robin was always too quick to act. Liza shows some of that impulsivity, but her fear tempers it. It's curious," he said with a one-shouldered shrug. "For instance, Mina showed her the basics of gates. Liza was reluctant to try, but Mina and Poppy goaded her into it. She made the attempt, she succeeded, everyone was pleased…and then she had to keep opening gates. The first five times worked well, but then she made one halfway up a tree, ran through, missed her footing, and broke her arm in the fall. Impetuous," he repeated. "If she's overly excited about something, she focuses and forgets to check the periphery."

"Sounds like Robin," I muttered.

"She's young, and this is new to her. I'd rather her be fearless for the moment—she's much easier to train that way." He hesitated. "Lady Eleanor has been visiting her. If you'll excuse me for saying so, you should do likewise."

Val had a point, as usual, and so I asked Liza and Poppy to dine with me that night. They agreed, but the meal began awkwardly—while Poppy ate in silence and gave Liza funny looks, Liza picked at her salad and sneaked glances at me, occasionally opening her mouth as if preparing to say something before snapping it closed again and turning away. Finally, having watched Liza cut her steak into little chunks and push it around her plate for half an hour, I put my utensils down and asked what was on her mind.

With the question posed, Liza chewed the inside of her lip and sought Poppy's eyes across the table. The shifter nodded reassurance, and Liza finally faced me. "I've, uh…I've been talking with Poppy and Ellie about the

Dark Company situation," she began, fidgeting under my gaze. "We think we might have an idea, but…well, I think Ellie wanted to run it by you first—"

"She'll get over it," I replied. "Go ahead."

Liza propped her elbows on the tablecloth and steepled her fingers. "Here's the problem, as I understand it. Moyna has an unknown group of friends, including at least one wizard. You and Ellie and the Arcanum can't find her, but there's a gang of werewolves in Idaho that probably can. You need someone to use them to get to her. Is that about it?"

"More or less…"

She spread her hands. "What about me?"

"*You?*"

"Why not? No one knows me. I've been in hiding most of my life—what are the odds that anyone with Moyna would connect the dots?"

"They don't have to know you, Liza," I protested. "Anyone with a little age could get into your head and—"

"Ellie's already though of that. Put up a smokescreen of false memories, and they'll never know."

"But if you were given false memories, how could you be of any use? You wouldn't be feeding us information if you didn't remember that you were on our team."

Liza flashed a grandmaster's smile. "Which is why I wouldn't be going alone. Kuni?"

Reaching into her blazer pocket, Poppy extracted the glowing piq, who seemed no worse for the close quarters. He squeaked at Poppy, who nodded and turned her attention to me. "Little guy says he's willing to help out. For an oversized firefly, he's damn good at going unnoticed."

"If you did the same thing to him that you did to Rebecca and Pete and me," Liza added, "he'd be able to understand whatever he overhears."

"And I'd be his handler," said Poppy. "Kuni gets what he can from Liza, comes to me, and I transmit it to you and the Fringe. Simple."

My headache was moments away. "Liza, I appreciate the offer, but you haven't thought this through. You're still learning to use your power—"

"Mina says I've come a long way," she countered.

"Fine, you've made progress. You're young. In a fight with someone twice your age—"

She snorted. "I don't plan to get into any fights. I go in, join them, and let things follow their natural course. They won't know I'm a spy because hell, *I* won't even remember."

"And what happens when Moyna sends you to do something for her? What if she tells you to kill someone, Liza?"

"She probably won't, because as you said, I'm young and not particularly useful. And can't you guys stick something in my reprogramming to keep me from going crazy out there?"

The three of them watched me as I struggled for a response more convincing than *This is a bad idea*. Finally, stumped, I muttered, "Eleanor's put a lot of thought into this, hasn't she?"

As they nodded, the dining room door opened, and the mastermind herself stuck her head through the crack. "It's a good plan, Coileán," she insisted, ignoring my glowering, then let herself in and pulled up a chair. "And yes, I'd be delighted to give you the preliminary details over dinner."

When the meal had ended and Poppy and Liza had taken their leave, I told Eleanor I'd think about her cockeyed scheme. "That's considerate of you," she replied as she swept toward the door, "and I'd appreciate your support, but the decision's been made. We're putting this plan into action next week after Helen and the Fringe have their little summit."

"What summit?"

She threw me a pitying glance. "Have you not spoken to Helen lately?"

"Not since she took office, no. Joey says she's staying busy—"

"You've not spoken to her in the last *month*?"

"She'd tell me if she didn't have the situation in hand," I protested, but Eleanor shut me down before I could elaborate.

"That's not the point. The way I see it, we can either sit back and wait for trouble to boil over, or we can be proactive, keep an ear to the ground at all times, and catch problems while they're still simmering. I'm not going to run intelligence for the both of us," she warned, gripping the back of a chair. "If you don't do the work, I'm not going to let you jump in whenever it's convenient. But this once, I'll fill you in."

"Generous."

She cocked her eyebrow. "Aren't I? Here's the latest from the silo: Helen's invited the Fringe's top brass over for a chat, and this is to be more than a 'getting to know you' social. She's nervous, but she's being stingy with the details. The meeting is on Saturday—be a dear and pry the other pertinent information out of Joey tomorrow, won't you?"

With that, Eleanor departed for the evening, leaving me with the nagging suspicion that I'd been outclassed.

I was waiting in the barn when Joey shuffled out of the loft midmorning the next day, dragging like he'd run a marathon. "Kicked you out of bed early again, did she?" I asked as a carafe of coffee appeared on the tack table. "How close are we to synchronization?"

"About five hours the wrong way," he mumbled, sleepwalking toward the caffeine. "And yeah. She's got a full plate today."

"She's having the Fringe over, right?" I asked, hoping

that sounded smoother than it felt.

But Joey was too groggy to notice subtleties. "Uh-huh. Got to arrange all the pickups, food, guest rooms if this goes long…"

"How many is she having over?"

He contemplated his answer while he poured. "Two dozen or so—Rick, Vivi, and a bunch of others. I don't have the full guest list."

A thought occurred to me as he drank. "Someone called Badger?"

"Yeah, that sounds right. Why?"

"Are you going to sit in on the festivities?"

"I'm not invited."

"But are you planning to be around the silo tomorrow?" Joey shrugged, and I said, "If you see Badger—Hannah Parsons, English, has a white streak in her hair—tell her we need to chat."

Even with his fatigue, Joey's eyebrow rose. "Since when do you buddy up with Fringers, boss?"

"Unfinished business," I replied, and patted his shoulder. "You know, you don't have to call me 'boss.' We're long past that."

Joey flushed. "I haven't mastered the court protocol thing, and I didn't want to piss you off—"

"You're not going to upset me over *protocol*, Joey. Let's make this simple: I'm Colin to you, all right? Coileán if you're feeling ambitious."

He grinned sheepishly. "Not that ambitious. You've heard my Irish."

I shook my head and topped up his coffee, then picked a path around Georgie's feet to the door. "Try to keep the missus from starting any wars, won't you?"

"I did tell you I'm not invited to the meeting, right?"

"You don't have to be anywhere near that meeting. You share her bed, and you have her ear. Why do you think the Council's so afraid of you, kid?"

He drained his mug and smirked as his hand swept to

encompass the barn and the lounging dragon. "I can think of a few reasons."

Strolling back to the palace, I let my thoughts run to Liza, who was eager to play at espionage. That impetuosity was more than a mere echo of Robin. She hadn't seemed swayed by my arguments the night before, but perhaps the failure was a result of the messenger. What if I conscripted Joey into dissuading her? Better yet, Rebecca? Surely one of them could convince her that walking into Moyna's arms was a poor life choice.

I was mulling over the best way to broach the matter with Joey when I rounded the corner toward my office and found Helen pacing the corridor like a caged tiger. "Looking for someone?" I asked. "I thought you were in the midst of party planning."

She paused in her circuit and ran her hands through her hair. "It's all going to hell. Help me."

The strain on her face was an unfamiliar tension that spoke of more than piecing together a jigsaw puzzle of seating arrangements. Helen wasn't merely stressed—she appeared to have spent the better part of a week inside a shallow foxhole. "What's the matter? Moon and stars, girl, what's after you?"

She met my eyes for only for a second before her gaze flickered to the dark patches down the hall. "I don't know. Someone keeps coming, and I can't even get a secure place for this meeting, and—"

I shepherded her into my office and locked the door, then headed for the bar while she slumped onto a couch. A moment of judicious pouring later, I presented her with a tumbler and two fingers of warmed brandy. "Drink it all," I ordered. "This is medicinal. If you get tipsy, I'll take care of it." To my surprise, Helen drank without protest, and I waited on the opposite couch while she finished and leaned back to rub her temples. "Deep breaths. Let the booze do its job."

"I'm warm all the way down," she murmured. "How quickly does this—"

"Keep breathing."

Five minutes and a considerable head massage later, Helen had lost enough of her edge to focus. "Someone's bugging my office," she explained. "I don't know who, and I don't know how, but every time I sweep, I find a new bug."

"Maybe you should let Aiden take a look. If any of this has to do with computers, he might spot something."

But she shook her head. "Not physical bugs—listening spells. Someone wants an ear on me, and he's great at covering his tracks. I haven't been able to pinpoint him yet, and that's with Toula taking a crack at it, too."

"You think it's a magus."

"I *know* it's a magus, but not which one of the bastards is responsible. Or two. Hell, it could be all of them, knowing the Inner Council," she muttered.

"Greg always thought the office was monitored," I replied. "This may be nothing new."

"New, tradition, or otherwise, it's got to stop. I can't work with the Council listening in on every word."

"Maybe it's a precaution."

Helen leaned forward and stared at me. "Coileán, *I don't trust them,*" she said, then laughed weakly. "God, this is absurd—I can't trust my own magi, and who do I turn to? *You?*"

"Come, now, it's not that strange. You're practically family." That earned a half-smile, and I settled into the cushions. "Am I to understand that the Council isn't invited to the powwow tomorrow?"

"No, they're not, and how did you know about the meeting? You're not bugging me, too, are you?" she asked, only somewhat in jest.

"Of course not. I talk to Eleanor, remember. Anyway, what's to be lost if some magus overhears? Surely you're not planning to embark upon a blood-soaked reign of terror."

"Not yet. If I should change my mind, you'd be the first to know." Picking up her empty glass, Helen coaxed a soda into being. "Greg left me with plenty of unfinished business. What concerns me most is that he didn't make any headway on finding the Arcanum mole you forgot to tell me about."

I declined to acknowledge the chastisement. "He said he wanted to root the spy out quietly."

"By which he meant putting the matter on the back burner and walking away. He was on the cusp of retirement—why launch an investigation that's going to annoy the wrong people when you can let your replacement handle the flak?"

"Which wrong people? I'd have thought the Council would jump on board if they knew there was a security breach."

"Ha," she muttered. "It must be lovely not to govern by committee."

"It *does* have certain perks," I admitted, "but what's the problem with your minions?"

"Precisely that: they're not my minions. The installation folks are still on my team, but I'm not going to have the Inner Council on my side until the current crop is replaced."

"How long will that take?"

Helen propped her elbow on the armrest and sighed. "The position is a life appointment, barring incapacitation or treason. It's going to be a while."

"Eh, you're young, they're mortal. It's only a matter of time. But I still don't see why the current Council would be against finding the wizard who's helping Moyna."

"That's because you're looking at this from the outside." She finished her soda, then stood and crossed to one of the windows. "Here's the trouble, and I'll be blunt," she said, addressing the garden. "The Council hates your guts."

I rose and joined her. "Can't say I'm surprised. And wow, you didn't even try to soften that blow—"

"I'm serious. They blame you for the siege."

"That was none of my doing! What, they think I put her up to it?"

"No, but they hold you responsible for letting her get to that point. You knew what she was like, and you put her back on the streets."

I pushed the unbidden image of Meggy's dead eyes from my mind. "The situation was complicated—"

"*Complicated*? She wanted you two dead, she had a boyfriend from the Gray Lands, and you slapped a light bind on her and hoped for the best. That's not complicated, Coileán—that's asking for a disaster."

"Meggy wanted—"

"Meggy was too emotionally invested to think straight, and you went along with her."

My hand began to ball up, and I forced my fingers to flex. "I don't have to explain myself to you," I replied, fighting to keep my voice level.

She maintained her calm as I twitched. "I'm not asking you to explain anything. I know damn well why you did what you did, and so does the Council, which is why they're putting the blame for Moyna squarely on you." Her face softened as she watched me drag myself under control. "Look, I've never been in that position. I know you thought you were doing the right thing."

"Wasn't I?" I muttered, leaning against the window. "What would you have had me do differently, Helen? Lock Moyna up forever and hope no one slips her a key in a cake? Execute her as a prophylactic measure? Wipe her memory again and relocate her somewhere, then cross my fingers that no one ever finds her?"

"I don't know."

"Exactly. So don't come in here and tell me I've been a fool unless you have a wiser answer than the one I chose."

She studied my expression for a moment. "I don't know what you should have done. The Arcanum has thoughts on the matter, none of which involve Moyna ever seeing the light of day again once you had her in custody."

"I should have killed her, you mean."

"That opinion has been expressed—"

I shook my head. "You're the grand magus now, kid. Stop hiding behind passive constructions. If you want to tell me something, say it."

"Fine. Nearly every magus in the silo thinks you're a fucking idiot for letting her go, and that includes Greg." She paused and winced as if anticipating an explosion, then mumbled, "Sorry. I suppose I could have softened that, too."

"Why bother? They're probably right. And you?"

She grimaced but held my gaze. "I might have killed her. Then again, she's not my child." Cocking her head, she asked, "Did Greg ever give you the Batman spiel? 'In this world, there is Batman, and then there's the mayor of Gotham,' she began in a fair impression of Greg's voice. "'Batman does what he thinks best and runs away when he's bored. The mayor has to think about the long term—about property damage and constitutional rights and keeping the lights on. Batman does what he wants, but the mayor makes the hard decisions for the good of society.' Yes?"

"Yeah, he gave me something like that once. Guess which one he thinks I am."

"Oh, I don't have to guess—he told me. But here's what he forgot when he was waxing rhapsodic on comic books: Gotham needs Batman."

I arched an eyebrow. "Meaning?"

"Meaning that sure, the mayor keeps the bills paid and the lights on, but when the shit hits the fan and he's got his hands tied, it's Batman who swoops in and saves the day. Take one of them away, and the city falls apart." Helen shrugged. "Batman's only one guy. He makes mistakes, he holds grudges. Maybe he doesn't always think about long-term civic health. But if he likes someone, he's going to go to whatever lengths it takes to make that person safe, even if it means blowing up a few buildings. That's the price Gotham pays to keep him around." She tapped one finger against the glass as she thought. "Do I agree with what you did concerning Moyna? No. But I understand why you did it, and I understand why certain options were never possibilities."

We stood in silence, staring out at the sunlight and the shifting shadows of the few clouds overhead.

"You're not actually twenty-two, are you?" I asked Helen.

"As of last month." She grinned. "Why, did I do something right?"

I squeezed her shoulder and watched a flock of sparrows swoop by. "Putting aside the question of whether the Arcanum's displeasure with me is warranted, you still haven't told me why the Council wouldn't leap at the chance to find the wizard assisting Moyna."

Helen sighed. "She's a massive sore spot. The Council's position is that we shouldn't be the ones spending time and manpower to track her down—*you* should be doing that because you started this. But Aid's priority last year was winnowing the candidates for Oberon's heir. His unwillingness to throw himself into the search irritated more than a few magi." She gave me a look of long suffering. "Aid *deeply* pissed off the Council last year. Not only did he not jump when they said to, but he gave them lip about it and shoved a few off the cliff in his place. I get it—I do," she insisted, "and I understand why he's a jackass to some of the magi. But Aid's not a politician, and the Moyna issue needed someone with a more delicate approach than his."

My face contorted as she spoke. "Do I want to know?"

"The worst meeting—this was the *very* worst, keep in mind—was the day that James Mulligan brought his son in to observe. It's not an uncommon practice, not for magi's children, and Greg had approved. Russell is Aid's age, so he'll be eligible for a magus slot in three years—"

"Russell Mulligan?" I asked as the name clicked with a face in my memory. "The boy who—"

"Used to beat the crap out of Aid, yeah. Nobody involved in that meeting thought it through. So the Council wanted an update on Moyna and got snippy, Aid had no new information and got snippier, and just when I thought I might be able to diffuse things, Russell stood up from the back of the room and said, and I quote, 'Why don't we do this without Dudley? He's useless, anyway.'"

I groaned, anticipating where this was going.

"My thoughts exactly," said Helen. "Before I could get Aid out of there, he'd thrown Russell against a wall and was about *this* close to setting him on fire. Then all the wands came out, and we had ourselves a nice little standoff while Russell cried and wet himself. The usual," she muttered. "Aid let him go, but he broke both of Russell's arms and an ankle in the process, and James almost started shooting when he saw how badly his kid was hurt. Anyway, I dragged Aid back to Faerie, and I think Val had a long talk with him, but there's no shortage of bad blood between him and the Council."

Resting my forehead against the cool glass, I mumbled, "I can't blame him…"

"Not for most of it. A seventeen-year-old with power, questionable impulse control, and scores to settle? I'd have been surprised if he'd played nicely. If Russell and the rest of those cretins had two brain cells to rub together, they'd stay out of Aid's sight. But I digress. Council's mad at you," she said, counting off on her fingers, "Council's mad at Aid, Council thinks we shouldn't be the ones searching for Moyna, and now *I'm* supposed to stroll in there and announce a hunt to ferret out a mole who's working with her? I won't hear the end of it."

"Whether they like it or not, there *is* a mole, which

means you have a security breach."

"Undoubtedly. But if there's a mole, then it's your fault or Aid's, which means that it's Joey's and my fault by association."

"Come again?"

Helen folded her arms. "Has Eleanor mentioned the number of times this month it's been suggested that I have my marriage annulled?"

I frowned. "Does Joey know?"

"Of course. He's heard me gripe every night since I moved in, and the Council isn't shy around him. A few magi have suggested that marrying him constituted treason sufficient to have me stripped of office. That hasn't gone far, but I'm not sleeping well." She held out her hand and whispered, and a shot glass full of a clear liquid that seemed suspiciously like vodka appeared in her palm. "Don't judge," she warned before she knocked it back.

I waited until her coughing fit subsided. "You know, I can't develop cirrhosis. The same doesn't go for you, kid."

"As you said," she managed between coughs, wiping her eyes, "I'm young. My liver can deal with a little punishment right now." She tossed the glass into the air and spoke a word to disintegrate it into atoms. "And that's where we stand: the Council's generally upset, I've got a spy I can't name, and someone's bugging my damn office. The Council's not invited to the meeting tomorrow because most of the silo magi have told me that they don't care what happens to the Fringe. I think we have a lot to gain from cooperation, but what do I know, I'm just the grand magus. More importantly, I don't want whoever's spying on me to overhear what we discuss in case that person is also the one working with Moyna. We've got to finalize the logistics on Hollywood, and I don't want Moyna getting wind of it before it even commences."

"Hollywood?" I echoed. "What's going on in—"

"Operation Hollywood. Putting Liza undercover. Sorry, the Fringe code-names everything."

"They know about all of that with Liza?" I folded my arms and scowled. "Okay, let's say that I may have heard about this proposal last night for the first time. How long has this been in the works?"

"About two weeks. If it helps, I don't like it, either, and Joey's not thrilled, but Liza's willing, and Eleanor thinks this has a decent chance of success. Do you have a better plan?"

"Honestly?" I mumbled.

She patted my arm and grimaced. "Want me to loop you in the next time Eleanor gets a great idea?"

"If you'd be so kind." I headed for the sanctuary of my office bar. "And I assume you need a bug-free meeting space, yes?"

"A room with chairs and doors. I'll bring my own coffee and donuts."

I considered my options, then reached for the trusty bourbon. "You think the Fringe's brass would be willing to come here?"

"As long as you offer safe passage." She joined me at the bar. "How about it? I'll even share my donuts if you let everyone go home at the end of the day."

I poured, lifted my glass in acknowledgement, and threw back the comforting fire.

CHAPTER 20

One of the perks of being the grand magus was getting to choose one's own meeting schedule. Helen set the events of her Arcanum-spy-free shindig around Montana time, and the rest of the attendees either thanked her or drank coffee.

Val placed a pair of guards at either door of the expansive meeting room I loaned Helen, both to assure the Fringers' safety and to keep them from snooping around. Aiden offered to sweep the place for electronic leavings when the horde departed, but I wasn't concerned about finding surprises in their wake. Slim was practically a friend, and Vivi had worked her way into my good graces, but for most of the Fringe, I was still an unknown lurking behind a triple-locked door with a bright red placard warning of teeth and worse on the other side. This arrangement suited me more than I'd realized. Perhaps it was a quirk of my mother's blood, but watching the delegates scurry past my guards, I couldn't help but think that Machiavelli was on to something.

Once the majority of the Fringers were sufficiently unnerved to behave themselves, I left Helen to her deal-making. I assumed that some of her guests were uneasy enough being in the presence of the Arcanum's top wizard—she didn't need me around to make matter worse. Nor, I insisted to our brother, was his attendance requested. "Come on," he wheedled, "I already know half the Fringe. Hel's not going to give you the full story, and I can sit quietly if I have to."

Joey laughed aloud, and I shrugged. "Your reputation precedes you," I told him. "And your sister ratted you out. When you told me you'd broken a few bones on the Council, I didn't think you were being *literal*."

Aiden slumped in his chair and sulked. "Like *you've* never lost your temper."

"I didn't say that," I replied, and yanked his ponytail before he could slap me away. "Leave them be. Helen will tell me whatever's necessary, and Joey will tell me the rest."

That pronouncement caused Joey to look at me askance. "I don't know, I never signed up to be a double agent. If Helen doesn't want you to know everything—"

"Trust me, she's anticipating that you'll let slip whatever's critical. The girl's no fool. Besides," I said, grinning, "you and I have an understanding, right?"

"Well, yeah, but I'm sleeping with *her*."

At that, Aiden groaned and covered his ears. "Dude, don't go there."

Joey chuckled and swatted him on the head. "Let's go, the Wii's still in my room. And if we're lucky, maybe we'll find another unicorn for you to befriend along the way."

Aiden slugged him in the gut and stalked out, but Joey, seeing my bemusement, shook his head. "They're so sensitive at that age," he declared with a wink, then followed Aiden toward the staircase.

Though perplexed, I let it go and settled in for a long day of treading water. With the glut of complaints to address, I lost myself—and much of the afternoon and evening—in my work. Only once I heard a knock that night did I look up from the bright glow of the computer and realize the sun was long gone, I was sitting in the dark, and I was starving. "Come in!" I called as the candelabra flared and a sandwich appeared beside me.

I paused with dinner almost to my mouth when Hannah Parsons stuck her head around the open door. "Bad time?" she asked.

My stomach protested, but I put my meal down and

stood. "Grabbing a bite. Come out of the hall." I beckoned her into the room, but I was surprised when Toula trailed her inside and closed the door. "Did Joey talk to you?"

"Helen. She said that he said you wanted to see me." The detective stood awkwardly beside the couches, clutching an oversized black valise, and watched me approach. "I've been meaning to call, actually. Is, ehm…is Dr. Richardson—"

"She's managing. Sit, please," I offered, and took the couch opposite hers as my other visitor perched on the back. "Toula, was there something you wanted?"

"Nah, I'm chaperoning," she said. "Don't mind me."

"Weren't you going to help Helen get the Fringe home?"

She shrugged. "Carver's got that under control, and since *someone* isn't off shift for another hour, I thought I'd stop in and—"

"Moon and stars," I muttered, resting my head in my palm, "tell Mina she can have the night off if it'll get you out of my hair."

Toula grinned and slid off her perch. "Ta, Gramps," she replied with a little wave, and the door slammed in her haste to depart.

My remaining companion frowned as Toula's rapid footsteps faded. "'Gramps'? Is she your—"

"*God*, no. Stick around long enough, and she'll probably find a nickname for you, too."

Hannah chuckled. "Thanks, but I've got plenty already. And I wanted to give Dr. Richardson this. I've only had it a week, so I haven't been holding out on her." She unlatched her valise, extracted a white cardboard cube, and carefully set it on the coffee table.

"Is that—"

She nodded. "No one ever claimed the body. I thought she'd want to have him." The detective hesitated, watching my expression. "I couldn't have him intact, but I said I'd take the ashes to a memorial garden since no one else seemed to want him. The...*cremains* came like this"—she nudged the box toward me—"and I didn't know what Dr. Richardson wanted done with them. If you think this would be too distressing to her now, I could keep them a while longer..."

I stared at the unmarked box, which squatted on my table like the world's worst batch of Chinese takeout. "She's ready. I'll see that she gets this, and, uh...thank you, Detective."

She nodded, visibly relieved to be unburdened, and sat back against the cushion. "Now that that's out of the way, what can I do for you?"

"Well," I said, mirroring her pose if only to distance myself from Walt's ashes, "I was curious about the investigation. Any progress?"

"Cold as ice. We ran down a few leads, but nothing of substance. No one even contested the wills, which was a pleasant surprise."

"Oh?"

"Wave a few quid around, and relatives come crawling out like cockroaches." She tucked her white forelock behind her ear. "With the sum they left to the university, I was expecting at least a call from some long-lost cousin. Nothing. It's like the Glastonbury Drummonds forgot he ever existed."

"Or opted to ignore an inconvenient fact," I murmured.

Her mouth twitched into a smirk. "Precisely. I asked Helen to look into the matter. If she wants to improve Arcanum–Fringe relations, she can start by seeing to it that our more talented kin acknowledge us." Hannah's voice hardened as she spoke. "That man was clever and kind and well respected. He deserved better than *that*," she said, jutting her chin toward the carton. "Not that I don't want his wife to have him back, but it's appalling that none of his family claimed him."

I paused to assess the detective's mood before pressing on. "Do you have family there, too?"

Her smirk reappeared and solidified. "Two aunts, two uncles, and some cousins. My father's the witch of the family. Went away, married my mundane mother, and never looked back. Don't waste your pity—I've never spoken to the lot."

"Is Helen aware of—"

"Not yet. Maybe someday. We've got more important matters to sort than getting me an invitation to the Parsons family reunion. Besides," she said, shifting in her seat, "what wizard gives a damn about his witchy kin? I'm Fringe by inheritance—I can barely do anything with magic. What would they do with someone like me?"

I didn't answer that, as Hannah didn't strike me as the type to appreciate a feel-good lie. "Want to tell me what Helen has in mind for this partnership, then? You know, in case it all goes to hell?"

She drummed her fingers on her knees, then seemed to reach a decision. "I suppose I could share a bit of intel without jeopardizing things."

"Nothing too sensitive, now."

"Of course not," she replied with a wry smile. "I have experience in interrogation, mind you—I know the tricks. Perk of the profession." She glanced at the table between us as a porcelain teacup appeared within arm's reach. "See you're playing Good Cop, then."

"Not at all," I replied as she sampled my handiwork. "I can't risk having you pass out on me from lack of tea in your bloodstream. Or are you not afflicted by your national ailment?"

She grinned over the rim. "One does what one must. Cheers."

With her thirst slaked, the detective set the cup aside and absently steepled her fingers as she inspected the ceiling mosaic. "Right, here's the meat of it. Helen wanted to bring us into the Arcanum fold."

"All of you?"

"*All* of us. There was some discussion of using only members with Arcanum connections as go-betweens, but that was shot down immediately."

I chuckled. "Vivi had thoughts, did she?"

"Not her," said Hannah. "Do you know Butterfly?"

"Maybe," I said, trying to bring her face to mind. "Brit, yes? Fifties, glasses, fat dog—"

"That would be Charles, also known as the Wonder Weiner, as in it's a wonder he can still walk about with his stomach dragging the floor. Butterfly's the senior coordinator for the south…we've got a regional bureaucracy, you understand," she explained. "Butterfly's based in London, and I cover the north—everything above Leeds."

"Ah. So Slim has what, the eastern U.S.?"

"And then some. Formally, he oversees the Atlantic states, but I understand he's the de facto coordinator for everything east of the Mississippi, and he has pull out to the Rockies."

"That's…surprising," I said, but quickly thought of the workshop beneath Slim's bar and the well-appointed apartment above it. What about my bartender *hadn't* been a surprise? "And Vivi? Alaska?"

But Hannah shook her head. "Vivi's a decent contender to replace Slim someday, but she's not a coordinator yet. Officially, she takes direction from him."

I smiled. "Unofficially?"

"You've made her acquaintance, haven't you? Anyway, it was Butterfly who put a stop to giving us an Arcanum-friendly front. She was *vehemently* opposed, and when she's set her mind on something, she doesn't have to look hard to find supporters."

"So what's her problem? Fae blood? Wants to stick this in the Arcanum's craw?"

"No to the first—she's a witch. As to the second, I don't know every corner of her mind, but she made a good point: the Fringe is the Fringe. No one else will have us, so we have each other. If the Arcanum wants to be cordial, that's all well and good, but they don't get to choose which of us they accept." She shrugged and picked up her teacup as it refilled. "The courts' recent dealings with our members didn't escape discussion."

"Oh?"

Her lips curled into a brief smile. "You've met almost exclusively with fae-blooded Fringers, aside from me, but that appears to have been happenstance. Dr. Richardson *did* marry a witch, so that balances the scales for now." She sipped and regarded me closely. "How about it? Any reservations in dealing with the rest of us?"

I linked my hands behind my head and stretched. "None. And lest it go unnoted, Slim's a witch-blood."

"Due credit was given. But back to Helen. She'd like to establish a more formal relationship with us—an alliance, I suppose. We wouldn't be answering to the Arcanum, but we'd be a dependable ally in case of trouble."

"So…the J.V. Arcanum, as it were?"

"That was her original thought. Also shot down."

I sat up and leaned toward her. "Do tell."

"Why so surprised?" she asked between sips. "We're an independent entity—we're no one's lapdog. Sure, we wouldn't mind having more formalized dealings with the Arcanum, and we wouldn't say no to a regular exchange of information, but I know plenty of Fringers who'll go sledding in Hell before they take orders from the grand magus."

"How'd she take the news?"

"Well, I thought. She's young, she's learning—and asking to meet with us is more than her predecessor ever did, so she's won points for effort. Honestly," Hannah confided, leaning toward me as she put her cup aside, "I think having the meeting here was a wise choice. This isn't exactly *neutral* ground, but it's better than meeting her in the heart of the bloody silo."

I kept my silence as to the reason for the location. "Happy to help."

She fixed me with a careful look, leaving me with the suspicion that I was on the wrong end of the interrogation. "You're in an odd position, aren't you? Both of you, but particularly you. You're tied to Helen through Aiden, and you're both connected to her through Joey…or is our information wrong?"

"That's fairly accurate," I admitted, "but if you think Helen has any special influence because of—"

"No, that's not what I was suggesting. What we see is an opportunity for the Arcanum and the courts to cooperate—a natural line of communication, if you will. That hasn't happened before, and we're watching with interest."

"You're not the only ones." I paused to read her practiced blank face. "Detective…if I may ask, what does the Fringe know about recent developments with the Company?"

"Since Jeanine's murder? Little and less. That's why we're so involved in Hollywood—a silent Company is a dangerous Company, and we've been cordial in the past. If their members are being threatened, we have a duty to step in."

"What duty? You're in a formal partnership now?"

Her dark eyes hardened. "Nothing of the sort. We work for the greater good, Coileán. If that means we come to the Company's aid, so be it."

I recalled what the Fringe had done in the last year. "In that case, want to tell me what this Hollywood scheme entails?"

The plan was a multifaceted relay system, and I hated every bit of it.

Either Eleanor or I was to put a bind of false memories on Liza, erasing her knowledge of the Bolins and the rest of us. We would knock her out and leave her in Idaho, having implanted in her a drive to seek out Moyna and join her band. Comparing notes with Vivi, Poppy agreed that the Fringe had probably gotten a lead on where the weres were based through Alpha's call. The biggest gamble was our assumption that *these* weres were working with Moyna, but waiting for further confirmation was out of the question, as far as Eleanor was concerned.

Accompanying Liza, Kuni would keep himself hidden—given the piq's constant glow, I had no idea how his kind managed the trick—and would spy without her knowledge. Every few days, he would report his findings to Poppy, who would pass them along to us.

"Wait, stop," I told Eleanor as she laid out the plan. "This has more holes than a sieve. First, even if we load Kuni up with the necessary languages, how's Poppy supposed to understand him?"

She cocked her head and fixed me with a look of incredulity. "He's fluent in Fae. So is she, we've seen to that. Just because you don't listen carefully when he squeaks doesn't mean everyone is similarly lazy."

"I'm not *lazy*. He speaks at frequencies common to bats."

"A little practice is all it takes. Poppy understands him well enough to pass his reports along."

"So this is to be a glorified game of telephone, then? Everything he sees gets filtered through her? What if she decides to filter in the name of Company security?"

Eleanor sighed and massaged her forehead. "Aiden's outfitting Kuni with enough equipment to produce a spy movie. Still cameras, audio recorders, video recorders, bugs—"

"How the hell is he supposed to carry it all? The little guy's what, six inches tall?"

Her incredulity deepened. "Aiden's building them at standard size and shrinking them with enchantment. He says he's had practice doing work for the Fringe." She shrugged. "Anyway, he's our best shot for gadgetry, and if that fails, we'll have to trust Poppy. You think she'd hold back, all things considered?"

She had a point, but I wasn't in a concessionary mood. "And what about Poppy? She'll have to stay close to Liza if Kuni's making these runs. You want to put her near the weres that have been trying to find her? They're *werewolves*. Someone's going to smell her, and then what's she supposed to do?"

Speaking slowly, as if she were explaining something remarkably simple to a petulant toddler, Eleanor replied, "We transform her. I understand that Toula has experience in this area if you're uncomfortable with it. All we need do is change her face and scent, and she'll be able to move about with ease."

"If we lock her into a transformation, she won't be able to shift if she needs to."

"She's aware of the risks. So that's Liza, Kuni, and Poppy sorted—"

"No, it's not. How's Poppy going to pass all of this along to us, then? Phone it in? Assuming, of course, that no one's bugged her phone…"

She waited until I ran out of steam, then folded her arms. "First, if we buy the girl a burner phone, it won't be bugged. Second, I'm sending Rufus with her as backup."

That got my attention. "The Stowe boy? Why him?"

"He's willing and able—he's only teaching one class this semester—but more importantly, he has Fringe credentials."

"I thought Vivi was the only Fringer of the family."

"She is," said Eleanor, though her veneer of patience was beginning to crack. "Rufus and one of their brothers were heavily involved in the mess in Montana. Vivi says they've been given associate membership, as it were. In any case, they can access the Fringe network—you know, their communication program?"

"It's more than that," I said. "They run their intel

operations through the network. Who signed off on granting access to more Stowes?"

"You'd have to ask Vivi. Anyway, the plan is that Kuni reports to Poppy and delivers his recordings, and Rufus stops in every few days to help disseminate. Plus, since he won't be using any Arcanum resources, Helen can learn what she needs to know without raising anyone's suspicion on the Council. We've thought about this. You're not going to be difficult, are you?"

Seeing as the necessary parties had colluded behind my back, there was little I could do to dissuade Eleanor from moving forward, and so I gritted my teeth and pitched in. The only other naysayer was Joey, who balked at the thought of sending Liza in under deep cover. "I'm not trying to make trouble," he confided in me one evening shortly before the operation commenced, "but…I mean, she's my great-grandmother, I've barely gotten to know her, and now she's going to go hang out with a bunch of psychos in Idaho. Mom wouldn't let her do this without a fight."

"Which is why Rebecca knows nothing, correct?" I replied.

His shoulders hunched. "I haven't said anything. And it's not my place to tell Liza what she can and can't do, but—"

"But you've seen combat, and she hasn't."

Joey nodded. "I know Val gave you the rundown of what happened while you were out of it, but…Colin, I was *there*. I saw what Oberon's people did here, and I saw what Moyna's did in Montana. That's not something you forget." He paused to judge my reaction. "Toula's not thrilled, either. She says it needs to happen, but she's not happy about it. Neither is Rufus."

"I thought Rufus was on board with it," I said, frowning.

His mouth tightened. "Rufus was there, too. When Eleanor approached him, he agreed, but mostly because he already has an idea of what he's up against. That doesn't mean he likes it."

Regardless of our misgivings and reservations, the operation proceeded as planned. On the morning of the team's departure, as we gathered in Eleanor's throne room, Aiden presented Kuni with a miniature satchel of electronic equipment—a cross-body bag by necessity, keeping in mind the piq's additional pair of limbs. Toula, who admittedly had more experience with transformation than either Eleanor or I did, performed the necessary work on Poppy, leaving her in the form of a sinewy, brown-haired man of perhaps thirty-five. Whereas Poppy had been on the cusp of beautiful, her new face was plain and unremarkable, a face that blended into a crowd and passed unnoticed. Once transformed, she patted her arms and torso, adjusting to the bizarre sensation of the stranger's body, then nodded and turned to Rufus. "Passable?" she asked, her voice suddenly lower and husky.

He waited while she did a slow turn, then held up his thumb. "I wouldn't know the difference."

"Good," she replied, but paused as a thought hit her. "And I don't care what this looks like," she added, tapping her flat chest, "if we bunk together, you do *not* get to see me topless."

"Not to worry," he replied, slinging his arm around her shoulders. "Hey, play your cards right, and I'll teach you to write your name in the snow."

Before Poppy could dive too deeply into the quirks of her new form, I slipped away to join Eleanor and Liza in Eleanor's office for the delicate work of the bind. "You may have heard about my track record on these," I said once I'd locked the door. "Meggy and Moyna's were imperfect—"

"That's still two more than I've attempted," Eleanor interjected, "so you're taking the lead on this."

Lying on Eleanor's new leather couch with her hands folded across her stomach, Liza looked up and smiled nervously. "Do what you need to do, all right? Whatever it takes. I don't want this bind to slip at the wrong moment."

I crouched beside her and met her dark eyes—Robin's eyes, but twitching with nervousness. "This won't hurt. I'll put you to sleep and craft the bind, and when you wake up, you'll be on your way to Moyna. Nothing to it," I said with false confidence.

Liza reached out to take my hand. "We're going to be okay. They know what they're doing, and I'm sure I'll muddle through somehow. I've made it this far," she added, trying to inject a bit of levity into her voice. "Already had angry wizards on my doorstep. What's a few werewolves, eh?"

Failing to match her smile, I settled for squeezing her cold hand. "You won't remember us or ever being here, not until the bind breaks. But if you can, try to remember to be careful. Look out for yourself, Liza. No one's going to be there if you get in trouble…"

She nodded too quickly. "Go ahead," she said, closing her eyes. "I'm ready."

I tried one last time. "You know you don't have to do this, right? Whatever Eleanor and Poppy and…and whoever else have told you, this isn't your responsibility."

Eleanor's eyes narrowed, but Liza tightened her grip on my hand. "I've run from an awful lot," she said softly. "I ran from the people I should have been protecting. This…" She sighed. "This is where I stop running. *This* is where I try to start making amends. To be the person I should have been for my son." She flashed a small smile. "Go on, now. Give me your best shot."

And, God help me, I did.

CHAPTER 21

Eleanor and I waited a long, troubling week for the first report. Still, we had plenty to keep us occupied in the interim—our courts' incursions onto the wrong side of the border were happening with increasing frequency. "I don't understand," she muttered one night as I compared our latest complaints to the database. "What's to be gained by harassing each other?"

"Old grudges, I guess," I replied.

"*Very* old," Val added from the door. "Separating the courts cured nothing."

Eleanor scowled at him. "You've been making enquiries, I suppose? Taking the pulse of the populace?"

He didn't snap at the proffered bait. "No need, my lady. I've seen this before—same problems, same patterns, and most of the same parties."

I slowly entered new information, cursing myself for never mastering a typewriter. "All right, Val, what are we facing?" I asked as I hunted for the elusive Z.

"Slow escalation." The wooden door creaked as he leaned against it. "Bloodshed is coming, that's inevitable— the question is from whom."

"You can't know that," Eleanor protested. "We've taken precautions, we've separated them, we've handled each complaint fairly—"

"You're missing the point." Val's voice sharpened with frustration and softened in the space of an instant. "May I speak frankly?"

She waved one hand in his direction. "Enlighten me."

Before he could begin, I rose and stepped between them. Eleanor had grown more agitated every day that passed without word from our spies, and Val, though superficially calm, couldn't hide his irritation. "We're listening," I told him. "What's bothering you?"

His eyebrow arched. "Are you sure? I suspect I'm about to cause offense."

I shot Eleanor a look, and she raised her hands and said, "All right, I apologize. Captain, if you please."

Val regarded us in turn. "You didn't take my advice last time. Hear me: the problem is that neither of you truly understands how to rule Faerie."

"And what would you know about it?" Eleanor snapped, flaring again.

He held her gaze until she glanced away. "Unlike you, I've seen what it takes to maintain order here. Coileán managed with only one court to consider, and Aiden had the sense to listen to experience, but now, with two courts and all of the old grievances resurfacing? You can't *negotiate* your way through this. You can't make rules and boundaries without muscle behind them. You've been trying for weeks—"

"Two months," I mumbled.

"As you like. A hand that crosses the line can't be slapped—it must be cut off. *That* is how you keep Faerie from disintegrating into chaos."

"That's draconian," Eleanor countered. "There's no need to resort to terror—"

Val groaned. "Child, you *do* understand who and what you're ruling, don't you?"

"I'm not a *child*," she said, bristling. "And yes, I'm well aware."

"Are you? You've spent your life hiding from our kind. Name one long-term connection you've had to someone at least half fae." She glowered in silence, and Val shrugged. "Exactly. And since I'm older than the two of you together, perhaps you could listen without fighting me on every syllable."

They stood locked in their uneasy standoff until Eleanor stepped back a pace. "Very well, I'm listening. Where have we erred?"

"You've been looking to the enemy beyond your border. I can't fault you for that. Moyna should be neutralized, and the Arcanum and Company situations bear monitoring. But you've been so focused on the smoke elsewhere that you've overlooked the fire within your own walls. For instance, that is a useful toy," he continued, pointing to my computer. "There's nothing wrong with the cataloguing that Aiden did. But looking at a record of a dispute doesn't tell you the whole story. It doesn't tell you who started the fight or what the true catalyst might have been. It doesn't tell you how many times Titania or Oberon was forced to step into the fray and hand down punishment. *I* could tell you, but no one has asked me."

I plucked a complaint letter off the desk and extended it to him. "What are we missing?"

Val read it carefully, then handed it back. "This sounds as if it's about a garden. A mutual reluctance to recognize the true borders. Yes?"

"Yes…"

He shook his head. "Raingol and Jermian have been squabbling for thirteen centuries. They're half sisters— Jermian's parents belonged to Oberon's court, but Raingol's mother was one of Titania's. Their father gave Jermian more attention, and Raingol was jealous." He pointed to the letter. "You can raise a fence between the two of them, but you'll never stop the fighting. They're *fae*. And you're foolish enough to think you're going to fix this with a few sternly-worded suggestions?"

Neither of us replied, and he began to pace the room. "Coileán, I told you how Titania kept the intra-court complaints to a minimum. You don't have to like it, but both of you need to look to your parents' example. If you don't show the courts that this behavior won't be tolerated, there may come a day when you *cannot* control them. Not without bloodshed."

"And I told you that I'm not a despot," I countered. "I don't think Eleanor is, either." She nodded, but I watched Val continue in his circuit, unfazed by my reply. "We can work these conflicts out. If we've even-handed with these matters, if we smooth the friction as much as we can—"

"They *invaded* us," he interrupted, stopping in his tracks to glare at me. "Or had you forgotten? This court hasn't. And now you two expect us to coexist?" He ran his hands through his hair in agitation. "When the silo was under siege, I was able to organize a volunteer force in short order because we had a common enemy. Oberon invaded, incarcerated, stole, *killed*. The moment anyone thought we had a chance of overthrowing him, the court came together. And when they'd routed his people here, they were only too happy to go after Moyna's. Now, I'd guess that almost all of the complaints you've received of late have been about inter-court matters. Yes?"

Feeling like a chastised child, I nodded glumly, and Eleanor did likewise.

"You've given each court a common enemy. Do you know how many died here during the invasion? We lost two hundred twenty, not counting the casualties from the silo. They lost ninety-nine, plus Oberon…plus the three hundred twenty-seven Aiden executed. There are grudges, and then there are *grudges*. You have half fae on both sides who lost family, and they have blood grievances. The rest want revenge. They're not openly at war yet, but these petty complaints are the preliminary skirmishes."

"You have theories?" said Eleanor. "Where do you see this fight beginning?"

Val nodded. "I have theories, but I've also asked Aiden to consider the available data and predict the likelihood of several scenarios. If you'd bring him here, he should be able to give you something more concrete than my conjecture."

"Go get him," I muttered, leaning against my desk as I processed Val's words. Aiden had killed *how* many of Eleanor's people in my absence? *Three hundred twenty-seven?*

Divining my thoughts, Eleanor waited until Val stepped out, then murmured, "I had no idea the boy had it in him. He showed me some of his encounters with my siblings, but *that...*"

Shaking my head, I said, "I dumped the court in his lap. The ones he executed—"

"Deserved what they got." Startled, I turned to Eleanor, who regarded me impassively. "The ones who went with Oberon were invaders. Perhaps if I'd stepped forward at the start and reasoned with Aiden, he'd have surrendered them to me. But I didn't, so some of the fault may be mine. The boy did what he did to hold your court together."

"You'd be wise not to repeat that sentiment outside this room."

She snorted. "I'm not an idiot, you know."

A few minutes later, Val returned with Aiden, who quickly set up his equipment. He created a wide screen against one wall with a flick of his wrist, but as he bent over his laptop, he could have been any teenager: wrinkled T-shirt, faded jeans, hair too shaggy to be anything but a phase. There was nothing about him that hinted at what he had done in the last year. And yet...

"Just a minute more. The file's huge," said Aiden, then frowned as he glanced at me. "You okay, Coileán?"

I forced myself to nod. Eleanor caught my eyes and shook her head, and I swallowed the question that burned to leap out at Aiden: *How could you do that?*

The presence at the back of my mind pushed its way to the fore. *He did what was required. Do not ask him about the executions*, Faerie warned.

"I need to know," I whispered.

Then know that he screamed himself awake every night for

*months. Know that he fears he is becoming Titania because he did
what she would have done. The necessary thing. I give you power, but
I cannot guarantee peace. That is for you and Eleanor to make—
and that is what Aiden did.*

"No one told me how many—"

*Because you could do nothing to change the past, and because the
boy isn't ready to discuss it. You made the choice to leave him in
charge. You can't blame him for making the decisions you should
have made.*

"I was *unconscious*. I wasn't in a position to make any
decisions."

Eleanor's brow arched, and I realized that the realm
had made her privy to our conversation. "Can you talk of
this later?" she whispered, cocking her head toward Aiden
and the projected image covering the wall screen, and the
alien voice retreated to its usual hiding place in my head.

If Aiden knew what was on my mind, he played dumb
with aplomb. "Here's what we've got for you," he said,
beckoning Eleanor and me to his side as ten columns of
black text filled the screen. "I asked the field guide team to
take a census a few months ago. Here's what we had as of
November. This is everyone in the court actually living in
Faerie, and as many of the ones outside the realm that we
could track down. We don't know of more than a dozen
on the other side, but I'm sure there are others."

"Liza," Eleanor murmured.

"Bingo." He tapped a button, and the image changed
into a massive diagram of colored circles and squares.
"Once we had an idea of what we were dealing with, I
nagged Toula until she helped me out."

She peered at the screen. "Good heavens, is that what I
think it is?"

"Court-wide family tree," Aiden confirmed. "Toula ran
the aural analysis spell when she had time, and this was the
result. Bright red is fully fae, striped marks half fae, and the
red gets pinker with distance. Deceased have gray borders,
and the fully gray ones at the top mark conjecture—Toula

found common ancestors, but no one knows who they might have been. The records here *suck*."

I stepped closer to examine the sprawling diagram, which more closely resembled a hedge than a tree. Then again, mine isn't a race known for monogamy. "And the other colors?"

"The usual. Blue for mundane partners, green for wizard. Anyone from Eleanor's court is in brown, Mab's is in purple, and Fringers got white outlines. Best I could do."

There was good reason for the size of the screen. I tried to count my deceased siblings, but the gray-rimmed blobs ran together before I hit more than two score. Many of them had children, and some several generations more than that. I located myself somewhere in the middle of the pack, then Aiden at the far-right end, a red and green square. He had included Helen on the edge of the screen, connected to Joey, whose square was an odd mixture of blue with pink and tan stripes.

After a moment of contemplation, Eleanor said, "This is impressive, but what does it have to do with the current situation?"

"Glad you asked." Aiden tapped the diagram into motion. As the trees shifted to the left, another set appeared in the empty space beside them, and he widened the screen to accommodate the spillover. The new shapes were predominantly brown instead of red, with plenty of blue stripes and gray markers. "Okay, some of this is our best guess because Toula hasn't had a chance to do her thing with the other court, and we don't have a full census. A lot of this came from Val and the Stowes."

She gnawed her lip in thought. "I could conduct my own census if you'd give me a few days—"

"Believe me, it'll take longer than that. Anyway, here's what you need to see." He touched a button, and the screen exploded in a riot of bright yellow arrows forming overlapping connections between the living and dead.

"This is a diagram of who's killed whom over the years."

The thick bundles of arrows coming from my mother and Oberon—and from Aiden—weren't lost on me. "That's, uh—"

"Depressing," Eleanor finished. "And more intra-court than I'd imagined."

"Yeah, that surprised me, too." said Aiden. "But ignore those. Here are the worst of the inter-court feuds." The trees vanished, replaced by five zigzagging rows of shapes. "Right, then," he said, and aimed a laser pointer at the start of the top row, a gray square bearing a name I'd never heard. "The upper line in each grouping is Coileán's, the bottom is Eleanor's. First link in the chain here died roughly five thousand years ago. His brother avenged him—I've written the killer under each victim in red, see—and one of *his* victim's sisters took him out. The next was a cousin, then another sibling…you get the picture." The laser vanished, and he gestured toward the screen. "The deaths come more quickly once you get half fae involved. Any faerie will defend his honor, right, but if you've got a situation where people are killing each other over the deaths of loved ones…" He shrugged. "We've got feuds that put the Hatfields and McCoys to shame."

Eleanor's face tightened. "You think these are the most likely to flare?"

"Well, these have been the most volatile over time. That's not to say that someone else couldn't snap first—"

"Who are the anticipated aggressors?"

A tight cluster of shapes appeared at the far-right end of each line. "I've listed close kin on both sides," Aiden explained, "since no one's mellowed in the time apart. It could be any of these, or it could be someone more remote. Or in another group entirely…" His voice faded while we stepped closer to the screen to read the names.

"Dozens," Eleanor murmured. "How are we supposed to keep them away from each other?"

I tried to ignore the knot in my gut. "Guards on the

border. No one crosses without authorization—"

"The border's a joke, and you know it. What about—"

"Listen," Aiden cut in, "I had a lot of success with—"

She wheeled on him and snapped, "I didn't ask your opinion, *boy*."

"Excuse the hell out of me," he muttered, and pressed a key. The screen blanked in an instant, and Aiden snapped the computer closed. "I'll be on my way."

"Stop, put that back up," she said, gripping his arm as he passed. "I need to see—"

He shrugged her off. "I'm not your personal assistant, and I don't take orders from you. If you want to see my work, fine, but you can drop the attitude first."

"*Attitude*? Of all the cheek—"

"Aiden," I cautioned.

He ignored me. "Sure, brush me off," he told her. "What do I know? I mean, I've been here longer than you have—"

"You're an impertinent child!"

"I kept the peace here for a year. You've been at it two months. How's that working out?"

Her fists clenched. "Mind your tongue."

"Or what, you're going to kill me? I'm telling you the truth. You wanted the writing on the wall, and I gave it to you. We're sitting on a powder keg."

"*Aiden*," I said sharply, and he fixed me with a stubborn glare. "That's enough."

His mouth twitched as he fought to keep his angry words inside, but he swallowed, gritted his teeth, and dropped his computer on the table. "Have fun. I'm out."

The door slammed behind him, and Eleanor met my eyes. "You know I can't afford to suffer tantrums like that."

"He's right," I muttered, opening Aiden's abandoned laptop.

"That may be, but I need to save face."

"With whom? Val? No one else saw that."

"*This* time. You must bring him to heel, Coileán."

I held up my hand. "He's bright, and he's frustrated, and you set him off."

"If I wanted advice from a boy—"

"You didn't have to yell at him!"

In the corner, Val sighed and rubbed his face. "Children, if you please."

"That's enough from you," she barked, and jabbed her finger toward the door. "Get out. I want a word alone with Coileán."

I met Val's questioning glance with a nod, and he gave us our privacy. As the door latched, Eleanor lowered her voice and stepped closer to me. "You're taking orders from your guard and the boy. Do you think that's wise?"

"They're right. You saw the data, Eleanor."

"I saw a teenager's attempt to reduce millennia of complex interpersonal relationships to probabilities, and he still had nothing solid for us. I don't see how we can prevent all inter-court contact. What are we supposed to do, put the likeliest contenders on house arrest?"

I made a face. "Well, for a time—"

"I was being facetious! We can have peace without a totalitarian state."

Her anger radiated in my direction like hot waves, and I struggled to keep my composure. "I hear you. But assuming Val and Aiden are correct, we have to do something before the situation worsens. What do you have in mind?"

"*If* they're correct. Which I'm not yet conceding."

"What do you see to the contrary?"

She moved uncomfortably close and murmured, "I see an old soldier with grudges to soothe. I see a little boy who had his favorite toy taken away. Now, we have two options. We can give in to fear, do as they say, and build all the useless walls we like, or we can accept that the courts are going through a transitional period and ride it out. Trust our instincts. Rule with justice instead of by fear.

What say you?"

Her gaze didn't waver, and I soon buckled. "All right," I sighed, "we'll keep trying. But it couldn't hurt to keep an eye on Aiden's targets."

"Aiden's *dozens* of targets."

"I'm not going to ignore his findings," I replied, stepping out of her reach. "He's trying to help."

"He's still a child."

"Val isn't." I paused, listening for noise in the corridor, but heard nothing beyond our breathing. "You do know who he is, don't you?"

Her brows knit. "Your captain?"

"He's Toula's brother," I said, then watched Eleanor's face while the realization set in.

"He…" She pointed at the closed door. "He's…but I thought he worked for you—"

"He does. But if things had been different—"

"Val would be the third of us," she murmured. "If the realm empowered him."

I nodded. "He hasn't misled me yet. If he thinks we're headed for a cliff, we'd be stupid not to listen."

She drummed her fingers on her arm, then met my eyes again. "You trust him?"

"With my life. Val doesn't want a court—he's not trying to sabotage us."

"Why would he need a court? He's had one for the last year, hasn't he?" My only response was a glower, and she huffed, "Fine, we monitor. But nothing more." With that, she opened Aiden's laptop and waited as the diagram reappeared. "I've got the names. You might want a pencil."

Three days later, dawn found me in my dining room with Aiden and our notes. He'd grudgingly agreed to discuss his findings again—a partial reconciliation in which I couldn't help but spot Val's fingerprints. I trod with caution, listening more than talking as Aiden walked me through his predicted scenarios, and I was scribbling down a few points to bring to Eleanor when Rufus poked his head into the room.

"Morning." He held up a sandwich baggie full of miniaturized equipment. "Want to retrieve the tapes, Aid? I'm not messing with the enchantment on these."

Aiden dropped his computer and jumped up from the table. "Lab. Let's go," he said, and the two of them were gone before I could ask for a status update.

Feeling suddenly sick, I flipped open my phone. "He's back," I said when Eleanor picked up. "They're pulling the tapes now."

"Did they find Moyna?"

"I don't know," I said, and ended the call. Putting the phone aside, I rested my head in my palms, waiting as the wave of anticipation, dread, and nausea crested. When Eleanor appeared a few minutes later, I forced myself to stand and open a gate to Aiden's suite. "Shall we?"

My brother had expanded his footprint in my absence, and his original room had multiplied threefold, branching off into the computer-heavy control room for the mapping project, and then, through a door posted with a warning placard, into his lab. As Eleanor led the way into his inner sanctum, Aiden muttered, "Touch nothing," and extracted a plastic card from one of Kuni's devices.

She surveyed the space—a white-walled, windowless chamber lit by humming fluorescents and ringed with deep workbenches. A generator powered the half-dozen computers Aiden had left running, but I couldn't name the other devices scattered around his space. I followed Eleanor's narrow-eyed gaze to the table on which a few sheets of thin-rolled steel rested and quietly explained, "Sometimes he needs custom pieces. It's best to avoid that side of the room."

Aiden and Rufus sat on wooden stools at a central island, their faces lit by the soft glow of a laptop. "I haven't vacuumed in a few days, so watch where you put your hands," Aiden said, not looking up from his work. "There's probably scrap floating around."

"You're a masochistic little thing, aren't you?" she replied.

"Pragmatic. And if you start enchanting in here, I *will* throw you out."

"Enchanting with what? There's barely any magic flowing in this room."

His fingers continued their rapid tapping. "There's a regulating enchantment around here because of the electronics. Don't like it, step outside."

She glared at me, and I cleared my throat. "Aiden, would it kill you to be civil?"

He paused to give me a look of weary exasperation. "I can do this quickly, or I can be charming. I can't do both with my caffeine this low. Choose."

I held up my hands and stepped back, and he resumed his typing. "Teenagers," Eleanor muttered, but she found a safe patch of wall to lean against while he worked.

After a few minutes, Aiden unmoored his computer and pointed us into the next room. When we'd assembled around his bank of dark monitors, he turned them on and filled them with collages taken from Kuni's cameras, grainy photographs and little snippets of video. "Okay," he said, swiveling in his chair to face Rufus, "when you see him, tell him to up the resolution on the still camera. He's got plenty of memory space, and I'd like to be able to tell faces apart."

"Got it," said Rufus. "What about the video?"

He stopped the playback, a shaky scene of shirtless men in jeans standing in a snowy clearing and howling at the crescent moon. "He's not going to win any awards, but it's usable. Tell him to lay off the zoom and try to hold the damn thing still."

"Forget the aesthetics," Eleanor interrupted. "Is Moyna there, yes or no?"

Rufus toyed with the strings of his university hoodie. "Yes. She pops in and out, but she's making regular visits to Idaho. Could I get a local projection?" he asked Aiden, who switched one of the monitors to a map. "Kuni doesn't pick up on every nuance, but he's thorough, and he takes notes. Here's what Poppy and I were able to piece together."

Rufus produced a pointer and shifted into professorial mode. "Our drop target for Liza was Bradley Knott, aka Alpha, last known residence Coeur d'Alene. As you'll notice"—he moved the red dot of the pointer onto the green expanse east of the city—"the Coeur d'Alene National Forest is in close proximity. Over a thousand square miles of woodland."

"Perfect for a pack of weres," I murmured.

He nodded. "And we've got the Lolo to the south and the Kaniksu and Kootenai National Forests to the east over the Montana border. Plenty of places to hide out there, and the snow's not bad right now."

"Is that by Alaskan standards?"

He smirked. "No, southern. I do know my audience." Eleanor twirled one finger to bring him back on track, and Rufus bent over Aiden to zoom in on the map. "Poppy's guesstimate was good, and we were able to drop Liza within five miles of the weres' camp. She woke, packed, and hiked the rest of the way in."

"Any trouble?" I asked.

"Kuni says no. The primary camp is here." He moved the pointer to a valley near the state line. "Off-trail, well away from roads, and quiet right now—early March isn't peak hiking season." Aiden switched the grainy pictures to a few shots of tents and campfires, and Rufus pointed to the nearest image. "It's a mixed camp—they've got the were pack and Moyna's court living in close quarters—but Kuni says there's little fighting. Alpha and his boys stay here"—he indicated a ring of army surplus tents—"and the fae contingent stay in this cluster," he explained, pointing to the larger ring of nondescript tents.

"They're not roughing it, I trust," said Eleanor.

"He got some interior shots in those tents…" Aiden brought up the requested photos, and the scene changed from the snowy campground to vast curtained pavilions full of bright candelabra and leather couches. "I should think they're making do."

"And Moyna's among them?" she pressed.

"From what we gather, she comes and goes. But I think there's a picture—"

"On it," Aiden muttered, and one of the monitors switched to a face by the firelight—a blurry face, but one I'd have known anywhere.

"Our working assumption is that she's split her forces," Rufus continued. "She spent a few days here this week— spoke with Liza and got her background, actually. Our girl seems to have passed muster."

I thought over the script we'd written: a lonely, unattached half faerie, attacked by rogue wizards and hassled by Eleanor's people, seeking out the charismatic young queen. Moyna couldn't help but be flattered, and she appeared to have bought the lie. "But you don't know where her other camp is?" I asked.

"Not yet. If Kuni gets any hints, Poppy and I can do a little scouting—we're in an extended-stay hotel in Coeur d'Alene. We could use a field trip, to be honest."

"*We*?" Eleanor asked.

Rufus shrugged. "I couldn't just leave her to sit in her room alone day after day. Anyway, to sum up, Liza's in, Moyna's around, and the weres are on guard duty."

"Any news about planned movements?"

"Unfortunately, no." He cast the pointer back into the ether. "We don't even have enough data to predict her movements between camps—"

"How soon will you be able to tell?"

He grimaced. "Hard to say, Ellie. We need time. Kuni's resting now, and he'll fly back to camp today, but a lot is going to depend on how involved Liza gets."

Her lips tightened to a thin line. "Very well. Coileán, a word?"

I followed her through Aiden's bedroom and into the hall. When we were alone, she murmured, "She's out there, we've got her. It's only a matter of time."

"Eleanor—"

"Tell them to have Kuni report more frequently. A week is too long. I want to know where she goes, and I want to know it as soon as possible."

I willed my roiling stomach to calm. "Patience. We still need to figure out which wizard is helping her."

"The Arcanum's problems are their own." She reached up to clap my shoulder. "Soon. For Walt. For Meggy."

I stood in the hallway until the gate closed behind Eleanor, waiting for my nausea to subside, then returned to the lab to find Aiden and Rufus carefully reloading Kuni's equipment. "Eleanor wants more frequent updates," I told Rufus. "And if Kuni sees any wizards, we need to know."

"Look at this," said Aiden, beckoning me to his computer, and I tiptoed across the minefield to join them at the island. He pulled up one of the photographs, a grainy shot of a figure in a hooded black robe. "Is he the one you're after?"

I mentally compared the poor shot to the picture Jeanine had shown me. "That's him. Does Kuni know anything about him? Or her? I mean, I can't exactly tell the gender…"

"Not yet," said Rufus, "but I'll tell him to study this one." He regarded me curiously. "Uh…my lord, are you feeling okay?"

"Tired," I lied, then squeezed Aiden's shoulder and saw myself out.

CHAPTER 22

All was calm in the wake of Rufus's report, if only because I made no attempt to contact Eleanor. I needed to think, to process, to *breathe*—but mostly, I needed to forget what I'd agreed to help her do. Feeling the walls of my office close in around me, I retreated to the one place where I knew I could find relative peace.

Unfortunately, our days had finally synchronized with Virginia's, and Slim's was locked up for the morning. Bereft of silent companions and booze, I plopped onto the bench across the street from the bar and sulked in the midmorning cold. A shapely brunette strolled by with a baby carriage, and I was appraising the curves of her yoga pants when the bar's door squealed open. "Hey," said Slim, "you know last call's at two, right?" He leaned against the doorframe in sweatpants and bare feet, and his arms folded across his dingy T-shirt as he gave me a quick once-over. "Get in here, I'll make coffee."

Slim led me upstairs to his immaculate, midcentury-Scandinavian apartment and left me in the main room to start the percolator. "How'd you know I was here?" I called over the rustling of the filter box.

"Got Toula to expand my wards after you stopped in last December. If the magic concentration veers too much from the baseline in a five-hundred-foot perimeter, the alert sounds."

"Gate."

"Yep." He shuffled back into the room and scratched his wide stomach. "How's the Dud Defender working out?

Is Joey practicing?"

"Yeah, but he can't do much without someone around to recharge it, and Helen's been so busy of late—"

"He's got the hang of it. Just needs to keep the rust off." The cushion of the white leather sofa wheezed as Slim plopped down beside me. "Now, what's so important that you're coming around here at ungodly hours?"

I rubbed my forehead. "Nothing. Needed some air."

"Liar." He chuckled. "What's on your mind? Girl trouble?"

His eyes drooped with fatigue, but the look he gave me was sharp enough to reveal the knowledge behind the query. "What have you heard?"

"Probably not much more than you have. Got the scoop from Poppy this morning. I'm not going to get a full day's sleep today, no matter what I do." The coffeemaker began to gurgle, and he pushed himself off the sofa to pour. "She didn't have any photos. What are the odds that you'd be willing to share with us?"

I waited until he produced two cups of tar-like coffee, then enchanted a fifth of Bailey's into existence to make the brew palatable. "Odds are good. Aiden got stills and video, but they're grainy."

"Mm." Sliding back into the depression he'd left, Slim sipped his disgusting drink and watched me doctor mine. "Kuni's holding up, I hear."

"Let's hope so. I don't have a spare piq on my hands."

"Couldn't you ask Lailu?"

"How do you—"

"Aiden didn't hide her." He shuddered as he forced the next sip down. "Maybe I used too many grounds in this pot."

"Like half the package?" I muttered, watching my coffee shift from pitch black to slightly brownish. "Anyway, no, I can't. She doesn't even know he's in the field."

"Sure about that?"

"Okay, *I* haven't said anything to Lailu about her nephew's whereabouts. Happy?" I took a test sip, grimaced, and sweetened. "You know how you used to threaten to offer Irish coffee for St. Paddy's?"

"Yeah?"

"Don't do it."

Slim watched me as I drank my highly adulterated beverage. "I understand we've had a Moyna sighting."

I wrapped my hands around the mug, focusing on the warmth. "That was what I wanted to drink to avoid thinking about."

"Sure."

We sat and sipped while the wall clock ticked off the seconds, until the silence pressed on me like a suffocating pillow. "I can't kill her," I blurted. "I can't do it, Slim."

He pried my mug from me before I could slosh coffee onto the pristine carpet. "So don't. Lock her up, throw away the key if you have to."

"But I told Eleanor I would help her do it."

"*Really*?" He shook his head. "Tell her you've had a change of heart. You want her alive."

"She wouldn't understand."

"If there's a shred of humanity in her, she will. She might not be happy, but she'll understand." He squinted over his mug. "You've got a thing for her, don't you?"

"Damn it, can you people leave *nothing* private?" I griped as my face flared.

"Oh, that's not Fringe chatter—that's me knowing what lovelorn bastards look like. The way I see it, you've got two choices, Colin. You can either go after Moyna with everything you have and hope Eleanor's impressed, or you can do what you think is right and risk annoying your non-girlfriend."

I mulled it over for a moment. "Moyna tried to kill me. She killed Eleanor's husband. She's the reason Meggy's dead. I don't want to think about how many people were involved in that mess with Oberon. So what would you do?"

He cocked his head. "You think she's incorrigible?"

"Probably."

"But she's yours. And her mother didn't give up on her, did she?"

"Never. So what, then? Catch her, lock her away forever?"

"Maybe. There's no good scenario here. But I believe that people change. For better or worse, they change."

"Maybe you're right."

He snorted. "As my mom always told me, do what you have to do. Just make sure you can look yourself in the mirror once you've done it."

I stood, leaving the little bottle of Bailey's where it was. "Thanks, Slim. What do I owe you this time? More dragonscale?"

"Nah, I'm set for it. Had no idea Georgie sheds the way she does. Got *pounds* of the stuff downstairs. But if you wanted to share those photos and videos with the Fringe, we'd be most obliged."

"I'll tell Aiden to leak them," I said, then nodded and opened a gate home as Slim's alarm began its warning blatt.

I could have done the mature thing, paid Eleanor a visit, and had a talk about dead lovers, revenge, and my minimum responsibilities as a parent. But it was far easier to sit back and hope she never decided the time was right to move on Moyna, thereby sparing me two nasty confrontations. Besides, every time I thought about addressing the issue, an image weaseled its way into focus: Eleanor's fiery hair in the candlelight, rubbing against my cheek as she sobbed in my arms. She was counting on me, and I didn't want to disappoint her.

But Meggy's hair had been that color, too. Meggy had cried on my shoulder long before Eleanor ever did. And even to the last, Meggy had tried to reach our daughter. I'd failed Meggy at every turn, but now, perhaps, I had a chance to do right by her.

Then again, Meggy was dead, and Eleanor was going to be part of my life for a long time to come. I had the chance to make her an ally, a friend…maybe something more…

At Moyna's expense. The infuriating child with Meggy's eyes and Mother's sensibilities, the lost little girl who was desperate to believe that Mother loved her. The look on her face as Toula struck the fatal blow…

I'd failed Moyna as badly as I failed Meggy. Of course she hated me—I'd done nothing to earn her love. In the space of two weeks, she'd lost her home, her mother, her power, and her own memories, mostly at my hand. There was only the most marginal of chances that I could shift Moyna's feelings toward me to something closer to disdainful than patricidal. Like it or not, however, I'd sired her. I owed her a chance at life.

And so I resolved to say nothing unless fate forced my hand.

If Aiden had shown us the writing on the wall, in the weeks that followed, the scribe returned with a Sharpie, a highlighter, and a set of glitter pens.

The night after Rufus's visit, one of my people, Hoim, threw a little fête, a lavish cross between a formal gala and a rave. She lived on a sprawling estate near the border, and for the evening, she put up a dozen brightly lit pavilions, each playing a different type of music at full blast, and invited a couple hundred of her closest acquaintances to dance, feast, and drink from the Versailles-esque champagne fountains. But the kicker was the deer. Hoim conjured up fifty or so white bucks and does, lit them like glow sticks, and set the herd loose to wander around the tents as living lanterns.

I was invited to this soirée, assuredly as a precaution against causing offense, but I sent my regrets and retired with a Dickens anthology and enough bourbon to give a fraternity brother pause. With Moyna on my mind, I had no desire to make small talk. I only learned the details of the party because Hoim begged an audience the next morning, after she woke from her champagne bender to find the glowing deer decapitated, the heads and bodies mingled with her guests who'd passed out on the lawn.

My first thought on seeing the carnage was that she'd neglected to send an expected invitation. Faeries are quick to act on perceived slights—the stories, at least, get *that* right—and the deer slaughter seemed like the sort of petty revenge an insulted neighbor might take. The culprit had left no sign of his identity, however, and so I stepped behind a tent, over a pair of sleepers wearing glitter and little else, and consulted the realm.

You need to talk to Eleanor, she replied.

"Please don't start that," I whispered, "I'm—"

Not about Moyna. The vandal is one of hers.

I groaned loudly enough to make the sleepers stir. "Damn it. Why?"

Talk to Eleanor, Faerie insisted, then went silent.

And so I found myself in Eleanor's office later that morning, having first retrieved a camera from Aiden and returned to the scene to take amateur evidence photographs. Eleanor scrolled through the snapshots and grimaced. "That seems...excessive."

"One word for it," I replied, watching her face contort as she reached the close-ups. "Faerie said the guilty party is someone in your court. Any ideas?"

"She didn't give you a name?"

"No, she's being coy. A hint would be nice," I said to an unoccupied corner of the room.

Anorian, came the reply. *I assume you can locate him without further handholding.*

I turned back to Eleanor, whose brow furrowed. "If I

didn't know better, I would think someone's feeling snippy," she said.

"Do you know this cretin?"

She grunted and waved her hand over the desk, and a three-dimensional map of her territory manifested in the space between us. "I wouldn't call him a *cretin*, per se, but yes, I know him. Well, *of* him. Boy got around, made a name for himself on the Med. He settled here," she said as a splotch of land on the border lit up. "Ah. I take it the victim is on the other side of the line?"

I nodded. "Neighborly spat. How do we want to handle this?"

She waved the map away and rose. "We present a united front. Visit him this morning. I'd rather avoid making a spectacle, if it's all the same to you. And are those two on Aiden's watch list?"

I fished my folded copy from my pocket. "Anorian…no. Hoim's not high on the list, but Aiden thinks she has connections that bear watching."

She sighed. "Well, sooner begun, sooner done. Who uses live deer for decoration, anyway?"

We summoned the parties to Eleanor's throne room, extracted a forced apology from Anorian, and suggested that Hoim keep the noise down henceforth. She went skipping on her way, he slunk home, and Eleanor and I called it a success.

And then, three nights later, Mina roused me from sleep when Hoim returned to court in a raging fit. Fighting my temper down, I called Eleanor and soon found myself on the border, wincing at the sonic onslaught from Anorian's estate.

Eleanor tightened her bathrobe sash and glowered at the illuminated tents. "He threw himself a damn music festival," she said, raising her voice to be heard over the ruckus.

I watched as half a dozen naked faeries drunkenly frolicked in a mud pit in front of one of the many stages and wondered how they could endure standing so close to the source of the bass. "What shall we do first, shut down the main stage or find Anorian?"

She scowled and pointed to the stone tower on the edge of the property, which was topped that evening by a lone bagpiper. "Do what you like, but I've reached my limit for 'Scotland the Brave.'"

Though I couldn't make out the piper's face, I could see his kilt, and something about sending an Englishwoman up there alone felt unwise. One long flight of stairs later, we reached the roof and the piper, who indeed was kitted out like a *Braveheart* extra. "Do you mind?" Eleanor shouted over the drone, and with a little wheeze, the pipes fell silent. "*Thank* you," she muttered, rubbing her ear. "Now, what the devil is going on?"

The piper gave me a sour look. "Defending ourselves," he replied, cocking his thumb toward Hoim's estate. "She can't bloody well treat us like that."

The piper wasn't native to the realm, and I had to concentrate to understand him through his brogue, but Eleanor seemed unfazed. "So Anorian threw a party, did he?"

He grunted. "*Aye*, my lady."

"Invited you to play?" He nodded, and she huffed in frustration. "That thing is a weapon. Put it away and get out of here before I become cross."

He hurried down the tower, and I was about to suggest heading for the house when twenty waving searchlights pierced the darkness on Hoim's side of the line, followed by the screeching blast of an electric guitar.

"Oh, *come on!*" Eleanor shouted toward the sudden noise. "That's not helping!"

As if accepting the challenge, the volume of the party around us jumped at least another twenty decibels. Hoim's searchlights flashed into a rainbow in reply, then began to strobe with her own pounding bass. In their flickering glare, I spotted the previous party's revelers, back with a vengeance—and with friends—dancing to the rock concert as it warmed up.

Eleanor watched the revelry escalate, then looked back at me. "That's it," she said, shaking her head. "I'm calling for reinforcements."

Our guards shut the parties down by dawn, and I glowered at the culprits from my throne as Eleanor stood by with her arms folded. "I'm only going to ask this once," I told the hosts cringing on the runner. "What the hell?" They started to talk over each other, and I held up my hand for silence. "Moon and stars, are you *children*? Is basic consideration so far beyond your ken—never mind," I muttered, catching Val's emphatic nod from behind the guilty parties. "All right, then, since you insist on acting like children, I'll treat you appropriately. Consider yourselves grounded. No parties for the next...two months?" I asked Eleanor.

"Make it three," she muttered, and pointed at Anorian as his mouth opened. "Complain, and I'll make it a year. You're dismissed. Don't try our patience again."

When the doors slammed behind them, I beckoned Val forward, and Eleanor's captain followed him to the dais. "I want a patrol on the border," I told them. "Those two aren't going to cooperate. Let us know if you sense trouble."

"It doesn't have to be a large patrol, but we need a presence," said Eleanor. "Understood?"

They departed, and I slumped against the throne as I produced a cup of coffee. "Bed?"

"Why bother?" She glanced at the jewels of light on the floor by the eastern windows. "They'll be up to their old tricks by noon, mark my words."

Fortunately, Eleanor's prediction was a bust. The day

passed without so much as a peep from the border—and then, before dinner, Rufus knocked on my office door. "Hi, sorry," he said, "we figured we'd let ourselves in and save everyone the fuss. Is Aiden around?"

"Ourselves?" I echoed. "You brought—"

Poppy's face—her *real* face—joined Rufus's at the door and flashed a strained smile. "Hey, it's me. Who were you expecting, Moyna?"

While Aiden took the equipment back to his lair for processing, Eleanor stood over the couch and scowled down at Poppy and Rufus. "The plan was for you to remain in Coeur d'Alene," she said to Poppy. "What are you doing here?"

She seemed unfazed by the attempted cowing. "Seeing to my mental health. I've been stuck at that motel for two weeks—I needed a breather. Change of scenery."

"I thought you were a *spy*."

Poppy shrugged. "We take breaks. Sticking someone in a room for days on end makes her less attentive, not to mention stir crazy."

"You have Rufus—"

"Who runs home every few days. Look, the situation's well in hand. Kuni's sleeping off the trip, you've got your latest batch of photos, and we've got nothing new to report from the woods. Now," she said, pushing herself from the couch—and using her few inches over Eleanor to full advantage—"*I'm* going to have a nice, long soak in a tub that I'm sure nobody's died in, and then Rufe and I are going out for pizza and Pac-Man. Got a problem with that, or are you going to tell me how to do my job?"

Eleanor bristled. "You realize that crossing back into Faerie breaks spells and enchantments, yes?"

Poppy glanced down at her female form. "I'd noticed. Your point?"

"How were you planning on putting that spell back in

place? The one that's keeping the weres in the dark about you? I can't replicate that. Maybe something close, but—"

"But it would be safer to ask Toula," I finished. "Unless you wanted to play guinea pig, Poppy."

She shrugged it off. "All right, I'll hit the tub, and you get the wizard. Any other problems?" As Eleanor began to speak, Poppy wheeled on her and held up a finger. "Before you light into me, remember that I'm not working for you, I'm working *with* you. Got it?"

"You're trying my patience, little girl," Eleanor murmured.

"I'm trying to keep myself sane." She brushed past Eleanor and headed for the exit. "Don't worry, I know my way back to my room," she added, and let the door slam.

Rufus stood and cleared his throat. "I'll make sure she's okay," he mumbled, and hurried off after the shifter.

When we were alone, Eleanor sat on the back of the couch and rested her forehead on her fingertips. "Coileán—"

"Let it go." I pulled out my phone and dialed the familiar number, and the line opened to a muttered greeting. "You busy, Glinda? I need a witch."

I braced for the expected comeback, but Toula only said, "Sure. Give me an hour. I'm working outside the silo if you want to stop by."

Frowning, I created a coat and boots, waved Eleanor away, then opened a gate onto the Arcanum's icy fields. Even in March, the ground was coated with hard-refrozen slush, and I skidded a few times before I located Toula behind one of the decaying trailers, standing out of the wind. Her flushed face steamed in the cold beneath a furry, ear-flapped hat, and I saw that she'd kept the puffed coat I'd made for her on our last such meeting. As I approached, my nose twitched with the smell of magic. "Not the wards again?"

She nodded and swigged from a thermos in her pocket. "Someone on the Council checked my work and found the holes I built in."

I skidded into the trailer and found my footing. "*Shit*, Toula."

"Can't trust a Pavli, right?" She drank again and tucked the canister away. "So now I get to close them—all but Carver's. Greg's is gone, I patched mine first, and I'm closing up Joey's." She cut her eyes to me. "Selectively, mind you."

"Oh?"

"I'm leaving him a pass-through, but only if he's with Carver. Even if he gets good at gates, he won't be popping in alone. That should keep everyone happy."

"Especially the ones who don't know about it."

"Precisely." She rotated her wrists, working out the tension and the chill. "What do you need?"

I leaned against the mildewing trailer. "Rufus brought Poppy over, and—"

"Spell broke. No worries. Give me time to finish the patch, and I'll fix the damage."

She sighed and peered at the wards I couldn't see, and I considered the tightness in her features. Her eyes were swollen, and that certainly wasn't a byproduct of the chill. "What's troubling you?"

"Nothing. I'm fine."

I gripped her shoulder through the thick coat. "Liar. What's happened? Is the Council being difficult again? Aside from the wards and the freezing wind, I mean."

That garnered a fleeting half-smile. "Really, I'm fine. Nothing for you to worry about."

"You know, I've learned that if you're concerned about something, I should pay attention to it." I watched her face for a crack in the mask. "What's going on?"

"*Nothing*," she insisted, but she wouldn't meet my eyes. "It's personal, okay?"

"Okay."

We stood in silence for a moment while the wind moaned through the holes in the trailer. Toula fumbled her thermos out of her pocket again, but before I could extract myself from the suddenly awkward situation, she mumbled, "Mina cheated on me."

I froze. "Toula, I'm sorry—"

"Went over earlier this week to surprise her. She was in bed with one of the other guards." Toula drank and shoved the thermos away. "Mina said she needed variety. I need commitment." She huffed and squinted into the wind, then muttered, "I should have known better. Stupid."

"You're not stupid."

"Don't patronize me. I was stupid—I'm big enough to own that." She stared at the gray snow until her face ceased its warning twitches. "Be my friend and don't tell Val, yeah? I don't want him to think I'm a complete idiot."

I slumped until we were on eye level. "You know he'll find out eventually."

"Then Mina can explain it. Don't tell him, *please*."

"Not a word, but not because of you. I'd worry for Mina's safety if Val knew the truth." Toula's brow creased, and I shook my head. "How do you think he's going to take it when he learns she broke his baby sister's heart?"

"I don't want him to get involved," she protested. "And you're forgetting that Mina's his second."

"You think that's going to make a difference to him?"

She snorted her displeasure. "It's none of his business, either. I don't need Val fighting my battles for me."

"See, Glinda, that's the problem with brothers," I said, smirking as she scowled. "I'm sure Vivi has stories. But you have my silence, for all the good it's going to do you."

"Thank you."

"Mm. And I've been waiting for a chance to ask: *Mina?* She's far too old for you."

Toula rolled her eyes and shoved me. "Look who's talking, Gramps."

"She's older than me!"

"She's fun, she's *hot*—"

"And twelve hundred years old. Really, Toula, there's a more appropriate match out there somewhere."

She considered that, then socked me in the arm and nodded. "If I didn't know better, I'd think you cared."

"Almost." I rubbed my battered arm and stepped away. "Come over when you're finished here, won't you? Poppy's having a soak, but she can't do that all night."

"You got it."

Toula turned back to her labor, and I stood aside and watched her hands wave in the weak afternoon light as the wind blew her sweaty hair from her face. After a moment, I flicked a finger, and Toula paused in her gesticulations as the first blast of warm air hit her back. "Do you work better in an arctic climate," I asked, "or would you like a space heater?"

Her eyes narrowed in her chapping face. "Don't you have somewhere to be?"

"Nah."

She nodded and returned to work. "Yeah, sure, you can hang out with me."

With Poppy cleaned, transformed, and on her way back to Idaho, the realm seemed to calm. I let Aiden show me Kuni's latest pictures, a disturbing slideshow of winter woods and unfamiliar faces. These pictures were sharper than the first set, and my gaze lingered on the frozen moments that had captured my daughter. But Aiden propelled us on to the images that caught his interest: the masked figure in the black hood, the constant shadow at Moyna's right shoulder. "Kuni told them he never saw the guy's face," Aiden explained, tapping the screen where the figure's eyes should have been. "He keeps it covered. But Kuni's positive he's male."

"Anything of use from the recordings?"

"Don't know yet." Seeing my confusion, my brother rose from his swivel chair and settled onto the ledge of his command room's narrow window. "Audio's not my specialty. I delivered the package to Vivi after I made copies of the files."

"Already?"

He nodded. "The sooner the Fringe can start picking it apart, the sooner we'll know if we have anything useful."

I frowned. "Such as…"

"A clue to our masked wizard's identity." He swung his feet onto the ledge and rested his back against one wall, folding himself into the tight space. "Every recording Kuni's made plays back with a different voice. He's hiding his real one."

"That's what Jeanine told me. How's the Fringe planning on stripping back the spell?"

"They can't. But the first recordings were enough to show us that his speech patterns remain constant. What the Fringe techs can do is extract those patterns and make a profile. What's his accent like, does he have a speech impediment, any quirks to his voice that the spell isn't masking? It's not a clear identification, but it's a start."

A start was better than nothing, and if Aiden made progress toward unmasking the wizard, maybe Eleanor would be interested enough to turn her attention from Moyna. I would take a reprieve, I decided, no matter who offered it.

I soon had cause to reassess my decision.

The following night, one of Hoim's neighbors, Marem, threw a raucous bash that put the previous revels to shame. Hoim was in attendance as a guest of honor, a survivor of continued assaults from the other court. The centerpiece of the extravaganza was a circular stage built around a grassy pit, where the partygoers drank and danced with abandon as an endless parade of instruments appeared and vanished around them. The pit was dark, by all accounts, and as the night wore on and the clothes came off, the action at its heart grew more intense.

Marem had neighbors on the other side of the border, a half-fae couple raising their first child, Henry. The boy was only six, and having grown up in Nebraska, he'd never seen anything like the light show outside his window. While his sensible parents constructed a noise-cancelling enchantment around the house and settled in for the night, the tyke slipped out of bed and across the lawns, drawn toward the party like a moth to a bonfire.

No one saw him enter the dance pit. The music blasted and thumped, the floating lights flickered above the dancers' heads, and if something small bumped into a pair of legs, no one paid it any heed. As a result, in the morning, no one could explain the little corpse trampled into the dirt at the center of the pit.

Eleanor tried to console the bereaved parents while I attempted to extract the truth from the sobered partiers, but neither of us had much success in our endeavors, and the realm refused to name names. At sunset, when I realized I hadn't eaten all day, I broke from my inquisition for a sandwich, only to find Aiden and Val waiting for me in the dining room with Aiden's tablet at the ready. "The child was a cousin," said Val as Aiden pulled up the appropriate revenge chain. "And so is Hoim. You have to take preventative measures, Coileán. *Now.*"

I sank into my chair. "And how am I supposed to lock her up for an accidental death someone else committed on another person's property? Marem says she had nothing to do with it. I mean, he doesn't remember much past midnight, but still—"

"Find a pretext." Val pulled up a chair beside me and stared until I reluctantly met his eyes. "I am begging you, my lord. Stop this before it ignites."

The intensity of his gaze made my guts knot, and I looked away first. "Double the guards on the border," I muttered.

"Coileán—"

"*Do it*," I said, and watched my hands clench until I was alone.

CHAPTER 23

I wasn't expecting to see Rufus the next afternoon, back only three days after his last appearance. With Henry's battered body haunting my thoughts, I was in no mood to look through Kuni's latest offerings, but Rufus insisted that I accompany him to Aiden's room to watch a video. "Moyna and Liza had a heart-to-heart last night," he explained, glancing at me over his shoulder as he led the way through the corridors. "Kuni made the trip as soon as he could get out of camp. Poor fellow's exhausted, but he wants to hurry back, so let's dump the tapes."

I half-jogged to keep up with his forced march. "Is Liza okay?"

"For now, he says." He rounded the corner, rapped on Aiden's door, and showed himself in. "We have footage," he announced as Aiden and Joey looked up from the television in the corner, whose screen froze on a warzone. "Sorry, boys, five minutes, I'll be out of your hair."

"I'd better not come back and find myself dead," Aiden warned Joey as he dropped his controller.

Joey waved his concern aside, and Aiden and Rufus disappeared into the lab. "Hey," he said to me, patting Aiden's vacated seat. "You all right?"

"No. You heard about the party?" I muttered as I sat.

"Horrifying." He glanced at the screen and shrugged. "That game's not the most sensitive response, but we decided to give ourselves something else to think about. Aid's worried sick—something to do with grudge matches?"

"That's about right." I met his waiting eyes—Mother's eyes, I realized with a jolt. The two looked little alike, but knowing the connection, I could spot the similarities. "Nothing to worry you yet, Joey."

He leaned back in his chair as he rubbed his temples. "Now, why do I have trouble believing you?"

"I'm sure you have more pressing concerns. How's married life treating you?"

"Can't complain, aside from the Council. Every time I run into them in the silo, they look at me like I might be wearing a bomb." He sighed. "Helen says it's going to take time, but she thinks they're starting to soften. *I* don't see any progress, but if she thinks they're coming around, I'll believe her. But you're changing the subject." He leaned toward me and murmured, "If you want help, say the word. I don't know how much good Georgie and I can do, but if you want us involved—"

"Hey, Coileán," Aiden called, cutting Joey's offer short as he threw open the door. "Movie time. Come in here, you want to see this."

"Do I?" I asked as I stood. "Honestly?"

Aiden grimaced. "Probably not. But I bet you'd like to see it before Eleanor does. Joey, you might want to watch, too. Looks like Moyna invited Liza over for tea."

From what I could see on Kuni's shaky video, my daughter's tent resembled a formal parlor, complete with velvet couches, mahogany end tables, and thick rugs. She'd hung a framed landscape on the canvas wall over the mantle, and a smokeless fire crackled below. Moyna herself had opted for a low-cut, floor-skimming black dress. There was still much of the blonde cheerleader in her face, but her eyes seemed older, wearier. She'd painted her fingernails crimson, and they clicked against the white porcelain teapot as she poured for Liza.

"I apologize for the short notice," she said, "but with

my schedule, you understand."

"Of course, my lady," Liza replied, her voice loud with the hidden microphone. Her hand moved into the video to take the proffered teacup. "I'd hoped to meet you, but I didn't think it would be this soon."

Moyna's rouged lips twitched as she poured for herself. "Someone wanders into my camp and says she wants to join us, and you think I wouldn't have an interest in making her acquaintance?"

"With your schedule—"

"I've been waiting for this meeting since the day you hiked in." She sipped slowly, but her eyes never dipped from Liza's face. "Your accent—American, I trust."

"Yes, my lady."

"You were raised here?"

"Baltimore, with my mother. She was, uh…"

"Mortal?" offered Moyna, filling the sudden silence. "It's nothing to be ashamed of. There are half fae in the ranks. And your father?"

Liza momentarily blocked the camera as she lifted her teacup. "I never knew his name. Neither did my mother."

"Who taught you the high tongue, then?"

I held my breath, praying that my work passed muster.

Liza's voice was bitter. "A gift, you might say."

"Oh?" Moyna leaned toward her, tea forgotten. "From whom?"

My niece was silent for a long moment. "Three men attacked me. I was fifteen. Couldn't defend myself. I tried, but they were stronger. Physically…magically." She took a shuddering breath. "They realized what I was, and one…he did something to me, made me understand them. He said it would be more fun for me if I knew what was coming next."

Moyna clasped Liza's free hand. "I'm so sorry," she said, and I frowned at the unexpected sympathy in her tone. "Could you identify them if you were to see them again?"

"I've been seeing them in my nightmares ever since. Yes, I'd know their faces."

"Which court?"

The camera shook as Liza shrugged. "I don't know. My lady…what I've learned, I've learned on my own. I know these courts exist, but I wouldn't know where to begin. You…I heard rumors that you were out here, that you might be willing to help me…"

"Absolutely," said Moyna, handing her a napkin from the tea tray. "Dry your eyes. Help me, and I swear you'll have your revenge."

Liza sniffled as her hand rose to wipe her face. "Thank you. I didn't know where to turn…"

"Believe me, I know what it is to need vengeance." She set her cup aside and rose to walk across the tent. "Let me tell you about the courts, Liza. This should make everything clearer."

I squinted at the video as Moyna lifted a tiny marble box from a side table and carried it back to her guest. "There were once three courts in Faerie. Mab was exiled, and her people were cast out with her. Until recently, they took refuge in the Gray Lands. Oberon brought his people into this realm on his own whim. And Titania ruled Faerie alone." Her fingers curled around the box as she spoke. "My grandmother by blood, my mother in truth. Do you follow?"

"I think so, my lady."

Whatever she was feeling, Moyna kept her mask in place. "She was wonderful. Kind and generous to me—I wanted for nothing. Her laughter was beautiful. *She* was exquisite."

"You loved her," said Liza.

She nodded. "Very much. She rescued me from all of this, you understand." Moyna waved one arm. "This realm. The woman who bore me would never have done for me a tenth of what Mother did."

Fabric rustled as Liza shifted on the couch. "What

happened?"

My daughter's jaw clenched as her composure threatened to slip. "When I was sixteen, she gave me a task. I was too stupid to see it, but she was testing me—showing me the truth about where I'd come from, what she'd done for me. She wanted me to bring Coileán to her." Moyna hesitated, then muttered, "My worthless father. I failed."

"She...threw you out? Because you failed?"

"*No.* Mother sent me out temporarily to test me, that was all. I returned to her with...well, with the woman who bore me. I won't call her my mother. Meggy," she spat. "One of Oberon's daughters. Here," she said, holding the box toward Liza, "look inside."

The camera couldn't follow the opening, but I saw a familiar flash of gold and recognized Moyna's baby locket when Liza lifted it to the light. "What's this, my lady?"

"The life in which Meggy wanted to trap me. Mother's test showed me what she saved me from." She held out her hand, and Liza returned the box and necklace. "Coileán told me horrible lies about Mother. He was going to leave me with Meggy—keep me from ever seeing Mother again." Her face twisted. "When I escaped, I accidentally brought Meggy to Mother. But Mother didn't mind—she said she would put her someplace where she could never hurt me. She welcomed me home. I told her everything Coileán had done, everything he'd said. She promised me I was safe."

Moyna fell silent, and Liza cleared her throat. "My lady...you don't have to—"

"You need to understand. Why we fight, what we fight against. You need to know this." She took a deep breath, then resumed in a monotone. "A few days after I came home, Coileán followed me. He sneaked into the palace with my idiot uncle and Mab's mongrel daughter...*Toula*," she muttered, looking as if she'd tasted something bitter. "They caught Mother unawares. Ambushed her with iron.

They killed her in front of me."

It was Liza's turn to take Moyna's hand.

"They killed Mab, too," said Moyna, "but I didn't see it. I was already their prisoner by then. Coileán stole Mother's throne with her blood still warm on his hands, and he…" She released a long breath. "He bound me. Locked all of my memories away and made me believe I'd lived my life with Meggy. That I was nothing but mortal. For months, she kept me prisoner with her in this realm, and he was always coming around—Meggy's *boyfriend*," she snarled. "I didn't remember who he was, but I knew—in my core, I *knew* he was evil. Does that make sense?"

From the shaking of the camera, I guessed Liza was nodding.

"One of Mab's sons saved me," Moyna murmured as Liza squeezed her fingers. "Geheret. He'd inherited her court. Broke the bind, gave me back my soul, took me to the Gray Lands with the rest of Titania's children—we were all refugees. But Coileán wouldn't let me go. He attacked—"

"Of all the revisionist histories," I began, but Aiden shushed me, and I reluctantly watched the rest of the tape in silence.

"Oberon helped him," she murmured, "though he regretted it later. They killed Geheret, and Mab's people were exiled again. They ran, and I went with them." She smirked. "After Meggy was dead. Coileán tried to kill me, and he killed his little pet instead. *Whoops.*"

Liza said nothing, and Moyna pressed on. "Oberon found us eventually. He wanted an alliance—he'd bring his court back to Faerie, and when Coileán was dead, I'd be queen of Titania's court. Mab's people would have a home again, and they were willing to follow me. Oberon said he'd handle Coileán, and I would stay behind at first and wipe out the Arcanum—you've heard of it?"

"Vaguely…"

"Wizards. Mortals, but an annoyance. I had them under

siege, ready to break...but Coileán overpowered Oberon, and we had to flee again. We've been hunted ever since." She sighed, extracting herself from Liza's grip to take up her cooling tea. "Mab's people, plus some of Oberon's who wouldn't follow his daughter. Eleanor, she's called. I gave her warning, but she sided with Coileán. No matter, I'll destroy them both." She sipped, keeping her eyes on her companion. "When I'm finished, there will be only one court—mine. Titania's is my birthright, Mab's is mine by her people's will, and as for Oberon's...well, I have blood there, too. And once I have my revenge, Liza, I swear to you that I'll give you the justice you seek." She put the cup down and grabbed both of Liza's hands, and as she leaned closer, I saw the fervent glint in her eyes. "You sought me out as your queen. I don't forget loyalty."

"Nor I, my lady," said Liza.

The camera angle was poor, but it caught Moyna's smile as she returned to her pose of serenity and lifted her cup.

"My lady," Liza began with a hint of trepidation, "may I ask you something? I don't mean to pry..." Moyna gestured for her to continue. "Your, uh, advisor...I heard he was a wizard."

"He is. Strange times make for strange alliances. The Arcanum's new leader is one of Coileán's pets—Mother's last child was a mongrel, and the troublesome little wizard is his sister. Coileán's fond of the mongrel, so I don't mind helping the Arcanum rid itself of the girl. In turn, they share information with me." She grinned and refilled her cup. "Let the wizards have this realm—we'll have Faerie, and when we're bored of it, we can take their realm from them. No more fighting, no more hiding, and peace in Faerie. How does that sound to you?"

"It sounds wonderful, my lady. And...the shifters?"

Moyna chuckled. "Such impressive specimens. It's always nice to keep cannon fodder on hand. I think they—"

At that, the video went to black. "Kuni said to tell you that the battery died," Rufus explained, "but the meeting ended pretty quickly." He hesitated, looking back and forth between Aiden and me, then settled on my brother. "If you could dump this, I'll get the gear back to Kuni and send him on his way."

"Sure," Aiden said, scooting his stool in front of the computer. "Who wants to let Eleanor know about this?"

I stood and patted his shoulder. "Congratulations, you've been deputized. I've got to go."

"Come *on*!" he protested as I headed for the door. "Don't make me do this—you know she's going to be in a bad mood."

I glanced back at the three of them huddled around the monitor. "Let her rage. I need a word with Greg."

"What about Helen?" Joey asked. "You heard what Moyna said—they're trying to get rid of her."

"Precisely. She's in the middle of the viper pit. Greg's on the outside, and he knows which ones have fangs. Tell her to watch her back," I added, and drew out my phone as I left the room.

Jermaine and Cynthia Polk had done well for themselves, I mused as I stood outside a wrought-iron fence in the Garden District. The address Greg had given me led to an antebellum home with a wide, columned porch, a showpiece in the middle of an immaculate yard. An ancient oak loomed to the left, draped with the requisite swags of Spanish moss, and the flower beds were riotous with fresh growth—a perk of the climate, I decided, not spellcraft. The only large construction I could detect was the ward system outside the fence, which made my skin tingle when I pressed my palm against it. Cindy Harrison may have married a mundane, but *she* was no slouch.

Spotting motion, I glanced at the shaded porch and picked an occupied rocking chair out of the gloom. With the late-winter sun sinking and the trees blocking the little light available, I couldn't make out the watcher's face or form, but I raised my hand. "Greg?"

"He'll be out in a second," the rocker called, and pushed herself to a stop.

I frowned, trying to place the voice. "Missy?"

"Getting warmer." She descended to the yard, and I realized she was far too young to be the magus—a handsome, dark-skinned woman in her mid-fifties with a complicated braided updo. She wore tailored jeans and a floral blouse, though she'd slung a light sweater around her shoulders as a concession to the fading afternoon.

"Cindy," I replied, barely recognizing her from Greg's old photo as she neared the fence. "You certainly grew up."

She smiled tautly. "Dad said you'd look like a kid. He wasn't wrong."

"A *kid?*"

Her smile crept toward a smirk. "My eldest is twenty-eight. They're still kids to me."

"If you'd prefer wrinkles, I could oblige."

"Not necessary." She stopped a foot from the latched gate and searched my face—for what, I couldn't say. After a moment, she murmured, "Dad retired, okay? That hellhole isn't his problem anymore."

"I understand."

"Then why are you trying to drag him back into it?"

I stared at Cindy until she glanced away. "You want to talk about kids? Helen's twenty-two. She doesn't even see the trouble coming her way, but I bet Greg does. Now, are you going to let me in, or are we going to continue this interview through the fence?"

Cindy sighed, but she snapped and whispered a word, and I felt the wards open. A twitch of her hand unlocked the gate, which swung inward. "If you hurt my family, I swear to God I'll come after you with everything I have."

"He's right about you." I brushed past her up the brick

walkway. "Has anyone ever told you that you take after your mother?"

"Sure. Usually when some foolish man thinks I'm being difficult."

"Touché," I muttered, and headed for the house.

Greg propped his elbows on the kitchen table and rested his face in his hands. "Run that by me one more time. *Slowly.*"

"Which part?" I asked. "The part where you never found your mole, or the part where someone in the Arcanum is plotting with Moyna to take Helen out?"

"How about you play this video for me?"

"It's at home. You can come over and watch—"

"Over my dead body," Missy interjected. She leaned one hip against the counter and folded her arms over her sweatshirt, an impenetrable blockade.

Greg grimaced. "Missy thinks it might be wiser if I didn't do the back-and-forth thing."

I glanced at his glowering self-appointed bodyguard. "You know, I'm asking for his help. I'm not going to hurt him."

"Unh-uh, faerie boy."

Rolling my eyes, I turned my attention back to Greg. "Moyna's still being advised by a wizard, the one you were supposed to hunt down, and now we know they're working together to oust Helen. Something tells me the wizard's not doing this as a solo initiative."

He spread his hands. "I don't know who the mole is, Coileán. There wasn't enough time before the transfer—"

"Then who are the likeliest candidates?"

"To get Helen out?" He sighed deeply and rubbed his forehead. "You got a list of the Inner Council handy, or do you need me to write the names down for you?"

"You're serious?"

"As a heart attack. Who do you think bugged my office

all those years? There's maybe two of them that I'd spit on if I accidentally set them on fire." He shook his head and glanced at his silent wife. "That's not counting present company, dearest."

"The silo magi wouldn't be upset if Helen took early retirement," she said to me. "She held on to that job only thanks to Greg's clout and an overwhelming majority of the installation magi. Girl needs to get out of the bunker."

"And go where?" I retorted. "Hang out here with you two? Spend some quality time with Eleanor and me?"

"She's got six other installations," said Missy. "Tell her to take my advice and go on a grand tour. Visit the magi, meet the local wizards, kiss the appropriate babies. Take Joey with her, and keep that boy on a tight leash. He needs to play the doting husband, and he needs to set everyone's mind at ease that he's one hundred percent Team Arcanum. But regardless of what he does, *she* needs to get out of Dodge. Go make friends."

"Your great idea is for Helen to run away for a while? Hope this all blows over and whoever's helping Moyna gets tired of waiting around?"

Missy's brows lowered. "Did I say that?"

"Well, more or less…"

"While she's away, you find Moyna and the mole. And you do whatever it takes to unmask him. Drag him back to Montana, call Helen in, and show solid proof that he's been helping Moyna. Make him name names. Helen will execute him for treason, and his friends will stay low if they know what's good for them." She shrugged. "Even if Helen had a name right now, it wouldn't do her any good. A name's nothing but an accusation, and if there were enough magi involved, she'd never get traction. But do your job while she's abroad, and you both might get somewhere."

I looked at Greg, then back at Missy. "You've put thought into this."

She flashed a well-edged smile. "How do you think *he*

kept that job for forty-five years? Greg played the game. I ignored the rules." Drumming her fingers on her arm, she said, "I'd give you the names if I could, if only to get you out of this house. But Greg's right—start with the Inner Council. Some magus knows Moyna's friend, and that's a guarantee."

I stood and regarded her over Greg's head. "Magus Harrison, I believe I underestimated you."

"You're not the first," she replied, and cocked her thumb toward the door. "Now beat it."

As Aiden expected, Eleanor was far from thrilled to watch the video. "At least we know the bind is holding," she said on my return from New Orleans. "Now, do we share this with the Fringe or wait and see what else develops?"

"Forget the Fringe, we share this with my *sister*," Aiden snapped.

Eleanor's mouth tightened. "Under the circumstances, and considering the Arcanum's security breaches—"

Before she could finish, the door slammed open, and Helen marched in with Joey a step behind her. "Okay, where's this video?" she demanded. "Joey says I need to watch it."

I glanced at Aiden in time to see him give Joey a little thumbs-up while Eleanor's back was turned.

We returned to Aiden's suite, and he directed Helen to a seat by the monitors while Joey and Eleanor loitered nearby, ready for a second viewing. After Aiden restarted the video, I pulled him back into his bedroom and muttered, "Taking the initiative, were we?"

"Doing what needed to be done, and Joey was right there with me. Best great-great-grandnephew-slash-brother-in-law *ever*. How's Greg?"

"Very retired. Missy seems to still be in the game, though."

"Any leads?"

"She suggested we keep an eye on the entire Inner Council."

Aiden grunted. "Heck, I could have told you that. So what now? Do we wait on Kuni to bring back more intel, or do we make a move on the tent city tonight?"

"We wait." He huffed through clenched teeth, and I explained, "There's no guarantee of catching Moyna if we move now. If we wait, we might be able to corner her. And even if we luck into finding her, we might miss the wizard—and then where would that leave Helen?" Aiden looked back at me glumly, and I patted his shoulder. "The more we know, the more precise an operation we can design, and the fewer casualties we're likely to suffer."

"The longer we wait, the longer they have to get their act together."

I couldn't refute that, and we lingered in uneasy silence while the tape played in the other room. When it ended, Helen emerged, paler than usual but otherwise hiding her discomfort. "Charming," she muttered to me. "Eleanor said you spoke to Greg?"

"To be fair, Missy did most of the talking."

"And?"

"They think you should go on an extended tour of the installations. Maybe spend some quality time in Mongolia, Australia, other places that aren't Montana."

"Hide, you mean." Her lip curled into a snarl. "Run and stick my head in the sand until the danger's past."

"Get the other magi on your side," I countered. "Make friends, influence people. Become too important to remove."

"By hiding from the Inner Council. This is supposed to show the rest of them that they can have confidence in me? Please, Coileán." She leaned against the windowsill and she stared out at the twilit garden.

I met Aiden's uncertain eyes, then joined Helen at the window. "You'll be safer if you put some distance between yourself and whoever's trying to get rid of you. Let us do the snooping, kid."

But she shook her head and continued to scan the horizon. "This job isn't about being *safe*. It's about doing the hard tasks, making the tough calls. Being the magus the others look to when everything's falling apart. Tell me how I'm supposed to be that magus when I turn tail at the first hint of trouble."

"This isn't a hint—we know that *someone* in the Arcanum is plotting against you."

"You think that never happened to Greg?" she retorted with defiance in her eyes. "You think it was all sunshine and roses? I've seen the records—I know how many assassination attempts he foiled over the years."

"Helen—"

"It's not your job to protect me. Not yours, either, Aid," she told him. "If I've got rats in my cellar, it's my responsibility to catch them."

"It can't hurt to go touring, can it?" Aiden protested. "You're not running away—you're checking things out in person. Say it's a fact-finding visit."

"It's transparently an attempt to put distance between the Inner Council and me. I don't run. I *can't*." Her eyes drifted toward the door to the control room, and she asked, "What do you think?"

I turned and found Joey standing on the threshold. After glancing at all three of us, he focused on his wife. "Honestly? I don't know what the right answer is, but you know the Arcanum better than anyone here. If you think you need to stick it out in the bunker, then I'm right behind you. Whatever you need me to do." Helen nodded, and a degree of tension dropped from her shoulders as she walked across the room to join him. "Just tell me how to make this better," he murmured as he wrapped his arms around her. "I'm here for you, babe. Say the word."

"It's a good sign for their marriage, but probably not *ideal*, all things considered." Eleanor watched from the couch as I paced in front of my office fireplace. "You can't fault the boy for being supportive."

"She needs to be careful—"

"She's a grown woman and a magus. Let her fight this however she sees fit." She produced a teacup and took a deep sip. "It's not your call, so stop fretting and sit down."

I wheeled on her in exasperation. "And do what, Eleanor? Twiddle my thumbs until Kuni gets the right video? Make a care package for our housebound shifter? Take tea?"

Her eyes dipped briefly to her cup. "You think this is *tea?*"

She held it out in offering, and I bent closely enough to catch a whiff. "Brandy?"

"That's the base. I added a few choice ingredients."

"Long day?" I muttered.

"You have no idea." She leaned into the cushion and closed her eyes. "How do you comfort a parent when the child was *six?* Did you get a good look at him?"

I settled onto the couch opposite hers. "Unfortunately."

"Yes, well, I did, too," she said brusquely, and drank. "And I fear I'm going to be seeing him for a long time to come."

The fire crackled and spat embers onto the flagstones, and when my empty hand itched, I soothed it with a half-full tumbler of bourbon. "It never gets any easier," I murmured, raising the glass.

Eleanor shook her head and stared into her teacup, seeing visions I didn't want to imagine. I had my own to haunt me.

CHAPTER 24

I don't know what I'd expected in the aftermath of Henry's death, but silence was far from the top of my list. While his parents mourned, I visited every house within twenty miles of the border and stressed that there would be no festivities for the immediate future. To my surprise, no one balked at the order, but still, I held my breath every morning until Val reported another quiet night.

"I wouldn't mind if this became a regular occurrence," I told him after two emergency-free days.

But Val was troubled. "This is the calm," he muttered. "It heralds the storm." He gazed out the window onto another of Faerie's perfect, temperate days. "The wind stills, the light changes, the birds go to ground—"

"I've seen my share of thunderstorms," I replied, rising from bed to join him. The view was postcard-perfect, a cloudless blue sky over the ever-blooming roses.

His eyes met mine, and I saw the tension in his face. "Do you feel it?" he asked. When I said nothing, he gripped my arm. "You've yet to see a storm here, but I've weathered enough to know the signs. Heed them," he insisted, and tightened his grasp. "*Please*."

I assured Val that I was keeping my eyes open, but as the days passed without incident, I couldn't help but wonder if the predicted storm hadn't actually blown over. Eleanor, too, was cautiously optimistic, which meant that she had more time to devote to the problem of Moyna. Kuni's work had shown us that she was active, but he had yet to bring back any clue as to her other camps, for which

I was grateful. Yes, I was burying my head in the sand, but it helped me avoid the unpleasant reality that I was at least nominally engaged in a plot to kill my daughter.

In retrospect, I can say many things about that season, but the overarching message is that it was far from my finest hour—and all of my poor decisions were about to pay dividends.

Rufus returned four nights after his last report, holding Poppy's hand. "*There* you are," he said with a touch of exasperation, stepping aside as Eleanor's escorting aide took his leave of her office. "We waited around your palace, but it took us half an hour to find anyone who knew where you'd gone," he told me. "Gave the guards the day off?"

"They're working elsewhere," Eleanor interjected with a peeved frown. "And what are you doing—"

"Before you get cross, we called Toula, and she'll put the spell back in place later tonight. We're taking a mental health break. Kuni's sleeping at the motel."

I regarded Poppy, whose charcoal sweater and shapeless jeans didn't suggest anything more exciting than a night in front of the television. "What are you up to?"

"Going to grab a bite," she replied, grinning at Rufus. "Get out of town for a few hours while you look over the footage. Hang out in my own body."

"Ah. And should we need to locate you?"

"You've got my number," said Rufus. "We'll be in Anchorage for the evening. Back well before midnight. We'll stop in and retrieve the equipment from Aiden."

To my relief, Eleanor didn't protest. "Where in Anchorage, in case of emergency?"

"The restaurant's called Avelina," he told her. "Little hole in the wall."

"Pasta night," said Poppy.

Rufus nodded vigorously. "Cannoli to *die* for. Anyway,

I'll drop the gear off with Aiden."

I watched as he opened a gate back to the palace and headed through, still holding hands with Poppy. When we were alone, Eleanor began to chuckle and shook her head. "What's funny?" I asked.

"He thinks he's so clever," she replied, plucking her phone from the cluttered desk. A few taps later, she said, "Lucian, I need a word with you. My office, please." He arrived almost immediately, a short blond in a stained chef's jacket. "Come in," she said. "I'm sorry for pulling you away from dinner prep. This won't take but a minute."

"Certainly, my lady." He gave me a polite nod. "Lord Coileán. Should I plan for guests?"

"Astrid might take offense," I said, and he flashed a broad smile—his little sister's, I realized.

"And we wouldn't want that," said Eleanor. "Lucian, are you familiar with the restaurant scene in Anchorage?"

His forehead shifted into bemused furrows. "More or less. Need a recommendation?"

"Have you heard of one called Avelina? Italian, I think."

At that, his smile returned full-force. "Oh, sure! Chef's talented. I've met her once or twice."

"A follow-up question: if I were to tell you that your brother is taking a female companion to Avelina this evening, what would you think?"

One of his thick eyebrows rose. "I'm sorry, my lady, but you're going to have to be more specific than that."

"Rufus, I mean."

"*Ah.*" He folded his arms. "This would be the shifter he's babysitting?"

"I didn't know you were privy to all of that," I interrupted.

Lucian shrugged. "Vivi might have let that one slip."

"To answer your question, yes, the shifter," said Eleanor. "Back in female form. First impression?"

He began to chuckle. "Boy's on a date. He may not be

aware of that fact, but it's a date. Avelina has a sommelier on staff. Kid thinks he's so smart, but sometimes, he's just *blind*. Anything else, my lady?"

A mischievous grin crept across her face. "One little thing. What do you suppose your sister would do if she knew what we know?"

"Give him hell about it," he replied without hesitation.

"Then perhaps you could make mention of this outing to the appropriate Fringe personnel. After all, they'd probably want to know that those two have left Idaho."

Lucian's expression mirrored Eleanor's as he considered the ramifications. "That's *cruel*, my lady."

"I know."

He pulled out his phone, nodded to us, then headed for the door. "Hi, Vivi?" he said as he took his leave. "Got something juicy for you and the boys…"

The door closed, and I turned to Eleanor, confused. "I thought you two were friends."

She seemed inordinately pleased with herself. "Rufus is a dear, but he's had this coming. NYU, 1986, he told a repulsive colleague that I was single and interested. Thought it would be amusing. We patched things up, but payback deferred is still sweet." Briefly, she savored the moment, then set her victory aside. "Shall we see what Kuni's sent us?"

Aiden looked up from his laptop and shook his head. "Nothing earth-shattering. The video's in snippets—I can extract stills from them, but not much else of use. There's nothing of Moyna besides a few photos."

"What about the wizard?" I asked.

"Four photos. Nothing helpful." He pushed back from the counter and popped his spine. "I should get that voice analysis from the Fringe in another few days. They're working as quickly as they can, but this takes time."

Eleanor seemed to deflate as he spoke. "So nothing

about Moyna's other base?"

"Nope. See for yourselves," he added, turning the computer to face our side of the counter. "I've got enough here to ID the weres and most of the faeries in a lineup, but Moyna's wizard knows how to keep himself covered."

She pushed the screen back for a better view, then muttered, "I don't understand."

"Kuni's doing the best he can," I protested. "He can't help it if the guy doesn't uncover his face—"

"But *why* doesn't he? Who in that camp would know him?"

"Assuming he's Council," said Aiden, "then there's a good chance he's known to the Dark Company."

"Spies," I added.

Eleanor looked up at me sharply. "You don't think they—"

"Not Kuni—how would they anticipate *him?* But a Company shifter with a small enough form could hide out and report back. Something that might get past the weres' noses." I shrugged. "The wizard isn't taking any chances."

"And he's the weak link," she said, tapping his photo. "If we find him, we can figure out how he's hiding Moyna."

"Keep Hel safe," Aiden murmured.

But Eleanor continued to scroll through the pictures. "To be perfectly frank, the wizard is the Arcanum's problem. I *will* have the girl."

If the Stowe siblings gave Rufus any trouble over his night on the town with Poppy, he made no mention of it in my hearing. Aiden assured me that our couriers had stopped back by in the small hours to collect Kuni's gear—"home before midnight" apparently referred to Alaska Time—and Toula had met them to ensorcel Poppy once more. "They seemed to be happy," Aiden reported over breakfast. "Giggly. I think they were drunk, to tell the truth."

I left my brother to his own devices that day and the next, trusting that his dragon-sitting chores would occupy his time. After a few sleepless nights, Joey had decided to stick close to Helen, and Aiden had promised to look after Georgie for him in his absence. I couldn't imagine that setup lasting—Joey would be little help to Helen in a firefight, and surely she'd tire of having him constantly underfoot. Besides, we knew that Georgie wouldn't suffer a long separation. Like it or not, Helen would have to share him eventually.

But with the situation stable for the moment, I turned my attention to whittling down the pile of letters on my desk. At first, as I tackled the complaints, I congratulated myself for being productive. By Sunday morning, however, I realized what the tickle at the back of my mind was trying to make me see: Val hadn't brought any new letters in days. Yes, I'd excavated down to the surface of my desk again, but only because nothing was coming along to cover it up.

The realm was calm.

I've weathered enough to know the signs. Heed them.

I was on the cusp of calling Val in on his off day when Aiden knocked. "Got the voiceprint," he announced, holding his tablet aloft. "Let's see what the Fringe did." He plopped the little computer onto my newly-cleaned blotter and turned up the volume.

The sound that came out was closer to a 1950s movie robot than a human voice. Only the pitch gave me any indication that the speaker was intended to be male. It spoke nonsense for ninety seconds, and as the track hissed to an end, I glanced at Aiden, expecting to see frustration on his face. Instead, he seemed thoughtful, and the wrinkle between his eyebrows suggested that the gears were turning behind them.

"You…recognized that?" I ventured.

He shook his head. "Not yet. Vivi said they did the best they could, but with the modulation the wizard's been

using, 'Mr. Roboto' was about as good as they could get."
He stepped away from the desk and rubbed his neck as he
turned to the window. "The voice itself is useless—it's the
cadence I'm listening to, the way he says certain words.
Quirks that set him apart from other speakers."

I joined him by the glass. "First impressions?"

"American, definitely. Region, now…" He worried his
bottom lip with his teeth as he thought. "That's tougher.
He's…*blah*."

"Blah?"

"You know, somewhere in the middle. Not Jersey, not
Texas, not a West-coast surfer—blah." He contemplated
the mystery for a moment longer, then pulled out his
phone and called his sister.

Five minutes later, Helen had listened twice to the
strange recording, and Joey, her shadow, had finally
perched on the corner of my desk. "I can't name him," she
told Aiden as her face scrunched. "I can *almost* recognize
something in that, but it's so distorted…"

"I know what you mean. Tip of your tongue?"

"Yup."

"Think he's Council?"

"That's still a solid bet. Send me a copy, eh? I'll keep
listening, and maybe something will pop out at me. I've
got Council meetings tomorrow and Wednesday—plenty
of time for someone to blow his cover. And while I'm
doing that," she added, turning to Joey, "maybe you
should run back over here and take Georgie out. I bet
she'd like to see you."

I fought back a knowing smile as Joey's eyebrows drew
together. "There's no reason why I couldn't sit in the
corner during your meetings. I could take notes or
something, whatever you need."

Helen rubbed his tense arms. "I need you to stand back
while I do my job. No one's going to attack me in front of
the whole Council. I'll call you as soon as it's over,
promise."

Though unconvinced, Joey nodded and hugged his wife. "Please be careful," he mumbled into her hair.

"We're going to be fine," she told him as she broke away. "You'll see. We've got his voice—all we have to do now is listen."

Once Helen and Joey returned to the silo, Aiden left me to continue my work in peace. The morning was silent but for my breathing, and as I read by the cold fireplace, I noticed a muffled voice floating from the micro-gate in the bookshelf. Curious, I rose and widened the gate, and the sound became clearer: a familiar nasal voice muddling through an off-key rendition of "Happy Birthday to You." Pushing the picture frame covering the gate aside, I continued to widen the hole until I could spy into Stuart's apartment and see who he was serenading.

I barely stopped my laughter in time. Stuart had strung paper banners around the living room, dumped balloons on the rug, and stuck a decanted can of tuna with a lit candle in the middle on the coffee table. The lunatic sat on the couch facing me, wearing a ridiculous party hat and bellowing his good wishes for the cat in his arms, a Siamese with a smaller hat affixed to its head, who meowed and struggled as Stuart sang. Once Stuart blew out the candle, he released the birthday cat, and the traumatized feline took off like a shot down the darkened hallway.

Stuart looked after the vanished cat, then pulled the candle out of the fish and put the plate on the floor. "Here, kit-kit!" he called, removing his party hat, but the guest of honor had apparently had enough of the festivities, and none of the other lurking cats wanted anything to do with fire, novelty headgear, or Stuart's unique vocalizations.

He looked so dejected that I spoke before I could stop myself. "How old?" I asked through the hole.

Stuart gasped and looked around wildly before he remembered the micro-gate. "Six, and don't scare me like that!"

"Sorry. I heard the party."

He glanced down at the untouched tuna, then shrugged. "Not much of a party, I'm afraid. I don't think Felix is feeling it today."

"Could be the hats."

"Could be." He considered the paper cone on the table, then tossed it onto the floor. "Wish I knew what they were thinking. My cats either love me or want to murder me, and there's not much warning when they change modes."

I told myself I'd regret it, then threw sense aside and widened the gate enough to slip through. "You really want to know? Bring me the damn cat."

After a hunt through every room and a brief chase, Stuart cornered the birthday cat and carried him back into the living room. When it saw me, the cat froze, then hissed and clawed at Stuart's arms. "No closer," I warned. "Not unless you want stitches."

He stopped and rubbed the spooked cat behind the ears. "Now what?"

Closing my eyes, I imagined the enchantment and willed it into being. The instant it coalesced, I could hear the cat's thoughts running through mine, a rapid jumble of sensory information. "He's scared of me," I told Stuart, stepping away. "Animals can sense magic, and I push all their 'danger' buttons. Yours wants to bolt. You're holding him too tightly, he doesn't like having his head scratched, and he thinks you smell weird. Have you been playing with paint thinner?"

"I brewed a few potions last night," he explained, giving his shoulder a sniff. "Certain ingredients are odiferous—"

"First, let the cat go." He obeyed, and I broke the enchantment as Felix streaked from the room. "What sort of potions are we talking about? You keep your eye of newt in formaldehyde?"

He crossed his freshly scratched arms. "Love potions.

A new line I'm carrying to go with the spells. Potions to find love, keep it, end it—"

"They *sell?*"

"Don't sound so surprised."

I sighed and headed for the gate. "I'm going to say this once, and only because it's your cat's birthday. 'Lord, what fools these mortals be.'"

The gate constricted behind me, and Stuart hurried to the wall. "Very funny. I still have cake," he offered, holding the picture frame aside to look through my bookshelf.

"Felix will enjoy it more if I'm not around. Take it easy."

"Yeah, you, too. Hey," he added as I started to move the router back into position, "you don't know of a recipe for a love potion that works reliably, do you? Or lust? My customer base isn't too picky about that distinction."

I rested my elbows on the shelf and stared back at Stuart's eye. "No. The Arcanum might, but what have we talked about?"

He huffed. "I'm still not convinced that with enough discipline and practice, I can't be—"

"You're not a wizard, Stuart."

"*Yet.*"

"Please don't make me quote Shakespeare again," I replied, and covered the gate.

As the long afternoon stretched into purple twilight, I pushed aside my doubts about the situation in Faerie and congratulated myself on a job well done. For the first time since awakening, I'd managed to clear my desk, and I was feeling accomplished as I sat down to dinner with my windblown brother. "Well," he said when we'd compared notes on the day, "since I was out with Georgie all afternoon, I'd say you're the momentary adulting champion."

"Considering that you're not yet an adult…"

Aiden reached for the breadbasket. "I've done my share of it. Building up a buffer so I can someday afford to goof off for months in peace." He bit one of Astrid's crusty dinner rolls in half, stuffing his cheeks like a chipmunk, and I hesitated while I considered whether the time was right to ask the question that had been plaguing me. Sensing my eyes on him instead of my plate, Aiden swallowed hard and stifled a belch. "What's wrong?"

The words forced themselves out before I was ready: "Did you really execute three hundred twenty-seven of Oberon's people?"

Aiden stilled, and I sought a way to retract the question while he regarded me in silence. After a few eternal seconds, he dropped his half-eaten roll and nodded.

"I'm sorry, we don't have to talk about this—"

His voice had flattened, and his face blanked as he held my stare. "No, it's okay. What do you want to know?"

"How?"

He blinked once, twice. "I'd filled the cells—the special ones Titania made, not the ones in the dungeon."

I stiffened as old memories surfaced.

"I'd packed the prisoners in so tightly that only half of them could sleep at a time. Softening them up for you in case you wanted to try to make them talk. They wouldn't tell me anything." He paused and squeezed his eyes shut, and I cautioned my nagging curiosity that I wouldn't like whatever was passing through his thoughts.

"I couldn't keep them like that," Aiden mumbled. "I was torturing them, Coileán. But I couldn't let them out— I'd have looked weak. And with you gone…"

He left the thought unfinished, but I saw where it was heading. Even wielding my power, Aiden would have had only a tenuous hold on the court at first. Had he shown mercy to the invaders, he might have lost even that. And Val certainly wouldn't have counseled parole.

"I understand," I told him.

Aiden's voice sped up. "Val didn't think you were going to be back for months, and I couldn't keep them penned up like that indefinitely. I had to do something. They didn't suffer, I did it quickly. Stopped their hearts— they were dead before they hit the floor. Most of them never saw me coming." He paused then, as if waiting for absolution. "I didn't want to do it. I *had* to."

"I understand."

If Aiden heard me, it didn't register. "They fell. All of them. Like I'd pushed over a domino. And I couldn't *leave* them there. I didn't know when you'd be up, and the cells…the cells were *packed*—"

"Aiden—"

"So I made them disappear. *Poof.*" He snapped and looked my way, but I could tell he wasn't seeing me. "All gone. Everything down there was nice and clean again, and I stood in the hallway and listened, and it was *quiet*. So quiet. Like they'd never existed." He stared into space. "I wasn't angry. I knew exactly what I was doing, and…" A deep breath, a long exhalation. "The realm approved. She wasn't happy about it, but she was satisfied."

At a loss for what to do, I trusted my instincts and embraced Aiden before he could protest. "I understand," I insisted a third time, holding on as he tensed. "Once or a thousand times, you don't walk away unscathed." Releasing him, I took a knee beside his chair and waited until his darting eyes lighted on mine. "Do you have any idea how many lives I've ended?"

To my surprise, his answer was immediate. "Fifty-seven. It was in the Arcanum file. I read up on you before…before Greg told me the truth."

"Ah." I wrapped my hands around his tight fists and shook my head. "Maybe fifty-seven wizards, but I haven't kept a separate tally. I stopped counting altogether once I thought I'd crossed the thousand mark. That was in 1834."

His eyebrows rose, but at least he was focusing again.

"I killed to save myself. Wizards, sure, but

highwaymen, bandits, run-of-the-mill cutthroats—I've seen them all. Mother's old changelings, you know. So many of them didn't want to take that last step." I swallowed, fighting down the gorge that rose with the memories I drank to drown. "Plenty of bad people. Plenty of good. Whatever I had to do. Mortals, witches, things out of the Gray Lands…and I've killed my share of faeries," I said, squeezing his fists so hard that my fingers ached. "More than your chart shows. I've killed in rage, and I've done it because it was the most convenient solution."

Keeping the words and the bile from mixing was rapidly growing more difficult. "Do you have any idea what it's like to blink the red away and realize you've stabbed someone to death? Maybe it wasn't hundreds at one go, but that…that's so *personal*. That's not an easy death, and even when you're clean again, sometimes you look down and think you see the blood still staining you." I waited for him to recoil in revulsion, but Aiden remained stoic. "I've got a lot of years behind me, kid. A lot of blood on my hands. So hear me—*I understand*."

He gave no reply, but his dark eyes had begun to turn glassy.

With a sigh, I stood and stooped to hug him again, the horrified child peeking out of the hardened youth. "You're not becoming Mother. I doubt she ever lost a night's sleep." He shook in my arms, and I held him more tightly. "Forgive me, Aiden. That shouldn't have been your burden to carry."

The shaking intensified, and then, with a hitching gasp, the pent-up floodwaters broke through. As he sobbed, I held on, knowing too well what was going through his mind.

Worn out, Aiden retired early, though not without extracting a promise that I would wake him if Rufus returned. In truth, I didn't want him anywhere near those cameras—every photo and grainy video was another step closer to a fight, and I wanted Aiden to do nothing more than hide out in Joey's loft and play Mario Kart for the next few years—but I assured him I'd be by if our spies appeared, then took my repose.

When I woke again, the windows were still black, and a hand was jostling me to consciousness. "Coileán. *Coileán*," Val prodded, shaking me until I was able to push him off.

"Is Rufus here?" I mumbled, tasting an unpleasant mélange of sleep-mouth and Astrid's garlic mashed potatoes.

"No. Get up."

Too groggy to question him, I imagined a bathrobe into being and stumbled across the hall on Val's heels. He threw open the door to one of the guest chambers, and I squinted at the odd sight beyond the window—a reddish flickering in the distance, sparks floating in the night. Only once he pulled me to the glass did the vision begin to resolve from dreamy to nightmarish.

"Hoim's estate is on fire," he said, pointing to one of the brightest spots. "So is Anorian's. And it's spreading."

Confusion and dread jockeyed for prominence as I stared out at the flames. A fire is easy enough to quench with enchantment…unless, of course, there's no one left alive to work the magic. "Moon and stars, what happened?"

He turned from the view. "I don't have all the details, but there are five guards waiting downstairs for you to put some shoes on and get to work."

By then, I was closing in on full alertness, and I dressed myself with a wave. "Stay here," I told Val, brushing past him as I headed for the door. "Wait for further instructions. Let Aiden sleep."

"My lord?" he asked, puzzled.

I glanced over my shoulder, barely slowing. "Aiden doesn't hear of this until morning. Keep him safe," I said, and marched into the night.

CHAPTER 25

By the time we reached the border, the estates were still burning, but the blazes were beginning to weaken. I turned to take in both fires and caught the flash of an opening gate as Eleanor and three of her guards ran through to join us. "What happened?" she demanded, pushing up her sleeves. "Who started it?"

"Damned if I know," I muttered. "Which looks further along to you? My money's on Hoim's."

She ran one hand over her face. "Just help me put them out," she said, and marched toward Anorian's home.

I bent my will toward Hoim's estate and pictured a smothering wet blanket. The flames responded appropriately, shrinking and darkening until all that was left was damp ashes and curling smoke against the stars.

"Any survivors?" Eleanor called from across the border.

The blackened heap of stone didn't seem promising. "I'm not holding out much hope. You?"

"No."

My guards were searching the rubble, but I knew what their report would be. "I'm stationing people here overnight. We'll deal with this at dawn."

Toula wasn't thrilled to receive an early-morning call, but when I told her what had happened, she hastened over and followed me to the site. A long look at the smoldering ruin of Hoim's house merited a pronouncement of "Damn," and a low whistle.

The air around us stank of acrid smoke, thanks to the domes Eleanor and I had erected over the estates to keep the curious at a distance. "Realm's being closed-lipped about the perpetrators," I told her as she grimaced. "Can you do a run-back, or do I need to ask Greg?"

One eyebrow rose. "You know about that, huh?"

"I've seen it worked once or twice. Can you manage it?"

"Solo? Probably, but be on standby in case I need you to fill in, okay?"

"You know," I hastily replied, "we could get Helen over here, too—"

"*Okay?*"

I sighed, surrendering to her scorn. "Okay. But I make no guarantees."

She huffed in exasperation, then stepped a few paces away, whispered, and snapped her fingers.

The world exploded into pulsing, searingly bright green ribbons—the enchantment of the barrier, I realized, as my pupils contracted to pinpoints. "*Ow.* A little warning, huh?" I said, creating a pair of sunglasses.

She smirked. "Big baby. You see the dome?"

"Painfully well. How the hell do you *live* like this?"

Toula flexed her fingers. "Eh, you get used to it. And it's not this bright—that spell lets you see a visual representation of the active magic, not the enchantment itself. Need me to dim it?"

"A few notches wouldn't hurt," I admitted, and the green lines faded from "industrial laser" to "airport beacon."

Having rectified my blindness, Toula cupped her hands and held them in front of her, palms a foot apart and facing each other. "The action's going to happen in here," she explained, nodding toward the space between her hands, then closed her eyes and mouthed her mantra of concentration. A new set of green lines swirled from the ether—a much neater set of lines than the chaotic mess above our heads—and as the spell coalesced, they connected Toula's palms to the sphere of white mist manifesting between them. "See anything yet?"

"We have a ball."

She cracked one eye open, noted her progress, and closed it again as the silent casting resumed. As she worked, the mist brightened, and a pair of figures appeared inside it—us, miniature and moving in real time. "Picture's up," I told Toula. "Can you rewind it?"

"I'm going to let you do that. Taking too much effort to hold this together."

"*Me?* I don't know—"

"Spin it. Counter-clockwise will go backward in time."

Hesitantly, I reached out and let my fingertips brush against the sphere, which felt like a captured cloud of fog, cool and damp. But as I held my hand in position, it solidified enough to give me something to push against. I flicked the ball like a desk globe and watched as the scene rewound, darkening to night, then lightening to the previous day, when the house beside us was whole. Having overshot the mark, I turned the ball the other way until I saw flames erupt.

"Got it?" Toula muttered through clenched teeth.

"Almost." I spun back a few minutes, watching…and *there*. "Anorian," I said, spotting him in the little knot that was slipping onto Hoim's property. "And half a dozen others. Can you show me his house?"

"Not unless we move."

"Hate to ask…"

She grunted, and the spell collapsed. "If you hated to ask, you wouldn't do it. Come on, then," she muttered, tromping through the grass toward the border.

A few minutes later, having rebuilt the spell, Toula gave me the go-ahead and hung on while I searched for clues. The image lightened as Hoim's house caught fire, and then the culprits were running back toward Anorian's place, slapping each other's backs. Anorian went inside, and the others dispersed...and then another mob ran into view.

"Hoim's neighbors," I said, freezing the picture. "Two cousins. And that one...she was at court this morning, shouting for blood. They must have started the second fire."

The visualization spells broke, and Toula groaned as she rubbed her hands together. "I'm guessing that the homeowners were dead before the fires began, yeah?"

"That's the working hypothesis." I surveyed the scene while Toula massaged out the kinks. "Time to tell Eleanor. You coming?"

"You need me?"

"I don't know," I replied, opening a gate to the mansion, "but it never hurts to have backup."

Eleanor and I agreed that we needed to throw the guilty parties into our dungeons, but past that, we failed to reach consensus. "I watched the replay," I told her as she nibbled at a hangnail. "This is clearly murder—we need to punish appropriately."

"Execute, you mean." Satisfied with the condition of her cuticles, she met my stare. "Yes, this is terrible, but they're been giving tit for tat for two weeks. If I execute Anorian's crew for avenging themselves—"

"That business was unprovoked! They *murdered* her, Eleanor!"

"Henry," she murmured. "You can't tell me Hoim didn't have a hand in his death."

"You can't tell me she did. He didn't die at her hands, on her property—"

"But it's all part of the back-and-forth. You've yet to execute anyone for Henry's murder."

"Because we don't know that he *was* murdered. Marem was disgusted by the body—if he'd done it on purpose, he would have shown some sign."

"Would he?"

I paused, trying to spot the truth behind Eleanor's poker face. "I can ask Toula to run back that night, but I don't think that was murder. *This* was. I have all the proof I need."

"I don't doubt your proof. But I'm telling you that I can't execute my people for avenging that child's death." She raised her hand to still my sputtering. "Coileán, what signal does it send to my court if I don't protect them? You haven't provided justice for Henry, so they made their own. I deplore it, but only within these walls." She glanced pointedly at her locked office door. "We can end this feud if you execute the people who killed Anorian."

My hands twitched. "And is there to be no justice for Hoim, then?"

"She was the instigator. She got—"

"Don't tell me she got what she deserved. You need to save face, I get it. I do, too. We execute everyone and wipe the slate clean. End of feud."

"No."

Fighting the urge to punch the wall, I settled for clenching my fists. "Whatever happened to presenting a unified front, huh? Whatever happened to justice?"

"This *is* justice," she replied, placid in the face of my rage. "We can agree that my plan is the proper course and preserve unity, but at this juncture, my concern is for the well-being of the court. If that means we can't agree on a course of action…"

Her voice trailed off, but the message was clear. "I think we're done here," I said, and left before I could do something regrettable.

I heard the crunch of Val's boots on the gravel path long before he found me at the center of my rosebush maze. He took in the scene—me, stretched on a wooden chaise in the dark with my head in the crook of one arm—then stepped into the clearing and glanced at the cloudless sky. "Good evening for stargazing."

I grunted noncommittally.

He eased his way closer. "Taking a rest?"

"Clearing my head. Or trying to." I shifted on the cushion and turned to the heavens. "It's boring viewing, Val. The constellations are gone."

He squatted by my lounger. "Do the shapes make the stars any brighter?"

"No, but there's a comfort in the familiar," I said, hating how petulant I sounded, "and I miss it."

A dozen bright lights streaked overhead in all directions—Faerie's version of a meteor shower, a once-and-done event—and Val chuckled. "She's never truly understood how that's supposed to look."

"Not going to quarrel with her. I've got enough fights to win without antagonizing the realm as well. Did you need something?"

"Just concerned about you."

"I'll be fine."

"No one's heard a word from you since you returned from Eleanor. And considering the events of last night, I can't help but think it unwise for you to be out here alone."

I gestured toward the hedge around us. "Built myself a fort, didn't I?"

"Oh yes, this is entirely defensible," he said dryly. "Come inside, or I'm staying with you. Your choice."

"Is that an order, Captain?"

"An offer. I cannot in good conscience allow you to mope in the dark without at least one guard."

I sat up and rotated the kink out of my neck. "I'm not *moping.*"

"No?" He gave the hedge a long look. "You returned from Eleanor without announcing a decision as to the prisoners, and then I find you brooding—"

"This isn't brooding."

Val shook his head and conjured up an orange fireball in his palm. "Mendacity isn't among your talents, my lord. Would you like to hear the latest news?"

"No, but you'd better tell me," I muttered, pushing myself from the chaise.

"Nico sent word shortly after sundown."

I frowned. "Nico…"

"Eleanor's captain. We share information."

That took me aback. "You think that's wise?"

Val's smirk blossomed. "Nicolaus was in Oberon's guard for a time, when you were a boy. Eleanor's in competent hands. Anyway"—he tossed his fireball from palm to palm—"we trust each other enough to share pertinent developments. She released her prisoners today."

I groaned, then marched across the clearing before I could lash out near Val. "Damn her," I muttered, and grabbed the rose hedge. There were no thorns to cut into my skin, but giving my hands something to do lessened the chance that I'd set the entire garden on fire.

As I dragged my anger down to a simmer, Val squeezed my shoulder and murmured, "Breathe, Coileán."

His presence was a comfort, and a few long exhalations later, I felt calm enough to release my grip on the hedge, though I winced as my fingers unclenched. "She told me we'd be even if I killed my lot," I said, watching Val's expression in the flickering light of his fireball. "I told her we needed to execute all of them, but she wouldn't budge."

He nodded. "That's what Nico conveyed."

"So what am I supposed to do?"

After a long moment of thought, he gestured toward my chaise and produced a copy beside it. We left the hedge and sat facing each other, and he tossed his flame into the air to free his hands. "I like your original plan," he began. "Wipe out both mobs and make an example of them. Obviously, that's no longer an option."

"And now? Do I follow Eleanor's suggestion?"

"That depends on what's more important to you, pursuing her or keeping this court together. I tell you in truth, as your man and your friend, that if you execute your prisoners while Eleanor's go free, the court will turn on you. And if you choose that path, I doubt that I'll be able to protect you."

I listened to the night breeze rustle the hedge as I considered his words. "If I set them free, then the odds are good that there's going to be retaliation again."

"I would think so, yes."

"But if I keep them incarcerated, the court will be on my doorstep again, worse than this morning. And there will *still* be retaliation."

"Undoubtedly."

"So you're telling me that the best plan is to release them? Because if I remember correctly, you were the one telling me to lock the likely instigators away."

"So I did," he replied with a slow nod. "You had a decent chance when the child was trampled. Yes, the court would have been upset if you'd incarcerated Hoim after that party—you probably should have taken Marem, too," he mused, "but you would have had a good reason for doing it. Eleanor's court would have been satisfied, and this court would have grudgingly accepted it. And if Eleanor's people had pressed their advantage after that, she could have come down on them. But now?" He shook his head. "Forget the child—you have fresh corpses on both sides of the border. Until the two of you can agree on what's to be done, I wouldn't do anything drastic, were I in your position. Let them go. Let this escalate—I fear it's inevitable. The next time this happens, remind Eleanor of what happened today and see if you can't work together."

"Of course, if I let my people go, she's going to be *peeved*."

"I should think so."

His face betrayed nothing, but the anxiety in Val's thoughts worsened mine. If I released the mob that had killed Anorian without punishment, Eleanor would surely take the gesture as a slap in the face. If I followed her plan, though, I'd ingratiate myself to her—and then I'd be a step closer to someday…

No.

Pushing my libido aside, I focused on the situation with cold logic. A tiff with Eleanor was survivable. A disintegrating court was another matter.

And remember what happened the last time you followed a foolish plan for another's affection, came the realm's whisper. Before I could protest, a too-familiar image flashed behind my eyes: an incongruous white rosebush among my oak trees, my reminder of the place where Meggy lay moldering. I cast the picture away before the realm could show me how Meggy had died, a vision I already saw far too often in my nightmares.

I had done everything I could to appease Meggy because I loved her. In my tainted, damned, catastrophic way, I *had* loved her. But Eleanor…yes, she had my Meggy's look about her, but as she had made abundantly clear, she wasn't her sister.

"My lord?" said Val, and I snapped back from my thoughts.

"Set them free." I rose from my chaise and disintegrated it. "If Eleanor wants to play that way, then so be it."

He offered me a little smile before opening a gate into the bowels of the palace and taking his silent leave.

Part of me expected to wake the next morning to rivers of blood, but it seemed as though the fires of the feud had been snuffed by the brief incarceration, and the parties had retreated to lick their wounds in private. I had no angry mob waiting and no stack of outrage-filled letters on my desk, which suited me well. I also had not a peep from Eleanor, which left me uneasy, but I resolved not to make the first move.

The day passed without incident, as did the next and the one that followed. By the fourth day after the fires, I'd begun to grow tense again, wary of the calm. Without waiting for my order, Val had called in all of the guards and their reserves, and he kept his team close to the palace.

With no pressing demand on my time that morning, I sought out Aiden for companionship, but I found my brother deep in his lab with his eyes locked on a monitor. "Coding," he said when I knocked. "Bug in the mapping program. I'm fixing it, but it's complicated."

"I suppose I could best be of help by leaving you alone, yes?" I replied.

He didn't look up, but he grinned wearily. "More or less. Actually, there *is* one thing—could you exercise Georgie? I've been at this for hours, and I'd like to crash once I get it sorted out. She needs a little time in the air— could you take her?"

That took me aback, as I'd never had occasion to ride without Joey at the reins. "Can she not go alone?"

"Sure, she knows her way, but she gets bored. Please?"

Seeing the circles under his eyes, I caved. But once I reached the barn, I found Joey already there, mucking the place out with his well-worn shovel. Confused, I slipped into the sheep pen before he noticed me and threaded my way through the flock toward Georgie, who was tossing unfortunate ewes and catching them in her mouth like bleating popcorn. "Is everything all right?" I asked the dragon. "Where's Helen?"

Georgie snapped her maw shut on the latest sheep and swallowed it in one gulp. *Silo. Joey's nervous about something. Needed to sweat it out.*

"Council again?"

She gave me the draconic version of a shrug, an exaggerated toss of her head. *He didn't say, and I didn't look.*

"Really?"

Her red eyes narrowed, and she snorted as she picked

out her next bite from the oblivious sheep. *It's something to do with Helen. That's as far as I looked—ah. Hello,* she thought, scooping a sheep into her mouth as it budded into two. *Doubles, I love these. Twice the mouthful for the same effort. But no, I didn't pry. She's his mate, and I don't need to know every detail of that mess.*

I folded my arms and watched her go after another morsel. "I've got to say, Georgie, that's mature of you."

She snapped up a sheep and swallowed it down—well, all but one leg, which dangled from her mouth like a wooly toothpick. *I know. And he'll tell me anyway.* She showed me far too many teeth. *He always does.*

A dragon's smile is anything but reassuring, and I left her to her meal. Pretending I hadn't tried to scout for information, I wandered into the barn and rapped on the wall to get Joey's attention. "You know, we have this thing called 'magic' that works wonders at making giant piles of lizard excrement disappear. Would you like a demonstration?"

He leaned on his shovel and smiled, but his face was taut. "Thanks anyway. Just needed some fresh air. Spending too many days in the silo makes me a little stir crazy."

"So go for a ride, I'll clean the barn. Get some air in your lungs that isn't quite so fragrant." When he made no move to release his shovel, I peered at him and frowned. "Girl trouble? Council on your back? Is Howard giving you grief?"

"No, not any more than usual, and Howard isn't speaking to us right now." Joey let the shovel drop and plopped onto a stack of bales. "Colin…there's something I need to tell you."

I hurriedly joined him. "What's wrong? Has the Council—"

"The Council's got nothing to do with this. Yet." He swallowed hard, then met my eyes. "Helen's pregnant."

"*What?*"

He laughed at my reaction, but there was a tinge of fear in his voice. "I know! She told me last night. Not yet three months along, so there's plenty that could still go wrong, but...yeah." Whether he was nodding or trembling, I couldn't say. "This is really happening, and I...I'm going to be a father."

"Joey, that—"

"And I am *so* fucking scared, man. I don't know the first thing about raising kids. Especially a little wizard kid! What happens if it throws a tantrum and stuff starts flying around the room? What am I supposed to do then?"

I grabbed his shaking shoulders. "*Whoa.* First, congratulations, kid. That's wonderful news for you both. Breathe. Second, was Peter a good father?"

"Huh?" he asked, momentarily thrown by the non sequitur. "Yeah, sure, Dad's great—"

"Then when you don't know what to do with the baby, you ask yourself, 'What would Dad do right now?' and try to do that. Or talk to Vivi's parents—I'm sure they have suggestions after thirteen rounds." I felt him relax a degree. "Now, I can't tell you how to raise a wizard, but I *can* tell you that they aren't born magi. Their talent grows with them, much as ours does. And anyway, Helen's not going to leave you with a baby you can't handle, right?"

I'd hoped that would reassure him, but another thought bubbled to the fore. "What if I mess the baby up?" said Joey. "What if it's a witch because of me? Or a dud? I mean, whatever it is, it's going to be witch-blooded, isn't it?"

Seeing his rising panic, I said, "Helen didn't get her position because she has a pretty face. Any child of hers is going to get a strong dose of talent, and the little sprinkling of fae genes you're bringing to the party may not make much of a dent against that."

"But what if it does? What if our kid's a dud, and it's my fault?"

I looked him in the eye and squeezed his shoulders.

"Then that kid's going to have the grand magus beside him, looking out for him. He's going to have a father who loves him and teaches him to ride dragons and joust and be brave. And if all of that somehow doesn't work, then he's going to have an uncle who will be *thrilled* to smash heads together if anyone gives the tyke trouble. So even if the next Bolin can't cast his way out of a wet paper bag, he'll have a support team in place." With that, I released him and smiled. "I still can't believe you're having a kid, whatever the hell it turns out to be."

"I know," he said with a nervous chuckle. "I'm scared, but I'm excited, just…surprised it was this soon."

"You and me both. I don't mean to pry, but how Catholic are your preventative measures?"

That earned a punch in the arm. "Not at all, but nothing's perfect. And on that note, I hope Father Paul won't mind baptizing the baby."

"I doubt he'd mind. Show up with a frilly gown and hope for the best."

"Well, you need a little more than that. We'll have to find godparents…" His voice trailed off, and one eyebrow slowly arched.

"No. *No*," I said, seeing the idea at the forefront of his mind. "That is an emphatic no. Forget it. I'm not even Catholic."

"Aw, come on, Colin," he wheedled, grinning. "You know you want to."

"I most certainly do not."

"But it would be perfect! If something happened to us—"

"Then I would be far down the line of conceivably responsible guardians for that child. Let's not be hasty about this, hmm?"

Joey remained undaunted in the face of reason. "Protest all you want, but you and I both know that you're dying to be Junior's faerie godfather."

I sighed and jabbed one finger toward the sheep pen.

"*Out.* Go retrieve your lizard before she eats the entire flock."

He slid off the bale and walked backwards toward the door. "That wasn't a no."

"This conversation is over, Joey."

"Still wasn't a no."

"*No,*" I called after him.

"What was that? Did you say something?" he teased, cupping his hand around his ear, and jogged off to retrieve the dragon before I could drive the point home in a firmer way.

Making the barn presentable was the work of a moment's thought, and I quickly returned to Aiden's suite to pass along the tidings. But his sister had beaten me to the punch, and I found him beaming at the silenced phone he still clutched when I let myself in. "This is *nuts!*" he exclaimed. "Great, but crazy. Hel's super-excited. She said Joey was coming over?"

"He went off with Georgie," I explained, but Aiden was too excited to focus.

He dropped the phone onto the workbench as his eyes widened. "You know what this means? I'm going to be somebody's uncle. This is…this is *big.* I'm not sure I'm uncle material yet—"

"Aiden, you're already an uncle dozens of times over. Liza? Mina? *Moyna?* Your entire surveying crew?"

"But this is the first one younger than me. It's different. There's a slim chance that this kid's going to look up to me, and I'm not certain that I'm ready for that level of responsibility."

"Sleep on it," I said, thumbing my hand toward the lab exit. "This will all make sense once you're thinking straight again."

"I'm thinking perfectly—"

The flow of magic into the lab was a mere trickle, but it was sufficient to build the tiny enchantment needed to push Aiden over the edge of his exhaustion into unconsciousness. I caught him as he slumped, dragged him out of the room and past the barrier, then floated him the rest of the way into bed. When I left, he was sprawled on his back and snoring, and I smiled to myself as I closed the door.

But as I wandered toward my office, a shadow crept across my thoughts. The Council would undoubtedly learn of this soon, if they hadn't already—and what would that mean for Helen? The other magi would have to accept that she wasn't inclined to divorce Joey, so would they finally give the kids peace? Or would the Inner Council step up their efforts to secure Helen's resignation?

And the spy…

Helen needed to leave the silo, end of discussion. Her own well-being hadn't been enough, but she had the baby's health to think about now—maybe, with a little persuasion, we could talk her into a vacation at a safer installation. Glastonbury, perhaps. Or Mongolia. Hell, even Giza would be safer for her than Montana was that season.

I latched the office door behind me, then leaned against the bookcase and tried to push the intruding fears from my mind.

When the Council learned of Helen's pregnancy, surely the spy would know about it, too.

Which meant that Moyna would also hear the news.

I squeezed my eyes closed in a futile effort to block Walt's severed head from my thoughts. That wouldn't happen again. I wouldn't *allow* it to happen again.

But I knew then, even as my memory held me hostage while it replayed the moment of Walt's unboxing, that I would be damned if I let Eleanor kill my daughter. Murderer, monster, or misunderstood, she was *mine*.

After letting the dragon stretch her wings and enjoying a few hours of daylight, Joey headed inside to accept Aiden's enthusiastic congratulations, then went home to his wife with a hot dinner in hand. I'd let slip to Astrid that Joey might be joining us that evening, and when he apologetically begged off, she insisted on making up a canvas sack full of doggie bags.

Still under-slept, but with a full belly and a slight buzz, Aiden retired shortly after dinner, and I stayed up in the comfortable solitude of my office, enjoying a roaring fire, a well-worn Poe omnibus, and an obscene amount of single-malt. The clock told me it was nearly dawn in Virginia—a bit ahead of the local time, which was somewhere in the wee hours—before I'd resolved to attempt to sleep, but I'd barely enchanted myself a bookmark when Rufus knocked and opened the door. "Got a moment?" he asked, keeping his voice low.

I took in his rumpled sweats and bed-tousled hair. We were nearly in synch with Montana, and the boy looked like he'd been pulled from deep sleep. "What's happened?"

Rufus opened his fist, revealing Kuni's backpack. "Liza visited the second camp last night. Want to pull the photos? Kuni couldn't videotape the best route in, but he said he took pictures of every landmark he could spot."

I reached inside to cure my already receding inebriation. "Where is it? Close to Coeur d'Alene?"

"No. She's pitched her backup tent somewhere in the Purcell Wilderness, up over the border in British Columbia. At least a five-hour drive north from us, and that just gets you to the edge of the park. *Where* she's hiding in there is still a mystery, but the people around Liza talked enough to get us that much information. They went in by gate," he explained, leaning against the doorframe. "Which is fair enough, I suppose. The roads in that park are less than minimal."

"I'm not familiar with it…"

"About half a million acres of rugged mountains, plus grizzlies, but that's a starting point. And there's more. Kuni only gave us a thumbnail sketch before he collapsed, but he got Moyna on camera talking about an attack plan." Rufus stuck out his laden hand. "So, do you want to give Ellie a call, or should I?"

CHAPTER 26

By the time Eleanor arrived, I'd shaken Aiden awake and steered him into the lab. I had no desire to see her—nor she me, judging by her frigid nod—but I could think of nothing to be gained by holding out on her, especially not with Rufus in the picture. Still, we stared each other down in silence while Aiden went to work. Sensing our hostility, Rufus excused himself, ostensibly to give Aiden a hand. Young and tired he might be, but the professor was no fool.

In a matter of minutes, Aiden had Kuni's video running, and the three of us gathered around his screen to watch the playback. When the clip ended, Eleanor barely had time to groan before Aiden's phone was at his ear. "Get over here, pronto," he muttered without preamble. "She's coming after you."

The video was no better on a second viewing, especially not blown up on the bank of monitors. Our quartet had ballooned for the repeat show: Helen, Joey, and Toula in their sleepwear, Vivi and Hal, only marginally less groggy than the Montana contingent, and Slim, who had yet to retire after a long Friday night and still smelled of beer. Val and Nico stood by the door, the only ones of us who seemed to have remembered how to dress in polite company.

"All right," said Vivi, pulling Hal's arm more tightly around her shoulders, "let's see what we're up against."

Aiden nodded and tapped a button, and the black screen switched to Kuni's shaky camera. "He's probably inside the hood of her coat," Rufus muttered. "Given the angles, I mean, He says she never pulls it on—"

"*Shh*," his sister ordered, and he ended his commentary as the voices spoke around Liza.

The first minutes of footage were mostly of evergreens and the back of Liza's head. It was the audio that mattered: quiet conversations in Fae, comments about the scenery from newcomers to the Purcell camp, and finally Moyna's voice calling them into a tent. Liza took a seat near the back, and Kuni pointed his camera toward Moyna and the masked wizard, who stood together near a wooden throne. As Moyna seated herself, the wizard took up a position at her right hand and surveyed the modest crowd.

"Thank you for making the journey," Moyna began, speaking over the throng until it quieted. "I'd rather address you without the wolves listening in." Affirmation rumbled around the tent, and she lifted her hand for silence. "Have patience. Their usefulness has almost been exhausted." She paused to smile. "The time is nearly upon us."

That earned another round of pleased mumblings, which Moyna permitted to run its course. "I've brought you here to explain the plan of action. All of your struggle, your sacrifice—you will be made whole again. The exile is almost over."

"Look at her face," Toula murmured beside me.

"What about it?" I asked.

"She's nervous. She's hiding it well, but she's—"

"*Shh!*" came Vivi's directive, and we acquiesced. But I could see what Toula had noticed—the tension around Moyna's mouth, the way her eyes either darted around or focused on an empty spot near the back, not to mention her stilted speech. That chat was heavily scripted, probably down to the pauses, and Moyna seemed to have a touch of stage fright.

"We will divide into two groups and attack the targets simultaneously," she continued. "All of you will join me in the conquest of Faerie. While we surprise the usurpers, the wolves will make their attack on the Arcanum's base of operations. We will cut them both down before they know we're upon them."

The heads around Kuni bobbed, but the wizard stiffened and clamped a gloved hand on Moyna's shoulder. "My lady," he interrupted, sounding troubled even under the voice-distorting spell, "that wasn't the agreement."

The room silenced as Moyna turned to look at the hand, then at its owner's covered face. "The agreement was that I help you remove the grand magus. A pack of werewolves in the silo should suffice, shouldn't it?"

"Without any magical support?"

"You'll be there. Once they're inside, they're your responsibility. I've protected the fleabags and fed them all winter, Magus," she said with disdain. "I'm not going to hold your hand while the pack does its job."

"The *plan*," said the wizard as his grip tightened, "was for the court to bring the necessary firepower. You have to send at least a few—"

Moyna pushed him off and stood to glare up at him. "You don't tell me what to do. You want to overthrow the girl so badly? Find your spine, and take what you want. I'm not risking my people to win your war for you."

"The deal—"

"*This* is the deal. You can have the wolves. Do with them as you like. Help them."

Though angry, the wizard managed to keep himself collected. "You know that's not an option. The rank-and-file would never understand."

"Then I suggest you find a way to be clever about it," she replied, resuming her perch on the throne.

He tried again. "Ten good wizards could kill the pack in minutes! If they don't have shielding, they'll die in there."

She shrugged. "Let them die, then, if you won't help them. But if I were you, I might at least get the door for them. I don't think paws are particularly useful with locks and such," she added, earning a chorus of titters.

But the wizard was having none of it. He slid closer to Moyna and planted his palms on the armrests, pinning her to her chair, then hissed, "I did everything I promised, little girl. All I'm asking is for you to honor your end of—"

Moyna cut her eyes to the left. "Kiet."

Hardly had the word left her lips when a blast of force flung the wizard across—and then through—the tent. Moyna stood and faced the sudden wind, then waved the canvas back together and sat with a huff. "Thank you, Captain," she said, and the old soldier nodded curtly before disappearing back into the mob. "Were there any further questions?" she asked the room. "No? Splendid. Return to your tents and await my signal."

The video cut off, and I looked at the others' faces. "Helen, Joey, you're staying here. Slim, Vivi, get your people out of the way—"

"Hold it," Helen interrupted. "Joey can stay, but my place is in Montana."

I thrust my arm toward the screen, flabbergasted. "There's a pack of werewolves coming your way, and someone on the Council wants you out. How much clearer can we make this, Helen? You're in danger."

"Or at least take the footage to the Council," Aiden suggested. "The *whole* Council. Someone has to know who the traitor is."

"Negative," said Toula. "Show the Council that tape, and our masked buddy's going to tell Moyna she has a spy in the camp."

"If he's still speaking to her," Aiden countered. "She did have him thrown through the wall."

"Granted, but that's a big *if*, man. You want to risk Liza and Kuni with those odds?"

Helen shook her head. "Of course not. I'm going back,

I'll keep my eyes peeled, and I'll carry a wand and a .38 at all times. As Moyna's friend said, ten of us can take out the pack. I'm not too concerned for my own safety."

"What about the rest of the silo?" Joey murmured. "The kids…"

"We'll have to respond quickly. And hey, we can tag-team this," she told Eleanor and me. "Moyna said the attacks are coming together, right? Whoever gets wind of movement first calls the other. If they don't have the element of surprise, they've lost their biggest advantage."

Eleanor considered Helen's plan, then pressed her lips together. "Or we kill her now and stop this madness from progressing any further."

I jumped into the fray before Helen could reply. "Out of the question."

Taken aback, Eleanor stiffened. "We have both of her camps. Let those two extract Liza"—she gestured toward Rufus—"and we'll launch a coordinated attack on the camps. She'll never see it coming."

"Slight problem with that," said Rufus. "Camp two is in the Purcell Wilderness—the place is *huge*. We don't know where in there she's holed up."

"Unfortunate," Eleanor said, shrugging, "but hardly insurmountable. If I have to set the entire forest ablaze to flush her out, I will."

"It's eight hundred square miles, Ellie! We can't do—"

"We *can*," she interrupted, giving him a look that forbade further debate. "Coileán, I suggest we wait for nightfall and synchronize—"

"No," I told her.

"Why hesitate? We have her where we want her!"

"I want her alive."

Folding her arms, Eleanor calmly said, "I don't care what you want. I'm going after her tomorrow night, with or without your blessing."

"Eleanor—"

As I reached for her, she slapped my hand away and

marched toward the door. "I'm cleaning up your mess. If you'd been smart enough to do this when you had her at your mercy, my Walt would still be alive. Meggy would still be alive."

"Meggy *died* to save her!" I bellowed, giving in to the upswelling of rage as the corona flared around me. "I won't let you do this!"

She wheeled on her heel as her own corona flashed into view, a white aura that heralded nothing good for anyone in a mile radius. "Try to stop me," she snapped, and strode from the room before we could come to blows.

Seldom did I have cause to address my entire guard, but dawn found all sixty in my office, primed for action. Val and one of his off-shift subordinates lurked near the door, trying to be inconspicuous with their coffee, but I was in no mood to quibble over protocol as I met the ring of eyes. "The captain's briefed you, I trust?" They nodded. "Good. I want half of you outside the primary camp tonight. Toula will guide you in. Under no circumstances are you to alert the shifter or the Stowe boy to your presence, understood?" The guards nodded again, and I glanced at Val. "Who's leading that group?"

"Mina." He gestured toward her with his mug. "The secondary camp will take more work to locate, and most of the senior guard are going with me."

I hesitated, and Mina sighed as she realized the cause. "We had a quarrel, Uncle," she muttered, "not a death match. I can work with Toula as long as she's willing."

"I've already run this past her," Val added.

"Well, thanks for keeping me in the loop," I grumbled. "Very well, you have your assignments. Assume Eleanor's guard will be in place by nightfall—the camps are roughly synchronized with us in terms of daylight. Bring Moyna back alive, if at all possible."

"And the rest of them?" Mina asked.

"Take prisoners if you can, but Moyna is the priority. If you can locate and extract her without alerting the rest of the camp, so much the better."

"What about Liza?"

Val cleared his throat. "Eleanor's guard has a retrieval plan. She's to be removed before the main attack."

"Nico's *still* talking to you?" I asked incredulously,

He smirked. "We didn't see the point in making redundant efforts to retrieve Liza. On that ground, at least, the two of you are in accord."

Before I could question the wisdom of Val trading tactical notes with his rival, the door opened, and he stepped aside to let Joey dart in. "Hi," Joey panted, raising a hand as he caught his breath. "Sorry I'm late. Couldn't find armor. Still in a moving box."

The boy was sporting full leathers, including his armored vest and flying duster, plus crossed belts carrying his nail gun and Dud Defender. He held his helmet under one arm, and the hilt of his sword peeked over his right shoulder.

"What are you doing here?" I asked. "Where's Helen?"

"Back at the silo. We figured I'd be of more use in the air than trying to skewer werewolves in the bunker."

"Joey—"

He held up his hands. "You've got an awful lot of terrain to search. Georgie and I can be your eyes in the sky."

"In the *dark*?"

"Aiden's putting a heat-sensing camera into her harness as we speak. We've used it plenty of times before. If Moyna's out there, we'll find her by infrared. So what do you say?" He spread his arms. "Put me in, Coach."

Val looked my way and nodded, and I rubbed my forehead against the headache coming on. "Fine," I sighed, "but you're not getting Georgie into that realm until well past sunset. And your role in this is purely reconnaissance, understood? No heroics, no aerial assaults, and no solo attacks. You get coordinates and get out. Is that *perfectly* clear?"

"Crystal."

"And Helen's on board with this?"

Joey flashed his thumb. "Why do you think I was late? She insisted that I stick around until we found my gear."

I could envision her calculus all too clearly: the odds of her husband making it through the next few days unscathed were greater if he were flying above the fray instead of fending off shifters in tight spaces. "Just remember who's going to be waiting for you if you get any silly ideas up there," I muttered, and continued the briefing while Val clapped Joey on the shoulder and produced another mug.

On Val's orders, the guards retired for the morning as soon as our meeting ended. "I want you alert," he said as they filed out. "Sleep, eat, whatever it takes. And *you*," he added, grabbing Joey by the arm, "to bed. Let Aiden test the equipment."

"He can't run the control room and fly simultaneously," said Joey. "And he's going to be busy getting the mobile unit together—"

Val snatched the helmet from his grasp and shooed Joey away. "He can test the camera first—I'll watch the feedback. Sleep, boy."

"But I just had a triple espresso."

The captain rolled his eyes. "If you're not unconscious by the time I get to the barn, I'll knock you out. *Go.* Unless you were planning on sleeping in the corridor…"

He took the hint, leaving me to brood alone about the many ways in which I could have avoided this path.

I could have reasoned with Eleanor from the beginning, I mused, staring out at the garden in silence. I could have told Aiden to prioritize finding Moyna in the few seconds I had with him before passing out for a year. I could have kept Moyna locked away indefinitely, putting security ahead of Meggy's feelings. I could have sent Moyna back to Mother the morning I met her, safety be damned.

Or I could have done the responsible thing and never taken Meggy to the beach.

Never followed Paul to Phoenix.

Never left Ireland.

Hell, if I was going that route, I wouldn't be in this position had I never left Faerie in the first place. If I'd been content with Étaín and our cottage by the lake…if I hadn't gone in search of the father who'd never imagined I existed…things would be different.

You would probably be dead, the realm chimed in.

"And how many others are dead now because I lived?" I shot back. "How many should be here in my place?"

You're playing with hypotheticals, child. Wallowing in self-recrimination. And you are overlooking your duties here because of your feelings for that girl. Open your eyes, Coileán. Whether Moyna lives or dies is not your most pressing concern.

"I know, it's Eleanor. I've got to work something out with her."

No, I speak of—

Before Faerie could finish her thought, my office door slammed open, and Poppy shouldered her way inside with Rufus two steps behind. "They're gone," she said as I leapt to my feet. "All of them. Camp's deserted."

"What do you mean, *gone*? Where did they—"

"I don't know, but Kuni says there's no trace of them." She held out her cupped hand, and I saw the exhausted piq sprawled in her palm, red-faced and gasping like he'd run a marathon. "He found—what was it," she asked him, raising her hand to her ear, "a fire pit?" He squeaked a breathless answer, and she nodded. "Fire ring. That was the only trace. Everything else—tents, tables, everyone—is gone."

I enchanted a piq-sized glass of water, which Kuni

began to chug, giving him the unfortunate appearance of a butterfly at a frat party. "They've moved everyone to Purcell?"

"That was our thought," said Rufus, "but we can't say. I need to tell Eleanor."

I suppressed the sudden urge to incinerate both his telephone and the jacket in which he kept it. "You can't. If she doesn't know, she'll still split her forces, and that might buy us some time. Please, Rufus." I grabbed his arm before he could slide out of range. "*Please.*"

His face twisted, but he shook his head and pulled free of my grip. "I'm sorry," he mumbled. "Truly, I'm sorry, but Ellie—if I don't tell her and she finds out—"

"We can worry about that later."

"She's my *friend*, not to mention my queen. I can't keep this from her."

"Then be her friend and help me. If she beats me to Moyna, she's going to kill her. Moyna's only eighteen." I stared at him until he averted his gaze. "She's a kid, Rufus. She's made some terrible mistakes, but Eleanor's going to *kill* her. Don't let her do that."

I thought I had won him over until Poppy slipped her free hand into his and squeezed. "Hey, Rufe, look at me," she murmured. His miserable face dipped toward hers, and she tightened her grip. "You didn't make this mess, okay? And you're not Eleanor's keeper. Do the job. Do what you need to do."

"What if she gets there first?" he asked her, momentarily forgetting me.

"That's not our call. We do the job. You can reason with her after that, but first, you do your duty."

Rufus hesitated a moment longer, then he pulled out his phone and left the room. As the door latched, Poppy turned to me with stony defiance. "We're the messengers. We said we would work with both of you, and you've got no right to guilt-trip him like that."

"Company rules?" I snapped, crossing to the windows

before I could do something violent. "Do what you're paid to do, and screw the consequences?"

"What pay?" She followed me with Kuni still in hand. "This gig was pro bono. Who's to say that Eleanor's plan isn't better for the general welfare? I can't answer that, and neither can Rufus. We're keeping our promise to you both. Make the best of it."

I turned from the glass to find her watching me impassively. "Have a care, girl."

"You're not going to hurt me. You know I'm right."

And as much as I hated to admit it, she was.

As I'd suspected, Rufus's phone call threw a wrench into everyone's plans.

"We can't wait for nightfall," Val told me while the rest of the guards made last-minute preparations. "They're leaving within the hour, and I'm not about to give them the afternoon's advantage."

I thought of several dozen heavily armed faeries running wild in the woods and hoped the only hikers out were of the uncurious sort. "How were you planning on getting in?"

"Two thoughts on the matter—" He paused at a knock, then called, "Enter!" and motioned Nico inside. "Quickly, out of the open," he muttered as the other captain closed the door and approached. "As I was saying, we had two thoughts—"

I stared at the newcomer, who had forgone armor in favor of fatigues and camouflage-patterned face paint. "Um…Val?"

He nodded to Nico. "The way we see it, both of you want to locate Moyna, but no one has any idea where in this wilderness she might be. We could open a gate with a sufficiently detailed photograph—that's how Aiden did much of his traveling—or we could follow a guide into the area and go our separate ways."

"What guide?"

"Peter Stowe," Nico replied. "Rufus's brother. He's been to the park—he can take us in."

I eyed him warily. "And you're sharing this information with me because…"

"Because, my lord, as Valerius said, you already have a way into the wilderness without us. Possibly deeper into the wilderness, judging by the pictures available. This levels the field. Makes the contest more interesting, as it were."

My nails dug into my palms. "This is a game to you, is it? 'Capture the flag and kill it'? You're getting fresh air and having a little friendly sport? Maybe a picnic in the park?"

To his credit, he didn't flinch. "Nothing of the sort. My goal—*our* goal," he amended, catching Val's eye, "is to get our people in and out with the fewest casualties possible. That includes Moyna." Seeing my surprise, one corner of his mouth twitched in a hint of a smile. "Recall Lord Oberon's last…campaign, shall we call it? He allied himself with the girl, and there are some within the court who haven't forgotten."

"You mean—"

"Not everyone is in favor of the queen's proposal concerning Moyna's continued viability. Whether she's aware of this seditious sentiment, I cannot say, and should she hear rumors of this conversation, I'll deny it with my last breath."

I nodded. "And should she learn that you came to me?"

"All part of the plan. If your people come in with ours, then we can watch them. Follow them." He glanced at the ceiling mosaic. "It would be a pity if they found her first, wouldn't it?"

Val was as serene as I'd ever seen him, and for the first time that day, I allowed myself to hope for success. "This conversation never happened," I told Nico. "But before you leave…you do realize that Oberon planned to dispose of Moyna once he had what he wanted, yes?"

"Can't prove that by me." He shrugged, but he paused for a moment's thought before meeting my gaze again. "Whatever his ultimate plans for her may have been, the court remembers that Moyna helped us go home. My lord, I don't think you're so naïve as to imagine that everyone was satisfied with the change in leadership."

"In her court or mine. Yes, I'm aware of certain frictions."

"Then you understand that if the queen were to harm Lord Oberon's last ally, the girl might be seen as a martyr in certain quarters."

That gave me pause. "You anticipate that degree of sentiment? *Here*?"

"Among the half fae, at least. Those among us of purer blood would probably take it as an insult to the king."

"By his half-fae daughter," I concluded, seeing the tumblers fall into place.

Nico permitted himself another brief, mirthless, smile. "I was his man once, but I'm hers now. And I *will* protect my queen, whether she likes it or not."

As he and Val turned to go, I caught my captain's elbow at the door and drew him back for a brief moment. "Dare I wonder what you do in my best interest when I'm not looking?"

His expression never shifted, but he couldn't hide the twinkle in his eyes. "You're still alive, aren't you?" he replied, and followed Nico to rally the troops.

With the guards leaving early, Joey's flyover had to be scuttled. "Temporarily," I assured him as he groggily shuffled around the barn. "You two can go over after dark, assuming they haven't found her yet."

And, I admitted to myself, assuming she was still there to be found. The guards' haste to reach the forest wasn't merely the product of friendly competition—if Moyna was consolidating her people, then the promised attack couldn't be far away.

With Joey sent back to bed, I took stock of the situation, deemed my most pressing fires extinguished, and called Helen. "Batten the hatches," I told her, ducking into my rose maze for privacy. "Moyna—"

"Is probably in Canada with the rest of her merry band, and you've got recon teams in the woods."

"How—"

"Rufus told Aiden, and he's been keeping me updated. Where's my husband?"

"Napping. I'm not sending him and Smaug out until they lose the sun. Are you safe?"

Helen snorted. "As safe as I can be fifty feet underground, locked in with at least one magus who hates my guts."

"They haven't blocked your shortcut through the wards, have they?"

"Considering that I opened a gate for Joey this morning from our apartment, no. Don't worry about me. I'm keeping the Inner Council where I can see them this afternoon, in case anyone decides to go on walkabout."

"Oh?"

"Impromptu meeting. I was presented with a proposal to build a new installation in India, and I've been putting off discussion for months. And by 'months,' I mean I got Greg to draft it this morning and forge a few magi's signatures. You know, I need the Inner Council to take a look and debate this before I present it to the installation heads."

"Clever girl."

"Aren't I?" said Helen. "Anyone who leaves early is on my short list of suspects. And before you ask, Toula's sitting in on this meeting. I'll figure out a pretext in the next few minutes."

I leaned against the hedge and smiled. "You've grown up so quickly, Grand Magus. What am I to do with you?"

"Just keep my boys safe, and we'll be cool. Go get 'em,

tiger."

We said our goodbyes, and I stood a moment longer in the shade of the hedge, smelling the warm flowers around me. The sky above was clear but for a few errant wisps of white cloud, the breeze refreshing, the hour perfect for a hammock and a beer.

Everything was well in hand. The guards would find Moyna and bring her home, and Liza would be extracted unharmed. Aiden and Joey were safe with me, Vivi and Hal had come over to visit Rufus, Poppy, and Kuni at the elders Stowes' new home while the espionage team decompressed, and Helen and Toula had each other's back in the silo. Eleanor would come around eventually, and we would put this mess behind us. Maybe we could start over, I mused as I headed up the gravel path toward the palace. Once she was satisfied that Moyna would never escape my keeping, perhaps Eleanor's anger would cool. We would work together again, and maybe—*maybe*—she and I would have a future as more than colleagues.

Satisfied with the rosy picture my imagination was painting, I sat down for a late lunch and waited for news from Val. Perhaps, I thought, they would stumble onto Moyna quickly. Maybe Joey wouldn't get a chance to take Georgie out after all.

And maybe someday I'll learn not to let my optimism out of its cage.

CHAPTER 27

Lunch was a waste—I was too wired to eat more than a few bites, and though Val had barely been gone an hour, I was impatient for news. Eschewing my office, I headed for the library, seeking solace in the cool silence of the cavernous room. A few shelves were in want of organization, and since my hands and head needed a distraction, I turned my attention to a neglected pile of dusty histories.

Time is a slippery creature in Faerie, and I had no idea how many hours I whiled away at my busywork. Every so often, I stole a glance at my phone to check for missed messages, but it remained obstinately silent. Eventually, the light began dimming to orange and pink, and I paused with a stack of books in my arms when I noticed how quickly sunset was approaching. I decided to finish my current shelf before rousing Joey, and when the night was sufficiently dark, I'd call Val and send the boy out to make contact. Perhaps it had been foolish to hope the guards would pick Moyna out of half a million acres of forest in the span of a single afternoon, but surely with an aerial heat-sensing camera…

Before I could finish the thought, the realm began to scream.

Startled by the deafening mental shout, I dropped the books and covered my ears, but there was no way to block Faerie's voice. Her scream was fearful this time, frightened and…angry?

I looked up at a flash of light as Aiden opened a gate.

"There you are!" he yelled over the realm. "We've got to move!"

"What's going on?" I asked, following him back to his chambers.

Aiden left me to close the rift and strode across the room. Rather than stop at his monitors, he veered to the left and pointed to the narrow window. "It's burning. Take a look."

I peered out at the unexpected black clouds rising in the distance—clouds lit from below with red lights like a dozen setting suns. "Moon and stars, what the hell is going on out there?"

Though the realm continued its shrieking, Aiden heard me over the cacophony and shook his head. "What do you *think*, Coileán?"

To the south, stretching over the horizon toward Eleanor's mansion, Faerie burned.

Aiden and I stood at the top of a tower to survey the chaos. My lands remained unscorched as of yet, but the estates abutting them were pocked with a fine crop of waving red flowers. The further south I looked, the worse the inferno raged, and the wind carried the choking smoke our way. I threw a shield around us to keep the air fresh, but that did nothing to improve the view.

The realm had ceased its alarm, but in its place, I heard the roaring of the fires and the screams of the figures darting through and above them. This wasn't even a riot—this was a battle in the streets.

"What are you going to do?" Aiden asked as a four-story castle imploded.

Before I could reply, a gate opened beside us, and Eleanor hurried through. In her pink twinset and jeans, she looked more like a soccer mom than an avenging warrior queen, and I might have laughed but for the fact that our courts were destroying each other. "Got the message?" I said as she waved the gate shut.

"Loud and clear." She joining us at the crenellated wall and muttered, "Well done, Coileán. You've managed to start a skirmish."

"*Me*? I had nothing to do with this!"

"You let your murderous prisoners go!"

"Only after you did!"

"I was being just! Defending my people. And *you*—look what you've given us." She gestured to the fires below. "If you'd listened to me, we wouldn't be in this mess right now."

"If I'd capitulated, you mean. Sorry, Eleanor, but I'm not going to roll over every time you snap you fingers and—"

"It was for the greater good!"

"For *your* greater good!"

As we shouted over each other, Aiden stepped between us. "Hey, guys," he said, shoving us apart, "save it! Realm's on fire. Stop acting like idiots."

Eleanor's eyes narrowed as the corona flared around her. "You *dare*, you arrogant child?" she yelled, and extended her hand.

Aiden flew across the tower and slammed into the wall, then crumpled to the floor, breathless and dazed.

"*You*," I spat, wheeling on Eleanor as soon as I saw his chest rise, and shot a burst of force at her, catching her off her guard. She flew through a gap in the crenellation but stopped her fall and hung in the air for an instant before she flickered and appeared in front of me, angrier than ever. For a moment, I thought her corona had brightened until I saw that mine had manifested as well.

With a scream of rage, Eleanor flung a bolt of lightning toward my face, and I threw up a shield in the nick of time. I countered with a volley of fireballs, but her shield held as true as mine, and we began to circle each other, crouching behind our respective walls of enchantment.

"Stop it," Aiden croaked as he clambered to his feet.

"Coileán, I'm fine. Eleanor, if you kill him, *Moyna* gets the throne. Damn it, *stop!*"

The kid was making sense, I realized, but only in the small part of my mind that wasn't roiling with fury. I hadn't felt this much rage since my fight with Oberon, but then, I'd been exhausted from my efforts to break free of his bind. I was strong now, and no one, no matter how much she looked like Meggy, was going to defeat me.

And then, somewhere between flinging a rain of fire at Eleanor and digging my heels in against the blast that tried to throw me from the tower, I heard Faerie whisper in the back of my mind: *Agreed.*

Another wave of force slammed me from my blind spot, and I flew into the air. Something caught me before I could fall, and an invisible hand wrapped its fingers around me, pinning my arms to my sides. As I struggled, I saw that the same fate had befallen Eleanor, then looked back at the tower below.

Bathed in a bright corona of his own, Aiden stood between us with his arms outstretched and his fists clenched. "If you're not going to fix this," he said, gritting his teeth as our pushback intensified, "then I will. Stop resisting."

Eleanor's eyes widened in confusion. "How…*what*…"

"I told Faerie that I'd be happy to try to salvage the courts if she'd power me up again. Now, I've got a realm to save, so if I put you down, will you stop shooting each other?"

I'd never seen Aiden so angry, but to my surprise, he wasn't flaring. His rage was a controlled weapon, a vise wrapped around me—and better contained than mine ever was once released. Whatever else Val had taught him, Aiden had discipline far beyond his years.

I went limp. "Fine. Put me down."

Eleanor slumped as well, and Aiden lowered us to our feet. "Call the guards back," he ordered. "I'll handle this until they get here."

"Not until they find Moyna," said Eleanor, sounding suddenly unsure. "I'm not letting her get away from—"

Another of the realm's painful siren blasts echoed in our heads, and when I opened my streaming eyes again, I found Aiden on one knee with his fingers pressed to his temples. "What do you want to bet she's here?" he said as he pushed himself upright. "Call the guards *now*, while you still have a realm to rule."

My hand, moving on instinct, dug in my pocket for my phone. "Aiden, what—"

But he already had his phone to his ear and was walking away from his shaken elders. "Joey, we're on. Get her saddled," he said, casually opening a gate, and vanished.

We stood in silence, listening to the fighting below us for a long moment.

"Coileán," Eleanor murmured, "what did he—"

"I don't know, and I'll deal with it later," I said, tapping out Val's number. "Something tells me Faerie is *pissed*, and I'm not going to argue with her right now."

"Yeah," she muttered, and produced her phone. "Ever fought off an invading army?"

"Can't say that I have. Hi, Val." I cupped my hand around the mouthpiece to block the ambient noise. "Everything's gone to hell here, and I think Moyna just made her appearance."

"On my way," he replied. "Where are the boys? Are they safe?"

A roar rent the air, and Eleanor and I leaned over the wall as Georgie rose against the sunset like a cloud of ash. Squinting, I could make out two figures on her neck, one in a flapping coat, the other with an oversized gun cradled in his arms.

"I wouldn't say that, no," I told Val. "Hurry."

I'd barely hung up when I heard Aiden's voice echo in my mind: *Mab's court is here to kill you. To me. To arms.* The air below Georgie rippled, and the fires died in their wake.

Invaders, to the east. To me!

"He's speaking to my court," I told Eleanor.

"And mine. How—"

Your task, said Faerie, *is to keep the peace. To prevent this. That is all I ask of you. If you will not do your duty, then I will find someone who will.*

"Understood," I mumbled, and turned to the red glow in the west. "Is there some reason why the sun is still setting?"

Aiden asked for light. It was the least I could do.

"Is there any way you could push the wattage higher?" Eleanor asked, as Val and the rest of my guards ran through a wide gate on the lawn below us. They froze in their tracks, taking in the destruction, and I waved from the tower to draw Val's attention as the sun began to reverse in its course.

"Aiden and Joey are out with Georgie!" I called down. "Moyna's somewhere to the east!"

Val leaned back to see me, then cupped his hands around his mouth and yelled, "I left you alone for an *afternoon*, Coileán! One afternoon!"

Eleanor sighed and stuffed her hands in her pocket. "If it's any consolation, Nico will probably express a similar sentiment when next we meet." She hesitated. "Temporary truce?"

"That would be for the best," I replied, and opened a gate into my office. "Come on, we're getting shown up by two kids and a lizard. Slightly embarrassing."

"Slightly," she agreed, and followed me through.

While some of Eleanor's people might have held a soft spot for Moyna, all bets were off when the tattered remnant of Mab's court came running out of the woods with shields up and fireballs primed. I watched through the realm's all-seeing vision as the first wave of invading faeries struck south of our border. By then, our people nearest the battle line had put aside their differences and jostled for place among the smoking debris to rebuff them. Our courts hated each other, but that evening, as the sun climbed from the west, they remembered that they hated Mab's more.

As the lines engaged, Georgie swooped overhead, and Aiden hefted his massive homemade gun to his shoulder. Instead of a bullet, a spray of metal flew from the long barrel onto Moyna's forces, who began to shriek at the aerial bombardment.

"Steel," Eleanor murmured, watching beside me. "He's loaded that thing with…birdshot?"

"Looks like lab scrap," I replied as the targeted faeries clawed at the metal. While they were distracted, Georgie made a second pass, and Aiden followed up with a long blast of bright green fire.

Rapid footsteps pulled me from the view as the captains marched in. "We've sent teams to organize the mob," Val began. "Aiden's made the preliminary arrangements. Were you planning on joining us?"

Eleanor opened a gate near the back of our line. "Where would you suggest we begin?"

He pointed to the eastern horizon through the gate. "They're coming from that direction, my lady. Maybe you should shoot that way."

"I'm being serious," she said with a scowl.

"As am I. Go, find your guards. Rally your court. Try not to get killed."

Nico left with Eleanor, but as I started to follow, Val pulled me back by the elbow. "We haven't seen Moyna yet. Do you still want her alive?" I nodded, and he released his grip. "Come, then. There's no reason to let Aiden have all the fun."

I followed him through the gate and choked on my first breath of smoke. The air stank with the remains of the house fires and burning flesh. As I scrambled for my bearings, I jumped as something thudded beside me, and

Aiden rose from a crouch. "Out of ammo," he said, tossing the gun aside. "I'm going to shield the mob. You in?"

"With you," I replied, pushing my way to the front of the line. The crowd's blood lust pulsed, and I scanned the opposing line for my daughter in vain as I powered a shield around my people. But more of Moyna's forces were streaming out of the woods to relieve the weary first wave, and Val and Nico shouted orders, moving our volunteer fighters into position.

And then, as the second wave barreled toward us, I saw Liza.

She panted at the edge of the trees and looked around in disoriented terror. "Aiden!" I shouted, and pointed through the fray. "Liza's here! Bind's off!"

He followed my finger and swore. "Hold the line, I'm going—"

"Allow me," said Poppy as she appeared from the crowd. "Keep up the fireworks—I'll extract her." She took two running steps and leapt, and in a split-second, the massive wolf was sprinting for Liza as Poppy's shredded clothes fluttered to the scorched grass.

She'd broken through the first part of Moyna's line when Rufus shoved his way to us and demanded, "Where?"

Aiden pointed to a gap, marred by a downed faerie with a bleeding arm, but grabbed Rufus's wrist to stay him. "You'll trip her up. She's got a trajectory planned." Rufus pulled free, but Aiden slammed him into the dirt with a twitch of his chin. "Dude, *no*. Let her work."

I held my breath as Poppy ran. To my relief, Liza recognized her, and when Poppy slowed to execute a turn, Liza jumped onto her back and clung to her neck. "They're coming," I said. "They're coming, they're going to make it—"

Seeing the wolf and her rider streak past, one of Moyna's people threw a focused bolt just before they hit the main line. Poppy yelped and fell, and Liza tumbled and rolled to a stop. As Poppy struggled to rise, the shooter pushed up his sleeves and advanced on her, one hand glowing with a yellow fireball.

"*No!*" Rufus screamed, and vanished. An instant later, he appeared between Poppy and the other faerie, who was too surprised to find a stranger behind the line to shield in time. Rufus struck hard, and his opponent flew a few yards through the air—a modest blow, had he not landed in a pile of Aiden's scrap metal. As he shrieked and burned, Rufus knelt beside Poppy and began assessing the damage, and Liza, stunned by the fall, tried to crawl toward them.

"You see them?" said Aiden.

"Of course," I replied, but saw him put his finger to his ear. He was wearing a headset, I realized, one with a wire-thin microphone, which meant...

A shadow passed overhead, accompanied by the thunder of Georgie's wingbeats. Quickly, I pushed my way into Aiden's surface thoughts to hear the other end of the conversation.

"I've got visual," said Joey. "Georgie can carry all four. Going to land."

"Negative. Stay high, maintain visual. I'm going to get a team to break through—"

"We don't have *time*, they've been spotted. I'm going down, I've got the Def—"

Joey's sentence ended in a high, piercing cry that froze my heart. I looked up in time to see the end of the flash, a bolt of lightning from below that had struck him in the chest, and then Joey tumbled from the sky.

Time slowed as I watched him plummet, boneless as a ragdoll. His coat was on fire, and I feared he was dead already even as my hand shot out with the enchantment to break his fall. As I ran toward him, I suddenly heard the realm cut through the turmoil of my thoughts: *This will hurt.*

Even as he fell, Joey's back arched, and he screamed

anew, over and over, like he was being washed with waves of pain. I forced myself to go faster, and then I was beneath him, holding him mere feet above the ground. I lowered him to the dirt and conjured a shield around us, and then, anticipating the worst, I pulled off his helmet.

Joey's eyes were closed, but he was breathing in ragged gasps, and I patted his cheeks. "Joey. *Joey.* Wake up," I begged, feeling for a pulse below his beard. "Please, kid, be okay." I beat out the last of the flames on his clothing, then found the buckles to his body armor and eased the vest off. The singed hole through the ballistic plate told me I wasn't going to like what I found underneath.

The next layer down was a black turtleneck, topped with the silver crucifix Joey never removed. For once, the metal wasn't my primary concern—rather, I focused on the catastrophic wound in Joey's chest, a bloody, gaping hole through which bits of charred ribs poked through. "Oh, no," I whispered as a towel appeared in my hands. "No, *no*, you are *not* dying like this…"

I barely noticed when Georgie landed and circled around us like a second shield, so focused was I on staunching the blood. One towel after another came away soaked, but by the fourth compress, the bleeding had lessened. I washed away the caked-on gore and peeled back the remains of his shirt to see the true extent of the damage, but to my shock, the hole was smaller. It shrank as I watched, covering the ribs, repairing the ruined muscle, knitting the skin back together. In another moment, there was no sign of an injury but for the wide, hairless patch on Joey's chest—and with a gasp, he opened his eyes.

"*Joey!*" I cried, laughing with relief. "Oh, my God, Joey, you *stupid* boy." I pulled him up into a bear hug. "Come on, we've got to get you out of here."

Distantly, I heard Aiden's thoughts mingle with mine: *We got them. Is Joey okay?*

Fine, I shot back, then stood. "Think you can walk? Or

ride?" I glanced at Georgie, who was swallowing a pair of legs. "She's busy. I can get you out of here—"

"Hang on," he mumbled. "Are we shielded?"

"Yeah, for another minute, but we need to move…"

Joey pulled the tough glove off his right hand, a concession to the wind at altitude and Georgie's rough scales, and stared at his skin as if he'd never seen it before. Ever so slowly, he reached for his necklace—and paused an inch away. "It tingles," he murmured. "I can't…I mean, I *could* get closer, but I don't think it would end well."

As I stared down at him, the truth hit me like a flashbulb in the face. "What the hell did she do to you?" I asked as Joey slipped his glove back on.

The gloves were thick, good for rough work but less than ideal for the fine task of working jewelry clasps. Protected against the silver, Joey gripped the crucifix and gave the necklace a sharp yank, snapping the chain. He climbed to his feet and tucked the crucifix into one of his duster's few intact pockets, then patted himself to check for his weapons. "She offered me the deal."

"What deal?"

"Like what she did for Aiden. Well, it's a little different, I guess." He reached over his shoulder, pulled his sword free, and examined the blade for damage. "All she had to do with him was suppress the wizard bits. I needed amplification. Hurts like *hell*. But she said it was the only way she could save me. Needed me to be able to help the healing." He finished his inspection but kept the sword at the ready. "Maybe I've damned myself, but Helen's still in danger."

"You mean—"

He pulled his left glove off with his teeth, cupped his hand close to his face, and regarded it with grim determination. "Focus," he whispered.

Before I could reassure him that these things took time, a blue flame flashed in his hand—small yet, but burning steadily. Joey regarded me over the fire, then closed his fist, leaving no trace of what he had done but a wisp of white smoke. "Looks like I joined the team. God help me, I said yes."

I gripped his shoulder and nodded. "Forget magic. Are you strong enough to fight?"

He gave his sword wrist an experimental turn. "I seem to be intact again, but I don't know how much of a charge the Defender has—"

"Leave the shielding to me." I gave Georgie's haunch a pat and told her, "Have fun, girl. I've got him. Finish your snack." Sparing a last concerned look for Joey, she uncoiled and lumbered toward the heart of the action, and I gestured at the approaching third wave. "All right, Percival, I've got your back. Show me what you've got."

Once re-gloved, Joey pulled his nail gun free and raised both weapons to the east. "Try to keep up," he said, and charged.

When one is trying one's damndest to keep a score of others alive, and the sun has decided that setting is for quitters, it's difficult to gain any sense of time. Later estimates suggested that our combined forces had routed Moyna's within an hour, but no one could provide a firm answer. Eleanor and I made a quick sweep through the casualties, sending the few live invaders back to my cells for keeping and separating our dead from Moyna's, but of Moyna herself, there was no sign.

"She's not the only one missing," said Val. "Kiet's probably with her. I can think of several others in the video."

"Forty-seven of her people dead, and twenty-two of ours," I told him, shaking my head. "She had to know this was suicidal."

"Probably. But that court is desperate for a leader, and she's standing in Mab's shadow. Anything less than a show of strength would have been disastrous for her. For any queen." He held my gaze. "Or king."

"Hint taken." I nudged one of the incinerated with my boot. "How are we supposed to sort out the rioters, Val?"

"I don't know, but perhaps that's a matter for tomorrow." He pointed across the field, where Aiden was grabbing Joey's hand to scramble onto Georgie's neck. "They're bound for Montana. Shall we?"

"But what about Moyna? If we hurry, we might be able to track her down—"

"Really?" He beckoned Eleanor into our huddle as she approached. "We were in the woods for hours, and we didn't cover a tenth of the ground. By the time we locate the camp, she'll be long gone."

Eleanor pointed to the aerial trio. "What about the heat-sensing camera? Nico said—"

"Again, too slow. And if you think you're going to keep the boys away from the silo for much longer, you've lost your mind."

She let the insult slide—Eleanor looked as weary as I felt. "I understand the geographical problems, but this is our best chance of locating her. Or we could set the woods on fire and flush her—"

"Look around!" Val gestured to the charred ruins scattered about us. "Don't you think we've had enough fire for one day? Let her go," he said, folding his arms. "She'll surface again in time. No one can hide forever."

"But—" I began.

He silenced us with a hard look. "Moyna isn't the immediate problem. The courts are going to destroy each other unless you focus on the trouble *here*. Work together, put an end to the feud. Play the long game—it's what we do best," he said, and grunted. "You'll have your chance with her. Make sure you still have courts to command when that day comes, hmm?"

Eleanor seemed poised to argue, but she considered the blood and ash around us, then sighed. "Very well, one problem at a time. But while we're waiting for Moyna, what are we to do with the survivors? We can't release them unless they join one of our courts—"

"Trust me," I interrupted, "that won't happen. We gave them that chance the last time we tangoed." I caught Val's eye. "But if, say, Mab's true successor wanted to come forward—"

"I'll be in Montana if you need me," he said, and hurried to join the others.

"Unbelievable," Eleanor muttered as he jogged away. "That court is his by right. Surely the realm would recognize him…yes?" she asked the darkening sky.

Faerie gave no immediate reply, and I headed for the dragon. "If memory serves, you weren't thrilled at the prospect of taking over, either."

She speed-walked after me. "I'm still here, aren't I? And Val's here already. It's not as if he'd have to move far."

"That's not the problem." I slowed my steps until Eleanor caught up. "He's spent ages here, he obviously has some idea of how to hold the realm together…what does he know that we don't?"

She flashed a tight smile. "Something along the lines of, 'Uneasy lies the head that wears a crown,' I would imagine." Pointing to the pair atop Georgie, she added, "You don't suppose Aiden's going to keep all of that power, do you?"

Only a loan.

"Oh, so you *are* listening," she said to Faerie. "You're not going to thrust power on Val like you did to me?"

There is nothing to thrust. I took Mab's from her when she broke our agreement.

"What if he were willing to claim that court? Take on the prisoners, solve one of our problems, yes?"

Faerie went silent again, and I thought she had decided not to answer when she said, *There are two courts. I will not create a third again.*

"Looks like he's off the hook," I said as Aiden opened

a gate into the Arcanum's pitch-black fields. "*Right*, the sun actually set on time over there," I muttered, then conjured an orb to light the path and led the way across the border.

CHAPTER 28

Though we marched into Montana primed for a second round, Helen met us outside the trailer park, sweaty but otherwise unharmed. She stood in the security lamp's puddle of light, overseeing a furry row of dead werewolves, and scanned the night for motion until she picked Georgie's bulk out of the darkness and yelled, "What took you?"

Georgie broke into an earth-shaking gallop, then skidded to a halt before she could plow into the rotting trailers and lowered her neck for the riders to slide off. *Hi! Are you going to eat those?*

Helen swept her arm over the corpses like a game-show beauty. "Snack away, sweetie," she said, then grabbed Joey and kissed him. "Hey, handsome, I was starting to get concerned. Any luck?"

"Moyna escaped," he replied, pulling her closer. "But other than that—"

"We'll worry about her later. I'm just glad you're..." She paused, then demanded, "Joseph Bolin, where on *earth* is your vest? And what the heck happened to your shirt?"

Joey's quiet resolve began to crack under his wife's interrogation. "Honey, there's something I, uh...can we go over there for a moment?" he asked, pulling her away from the grazing dragon.

She let him lead her into the shadows. "What's wrong, babe?"

"Moment of truth," Aiden murmured once they'd disappeared around a single-wide. "He's terrified. Don't tell him I told you, okay?"

Ten seconds later, Helen's voice echoed like a gunshot: "*What?* Oh, my God, *where?*"

We waited for a few minutes, listening to a pair of owls hoot across the pasture and Georgie contentedly crunch through bones, before they returned to the huddle. Joey looked pale, and the hand he'd locked on Helen's had acquired a new tremor. "Well?" I asked. "Have we finally reached an impasse?"

Helen's eyebrow arched. "You're not making my job easier, that's for certain. We're going to keep this quiet for now."

"You're not throwing him out, then?"

She squeezed Joey's hand. "Look, as far as I'm concerned, he's the sweet guy who got stuck with a wizard."

"There's no one I'd rather be stuck with," said Joey, slouching to peck her cheek.

Helen turned to kiss him properly. "We married each other's crazy," she told me. "I'm okay—I mean, look at Aid. Didn't think *this* would happen, now, but I'm not calling a divorce lawyer."

"Who's getting divorced?" asked Toula, slipping out of the shadows beside the wolf carcass she was floating down the road. "What'd I miss? And where are the rest of the— oh, hey," she said as Georgie snorted a quick burst of flame. "You still hungry?"

Gimme.

She dropped the wolf at Georgie's feet, and Val wrapped his arm around her shoulders. "Everyone okay?" she asked, looking at the rest of us for a clue. Val whispered a rapid explanation, and Toula's eyes bugged. "*Seriously?*" she said to Joey. "And you still got to keep the fuzz?"

He ran one gloved hand over his beard in thought. "She didn't say anything about that. I was more concerned with the internal bleeding and—"

Toula raised her hand for silence, then beckoned everyone closer. When the knot had constricted, she muttered, "Where have we been discussing this?"

"Right here," said Eleanor, "and they went behind one of the buildings…"

She squeezed her eyes closed and groaned. "*Carver.* Security cameras."

Helen stiffened, then softly swore. "Maybe no one's watching—"

"And maybe I'm Merlin. I give it an hour before the magi get wind of this."

"At least give us some good news," Aiden interrupted while his sister's cheeks reddened. "Who's the spy?"

But all Toula could offer was a shrug. "The meeting lasted until the moment the wolves came running down the hall. Every magus was present the whole time—we didn't even break for dinner."

He scowled at the gravel, then turned to Helen. "Moyna called him 'magus.' If he's not in the Inner Council—"

"Could be an installation head faking an accent," she finished.

"Or Moyna could be mistaken," said Toula. "Maybe he's not a magus at all. Maybe he's working *for* a magus. Or magi."

As that unpleasant thought hung, I took Helen's free hand. "Come back with us, both of you. Let this blow over, then figure out how you want to find the spy. I'll help you if I can. But don't do this to yourself. You survived a werewolf attack, kid. Don't let the Council eat you alive."

Helen looked up at Joey, who took his turn at giving reassuring squeezes. "Whatever you think best," he told her. "If you want me here, say the word. If you think I should go…"

She hesitated before she mumbled, "Maybe for a couple of days."

Joey nodded and held her, and Helen slumped against him. "It's going to be okay," he whispered into her hair. "I love you."

"Now and forever," she replied, hanging on against the moment of departure.

We returned to a quiet, starry night. The guards had finished the cleanup of the dead in our absence, and a few remained near the site, watching the woods in case of lurkers. Hungry but too weary to eat, I collapsed and allowed myself to drift until morning, when Mina woke me to announce that Eleanor was waiting in the dining room.

When I shuffled downstairs, I found her sitting behind a pot of tea and a pound of thick-cut bacon. "No judging," she warned. "Aiden recommended it, and he wasn't wrong."

I glanced down the table at my brother, whose chipper smile seemed out of place. "Aren't we perky."

He sawed through his pancakes and shrugged. "Realm took the boost back when I went to bed, and I slept like the dead. Too tired to do anything else." Stuffing his mouth, he added, "Joey's been up since dawn. Val put him in basic training."

"What does that entail?" Eleanor enquired.

Aiden's smile dimmed at the question. "Believe me, you don't want to know."

Once fed, hydrated, and sufficiently alert to feign competence, Eleanor and I went to the border between the piles of rubble that had been Hoim's and Anorian's houses, constructed a canopied platform for ourselves with a pair of thrones, and sent out a summons. Half an hour later, I scanned the crowd for familiar faces, picking out my kin, then the many members of Eleanor's court whose noses I'd bloodied. The Stowes stood in a clump, and to my surprise, I spotted Vivi and Hal near the front. Behind them stood Rufus—and, I noted, Poppy, who supported her weight on his shoulder and a crutch. Though her shattered arm and leg had been mending overnight, the bones were still soft, and her not-so-secret admirer was playing nursemaid. Bringing up the rear were Aiden, Val, and Joey—and beside Joey, lingering on the edge, stood Liza, who seemed to be doing her best to blend into the scenery. A golden orb flew to her shoulder, and Liza looked down at the piq with an uneasy smile.

Eleanor shifted in her seat and leaned closer. "Would you like to kick this off, or shall I?"

"Happy to begin." The crowd quieted as I stood, and I cleared my throat. "Good morning. Let's talk about yesterday—"

"Try another stunt like that," Eleanor interrupted as she joined me, "and I'll skin the instigators alive and throw them into the sea. Oh, I'm sorry," she said, seeing my surprise, "were you going to say something else?"

"Well, uh…I thought I was going to begin."

"You did. Now, as for the lot of you miscreants, this nonsense is going to *end.*"

I stepped back and met Aiden's eyes while Eleanor promised new forms of pain for anyone foolish enough to break the peace. *Creative*, I thought.

She's got a great "angry teacher" voice, he replied. *Is she going to be the bad cop now?*

I don't know. Eleanor's pitch rose as she hit her stride, and the crowd shrank back as she made plain how exasperated she was. *She seems to have this in hand.*

Five minutes later, Eleanor turned to me and smiled. "I think Coileán has a few words for you as well," she told the terrified throng, then stepped aside and gestured to her vacated spot. "Got them warmed up for you," she whispered. "I may be mistaken, but I *think* they're listening."

By the time we allowed the crowd to disperse, I

thought we'd instilled enough fear in our courts to keep future feuding to a minimum. "Of course," said Val as the last of my people slunk off, "the test will be your response once someone starts trouble anew. As long as you follow through with half of what I heard..." He patted my shoulder. "I heard echoes of Titania this morning. The necessary echoes," he explained as my expression darkened. "The ones that give me hope for the future of this realm. Like it or not, the court needs a firm hand."

"Perhaps," I said, and opened a gate. "My office?"

He followed me and accepted a seat on one of the couches. "What's troubling you? Beyond Eleanor's imagination, I mean."

I sat opposite him and glanced over his shoulder at the door, ascertaining that we were alone. "How's Joey?"

"Difficult to say," he finally replied. "His training is progressing well. Joey watched me work with Aiden—he knows the theory. Beyond that?" He shrugged. "He's quiet. Worried about Helen, but more than that, I can't say with certainty."

"So he hasn't had a breakdown or—"

"Perhaps once the Arcanum situation calms, his thoughts will turn to himself." Val mulled over his words. "Joey's only a few years older than I was when I discovered...*this*. If memory serves, he'll need a little time to come to terms with it."

I ran my hands through my hair and slowly exhaled. "He almost died out there."

"True, but he's had less than a day to dwell on it, and he's been occupied much of that time. The shock will come later, I imagine."

"He almost *died*, Val."

My captain stood and regarded me. "You can't protect his every moment, Coileán. Remember that he lived, and save your worry for the true problems. Now, if you'll excuse me," he said, glancing at the door, "Joey's waiting at the barn, if he knows what's good for him."

I waved him on. "Go easy on him, all right?"

He paused with his hand on the doorknob and smiled. "I'm not going to insult the boy by coddling him."

When Val had taken his leave, I locked the door and leaned against the couch with my eyes closed, thinking of the look on Joey's face when he'd ripped off his crucifix. A gold one wouldn't be difficult to acquire, but something told me that the necklace wasn't the real issue. Joey needed some quality time with Paul, that much was plain—but it wasn't my place to call the priest. Maybe in a few days, when the waters calmed in Montana, Joey would take stock of his situation and fall apart, but there was nothing to be gained by trying to force him into an existential crisis.

At the buzz of an opening gate, I opened my eyes to find Toula standing a few feet away, wearing a fraying backpack on one shoulder and waving. "Hey, Colin. Any chance that I could crash here? I don't want to be a bother, but Val's apartment is tiny."

"Help yourself," I said, rising from the couch. "What's going on in the silo?"

"Oy," she sighed. "The magi are *not* amused."

"Is Helen—"

"She's dealing with them. But with the werewolves and Joey to work through, her thought is that anyone even remotely connected to Faerie should take a walk for a few days, let things cool down. Since I'll never be Miss Popularity…" She shifted her pack. "Didn't have anywhere in particular to go, so I was hoping to borrow a futon."

"You can even have a real bed. But be honest with me, is Helen safe?"

Her lips tightened to a pale line. "I don't know. I didn't want to leave her, and I didn't go until Greg got into town."

"*Greg?*"

"Council called him and Missy for the emergency

meetings. Maybe they'll finally flush the mole out, now that Moyna's on the run again. Locating him would take some of the heat off of Carver, at least, but in any case, I'm staying away until she calls. Where's Val?"

"Out at the barn, showing Joey the ropes—"

She rolled her eyes. "He'd better not be beating Joey up. Okay, sorry to interrupt. I'll go drop my gear, and I'll be out there if you need me, playing referee. Thanks again," she said as she headed for the door.

"Toula."

She whirled on her heel. "Mm?"

"If you hear word from Helen, let me know. I don't trust the Council."

"You and me both, bub," she replied, and slipped out.

I had just sat down to lunch when my phone rang. Though the number was unfamiliar, I was curious enough to take the call as I poured my wine. "Hello? Who is this?"

"Lord Coileán, I presume?" said the man on the other end.

"That depends. Again, who is this?"

His voice was silk over stone, simultaneously reassuring and commanding. "My name is Tanner Adler. I'm calling on behalf of the Dark Company."

"Ah." I relaxed into my chair. "May I ask how you found this number?"

"Jeanine's phone. The Las Vegas PD released her effects to us a few weeks ago, but as you surely understand, I've been too busy to touch base. Jumping into one's predecessor's position is never simple."

"I hear you." The wine wasn't bad, but I adjusted the tannins and tried another sip. "If you're calling about the weres, the Arcanum handled that mess. I hope you don't want the bodies—we had a hungry dragon, and the wizards were eager to be rid of the corpses."

"That's disturbing, but no harm done."

"Great. And I want to tell you how helpful Ms. Kane has been. I don't know what commendation system you people use, but I'd give her a gold star."

The line was quiet for a moment. "Actually," said Tanner, "I was calling about her. Our intel suggests she's over there."

"She was injured. The enchantment works more effectively here, but I can send her back now if it's pressing—"

"Don't bother. She's fired."

I pulled the phone away in surprise, then pressed it back to my ear. "*Fired*? Whatever for? She's been of great assistance—"

"Exactly. She hasn't checked in with us in three months."

"Because the weres were after her. We kept her here for her own protection after Jeanine was murdered, and she spent the last month undercover in Idaho."

"We're well aware of her movements. We've had a tail on her for three weeks."

Something in his tone made me bristle. "And you couldn't have offered us any assistance?"

"Why bother? You had it in hand."

"This was a joint initiative."

"No, *Jeanine* had planned for a joint initiative. The plans changed. If Ms. Kane had bothered to check in, she would have known."

My fingers clenched around my wine stem. "If I may ask, what was your plan to deal with the weres, if not work with us?"

"They were going to get themselves killed," he said with as much nonchalance as if we'd been discussing the weather. "Jeanine's loss was a blow, but there was no need to risk other Company resources when the problem would sort itself out. We were watching them—the idiot werewolves were playing with fire."

"So you knew where Moyna was encamped?"

"The Idaho camp? There was one over the border, but our targets never traveled, so we had no reason—"

"You knew where a rogue court was hiding, and you never saw fit to alert either of us? Or the Arcanum? The Fringe? No one?"

Tanner's voice was cool. "We were on no one's payroll."

"Son of a bitch," I muttered, but wrestled my temper under control. "Poppy did us all a favor—she didn't hurt your interests. Don't punish her for taking a job pro bono."

"The job is only part of the reason for her termination. Her disregard for protocol might have been overlooked had she not been blatantly fraternizing with one of your people."

"Who, Rufus? They were working together!" I protested. "She wasn't *fraternizing*—"

"You're right. There was nothing fraternal about that kiss."

"What kiss?"

He chuckled softly. "Your little glowing friend isn't the only one with miniature equipment. Some of the pictures I've seen…well, they're an eyeful."

"All right, they had one date. Big deal. Pasta, wine, maybe a little too chummy."

"And completely against Company regulations. She knows the rules."

I drummed my fingers on the table. "What if they broke it off?"

"She's tainted. A proven liability. Besides, we've decided that it's in the Company's best interest to phase out lupine shifters, considering their track record. There's not much call for wolves these days."

"I see. So why are you telling me? Why not call Poppy yourself and deliver the bad news?"

"I wanted to introduce myself in case our paths cross in the future. Since she's in your custody, I assumed you wouldn't mind forwarding the message."

"She's not in my *custody*, she's a guest."

"Same difference, and it's no concern of mine. She's free to do what she likes," said Tanner. "But as of now, she's no longer employed. Good day."

He hung up before I could say another word, and I threw the phone across the room, which seemed like a better idea than setting it on fire. After a few minutes and a couple glasses of wine, I picked at my lunch, repaired my broken phone, and set off to bear the bad tidings.

Martin and Rohese Stowe had constructed a charming manor for themselves and any of their brood who happened to be in the neighborhood. Tucked back among a grove of hardwood trees, the house boasted three floors, at least fifteen bedrooms, and an Olympic-sized pool out back, where I found Poppy and Rufus sunning on vinyl chaises. Having shown me the way, Rohese awkwardly stood by, unsure what to do but reluctant to leave me alone with her little boy.

"How's the leg?" I called to Poppy as I headed down the deck.

She raised her head and waved her good arm as Rufus stood. "Hey! It's hardening. Rohese says I should be set to go in the morning."

"About that." I looked down at Poppy while she regarded me over the top of her frameless sunglasses. "I had a call from the Company's new head. Someone named Tanner?"

"*Adler*?" she groaned. "Fantastic. The guy's a prick. What did he want?"

"You're fired. I'm so sorry," I hurriedly added as she gaped. "Something about protocol and getting rid of all the wolf shifters…"

Her eyes narrowed. "You know what Adler's shifted form is? A friggin' *cougar*. He hates anyone canid on principle." She sat up and rested her head in her hand. "*Shit*. What am I supposed to do? Mom and Dad are going to kill me—"

"It's only a job."

"They're Company! Not like they're going to help me now. Hell, they don't even have a basement I could move into—they live in the barracks."

"Come with me," Rufus offered.

We turned to him as he took Poppy's hand. "Back to Alaska. I've got favors to call in at the university—we'll find a job for you. The pay's not spectacular, but I've got a guest bedroom. You could stay with me until you're ready for your own place, rent-free. What do you say?"

Rohese twitched, but Poppy had eyes only for Rufus. "Really?" She gave him her other hand. "You'd do that?"

"We make pretty good roommates, right?"

Her smile slid toward mischievous. "Pretty good. And I wouldn't have to look like a dude this time."

At that, his expression clouded. "Uh...do you remember what I told you about the glamour situation?"

"What, that you get wrinkly for class?"

"And...you know, for going out in town," he said, reddening. "I mean, the glamour's off behind closed doors, but—"

"Rufe, I spent most of the last month as a *guy*. Do what you need to do."

"You don't think that'll be too weird?"

"Well," she said, grinning, "we'll have to be careful in public so no one knows you're cradle robbing, but other than that..."

"Are you sure?" he mumbled.

Poppy squeezed his hands and leaned closer. "If it'd make you feel better, I'd be happy to shed around the place."

Rufus's face finally began to lighten. "I'll have to check the lease, but I think there's a ban on dogs over fifty pounds."

"Aw, fifty? That's cute. So fluffy. So tasty."

As their heads bent together, I joined Rohese in the shade. "I had nothing to do with that," I muttered.

She nodded. "They seem to have a connection, my lord. As long as she doesn't hurt my son…" Rohese shrugged. "They're adults, aren't they?"

I glanced at the oblivious couple, then back at Rohese. "You're all right, you know."

"I do my best," she said, and sighed. "Anyway, it's not as if my children have never fallen for mortals before."

With Poppy's plans sorted, I went home, intending to make sure Joey was intact, but Mina found me first. "Liza would like a word," she reported. "Are you busy?"

Putting the barn trek on hold, I found the guest room where I had left my niece. Liza sat by the window with her cupped hand close to her face, and I spotted Kuni's glow in her palm. "Uncle," she said, rising at my knock. "I'm sorry, I didn't know when—"

"Good time?"

"Certainly." She sat, and Kuni flitted to the window ledge. "I've been hearing about what I missed," she explained as I leaned against the wall. "Most of it…well, it seems like a dream, you know? I look back at the last month, and it's as if I'm watching someone else's life…" Liza's voice faltered, but she smiled. "Kuni remembers it better than I do. I can't believe you *hid* that long," she added, turning to the piq, who squeaked something suspiciously like laughter.

"How are you feeling?"

"Much better, thank you. Is Poppy—"

"On the mend."

"Good. And, uh…Joey?"

"He's been with Val all day, but more than that…" She nodded in understanding, and I changed the subject. "You're free to go whenever you like. If you're ready to return to Baltimore, say the word, or you're welcome here. I can't see Eleanor making you leave."

Liza's eyes dropped to her lap as she thought, then rose again. "I have to do what she says, right? That's how this works?"

"More or less, but if you don't start riots, she won't step on your toes."

"Because my father chose Oberon, yes?"

"That's right."

"But I can choose for myself."

I tried to be political. "Yes, you're free to switch courts, but this isn't something that has to be decided today—"

"Joey chose you?"

"Unless something's changed of late and he's trying to spare my feelings."

"Then I do as well." Seeing my surprise, Liza shrugged and held out her hand for Kuni. "Eleanor's been kind, but since Joey's here…it makes sense. And it's a clean start for me. I'm getting a little tired of making muffins."

I nodded, pushing aside thoughts of how I was going to break the news to Eleanor that Liza was defecting. "In that case, welcome home."

When I finally reached the barn, I found a familiar scene: Val and Joey in the dirt—the former instructing, the latter sweating—with Aiden sitting on a stack of bales by Georgie's head, keeping her calm. By then, the dragon knew what training entailed, but she didn't have to like it. Toula leaned against the doorframe with her arms crossed, watching as Joey struggled to hold a shield intact without his Defender on hand.

"Is it time for a break yet?" I asked, joining Toula on the edge of the practice yard.

Joey turned at the sound of my voice, letting his concentration waver, and Val took the opportunity to send him sailing into the grass. "Focus," he said as Joey groaned and started to pick himself up, then joined us at the door. "Strong progress. I'm pleased," he murmured, and jutted his thumb toward the barn. "You have a visitor."

I headed inside, but before I could ask Aiden where the visitor was hiding, something landed on my shoulder, and I jerked and tripped over myself in surprise. It grabbed my ear to steady itself, and as I caught my breath, I could make out Lailu's purple glow from the corner of my eye. "Hello," I managed. "Sorry, wasn't expecting that."

"Be calm," she said slowly. "It has been days, Coileán. I wish to speak of my nephew."

"Of course." I walked to the back of the barn, and Lailu flitted onto a convenient tack shelf, the better to look me in the eye. "We could go somewhere more comfortable—"

"This is sufficient." She eased herself down, letting her legs dangle over the side of the shelf, and tucked her wings out of the way.

"I'm sorry for the silence. Things have been a little...tense."

"I know. The Lady told me all." She clasped her hands in her lap and smiled. "Kuni is a good boy, but he has been unsatisfied for a time. Many of my daughters have made their way in that realm—I have no complaint with his actions. Or yours," she added with a wry smile, "in permitting him to go."

"He's been a great help. A real credit to you."

She waved the compliment aside. "I had small part in his rearing—my brother and Kuni's mother would deserve your praise, were they living yet."

"I'm sorry, I didn't know—"

"My thanks, but they've been gone for days and days and *days*." She smiled sadly. "I had sent them among the daig as my emissaries for a time. When the daig warred, they were caught unawares. Their deaths were accidental, but we went to safety in the forest. There are far too many ways to be injured by fighting daig, you understand."

I paused to put the details of her story into the timeline I knew, then frowned as the pieces aligned. "Wait, *how* old is Kuni?"

Lailu shrugged. "Younger than some, older than others. I don't know his days."

Nor did I—no one could say exactly when the Three had made their uneasy peace, but it had been well before the flourishing of Rome or Athens or Egypt—possibly before the first huts were erected by the Tigris and Euphrates. And if Kuni was still young in Lailu's estimation…

Seeing my shock, she laughed, then leapt back onto my shoulder and patted my cheek. "Child, you have much yet to learn. In the meanwhile, Kuni may remain with you. If I know his mind, he is enjoying himself. Kuni…well," she said with a hint of frustration, "he is seldom *still.*"

"Believe me," I replied, glancing at the dragon, "you're not going to find any disagreement out here."

As I retired late that evening, my heart wasn't precisely light, but I realized that I felt *better.* Not fantastic, not altogether at peace, but more comfortable than I'd felt in weeks. Nothing was burning. Val and Aiden weren't foretelling doom and destruction. Eleanor was speaking to me. Yes, I had a dungeon full of Mab's people to deal with, my daughter was once more on the lam, the hornet's nest of the Inner Council had been kicked, and Joey, I suspected, was being kept too weary to think about his situation, but I didn't feel guilty about taking my repose. Something in my chest had unknotted, allowing me to close my eyes and burrow against the breeze blowing through the open window. Breathing deeply, ignoring the background scent of magic, I smelled roses on the wind and linen around me, a soothing perfume that seduced me toward dreamless sleep.

That's the problem with seduction. So intent are you

on the beautiful woman at the bar that you miss her boyfriend's fist until it connects with your chin.

My phone's fugue dragged me back to consciousness shortly before dawn. Reminding myself for the thousandth time that I needed to choose a ringtone that didn't make me want to stab myself in the ear, I slapped at the nightstand and answered with a half-mumbled, "Hello?"

"I figured out the voice," said Helen, who sounded decidedly more alert than I felt.

With a grunt, I pushed myself onto one elbow and squinted into the paling morning. "What voice?"

"Moyna's wizard friend, the one with the masking spell?"

That—or perhaps the edge in her tone—made me sit up in earnest. "The magus? You figured out the magus?"

"He's not a magus at all. He's my dad."

CHAPTER 29

The rogue wizard's voice had bothered Helen for a week. Even modulated beyond recognition, it remained lodged in the back of her mind, an annoyance she'd allowed her subconscious to puzzle out. She'd had no success, but then, by chance, she'd needed a scroll from the Archives.

As a rule, Helen avoided the older corners of the Archives. But then she had set in motion her Indian installation ruse to bring the Council together—which, to her surprise, had generated interest. Finding herself with support for an eighth installation, Helen had ventured into the Archives to see how the other seven had come about. Eventually, having turned her attention to the oldest of the Arcanum's former outposts—the ones founded in the days when writing on dead animals was the best option—she had resigned herself to spending quality time with the digitized scrolls and called up the instructional video for the software. The video was a concession to the technologically inept, and the digitization project's head, Howard Carver, had provided the reassuring narration.

"I had it going in a minimized window," she explained over the phone as the small crowd in my office listened in. "I was listening to Dad drone on about the software features, and then it clicked. If you think I'm crazy, tell me…"

Aiden, who had already listened to the video alongside the voiceprint three times, leaned toward the phone on my desk. "You're not crazy. How did we *miss* that?"

"Because we thought he was a magus," Toula offered,

"and without context, that voiceprint sounded like gobbledygook. Carver, listen to me. Get out of there, *now*."

"And go where?" Helen asked. "I can't slip over to Faerie—I'm in enough trouble with the Council as it stands."

"Pick another installation, then. It's better than nothing."

"What's my cover? I've got no reason to go traveling—"

Toula huffed and picked up the phone. "Screw your cover. I'd bet my life that Howard isn't working alone. You've got to get out of the silo, Helen."

"I can't."

"*Why*? Go take tea in Glastonbury, see the pyramids, it doesn't matter. Go!"

Helen's tone was quiet but resolute. "If I leave now, out of the blue, then Dad and whoever else is working with him will suspect that I know something, and the rest of the Council will assume I'm sneaking off to Faerie. Guys, I've got to toe the line for the time being."

Aiden took the phone from Toula. "What if you were to go to India on a scouting—"

Before he could finish, Joey yanked the phone out of his hands. "Please, hon," he murmured, "listen to Toula. Either get out of there or let me come back."

"Joey," she sighed, "I'm doing the best I can—"

"I don't know what I'd do if something happened to you and I wasn't even there. *Please*, Helen."

The phone went silent, and I'd begun to think the connection had been severed when Helen said, "Greg and Missy are here. Nothing's going to happen, sweetie. We'll get to the bottom of this mess, and I'll be careful, I promise you…"

Joey's eyes were suddenly too old, weary and sick with worry, and I took my turn with the phone. "Okay, Helen. What's the plan?"

"Business as usual. I've got a couple of meetings

scheduled today, and other than that, I'll probably be trying to parse thousand-year-old script. What can I say, it's Monday." She paused. "I'll check in. Don't worry about me. And Joey? Are you still there?"

I handed him the phone and watched his fingers tighten around it. "Right here," he said, staring into space as he listened to her breathing.

"Everything's going to be fine. The installation magi are coming around, and the Inner Council will cave soon. Wait a little longer, and we'll be back together. I love you, Joey." He said nothing, and Helen asked, "Hello? Can you hear me? Joey?"

"I love you," he mumbled. "Please be careful."

Aiden pried the phone from Joey, and with artificial ease, he told his sister, "Joey's fine, Hel. Let me know how I can help."

"Will do. I'll call by dinnertime," she promised, and the phone went dead.

Eleanor and I took breakfast alone in her marble-walled dining room. "I don't understand," she said as she doctored her second pot of tea. "Her *father*? What the devil would Helen's father be doing with Moyna?"

I gave my coffee cup a swish and watched the cream spiral. "He's Aiden's father, too—"

"Yes, but that still doesn't make sense. What did he stand to gain from Moyna's victory?"

I mulled the matter over while I drank. "My first thought is that he was an Arcanum plant. He gained Moyna's trust, made her think he was helping her, then encouraged her into a suicide mission."

"Which would be clever if it fit the facts. He would have been acting at the direction of the Council, yes? Surely Greg would have known of the plan, and he'd have told Helen." Eleanor shook her head. "And remember the last video. The wizard was trying to make Moyna send faeries against the Arcanum. A dangerous move, if he'd been playing that game."

"So he probably wasn't." I took another sip. "Which leads me to my second thought."

"He's a mole, and he has a Council handler. I concur. But *why*? How does the Arcanum benefit from hiding Moyna?"

"I suppose he blocked the blood trace because he assumed that Toula would run one for us eventually. If we couldn't see Moyna coming—"

"—then we couldn't defend against her as well. But how would that help the *Arcanum*? Why would they prefer to take their chances dealing with Moyna instead of dealing with us?"

"Or Aiden."

Her brows drew together. "I beg your pardon?"

"They had to deal with Aiden for a year, and he wasn't the most diplomatic."

"Bad blood, hmm?"

"*That's* an understatement. But he said the Council kept pressuring him to stop looking for you and put his resources toward locating Moyna—"

"—which would have been a waste of time because they were hiding her."

I regarded Eleanor closely. "Are you assuming that the entire Council is involved in this?"

"Not necessarily. Say it's only a few. The bulk want Aiden to find Moyna for the obvious reasons, and the conspirators go along with it because they've nothing to lose. But I still don't see—"

Maybe I had the caffeine to thank, but the pieces snapped into place, and I slammed my cup onto the table. "This isn't about Moyna," I told my startled hostess.

She waved her hand to clean the sloshed coffee from her lace tablecloth. "I don't follow—"

"Nobody on the Council wants anything to do with me but Greg. Suddenly, I'm gone, and they're stuck with

Aiden, who has a list of heads to smash. All along, they're looking around the room and realizing that Helen's about to take Greg's place—Helen, who never turned her back on her little brother. Who's engaged to the nice mundane boy living in my backyard. This isn't about Moyna," I said again, pushing my plate away. "It's about *Helen*." I stood and began to pace the length of the table. "Hide Moyna, build her confidence, and send her forces against us and the silo. She's almost guaranteed to lose, but faeries in the silo could have caused problems. Maybe they could have gotten to Helen."

"But Moyna didn't send any."

"Precisely. All she sent were the werewolves, and the wizards made quick work of them. But that attack—don't you see?" I wheeled to face Eleanor. "They *wanted* Moyna to send faeries against the silo. Why take that risk unless they were desperate to have someone removed?"

"Moyna's forces might not have reached Helen. There was no guarantee."

"No, but what does it say about the grand magus if she's so weak as to allow faeries in the silo? Either she's too weak to protect the community or she's been dragging the Arcanum into court matters, and that's a big no for them."

"So Helen is dead or out of a job," Eleanor mused, "and the conspirators win. But why would her *father* be involved? To put his daughter's life on the line—"

I sank back into my chair and rested my head in my palms. "Mother stole and killed Howard's sister, then raped him," I muttered. "Aiden was the result. Val took him to the silo, and Howard's wife insisted that they keep him. They raised him as a dud."

When I looked up, her face was drawn in dawning horror. "Good God. And once Aiden became regent…"

She didn't have to finish that thought for me to see the picture. Howard's secret shame, the nasty little truth known only to the Council for so long, was suddenly in the open. His son was half fae and kin to me, making Howard either a victim or a fool. Was Howard pitied? Reviled? A punchline? In the span of a few months, he'd gone from being the proud father of the rising grand magus to the reluctant progenitor of one of the most powerful faeries alive—how had he coped with the shame?

Then Helen, his pride and joy, had the audacity to hook up with a mundane. And not just any mundane—a boy who lived in Faerie and palled around with Aiden. Perhaps that could have been tolerated, but when the secret in Joey's ancestry had been revealed…

And now that Joey had thrown his lot in with us, and the whole silo knew the truth about the grand magus's sympathies…

"She humiliated him," I told Eleanor. "Aiden was bad, but when Helen slid in such spectacular fashion, it must have pushed him over the edge."

But she shook her head. "Howard was hiding Moyna before Helen got engaged, was he not? *Someone* was keeping her hidden all that time. Perhaps that business with Aiden alone was enough to win Howard's cooperation—but why recruit him in the first place? Why not a proper magus?"

I kicked myself for being so blind. "Because Howard's an archivist. Think of all the interesting texts he must have seen. Maybe a scroll with a technique for, oh, hiding someone from a blood trace."

She lifted her teacup, reconsidered, and put it aside. "One way or another, we're getting Helen out of there tonight. When is she due to phone?"

I pulled out my flip phone and glanced at the clock. "Within the next nine hours."

Eleanor folded her arms on the tabletop and scowled. "We could make a gate into her office and snatch her—"

"Out of the question. Toula re-warded the place. We can't get into the silo by gate—only Helen can, and Joey if he's with her. Since they're split up, though…"

Her eyes dipped to my phone, then back to her forsaken tea. "Nine hours, then," she said as the tea won and she reached for her cup. "Get ready to be persuasive, Coileán. Lie if you must. I don't like this at *all*."

Later that morning, we shared our suspicions with Toula, Val, and Nico, but Eleanor and I decided that nothing good would come of discussing them with Aiden and Joey. Toula concurred. "The things I heard before Helen made me leave did *not* give me the warm fuzzies," she muttered. "If those two were to go storming through the trailer park right now with guns drawn…"

The realm had left Aiden with a boost as a gift for his regency, but Joey had been empowered for less than two days and was still making sense of the mechanics. And so, in the interest of keeping the boys from running into a pack of well-trained wizards, we held our silence and waited for Helen's call.

As I loitered in the barn after lunch, watching Val demonstrate to Joey the many ways in which pain could be magically inflicted, my pocket began to vibrate, and I yanked the phone free with a surge of relief. "Hello, Helen?" I began, heading toward the rear of the barn to block the noise of Joey's grunts and yelps. "Change of plans?"

"Check your ID," said a male voice.

I stopped in my tracks. "Slim? What's up?"

"Well, I'm not sure, but I've got Wizard Stu in my apartment right now, and, uh…I think he's shot someone. I've dropped the wards, so could you—"

Before Slim could finish the request, I'd opened a gate into the bar. "I'm downstairs."

The apartment door opened, and Slim hurried down in his flapping bathrobe. "Let me turn the wards back on," he said, brushing past me to play with the panel on the wall, then beckoned me aside and whispered, "He's shaking like a leaf. I don't know what the hell happened, and the shots of Jack haven't taken effect, so Stuart's a mess."

I trailed Slim upstairs. "*Stuart* shot someone?"

"I know." He paused at the landing. "I wasn't able to get much out of him, but I think he bought a gun after the wolf-mantis rampage."

"Makes sense."

Slim's eyebrow rose. "You like the idea of *him* strapped and loaded?"

"No, but better a pistol than a fancy stick," I replied, and followed Slim into his immaculate apartment.

Slumped on the Swedish couch, Stuart twitched as Slim locked the door behind me. The little man seemed to curl into himself as I approached, and I noticed that his jeans, too wide and light to be fashionable, were streaked with mud...

No, not mud, I realized as Stuart's wide eyes met mine. The stains were blood, and they continued onto his jacket, his hands...his *cheeks*...

I slid onto the coffee table to search Stuart's face for clues. "What happened? Tell me what happened, Stu, and I'll try to make it right."

His hand clenched around a coffee mug that smelled like an offering from the bar. "I think I killed them."

"Killed who?"

"Wizards. Two of them. Like the ones who killed Auntie Eunice." He jerked, retching, but covered his mouth and kept his stomach under control while Slim ran for a trash bag.

"How do you know they were wizards?" I asked once he'd swallowed.

"All in black. Carried wands. They—"

Slim shoved the plastic bag in his lap, and I urged, "Take your time. Where did you see them?"

He swallowed whatever bile was trying to make its escape, then closed his eyes and squeezed his mug. "I was in the shop, cleaning and doing inventory. I was behind the counter, and I heard someone rattle the doorknob, and when I looked up, they blasted the door in. I…oh, no, I…"

I gripped his shaking shoulders until he opened his eyes. "Tell me, Stuart."

"I shot them," he whispered as his eyes welled. "My gun lives by the cashbox. They'd broken in, and I…I don't know what I was *thinking*, but they were on the floor, and the gun was in my hand—"

"Could they still be alive?"

His mousy mop flew about his face as he shook his head. "I shot them again to be sure. Shot them until I didn't have any bullets left. And then…the athames were right there, and I had to be sure they were dead…"

"Jesus," Slim muttered as Stuart covered his eyes and wept. "And then he called me."

I rose and patted Stuart's shoulder. "Stay here. We're going to assess the damage."

He looked up through streaming eyes and gripped my wrist. "My cats—"

"That's why I'm bringing Slim," I said, carefully extricating myself. "We'll get the cats. Uh…sit tight, okay?"

Two minutes later, as we headed up the sidewalk, I realized that Slim was still walking about in a bathrobe and beach shoes. "Would you like some real pants?" I asked as he puffed along beside me.

"Nothing wrong with sweats. And no time to waste. If someone called the police for suspected gunshots—"

"Say no more." I glanced down a side street at the long-empty remains of a barber shop, and the wood-framed building burst into flames. "There, that should buy us a few minutes. I'm surprised no one took that wreck down during the rebuilding."

"Because a nice kid from Richmond is trying to flip the property. Or was," Slim retorted, followed by a quietly grunted, "Faeries."

"I heard that."

"Good."

When we reached my old building, a siren was wailing in the distance. The sight through the plate-glass window, however, silenced my planned smug remark to Slim. Two bodies, clad in black, lay sprawled on the wooden floor in pools of blood. Both still bore multiple decorated knife handles in their chests, and an overturned table and haphazard scattering of fallen candles showed me where their assailant had been. One of the corpses clutched a wand, its hand having tightened in a death grip.

"Wow," I whispered.

Slim whistled, then pushed open the broken front door and squatted to lift the smoked visors of the victims' black helmets. "Assassin squad. No patches. They were here to kill him."

I enchanted window shades into being, blocking the gristly scene from passersby. "*Stuart*? The guy couldn't cast a spell if his life depended on it. Why would they—"

He pried a flat box from the hand of one of the corpses and showed it to me. "This detects fluctuations in background magic. Isn't there still a tiny gate into Faerie up in the apartment?"

"Shit," I muttered. "Is it spiking?"

Slim flipped it on and glanced at the readout. "Big time. This building is an anomaly—this one, and mine, with the wards. But why would the Arcanum send assassins after Stuart? He's as mundane as they come."

Before I could hypothesize, a chiming sounded, and Slim pulled his phone from his robe pocket. "Candice?" he asked, frowning into space. "What's up?" He listened for a second, then nodded and headed for the stairs to Stuart's apartment. "I don't know, but I don't like it. Get the kids and go to ground. Better yet, head into Jersey—try to get some distance."

I started to follow him, but Slim held up his free hand.

"Hang on," he told the woman, then said to me, "Stay there. I've got to get the cats, and you've got to get Stuart out of here. We've got assassins in Brooklyn, too."

For an interminable ten minutes, I remained in the store while Slim clomped around upstairs, flushing Stuart's cats from their hiding places. I reduced the corpses to atoms and tidied the shop to pass the time, but I couldn't help but hear through the ceiling every time Slim's phone began to ring. And ring it did—he'd no sooner hang up than the chimes were playing again, and his voice was becoming agitated.

When he descended with a stuffed cat carrier in each hand, his face was drawn. "What's happened?" I asked.

"Walk and talk." He headed for the door, and I held it open while the cats hissed. "We've got reports of assassins up and down the country," he said as he started up the street. "And word is we're seeing the same thing abroad. I've got to get on the network—"

I grabbed him by the back of the bathrobe, opened a gate into the alley beside his store, and shoved him through before anyone could notice. Though startled, he quickly regained his composure and turned off the wards long enough to let me through again. "They must have come for me," he said as he climbed the stairs to his apartment. "Those two were young—maybe they didn't have the address. Or maybe someone warned them to look for traces of faerie activity in this town. Who knows? But we may have time before anyone notices they're out of commission. You got rid of the evidence?"

"Everything I could see. Bodies, blood, that sort of thing."

"That'll do." Slim grunted and shouldered the door open to reveal Stuart still on the couch, staring into the depths of his empty mug. "Time to go, Stu," he said, dropping the cat carriers to a chorus of yowling. "It's not safe here. Colin—"

"You're going home with me," I interrupted, stepping

around the cats. "You, too, Slim."

But the bartender shook his head. "I've got people in danger—my place is here."

"*Slim*—"

"Forget it." He marched across the room to retrieve his laptop from his desk. "I'm a coordinator. When there's trouble, we're the first ones in and the last ones out."

"Which I appreciate, but you said those two were after you. What do you want to bet they can get through your wards?"

"Guess we're going to find out," he muttered as he began the long process of gaining access to the Fringe's network. "Where's Vivi?"

"Visiting her parents, I think. Hal's with her—"

"Good. Do me a favor and call her. Use my phone."

While Stuart tried to console his panicked cats, I did as Slim bid and got Vivi on the second ring. "Something's happening, he wants to talk to you," I said in greeting, then put the phone on speaker beside Slim's computer and backed away. "I'll be in the kitchen. I need to call Helen—"

Before I could finish the thought, my phone began to ring, lending its voice to the growing cacophony of the apartment. Though hoping for Helen, I was relieved to see Greg's name on the ID line. "Could someone tell me what's going on?" I said as I answered the call. "We've got hitmen all over the place, and it looks like they're going after Fringers."

Greg's voice sounded odd, his typical cadence exchanged for the tones of artificial formality. "I'm calling on behalf of the grand magus."

"Is she okay?"

He paused. "Grand Magus Mulligan wishes to convey a warning."

My gut twisted as I leaned against Slim's granite countertop, and in that moment, I knew two things with certainty: something was deeply wrong, and Greg wasn't in a position to tell me the details. "I'll hear it in a minute," I replied, struggling to keep from shouting. "First, tell me where Helen is."

"Ms. Carver is now a ward of the Arcanum."

"Where is she?"

"Her whereabouts are of no concern to you. She's safe. For now."

The threat made my blood boil. "Damn it, Greg, give me *something!*" I yelled, vaguely aware that Slim's dishes were rattling in the glass-fronted cabinets.

"I'd advise you to let me finish."

My fingers ached, and I realized I was squeezing the phone hard enough to cut off circulation. "All right. Talk."

Greg cleared his throat. "As I was saying, the grand magus has a warning for you and the rest of your ilk."

"By which you mean Eleanor, I take it?"

"And Aiden. Any of your people." He paused. "That includes Mr. Bolin."

"Go on."

"Henceforth, the mortal realm is off-limits to you. Do as you like with the Gray Lands, but this realm is under the Arcanum's protection and control."

The dishes began to rattle again, and a crack shot through the nearest pane of glass. "And if we should tell the grand magus to stick his warning where the sun doesn't shine?"

"Then Ms. Carver's life is forfeit."

Silence hung between us until I finally managed, "You're not serious."

"Consider her a bond for your good behavior, Coileán. She's in forced sleep, she's not in pain."

"You can't do this. Forget *us*, Greg, you can't do this to Helen. She trusts you, she—"

"The decision isn't mine," he said stiffly. "Any attempt to remove Ms. Carver from Arcanum custody will be treated as a violation of this agreement."

"What *agreement?* You've kidnapped—"

The cabinets exploded in a shower of shards, and I shielded on instinct. As Stuart screamed and the glass tinkled onto the tile, I dragged myself under control and focused on Greg's voice. "Suppose I reject the Arcanum's terms," I said through clenched teeth. "Suppose I count Helen as a necessary loss and turn the fucking silo into a crater. What's your grand magus's plan then?"

"That would be unfortunate, since Ms. Carver isn't the only person being taken into protective custody." The ease of Greg's response suggested how much he had been coached. "Witches are being...*collected.*"

I heard his distaste, but I wasn't about to give him slack. "Collected? You mean *killed*, right? Since when do you spend assassins on retrieval missions?"

"Witches are being collected," he slowly repeated. "*Witches*, Coileán."

The sick feeling doubled as I realized what he wasn't saying. "Tell Mulligan or whoever's running the show to stand down. We'll get the rest of them out of your way."

"I'm not sure if that's an option," said Greg. Suddenly, his voice dropped to a frantic whisper. "Find Rick. Tell him it's unravelling. *It's unravelling.* Got—"

The phone went dead, and I ran over the broken glass back to the main room. "They've stashed Helen somewhere, and they're picking up the witches in the Fringe," I told Slim, who had half a dozen video calls running at the sides of his screen. "I think they're going to kill the fae Fringers."

"What was that?" one of the tiny heads in the computer asked, cupping his hand around his ear. "Who's trying to kill whom?"

"Hang on, Ralph," said Slim, then swiveled to face me. "And run that by me again, Colin. *What* is happening?"

"Helen's been snatched to ensure my good behavior, and the Arcanum's after your people. Witches get kidnapped, lesser bloods get killed."

His forehead scrunched. "How would they know? We

don't make distinctions."

"I have no idea, but Greg said to tell you it's unravelling. What does that mean?"

The blood drained from Slim's face, and he began typing furiously. A few seconds later, the border of the screen began to flash red, and the babble of the video streams rose in fervor. "This is not a drill," he said. "The network's been compromised, probably through Greg Harrison. Get to safety. I repeat, this is not a drill. Take immediate precautions…"

On the third iteration of Slim's warning, a gate opened across the room, and Rufus stepped aside as his sister ran through. "Got the memo," she said to me. "What the heck is—"

"You, back across," Slim ordered, looking over his shoulder. "Get her out of here, Colin. Take Stuart, too. There are assassins after us," he explained to Vivi, "and I've got to work here. Go to your parents."

"Like hell I will," she snapped. "What can I do to help?"

As mentor and mentee bickered and the terrified cats yowled, I pushed Slim and his chair out of the way, then crouched in front of the computer screen. "Is this thing on?" I asked the worried Fringers, who nodded. "We're going to evacuate you. I need a prioritized list of pickup locations—coordinates, pictures, anything that will let us open gates. Major landmarks are easiest. Send the information to Slim and Monkey, yes?"

The watchers nodded again and began typing. Stepping back, I pointed to Vivi. "You, to Faerie, coordinate with Slim. Rufus," I said, turning to the open gate, "call Eleanor, Toula, Val, your brothers, and mine, in that order. Stuart, get the damn cats and get over there. Slim…"

He shook his head. "Someone needs to be here. I'll keep a line open to Vivi."

I squeezed his shoulder. "Don't be a hero, man. Keep the wards up."

Slim nodded and slid back into place, and I hurried across the border.

CHAPTER 30

Rufus proved skilled with a phone tree. By the time Vivi had finished converting Aiden's room into her command center, the last of her brothers was running through the door, joining Val, Nico, Toula, and half the guards. "Preliminary list is coming in," she told us, watching the main screen. "Anyone fae gets priority, followed by witches with small children—ah. Okay, we've got a clump in London, rendezvousing at Trafalgar in five. Can someone—"

"I've got it," one of the Stowes interrupted.

"Ned, good. Harry, you're backup," she said, pointing to another brother, who did as she instructed without protest. "There's another clump in Paris…Luce? Arc de Triomphe?"

As Vivi marshalled her forces, I glanced across the room at Eleanor. She'd strategically positioned herself beside Aiden, who was doing his best to prevent Joey from running through an open gate. While the first pickup teams departed, I headed for their huddle. "We're going to get her back," I told the boys. "Probably not today, but we're going to find her."

Joey didn't try to hide his panic. "*How?* If they've got her somewhere in the silo, how are we supposed to sneak past the wards? And the baby, what are we going to do about—"

"Uh, Joey," Hal interrupted, handing him a tablet, "you've got another problem to deal with first."

He scanned the screen. "What am I looking—"

"There," said Hal, pointing over his shoulder. "Greg has full Fringe credentials. 'It's unravelling' was a code he had in case someone used his creds to mine the network. Someone's pulled the entire database—names, codenames, family ties, locations…"

Joey's eyes widened as he followed Hal's finger. "Oh, my God, *Mom*," he whispered, his panic blossoming to full-blown terror. "I've got to get them out of there—"

"Calm down," I interrupted, and pulled him from his seat on the window ledge as I recalled the Bolins' farmhouse in my mind's eye. When I had a clear picture, I aimed for the front door and opened a gate—and found myself staring at the muzzle of the shotgun pointed through the nearest window.

The gun jerked and withdrew into the house, and the door open to reveal Peter in the foyer. "*Wow*, I'm glad to see you," he said, pulling me inside. "There's a man and a woman in black helmets, and they've been circling the house for the last ten minutes…Joey, no, get in here," he said, yanking his son through the door before Joey could investigate. Latching the door behind us, he returned to his post at the front window and slipped the gun into position. "They've been yelling for Rebecca to come out. Want to tell me what's going on?"

"Nothing good," I replied, "and why didn't you call me? You have my number—"

"They can't get past the fence. See?"

Looking out the window, I spotted the wizards circling around to the front of the house. "Toula's wards?"

"Yep. Rebecca hit the button as soon as they turned up." He frowned at us as a thought struck. "How'd y'all get in here?"

"She must have built exceptions in. Joey, find your mother. I'll handle—"

"*Rebecca Bolin!*" came the amplified shout from the dirt road. "*This is your final warning! Surrender now, and no one will be harmed!*"

Flushed, seething, and muttering incomprehensibly, Joey reached for the steel door bolt, then yelped and yanked his burned fingers away. "Damn it, that's *it*!" he cried, and stretched out his uninjured hand. The front door exploded into splinters, and as Peter gaped, Joey marched past the still-open gate to confront the lurking wizards. "Hey, you!" he bellowed. "You with the sticks! You want a Bolin? Come and get me!"

"What is he—" Peter began, but I pushed him aside and dashed out after Joey.

The wizards, who had been approaching the wards with interest, stopped in their tracks as I appeared. "Leave!" I yelled, then flickered through space to close the gap between Joey and me. "Final warning. Get out of here."

Orders or no orders, the assassins sent to retrieve Rebecca were wise enough to know when they were outgunned. The two fled toward the highway, and I grabbed Joey's shoulder before he could give chase. "Let them go. Don't give them an excuse to start shooting."

"But they—"

"You aren't ready to tangle with two trained wizards, kid. Back to the house."

Joey looked after them a moment longer, torn between anger and sense, and finally turned away. "They've got Helen," he mumbled. "Those bastards have Helen."

I steered him toward the hole that had been the front door, where his anxious parents waited with their guns. "We're going to find her, I promise. But one problem at a time, Joey."

"What are we going to do?"

I sighed. "Sometimes, the long game is the only option. Right now, though, I think you've got some explaining to do," I added, catching the looks on his parents' faces. "That was a nice door you shredded."

"Huh? Oh, *shit*," he muttered, realizing the extent of what he'd done. "What do I tell them?"

"I'd recommend the truth," I replied, and beckoned the Bolins out of their hiding place. "You're coming with us," I called to them. "You've got about ten minutes to pack whatever you can't live without."

"Why? And who were *they*?" Rebecca pressed, pointing toward the dust trail settling in the wizards' wake.

"Assassins. Joey will tell you everything, but we have to hurry."

Peter nodded and ducked into the house, but Rebecca lingered on the stoop to hug her boy. "It happened to you, too, didn't it?" she murmured. "The door exploded, like the TV and Grandma's crystal—"

"It's a little worse than that," he said, retreating from her embrace. "And they've taken Helen, Mom. They're hiding her, and—"

"We'll deal with that later," said Liza as she ran through the rift. "Rebecca, you've got to come now. Where's Peter? And Ellie wants to know what's to be done with the refugees," she added, glancing at me. "Where are they going to camp?"

I flipped through my mental map. "There's a meadow north of the palace—ask her to make them comfortable however she sees fit. Tell her to post a guard, too." I sighed and rubbed my neck as she departed, then shooed Rebecca into her house. "Grab what you need. We'll take care of the rest."

The Stowe boys were efficient, and they ferried Fringers without complaint as Vivi and Hal assigned locations and reference shots. Not every pickup was a success—the Arcanum teams reached some of the targets first—but by the end of the first half hour, they had successfully made three-quarters of their preliminary runs. To my surprise, Faerie said nothing about the influx of witches. The realm was picky, but perhaps she had a conscience.

When Joey and I returned, Eleanor was already in the

meadow, ushering the dazed refugees into her temporary housing. I had no time to assist her, as the surveying crew had arrived to pitch in and needed to be briefed. While I was giving them the short version, my phone rang, and I stepped into the corridor to take the call. "Yes?" I said as the door shut behind me, blocking the hubbub of Vivi's command center.

"I thought Magus Harrison made the terms of our arrangement clear," said a male voice—American, but otherwise unknown.

"Mulligan, I presume."

"Indeed. James Mulligan, but you can call me 'Grand Magus.'"

"And you can rot in hell. You're making a serious mistake, boy."

He tutted on the other end. "Such manners. I would think you'd have a care for Ms. Carver's sake."

With great effort, I forced my tongue into civility. "What do you want, Magus?"

"*Grand* Magus, if you please."

"What do you want?"

"Well, for one, I'd like to know what the hell you think you're doing. Interfering with Arcanum business *already*?"

"I'm preventing you from murdering innocent people," I spat. "Let me take them. Twenty-four hours, and I'll have that realm cleansed of fae-blooded Fringers."

"Tempting, but no. Then again, I'm feeling generous today—I'll give you an hour. My team could probably use a water break by now."

"An *hour*?"

"One hour." His voice sharpened. "And if see a hint of you here after that hour's up, I'll kill the bitch myself. Got it?"

"Time starts now?" I snapped.

The dial tone buzzed, and I returned to Aiden's suite. "Who was that?" Vivi asked as I slammed the door open. "Pickup?"

"We've got an hour, and it's running," I replied, then called Slim. "Drop the wards, I'm coming over," I told him. "It's urgent."

When he gave me the go-ahead, I opened a gate to his apartment and found him puffing upstairs. "Arcanum's giving us a one-hour cease-fire. Vivi's got this in hand. You can't do anything more from here."

Slim looked around his trashed apartment, then tightened his robe belt and sighed. "I, uh…I think I'll put those pants on now."

I waited outside his bedroom while Slim made himself presentable. "Don't worry about packing. We'll make you anything you need."

"Understood," he called through the door, "but want to grab the Johnnie Blue from my cabinet, anyway? Bottom shelf in the pantry. And I've got all my gear in the basement—"

"You'd never get that room packed in time."

"Give me a chance. Come back for me last, huh?"

"Slim—"

"That's my life's work down there. I can't just leave it, Colin."

I leaned against the wall and closed my eyes. "Okay. But I'm serious about the timeframe."

"Understood," he said as he emerged. "While you're waiting for me, there's someone nearby you should pick up."

"Who?"

Slim folded his arms. "Since he's been so helpful, Father Paul's been on our roster for a while now. Friend of the Fringe."

"Jesus," I muttered, and opened a gate to Sacred Heart's parking lot. "Leave the wards down—I'm coming back soon to get you," I told him, then set off to find my priest before the Arcanum did.

Doris wasted no time when I marched through the parish office's door. Leaping from her chair with surprising speed, she grabbed a plastic misting bottle and an unfolded stapler, then snapped, "No closer, I'm warning you."

I paused to assess the risk—one squat, doughy woman in bifocals and a straining denim jumper, armed with holy water and a Swingline—and put up a shield on the off-chance that she had something with more firepower tucked away behind her desk. "Hello to you, too, Doris. Where is he?"

She gave the bottle a warning squeeze, which succeeded only in misting the pamphlets on the counter.

"I'm fae, not a *cat*," I said, "and this is urgent. Where's Paul?"

"Meeting with the bishop. You can't go back there."

I looked around the waiting room and noticed a basket of plastic eggs on the side table. "Are we in Holy Week or something?"

"Easter Monday. The office is closed—"

"Then maybe you should lock up. Go home."

"I'll do no such—"

I moved close enough to her desk that my shield blurred with the incoming squirt of holy water. "If I'm right, a couple of trained assassins are going to be here for Paul in the next hour or so. Now, be a good girl and let me save your life, okay? Surely there's someone you'd like to live for." I hadn't missed the modest diamond on the hand wrapped around the squirt bottle.

Doris hesitated, then stepped back, still holding her makeshift weapons. "If this is a trick—"

"It's not. Get out of here."

She nodded curtly, then squeezed out of her counter fortress and beat a retreat to the back door. As it slammed, I headed to Paul's office and rapped. The muffled voices inside stilled, and he called, "Come in!"

Hoping my sleeve would hold, I tucked my hand inside and gave the steel doorknob a turn. "Afternoon, Paul," I said as the bishop, with all the dignity befitting a well-respected man of fifty, squeaked and jumped from his chair. "You're coming with me."

The elder priest looked at the other men in the room—his freaked-out superior and Isaac, the would-be exorcist—and crossed his arms. "Can it wait?"

"Nope. There's been a coup in the Arcanum, and the new grand magus is either taking Fringers to Montana or killing them outright. You're in the files. Given our association, I can't see why they would leave you alive."

Paul stared at me, then bent to grab the jump bag behind his desk. "How long should I plan to be away?" he asked as the bishop sputtered.

"I don't know, but I'm not leaving you here."

"That *does* complicate matters. Nick," he said to the bishop, who by then looked sick enough to match his gray cardigan, "it looks like I'm taking leave. Sorry for the short notice. And Isaac…" He regarded the young priest carefully, then shrugged and shouldered his bag. "Good luck. You'll need it."

As Paul moved to join me, the bishop finally recovered his voice. "You can't go with *him*! That…that *thing*—"

Paul turned on his heel and jabbed a gnarled finger at him. "Colin is my friend," he said over the bishop's incredulous babbling. "And when it comes to wizards, I trust his judgment far more than I trust yours. If anyone asks, I'm golfing." He limped to my side with a smirk, then gestured to an empty space. "Ready when you are."

"I don't know how long this is going to take," I told him. "If there's something at your place that you can't live without—"

"I've got clean socks and a copy of *De Exorcismis*, so I'll be set if you've got a cot."

"Not a problem," I replied, opening a gate to Aiden's rooms. "Go on—I've got to swing back to Rigby for Slim. Do me a favor and see if you can't find Joey, eh?" I added as he crossed through. "He probably needs to talk to you."

"Understood. Hello again, Hal! Who wants to fill me in?" I heard him call as I closed the gate.

"As I told Doris," I said to the shock-silenced clergymen, "you might want to go home early today." With that, I opened another gate and saw myself out before they got any bright ideas.

Slim's apartment was silent, but I spotted his prized bottle of Johnnie by the door and picked it up on my way downstairs. "I'm back," I called. "Slim? Where are you?" Finding the trapdoor behind the bar raised, I headed into the basement. "It's me," I said as I pushed on the workshop door. "Are you ready to—"

The words caught in my throat. In the reddish glow of the safety bulb, I could pick out Slim, who stood on one side of the wooden table with a sack of tools. Blocking the exit was Howard Carver, who pointed a wand at Slim's head.

"Drop the stick," I ordered as a fireball ignited in my free hand.

The wizard gave me a cursory glance over his shoulder. "I wouldn't do that if I were you."

"Let him go, Howard. Your boss called a cease-fire."

"Not for this one. The mongrel's going to join us in Montana," he replied calmly. "Crafters have their uses, after all."

"He's coming with *me*."

"No, he's not." Howard lowered the wand a degree and fixed me with a frigid smile. "Interfere, and I'm afraid the agreement is void. Your choice."

I searched his face, hoping to see a twitch of doubt that I could exploit, but Howard was glacially cool and equally unyielding. "You're doing this your daughter. Your *daughter*, Howard."

"Magus, if you please."

"Oh, they gave you a promotion, did they? A pat on

the head for betraying Helen? What are you going to do with it? You're no magus. You're not strong enough."

His smile never faltered. "And yet, I seem to be holding you at bay."

I switched angles. "What's Rachel going to say when she finds out? You helped Moyna escape us, you've got Helen locked away—"

"Helen is a traitor. I'm doing my duty."

"She's your *child*. She's carrying your grandchild. For mercy's sake, Howard, let her go," I pleaded. "If the Council doesn't want her around, I'll take her. But don't do this. Joey's frantic, and Aiden—"

That, at least, managed to penetrate his shell. "*Damn* him," Howard said, and spat on the floor. "And damn you all. You can tell him that for me," he added, and beckoned to Slim. "Time's up, mongrel. We're leaving."

"Howard—"

"It's okay," Slim interrupted, and shoved a few last things into his bag. "I'll be okay, Colin. You heard what he said—I'm useful to them. They can't make their own wands. Not *well*, I mean." A flicker of contempt crossed his face. "I'll be fine, man. Take care of Vivi, okay?"

"Slim, I—"

"*Okay?*"

"Okay," I mumbled, and stepped aside as Slim and Howard left the workshop. I followed a few paces behind them back up to the bar, hoping that Howard would have a flash of conscience and kicking myself for telling Slim to leave the wards down. But when I finished the climb, I had only a second to see Howard pull a metal ball from his pocket—a single-use spell, no doubt—and toss it into the air. A gate opened to the road outside the trailer park, and he shoved Slim through the rift. By the time I'd vaulted the counter, the gate had slammed shut, and I was alone in the bar, still holding Slim's forgotten bottle of whisky.

We evacuated a fair number of Fringers, but not enough. Some had been snatched or killed by the time we found them, while others went on the run the moment Slim sounded the alarm. But at the end of that day, we had several hundred frightened refugees on our hands, a collection of witches, duds, and lesser bloods of all ages and nations. A few polyglots among them had stepped up to coordinate, helping people find friends and family and tending to immediate needs. Little knots of people huddled around beds or by one of the fireplaces in Eleanor's massive new bunkhouse. "Astrid fed them," she told me when I checked in, "and I've put a team in place to field needs as they arise, so I believe we're treading water for the moment." She stuffed her hands in her pockets and sighed. "What's to be done with them?"

"Post a guard," I replied, suddenly weary. "Everything else is a question for the morning."

She patted my shoulder. "Be with the boys. I'll handle this tonight."

I walked away, but when I looked back, she was still standing in the moonlight, contemplating the controlled chaos as her red hair waved in the wind. For an instant, I thought I saw Meggy in the slump of her shoulders, but before the image could come into focus, Eleanor started toward the bunkhouse, weary but holding a confidence Meggy had never possessed.

I watched her until she disappeared inside, then took my leave.

At the end of the grace hour, Vivi sent a final message to the Fringe before shutting down: *Network is compromised. Stay off. Be careful.* Though there was nothing else she could do, she lingered in Aiden's room that evening, leaning against Hal and staring into space. Occasionally, Hal locked eyes with Rufus, who had created chairs for Poppy and himself. That the shifter would remain was obvious—

without the Company's protection, Poppy would be an easy target.

When I'd last seen Aiden, he was monitoring his phone in vain for any messages from Fringers on the run. He seemed to have resigned himself to radio silence when I returned to his rooms, however, as I found him talking with Father Paul and Stuart when I arrived.

Noticing me come in, Paul motioned me toward their huddle. "Where's Joey?" I asked as I joined them.

Paul shook his head. "Poor boy's beside himself. He went back to the barn with his parents and…Lisa, was it?"

"Liza," said Aiden. "Val went with them."

He didn't have to elaborate—the only way Joey was going to sleep was through forced unconsciousness. "Eleanor did a nice job with the bunkhouse," I told Paul and Stuart, "but I'm sure it's crazy tonight. If you want to sleep here, be my guest. I'm not hurting for space."

Paul nodded. "Thanks, I'll take you up on that."

"My cats are in a spare room," said Stuart. "If I could trouble someone for a litterbox and kibble—"

"I'll handle it," Aiden offered. "Want a cat tree, too? I think I could work something up—"

"Thank you, but I don't plan to be here long," he replied, and turned to me. "You're going to need eyes in Montana. Send me back."

"Are you out of your *mind*?" I protested. "You had wizards on your doorstep—"

"They were probably looking for Slim and got turned around. And if they got a good look at me…well, they're not going to be talking without a spirit board. I know what you're capable of doing—forge my papers and send me to Montana. I'll keep my ear to the ground and see what I can learn about the Arcanum situation. Besides," he pressed, "I can't keep my cats here forever. The poor things are nervous wrecks."

"Stuart," I said slowly, "if some wizard were to become suspicious and looked closely enough—"

"I'm aware of the risk."

"You'd be dead before anyone could get to you."

The little man shrugged. "Then I won't give anyone a reason to suspect me. Come on, I *want* to do this. How are you going to find Helen if you can't get within a mile of the silo, huh?"

Much as I hated to admit it, he had a point, but the risks loomed large in my mind. "Why you?" I finally asked. "Why step in front of a gun?"

His smile was small but determined. "Because I'm a wizard. I'm sworn to the Light, Colin, and the Light must always fight the Dark."

"But you're *not* a wiz—"

Stuart held up his hand. "I am. And if you're still not convinced, think of it this way: everyone needs a goal, right?"

I tried to counter that, then gave up and looked away from his placid stare. "I'll...think about it. Not tonight, Stu. But I'll think about it."

Weary and worried, I retreated to the solitude of my office. But when I walked in, I found the fire blazing and Toula and Val sitting on one of the couches, her with her phone in hand, him with his arm around her, holding her close. "Looking for me?" I asked as I shut the door.

Val glanced up at the noise. "Toula's received a message from the silo."

"Really?" I hurried to the couch opposite theirs. "From whom? What's it say?"

Toula raised her eyes, and I saw the tracks of her mascara running down her face. "Missy Harrison," she mumbled. "She said...here, read it yourself." She thrust the phone across the table as her voice cracked.

Val tightened his protective grip, and I began scrolling through the long message:

Fotoula,

I hope you're safe. Don't reply. As soon as this goes through, I'm breaking this phone.

James Mulligan, with help from most of the IC, has hidden Helen. They took her early this morning. The official line is that she and Joey were killed by faeries lurking outside the silo. I trust she's still alive, but I don't know where. James sent the special units after the Fringe. He's set up a prison here for the ones they brought back. They're being housed underground somewhere, but we're not allowed contact. I suppose the full cover story is forthcoming.

If you're not there already, get to Faerie and stay there. And when you see C, tell him this wasn't Greg's fault. James was going to send units after our girls and their families if Greg didn't give him the Fringe information.

I don't know when, or if, this situation will improve. In case I don't see you again, there's something that's been weighing on my mind, and I need to tell you the truth while I have the chance. Apollonios made mistakes, and I don't condone what he did, but your father wasn't a monster.

I paused and looked at Toula, but she had tucked her head against Val's chest and closed her eyes.

I don't know what you were told of your father's family. Apollonios was new-blooded, and his parents died when he was a child, maybe seven or eight. A half-fae neighbor took him in—another Fotoula. No one in the Arcanum knew about him until a unit took her out. She had a long list of dead wizards to her name. A few days later, he showed up in Glastonbury, demanding justice. She'd told him enough about us to know where to go.

As you'd expect, this didn't go over well. The magi explained that she had been on our list for a long time, but he wouldn't take no for an answer. Anyway, Glastonbury sent him to the silo to address the Council, and Greg told Apollonios the facts of life. He offered your father proper training, but Apollonios turned him down and disappeared.

You know what happened next—the training, the camp in North Dakota, and the deal he made with Mab. We still don't know how she found him. What you haven't been told is that his victims in Chicago were training for the assassin corps.

Apollonios put on a good show of nonchalance about you, but anyone who spent time with him knew it was only an act. He loved you. He was so proud of all you did, in spite of the bind. He begged me to let him tell you, but we thought it best that you not grow attached to him. That was part of his bind—he probably seemed cold, but that was the dampening spell. He simply couldn't show you positive emotions, and he couldn't tell you what was holding him back.

What we did was wrong. You should have known your father, if only for a few years.

"Toula," I whispered, "this is—"

"Awful?" Val ventured. "Cruel? Inhumane? I could go on, if you'd like."

"Did you get to the end?" Toula asked me, not bothering to open her eyes.

"Not quite—"

"Finish it."

Feeling nauseated, I continued to read Missy's letter:

It's said that Apollonios went to his death screaming, which is true. Greg said he told you that your father was screaming for Mab to remember their bargain, but that wasn't the case.

He was pleading with us to let him see you one last time.

Before we gave you his belongings, we removed everything you'd given him so as to keep up the illusion that he hadn't cared. I know it must have hurt you, but again, we thought it best at the time.

I knew your father better than many did. If his situation had been different, he probably would have been a magus. Apollonios was clever and passionate, and even incarcerated, he had a wicked sense of humor. While I abhor what he did, I understand the impetus. He came to us for justice, and when we refused, he did what he thought was necessary.

I see much of the good in him in you. You're a remarkable woman, and I know you've been a help to Greg and Helen. I'm so sorry it's come to this.

Please be safe, Toula.

M.H.

I put the phone on the table, sat back against the cushions, and whistled. All of Toula's life, all that weight she had carried—rejected by her father, her peers, the Arcanum that had raised her...

Toula opened one eye. "Do you know what my father would have done right now?"

I shook my head. "Tell me."

"He would have waited. Made himself stronger. Bided his time. And then he would have thrown every bit of his firepower at the Arcanum and watched it burn." She straightened, then reached across her chest to take Val's hand. "Do we know how many died today? How many witches they kidnapped?"

"If Vivi has a guess, I haven't heard it."

"Doesn't matter. This is the waiting time. But someday,

there's going to be a reckoning." She stared into the fire, then looked back at me. "Maybe I *am* my father's daughter after all."

"You want to destroy the Arcanum?"

She pondered that, then shook her head. "Maybe not the whole thing, but I've got a list of magi with whom I'd like a few words. You?"

"I wouldn't mind sitting in on those conversations."

Toula grinned. "Then it looks like you've got yourself a partner, Colin."

The fire began to smoke, and I pushed myself off the couch to throw open a window. Below me spread my night-dark rose garden, and beyond that, the realm that was now both birthright and prison. "You're right," I said as I turned to her. "There will be a reckoning."

"Yeah?" she said with a sad smile.

"Yeah." I sat at my desk, cracked my knuckles, pulled my phone from my pocket, and dialed. "Because if there's one thing you shouldn't do, it's piss off a faerie."

Aiden answered on the second ring. "What's up?"

"Is Stuart still there?" I replied. "Tell him I'm in the market for a wizard."

ACKNOWLEDGEMENTS

Many, *many* thanks to you for coming along with me through four books now. There's much more ahead, I promise...

As always, my gratitude goes to the Novel Chicks for their advice and friendship. Once again, I owe thanks to Adam Domby, beta reader extraordinaire.

And yes, here's to you, Mom and Dad.

ABOUT THE AUTHOR

When not writing fiction, Ash Fitzsimmons is an appellate attorney and an unrepentant car singer.

Find her online:
www.ashfitzsimmons.com